PLAY TO THE END

Robert Goddard

BANTAM PRESS

LONDON · NEW YORK · TORONTO · SYDNEY · AUCKLAND

TRANSWORLD PUBLISHERS
61–63 Uxbridge Road, London W5 5SA
a division of The Random House Group Ltd

RANDOM HOUSE AUSTRALIA (PTY) LTD
20 Alfred Street, Milsons Point, Sydney,
New South Wales 2061, Australia

RANDOM HOUSE NEW ZEALAND LTD
18 Poland Road, Glenfield, Auckland 10, New Zealand

RANDOM HOUSE SOUTH AFRICA (PTY) LTD
Endulini, 5a Jubilee Road, Parktown 2193, South Africa

Published 2004 by Bantam Press
a division of Transworld Publishers

A catalogue record for this book is available from the British Library.
ISBNs 0593 04605 (cased)
0593 047664 (tpb)

Typeset in 11½pt/14pt Times by
Kestrel Data, Exeter, Devon.

Printed in Great Britain by
Clays Ltd, Bungay, Suffolk.

1 3 5 7 9 10 8 6 4 2

Papers used by Transworld Publishers are natural, recyclable
products made from wood grown in sustainable forests.
The manufacturing processes conform to the environmental
regulations of the country of origin.

PLAY TO THE END

By the same author

Past Caring (1986)

In Pale Battalions (1988)

Painting the Darkness (1989)

Into the Blue (1990)

(Winner of the first WH Smith Thumping Good Read Award
and dramatized for TV in 1997, starring John Thaw)

Take No Farewell (1991)

Hand in Glove (1992)

Closed Circle (1993)

Borrowed Time (1995)

Out of the Sun (1996)

(a sequel to *Into the Blue*)

Beyond Recall (1997)

Caught in the Light (1998)

Set in Stone (1999)

Sea Change (2000)

Dying to Tell (2001)

Days without Number (2003)

For
Marcus Palliser
1949–2002
Sailor, writer, debater, debunker and much missed friend

*A transcription of tape recordings made in Brighton
during the first week of December 2002*

SUNDAY

What I felt as I got off the train this afternoon wasn't what I'd expected to feel. The journey had been as grim and tardy as I suppose it was bound to be on a December Sunday. Most of the others have chosen to go via London and they won't be coming down here until tomorrow. I could have joined them. Instead I volunteered for the slow South Central shuffle along the coast. I had plenty of opportunity to analyse my state of mind as a seamless succession of drab back gardens drifted past the grimy train window. I knew why I hadn't gone up to London, of course. I knew exactly why bright lights and brash company weren't what the doctor had ordered. The truth is that if I *had* fled to the big city, I might never have made it to Brighton at all. I might have opted out of the last week of this ever more desperate tour and let Gauntlett sue me if he could be bothered to. So, I came the only way I could be sure would get me here. Which it did. Late, cold and depressed. But *here*. And then, as I stepped out onto the platform . . .

That feeling is why I'm talking into this machine. I can't quite describe it. Not foreboding, exactly. Not excitement. Not even anticipation. Something slipping between all three, I suppose. A thrill; a shiver; a prickling of the hairs on the back of the neck; a ghost tiptoeing across my grave. There wasn't supposed to be anything but a protraction of a big disappointment waiting for me in Brighton. But already, before I'd even

cleared the ticket barrier, I sensed strongly enough for certainty that there was more than that preparing a welcome for me. More that might be better or worse, but, either way, was preferable.

I didn't trust the sensation, of course. Why would I? I do now, though. Because it's already started to happen. Maybe I should have realized sooner that the tour was a journey. And this is journey's end.

The tapes were my agent's idea. Well, a diary was what she actually suggested, back in those bright summer days when this donkey of a play looked like a stallion that could run and run and the mere prospect merited a lunch at the River Café. A chronicle of how actors refine their roles and discover the deeper profundities of a script before they reach the West End is what Moira had in mind. She reckoned there might be a newspaper serialization in it to supplement the two thou a week Gauntlett is ever more reluctantly paying me. It sounded good. (A lot of what Moira says does.) I bought this pocket audio doodah on the strength of it, while the Cloudy Bay was still swirling around my thought processes. I'm glad I did now.

But it's more or less the first time I have been. I abandoned the diary before I'd even started it, up in Guildford, where the Yvonne Arnaud Theatre hosted the world première of our proud production. Is it only nine weeks ago? It feels more like nine months, the span of a difficult pregnancy, with a stillbirth the foregone conclusion since we had word from Gauntlett that there was to be no West End transfer. I thank God for the panto season, without which he might have been tempted to keep us on the road in the hopes of some magical improvement. As it is, the curtain comes down next Saturday and seems likely to stay there.

It shouldn't have turned out this way. When it was announced last year that a previously unknown play by the late and lauded Joe Orton had been discovered, it was widely assumed to be a masterpiece on no other basis than its authorship. What greater proof was needed, after all? This was the man who gave us *Entertaining Mr Sloane*, *Loot* and *What the Butler Saw*. This was also the man who sealed his reputation as an anarchic genius by dying young, murdered by his lover, Kenneth Halliwell, at their flat in Islington in August 1967. I have all the facts of his extraordinary life at my fingertips thanks to carting his biography and an edition of his diaries around with me. I thought they might inspire me. I thought lots of things. None of them have quite worked out.

The script of *Lodger in the Throat* was found by a plumber under some floorboards in the flat where Orton and Halliwell used to live. I imagine Orton would have been amused by the circumstances of its discovery. Maybe he actually planted it there as a joke. Or maybe – my preferred theory – Halliwell hid it during the final phase of his mental disintegration, not long before he bashed Orton's brains out with a hammer and then killed himself by swallowing a fatal quantity of Nembutal tablets. The Orton experts date the play to the winter of 1965/66 and reason he gave up on it when *Loot* was revived after a disastrous initial tour. Now I come to think about it, that tour bore eerie similarities to the experiences of the cast I've been trying to lead this autumn. *Loot* worked second time around, of course, because Orton was alive and well and willing to revise it. The irony is that he's not available to salvage *Lodger in the Throat*, the play he consigned to a bottom drawer (or maybe the floor-space) in order to return to *Loot*. We're on our own. And, boy, does it feel like it.

Enough about the play. We've analysed its potential and its problems, my fellow performers and I, till we're sick of the subject. Sick *and* tired. It was supposed to put my career back on the rails, or at any rate haul it out of the siding into which it was unaccountably shunted a few years ago. I'm the man who was in with a chance of being the new James Bond when Roger Moore packed it in, something I now find hard to believe, even though I know it's true. What's also true is that you don't realize you've stopped going up until you start going down.

There are plenty of signs if you're smart enough to spot

them, of course, or if you're willing to let yourself spot them. My name tops the bill, but Martin Donohue, who plays the part of my younger brother, has somehow managed to emerge from our dismal run with enough credit to make my primacy look shaky if we were ever cast together again – which, naturally, I'd move heaven and earth to prevent. Time was when Mandy Pringle, our ambitious deputy stage manager, would have set her sights on me, not Donohue. But that time is past. Not long past, but past none the less. Maybe they're looking forward to a week in Brighton. What they certainly won't be thinking is that I'm looking forward to our week in Sussex-by-the-sea. But I am. At least, I am now.

It rained all last night in Poole and was still raining when I got on the train this morning. Brighton must have caught the deluge too, but it was dry when I left the station and trudged south along Queen's Road through the mild grey dusk towards the darker grey slab of the sea. I'd already written off my weird presentiment. I'd accepted the exact and un-appetizing character of the next six days. And the idea of making any kind of a record of them was about as remote as it could be.

I turned east along Church Street, a fair enough route to take to my destination, but one that also permitted a detour along New Road, past the familiar period frontage of the Theatre Royal. This will be my fourth professional engage-ment on its antique boards and I'd happily swap any one of the others for the eight renderings of *Lodger in the Throat* that the near future holds.

I stopped and examined the poster, wondering whether I'd visibly aged since the photograph was taken three months ago. It was hard to tell, not least because I haven't been taking any lingering looks at myself in the mirror lately. But it was me all right. And there was my name, listed with the others, to prove it. *Leo S. Gauntlett presents Lodger in the Throat, by Joe Orton, starring Toby Flood, Jocasta Haysman, Martin Donohue, Elsa Houghton and Frederick Durrance, Monday 2 to Saturday 7 December. Evenings at 7.45 p.m. Thursday and Saturday matinées at 2.30 p.m.* Part of me longed to see a CANCELLED sticker across the poster, but it wasn't there and it isn't going to be. We're on. There's no way out. Until the end of the week.

I didn't linger, cutting round by the Royal Pavilion to the Old Steine, then heading east along St James's Street. The Sea Air Hotel is neither the chicest nor the cheapest B & B establishment in Madeira Place, one of the guesthouse-filled streets running down to Marine Parade, but Eunice is as actor-friendly a landlady as they come, willing to suspend her winter closure just for me. As the tour's gone from bad to worse and the play's immediate future has shrunk, I've started economizing on accommodation in order to have some dosh to show for my efforts even if kudos is out of the question. I'd probably have opted to stay with Eunice anyway, but just now the Sea Air has a number of crucial advantages apart from the tariff, principal among them being the fact that none of the others will be staying here. I have Eunice's word on it. 'I couldn't cope with a party, Toby. All that coming and going. All that bathwater. I reckon you'll do for me.'

I've only ever been here out of season, to share the dining room with the ghosts of summer holidaymakers. It's a peaceful house, thanks to Eunice's serene temperament and aversion to noise of all kinds. Even Binky, her cat, has learned not to purr loudly. Eunice is *Mrs* Rowlandson, complete with wedding and engagement rings, but Mr Rowlandson is a subject never touched upon, sometime existence presumed but fate unspecified. It's true to say, mind you, that Eunice might not be able to discard the rings even if she wanted to. A thin woman she is not. And less thin than ever. An aroma of baking wafted up from her basement flat as she ushered me into the speckless, flock-papered hall and up the Axminster-carpeted stairs to the first-floor front bedroom, furnished like an Art Deco museum and with a bay-windowed view of its shabby twin on the other side of the street.

'Do you want some tea?' Eunice asked, watching me from the doorway as I dumped my bag and returned the room's silent welcome.

'That'd be great,' I replied.

'And some cake? You look as if you need building up.'

She was right there. She was indeed spot-on. I smiled. 'Cake would be great too. Oh, and do you have yesterday's *Argus*, Eunice?'

'I dare say I could put my hand on it. You'll not find much in it to interest you, though.'

'I only want the cinema schedules. I thought I might catch a film tonight.'

'Mmm.' She looked seriously doubtful.

'What's wrong?'

'I wouldn't make any definite plans if I were you.'

'Why not?'

'There was a phone call for you earlier.'

I was puzzled by that. Those who knew where I was staying were more likely to have rung me on my mobile. 'Who from?' I asked at once.

'Your wife.'

'My *wife*?'

The puzzle instantly became a mystery. Jenny and I *are* technically still married, but only because the decree nisi is a month or so short of becoming absolute. Given that her husband-to-be's country estate (well, that's what Wickhurst Manor sounds like to me) is only a few miles north of Brighton, I'd caught myself wondering on the train whether Jenny was thinking of coming along to one of the performances. I'd reckoned not. She'd keep her distance. She'd put my presence in the city out of her mind. But it seemed she hadn't.

'Jenny phoned here?'

'Yes.' Eunice nodded. 'She wants to see you, Toby.'

It's time to own up. It's time to say what I've long since known. I love my wife. My soon-to-be-ex-wife, that is. I

16

always have. I just haven't always acknowledged the fact, or behaved accordingly. Actors' marriages are notoriously unstable, like actors themselves, I suppose. We sometimes forget where the part ends and we begin. Sometimes, in the absence of a part, we invent one. Usually, because we perform rather than create, it's a character from stock: the hard-drinking, fast-driving womanizer, forever on a spree of one kind or another. It's easier to keep a mask in place for fear of what peeling it off would reveal.

That's only one of the problems between Jenny and me. And, ironically, it's a problem the last few years have abundantly solved. I know myself now, perhaps too well. But self-knowledge has come a little late. You're not supposed to wait until the brink of your half-century to understand the workings of your own mind. Better than never at all, I suppose, although some might disagree.

We'd still have made it, I reckon, despite the infidelities and indiscretions, the lost weekends and broken promises, but for something else neither of us could have anticipated. To have a son. And then to lose him. There. I've said that too. His name was Peter. He was born. He lived for four and a half years. And then he died. Drowned in the oversized swimming pool that went with the oversized house that went with the lifestyle we thought we were supposed to enjoy.

We blamed each other. We were right to. But the blame should have been shared, not contested. You can't alter the past. And maybe you can't alter the future either. But you can wreck the present. Oh yes. You can lay that thoroughly to waste.

When Jenny left me, I told myself it was for the best. Platitudes like 'Time for us both to move on' fell regularly from my lips. I think I may even have believed them. For a while.

Not any more, though. I should never have let her go. I should have done things differently. Very differently. Hindsight is the sharpest sight of all. It lays bare the truth.

And the bleak truth is that there's nothing I can do to

17

repair the damage I've done. There's no way back. At least, that's what I would have said. Until tonight.

Jenny had left a mobile number with Eunice. When I rang it, she answered instantly. And all I could manage by way of greeting was, 'It's me.'

'I expect you were surprised to hear from me,' she said after a long pause.

'You could say that, yes.'

'Can we meet?'

'When have I ever objected to the idea?'

I heard her sigh before she answered. 'Can we?'

'Yes. Of course.'

'This evening?'

'All right.'

'You're not busy?'

'What do you think?'

Another sigh. 'There's no point to this if you're going to be—'

'I'll be whatever you need me to be, Jenny. OK?' I could, perhaps I should, have asked why she wanted to see me. But I didn't dare to. 'Where and when?'

The Palace Pier at six o'clock was about as quiet as it ever gets. Most of the bars and attractions were closed, although the Palace of Fun was open for the benefit of anyone determined to pump money into its fruit machines. The sea sucked sluggishly at the beach below, while a couple speaking what sounded like Hungarian huddled in one of the shelters, sharing a bag of chips. All in all, the venue struck me as improbably distant from Jenny's natural habitat.

Then, as I reached the end of the pier, where the helter-skelter and merry-go-rounds were shrouded in wintry darkness, another thought struck me. Perhaps Jenny had chosen to meet me there just because of the shortage of witnesses, especially witnesses likely to know her. She didn't want to be seen with me. That was the point. The pier

18

was somewhere she could be confident of a very private word.

She was leaning against the railings halfway back along the other side, dressed in a long dark coat and boots, gazing vacantly down at the beach, her face obscured by the brim of a fur-trimmed hat. If I hadn't been looking out for her, I might not even have noticed her. Though she, presumably, would have noticed me.

'Great night for a promenade,' I said stupidly as I approached. 'How about a barbecue later?'

'Hello, Toby.' She turned and looked at me, a tight half-smile flicking across her face. 'Thanks for coming.'

'You look well.' (This was something of an understatement. Separation from me had evidently agreed with her. Either that or she's found a good beautician in Brighton. I prefer to believe the latter.)

'Shall we sit down?' she asked.

'If we can find a seat.' This didn't raise even half a smile.

The bench in the nearest shelter was dappled with droplets of rainwater, shimmering in the lamplight. I thought I caught a few words of Hungarian drifting over from the other side of the structure as I brushed some of the water away. We sat down.

'The chippy's open,' I said, nodding over my shoulder towards the kiosk I'd passed earlier. 'Fancy sharing fifty penn'orth?'

'No, thank you.'

'When was the last time we shared a bag of chips on a draughty sea front, would you say?'

'Have we ever?'

This wasn't going well. Jenny didn't seem remotely pleased to see me. Which was odd, since we were meeting at her request.

'How's the play going?' she asked suddenly.

'Do you really want to know?'

'I read about Jimmy Maidment.'

Well, that was no surprise. The apparent suicide of a

famous comic actor, albeit one not as famous as he once was, makes plenty of headlines. Throwing himself under a Tube train the day before he was due to open in *Lodger in the Throat* may have been Jimmy's characteristically pithy way of telling the rest of the cast that he doubted the play would resurrect his career, or anyone else's. Alternatively, maybe he was just drunk and missed his footing. The coroner will say his piece in due course. Either way, though, it wasn't a good omen. I miss him. And so does the play.

'It must have been a shock,' said Jenny. 'Was he depressed?'

'Perpetually, I expect.'

'The reviewers seem to think . . .'

'That we're lost without him. I know. And it's true. Fred Durrance isn't in Jimmy's class. But that's not the only problem. And I'm sure you didn't suggest meeting so we could analyse where it's all gone wrong, so—'

'Sorry,' she interrupted, her voice softening.

A brief silence fell. The sea hissed soothingly beneath the pier. 'Me too,' I murmured.

'Will it go to London?' she asked.

'Not a chance.'

'So, this is the end.'

'Apparently.'

'I *am* sorry, you know.'

'Sorry enough to have me back?' I smiled thinly at her in the lamplight. 'Just joking.'

'I'm very happy with Roger,' she said, apparently assuming I doubted it, which actually I didn't. 'We've set a date for the wedding.'

'Pity I left my diary at the Sea Air.'

Jenny sighed. I was trying her patience, an art I unintentionally perfected a long time ago. 'Let's walk,' she said, rising before the words were properly out, and striding off towards the shore, boot heels clacking on the planks of the pier.

'Where are we going?' I asked as I fell in beside her.

'Nowhere,' she replied. 'We're just walking.'

'Look, Jenny, can I just say . . . I'm glad you're happy. Strange as it may seem, I've always hoped you would be. If there's anything I can—'

'There is.' Her voice was firm but far from hostile. That's when I guessed what was really making her so edgy. She had a favour to ask of me. Since the last favour she'd asked of me was to get out of her life and stay out, it was, however you cut it, a delicate situation. 'Will you do something for me, Toby?'

'Gladly.'

'You haven't heard what it is yet.'

'You wouldn't ask me to do it if it wasn't the right thing to do.'

She might have smiled at that. I can't be sure. 'I have a problem.'

'Go on.'

But she didn't go on until we'd turned off the pier and started west along the promenade, the empty beach to our left, the thinly trafficked sea front to our right. A full minute of silence must in fact have passed before she started to explain, which she did with the bewildering question, 'Have I told you about Brimmers?'

'No,' was the best answer I could give, sensing this wasn't the time to point out that she hadn't told me anything at all in a good long while.

'It's a hat shop I own in the Lanes. I've really enjoyed making a go of it. It's quite successful, actually.'

'You always wanted your own business.'

'Yes. And now I've got it.'

'That's great.'

'Roger's fine about it.'

'Good. And what line of business is Roger in?'

'Corporate investment.' I was still puzzling over what precisely that meant when she briskly continued: 'Look, this has nothing to do with Roger. The thing is, some weird bloke's been hanging around the shop. There's a café opposite where he sits in the window, sipping endless cups of

21

tea and staring across at Brimmers. I find him standing around outside when I open or close up. I've seen him out at Wickhurst too. There's a footpath that runs close to the house. I can't walk along it without bumping into him.'

'Who is he?'

'I don't know.'

'Haven't you asked him?'

'I've spoken to him a couple of times, but he doesn't respond. He answers "Can I help you?" with "No", then stares some more and wanders off. He's beginning to prey on my nerves. I think he's harmless, but he just won't go away.'

'Have you spoken to the police?'

'To complain of what? A man patronizing a café and walking along a public footpath? They'd think *I* was persecuting *him*.'

'Is he persecuting you?'

'It feels like it.'

'Sure you don't know him?'

'Positive.'

'What's he like?'

'Creepy.'

'You can do better than that.'

'All right. He's . . . middle-aged, I suppose, but a bit childlike at the same time. There's something of the overgrown schoolboy about him. The nerdy, socially dysfunctional kind of schoolboy. Wears a duffel-coat, with all sorts of . . . badges on it.'

'Obviously dangerous, then.'

'If you're not going to take this seriously . . .' She tossed her head in a well-remembered gesture.

'What does Roger say?'

'I haven't told him.' It was an admission she seemed reluctant to make, even though she must have known she'd have to.

'Really?'

'Yes. Really.'

I can confess now to deriving some small but twisted pleasure from the discovery·that Jenny had a secret from her affluent and no doubt handsome fiancé – and was sharing it with me. The pleasure distracted me to some degree from the mystery. Why hadn't she told Roger? She supplied an answer swiftly enough.

'Roger travels a lot on business. I don't want him worrying about me or staying home on my account.'

But it didn't ring true. Jenny should have known better than to feed me such a line. I know her too well. Whatever she said, I had Roger down as the protective, not to say possessive, type. Her real concern is that her independence is at stake if she asks the new man in her life to save her from the stalking nerd of the Lanes. And Jenny values her independence. Very highly.

'Besides,' she added, 'what could he do?'

Several possibilities sprang to mind, but I didn't put the more extreme of them into words. After all, by the same token, what could *I* do? 'He might recognize the bloke.'

'He doesn't.'

'How can you be sure?'

'We were together when chummy walked past us recently. On the footpath I mentioned. I asked Roger if he knew him. He said no. Definitely not.'

'But you didn't explain the significance of the question.'

'Obviously I didn't. Besides . . .'

'What?'

'I think I might know what chummy's connection with me is. And it isn't Roger.'

'What, then?'

'You mean *who*.'

'OK, who?'

'You, Toby.'

'What?'

We both stopped and turned to look at each other. I couldn't make out Jenny's expression clearly in the shadow of her hat. But I dare say she could read me like a book. She's always been able to. And what she must have read was disbelief.

23

'Me?'

'That's right.'

'But it can't be. I mean . . . that doesn't make sense.'

'Nevertheless . . .'

'How can you be sure?'

'I just am.'

'OK.' I relented. 'What made you think it?'

Jenny glanced over her shoulder. She'd noticed before I had that a group of youngsters was approaching. With a touch on my arm, she steered me to the side of the promenade. The precaution turned out to be unnecessary, because the youngsters promptly dashed across the road towards the Odeon Cinema. But still she lowered her voice as she spoke. 'Sophie, my assistant at Brimmers, often goes to the café where chummy hangs about. She's noticed him too. Well, last week, she spotted a video he'd bought lying by his elbow. He'd taken it out of the bag to look at. Guess what it was.'

I turned the puzzle over in my mind for a moment, my gaze drifting towards the carcass of the West Pier, a hump of black against the blue-black sky. '*Dead Against*,' I murmured.

'How did you know?' Jenny sounded genuinely surprised. *Dead Against* was the last of my all too few Hollywood engagements, released to vinegary reviews and absentee audiences all of eleven years ago. A sub-Hitchcockian thriller in which I play an English private detective pursuing a glamorous hit-woman in Los Angeles, *Dead Against* turned out aptly to have nothing going for it. My co-star, however, Nina Bronsky, has gone on to better things, which is why, according to Moira, some of her earlier films are suddenly making it to the video-store shelves. Perhaps a royalties cheque eighteen months from now will quell my resentment. Then again, perhaps not.

'There aren't that many videos out there in any way connected with me, Jenny. *Dead Against* it had to be. But it could mean nothing. Maybe chummy's a Nina Bronsky fan. He sounds her type.'

'Be serious, Toby. Please. I'm worried about this man.'

'Well, if he's a fan of mine . . .' I shrugged. 'I guess that makes me in some way responsible for him.'

'I'm not blaming you, for God's sake. I just want this weirdo off my back.'

'How can I accomplish that for you?'

'Go to the café tomorrow morning. See if you recognize him. Or if *he* recognizes *you*.'

'I haven't changed that much in eleven years. He *should* recognize me.'

'Then speak to him. Find out who he is; what he wants. See if you can't . . .'

'Get rid of him?'

'All I want him to do is lay off, Toby.'

'Plus tell me why he's on your case. *If* he's on your case.'

'It's something to do with you. It must be. The video proves that. He's found out we used to be married and—'

'We still are, actually. Married, I mean.'

Jenny addressed the quibble with a seaward glance and a brief silence. Then she said, 'Will you do it?'

'Of course.' I smiled. 'Anything for you, Jenny.'

I meant it. I still do. But there's more to it than that, as I suspect Jenny's well aware. The video alone proves nothing. If our duffel-coated friend is interested in me, he could also be interested in Roger. Jenny says she doesn't want to worry Roger. But maybe she doesn't quite *trust* Roger. Maybe she wants to find out on her own terms what this is really all about – if it's about anything beyond the daily habits of a millinery fetishist. And maybe she knows she can rely on me to dig out the truth, because I still love her and haven't given up hope of making *her* love *me* all over again. She's playing a dangerous game, my once and future Jenny.

'What time should I show up?' I asked.

'He'll be there by ten. Without fail.'

'I'd better get an early night.'

'Don't come to the shop. Don't let him think I've sent you.'

'I'll do my best. Ad libbing's always been my forte.'

'Thanks, Toby.' There was genuine relief in her voice and maybe fondness too, although there I admit I could be kidding myself. 'I'm more grateful than I can say.'

'Shall I phone you . . . afterwards?'

'Yes, please.'

'But you'd rather I didn't pop round to report?'

'It's not that. I . . .'

'Perhaps Roger wouldn't be pleased. If he got to hear about it.'

'This has nothing to do with Roger.'

Jenny brushed a strand of hair back beneath the brim of her hat, exploiting the action to avoid my gaze. 'As it happens,' she said, 'Roger's away on business at the moment.'

'Is that so?'

'Yes,' she replied coolly.

'So, this is just between us.'

'I'd like to keep it that way.'

'I understand.' So I did. And so I do. We have an understanding all right. But it depends on not being made explicit. Neither of us is being entirely honest.

'I'd better be going,' said Jenny, with a sudden conclusive motion of the head. 'I'm meeting friends for dinner.'

Jenny's always been good at making friends. I didn't realize how good until she left me, taking most of them with her.

'Goodnight, Toby.'

I watched her cross the road and head up West Street past the cinema. Then I started back along the promenade, towards the Palace Pier and the Sea Air beyond.

Eunice said I was looking cheerier when I got back than I had been earlier. She'd probably have said that whether it was true or not, harbouring as she does a romantic Burton and Taylor vision of me and Jenny. But a glance in the hall mirror told me she was right. I saw reflected there what I haven't glimpsed so much as once during our long weeks on the road: a faintly optimistic sparkle in the eye.

*　　*　　*

After tackling Eunice's steak-and-kidney pud, I needed a walk. Time spent in reconnaissance being seldom wasted, as my old dad used to say, I made my way to the Lanes and prowled around, until, after several double-backs, I found Brimmers.

Jenny's good taste is pretty obvious just from the stylish window display and candy-stripe colour scheme. I couldn't see much of the interior and, if I'm to obey Jenny's orders, I'm not about to. But who knows? Not me. I'm just hoping.

The Rendezvous café was also closed, as you'd expect. The sign promises morning coffee, light lunches and afternoon teas. There's a counter at the rear, tables and chairs in the centre and a broad ledge along the glazed frontage, with stools, where customers can perch and watch the world of the Lanes go by as they sip their beverage of choice. You can easily keep Brimmers under observation from there, of course, though not without being observed yourself, which may or may not be the object of the exercise for my alleged fan. We'll see about that. Tomorrow, as promised.

Reconnaissance done, I ambled off to a pub I generally end up in at some point during Brighton runs – the Cricketers in Black Lion Street, allegedly Graham Greene's favourite – and downed a reflective pint. Sunday in Brighton had already exceeded my expectations, which admittedly wasn't difficult, but little did I realize that it still had a surprise in store for me.

I was at a table in the corner of the bar not visible from the door, idly watching a middle-aged married man and a woman who clearly wasn't his wife getting slowly sloshed. Sunday night can induce more than its fair share of morbidity. It's my only free night of the week at present, so I should know. Tonight, however, I was feeling just fine.

That's probably why my heart didn't sink when a bloke sidled over from the bar, said, 'Mind if I join you?' and plonked himself down next to me.

He struck me at first sight as your typical garrulous pub bore. Short and stout, with moist blue eyes, veinous nose and cheeks, thin sandy-grey hair and a tongue that seemed too large for his mouth, he was dressed in a crested blazer that could surely never fasten round his paunch, off-white shirt and stained cavalry twills. In one hand he held a glass of red wine, in the other a flier advertising *Lodger in the Throat*.

'You're Toby Flood or I'm a Dutchman,' he announced.

'And you're not a Dutchman,' I replied.

'Can I buy you a drink?'

'I'm fine for the moment, thanks.'

'It's a relief to see you, to be honest.'

'A relief?'

'I've got a ticket for Tuesday night.' He held up the flier. 'So, it's good to know you've made it down. Syd Porteous. Pleased to meet you.' He extended a large, saveloy-fingered hand, which I had little choice but to shake.

'You a regular theatregoer, Syd?' I ventured.

'No, no. Leastways, I didn't used to be. But I've been trying to . . . broaden my horizons . . . since I've had more time on my hands.'

'Just retired, have you?'

'Not exactly. More . . . downsized. You've got to duck and dive in this town. Well, *city* they call it now. Nice for the councillors, that, but bugger all use to those of us who keep them in expenses. Anyway, I can't claim to have been to the theatre' (or thee-eight-er, as he pronounced it) 'more than the gee-gees this year, but maybe next, hey? It'll soon be New Year resolution time and I've turned over more new leaves than the average rabbit's eaten, so . . .'

The way he'd started gave me the impression I could be on the receiving end of a stream-of-consciousness monologue till last orders. I was just beginning, in fact, to devise an excuse to leave him to it when I became aware that there was a small, still point to the turning world of his rambling thoughts. And I was it.

'Any chance of a new series of *Long Odds*, Toby?' Syd suddenly asked. 'I used to be glued to that.'

Sad to say, Syd was in a small minority there. My 1987 TV series about a compulsive gambler who dabbles in private

28

investigations on the side (or was it the other way round?) is about as likely to be revived as Empire Day. 'No chance, I'm afraid.'

'Don't seem to have seen you much on the box lately.'

'I'm concentrating on the theatre. Live performance is more challenging.'

'Yeah, well, there's that to it, I suppose. Your fans get to see you in the flesh.'

'Exactly.'

'This play must be getting you a lot of attention. I'm looking forward to it.'

'Good.'

'I met him, you know.'

'Who?'

'Orton.'

Against my better instincts, my curiosity was aroused. 'Really?'

'Oh yes.' Syd lowered his voice melodramatically 'Here. In Brighton. Just a couple of weeks before he died. Summer of 'sixty-seven.'

I'm familiar enough with the diaries Orton kept from December 1966 until his death in August 1967 for Syd's reference to have struck me as at least superficially authentic. Orton and Halliwell came to Brighton in late July, 1967, to spend a long weekend with Oscar Lewenstein, co-producer of *Loot*. Orton was bored out of his brain by the visit. I didn't recall a younger version of Sydney Porteous lurching onto the scene, however.

'How did you come to meet him?' I casually enquired. A public lavatory sprang to mind as the venue, given Orton's sexual habits, but Syd's answer was rather more disconcerting.

'Bumped into him in this very pub. A Sunday night, it was – like now. We chatted about nothing much. He didn't say who he was, though the name wouldn't have meant a thing to me if he had. I was an ignorant young shaver. Clocked his face in the papers a fortnight or so later, though. A bit of a shaker,

29

that was. Looking back, I think he was trying to pick me up. Weird, isn't it?'

'What is, in particular?'

'Well, him and now you, in the Cricketers on a Sunday night. What would you call that if it isn't weird?'

'I'd call it coincidental.' (If it was true, which I rather doubted.) 'Faintly coincidental.'

'Even so, you want to be careful. I'm not the superstitious type myself, but you actors are supposed to be. The Scottish play. The Superman curse. All that sort of malarkey.'

'I'll try not to let it worry me.'

'Look, I'm an old Brighton hand. My ma had a bit part in *Brighton Rock*. And I'm in a crowd scene in *Oh What a Lovely War!* So, I almost feel like an honorary member of the acting profession. Anything I can do for you while you're here – anything at all – just say the word. I'll give you my mobile number.' He scrawled the number on a beer mat and thrust it into my palm. 'Not much I can't lay hands on or find out in this town. Know what I mean?' He winked.

Unsure whether I really wanted to know what he meant, I smiled weakly and pocketed the beer mat. 'I'll bear the offer in mind.'

'You do that, Toby.' He gave me a second, more exaggerated wink. 'I wouldn't like to think of you getting into trouble for the lack of a word to the wise.'

Shaking Syd off wasn't easy. He was all for 'going on somewhere'. I had to dredge up considerable reserves of charm to avoid offending him. Somehow, though, I doubt he takes offence easily. He can't afford to with his personality.

Back here at the Sea Air I've had the opportunity to check Orton's diaries for late July, 1967, which have raised more questions than they've answered. He and Halliwell arrived in Brighton on Thursday 27th and spent three days cooped up discontentedly at the Lewenstein house in Shoreham, leaving on Monday 31st. Just about the only time Orton was alone, oddly enough, was Sunday evening. He had gone with

Halliwell and the Lewenstein family to see the new Bond film, *You Only Live Twice*, at the Odeon Cinema, but it was sold out. The others opted to see *In Like Flint* instead, but Orton preferred to cruise off in search of casual sex. He succeeded in getting himself sucked off by a dwarf in a public convenience. (Orton seems to have given the word 'convenience' a very liberal interpretation.) Then he had a cup of tea at the railway station and walked back to Shoreham.

No mention of the Cricketers, then, nor of anyone who could be Sydney Porteous as an ignorant young shaver. Orton wasn't much of a pub-goer by his own and others' accounts. The incident doesn't ring true. Syd, I conclude, was spinning a yarn.

Or was he? No Orton scholar for sure and certain, how did he manage to get as many facts right as he did? As it happens, Sunday, 30 July 1967 was the only evening when he *could* have met the great and soon to be late Joe Orton in a Brighton boozer.

Besides, I can't deny that there's something slightly disturbing about Porteous's story. Orton's weekend by the sea wasn't wholly lacking in superstitious significance. His agent, the legendary Peggy Ramsay, had a house in Brighton. She met up with the party on Saturday night and they dropped by her place on the way out to dinner. There Orton made some characteristically scornful remarks about a horus she showed him – an Egyptian wood carving in the likeness of a bird, traditionally placed on graves to escort the souls of the departed to heaven. Peggy thought such disrespect was tempting fate. Sure enough – if you're that way inclined – Orton was dead within a couple of weeks.

I'm not, of course, that way inclined. At least, I try not to be. But Eunice brought yesterday's *Argus* up to me earlier, as I'd asked her to, and I see the Odeon is showing the latest Bond film. Just as it was in July 1967. I haven't been to see it. I might have done, if only to glare in envy at Pierce Brosnan. But circumstances conspired to prevent me. Just as they prevented Orton.

And now I find myself keeping a diary of sorts. Just like Orton.

Thinking, drinking and talking. I've done too much of all three. I should get that early night I promised myself. But my body clock's geared to the rest of the week, when I'll be up till the small hours. I can't seem to relax. I can stop talking, though. That at least is in my control. Besides, there really is nothing else to say. For now.

MONDAY

The alarm clock roused me at half past eight this morning, *hora incognita* as far as I've been concerned recently. Novelty did not lend enchantment to the experience. A squint through the window revealed a grey sky and a wind-driven burger carton bowling up the street. The man whose face I met in the shaving mirror didn't look to be at his best.

He still wasn't after breakfast and a walk down to the sea front. But I had a promise to keep. And it wasn't going to wait until my biorhythms were in synch. I headed for the Lanes.

It was gone ten by the time I reached the Rendezvous, but not long gone. I spotted chummy as I moved at a practised amble towards the door, but didn't look at him, any more than I glanced into Brimmers. A duffel-coated shape in the window seen from the corner of the eye was enough to justify the witheringly early start. Whether the proprietress of Brimmers was watching I didn't know, though I hoped Jenny would have the good sense to lie low. This was one show that didn't need an audience.

The Rendezvous was in a lull between workers looking for a caffeine fix and shoppers resting their feet. It aims for a Continental ambience, with lots of dark wood and sepia photographs of Third Republic Paris, but doesn't quite hit the mark, thanks to the bright and breezy staff and manifestly *un*Continental customers. Chummy was a case in point. The duffel-coat, jeans and desert boots were more Aldermaston March than Champs-Elysées. From where I parked myself with a double *espresso* and a complimentary *Indie*, I couldn't make out what the badges were, but there had to be at least half a dozen of them on his coat, dimly reflected in the window through which he was gazing across the lane towards Brimmers. He had a book open in front of him, but it wasn't getting much of his attention.

Nor was I, come to that, which called into question Jenny's contention that I was the key to his interest in her. It also raised the issue of how I should best approach him, an issue I hadn't really thought about beforehand. He didn't have the video of *Dead Against* with him and had displayed no interest whatsoever in my arrival on the premises. He hadn't so much as twitched a toggle in my direction.

My impression, based on a three-quarters profile view, was that Jenny had him about right. A middle-aged mummy's boy, whether his mummy was still around or not. There was an obviously home-knitted sweater visible beneath his coat. His hair was a pudding-basin mop of brown and grey. The glasses perched halfway down his nose were about fifteen years out of fashion. When he drank from his cup, he used both hands to raise it cautiously to his lips. He wouldn't have been out of place standing at the end of the platform, notebook in paw, as my train drew into Brighton station yesterday afternoon.

But stereotyping, as every actor knows, is a treacherous business, as miserable to experience as it can be misleading to apply. I needed to handle this sensitively. I followed up the *espresso* with a *latte* and cobbled together the least worst cover story I could contrive. Then I moseyed over to join him.

'Excuse me,' I said, 'are you local?'

'Yes,' he replied, turning his head slowly to look at me. 'I am.' He spoke as slowly as he moved, with a slight lisp. Recognition failed to flicker in his eyes.

'I'm a stranger to Brighton. I wonder if you could help me with some directions.'

'Maybe I could.'

The badges, I now realized, were actually painted enamel brooches, depicting characters from Hergé's Tintin books: Captain Haddock, Snowy, Professor Calculus, the Thomson twins and, naturally, the legendary quiffed one himself. 'I'm looking for the public library,' I pressed on. (Pretty lame, I know, but there it is.)

'It can be . . . difficult to find.' He smiled wanly. 'They moved it, you see.'

'Did they?'

'It's in New England Street.'

'Right. And that is . . .' My gaze drifted down to the book he'd been reading, which ironically had the yellowed margins and cellophaned cover of a library book. Then I noticed the title at the top of the page. *The Orton Diaries*. I said nothing, though my eyes must have widened in surprise.

And at that moment – of all the hellishly inconvenient ones – my mobile rang. 'Someone's after you,' said chummy, as I wrestled it out of my pocket.

'Sorry,' I blurted out. 'Excuse me.' I had the blasted thing in my hand now. I turned and moved back to the table where I'd been sitting to answer. '*Yes?*' I snapped.

'Toby, it's Brian. Not too early for you, I hope.'

If Brian Sallis, our indefatigable company stage manager, had woken me from a well-deserved lie-in, I'd have felt less irritated than I did. What in God's name could he want? The question was swiftly, though to my mind far from adequately, answered.

'I just wanted to check you had a smooth journey yesterday.'

'I made it, yes.'

'Good.'

'Look, Brian—'

'You haven't forgotten our press call this afternoon, have you?' So that was really why he'd phoned: to ensure I wasn't likely to cop out of our meet-the-media session. 'Two thirty, at the theatre.'

'I'll be there.'

37

'With the technical to follow at four.'

Every Monday afternoon of the tour had been the same: press call at 2.30; technical rehearsal, to get the feel of a new stage, at 4.00. Brian could hardly have thought I'd forgotten the schedule. My state of mind was probably his more immediate concern and it was actually none too good, though for reasons he could have no inkling of. 'I'll be there,' I repeated. 'OK?'

'Splendid. I just—'

'I've got to go now.'

'You are all right, aren't you, Toby?'

'Fine. See you later. 'Bye.'

I ended the call before Brian had a chance to say his own goodbye and turned round to re-engage chummy.

But he wasn't there. His stool was empty, his coffee-cup drained and abandoned. Chummy, complete with *Orton Diaries* and Tintin badges, had vanished.

Cursing Brian Sallis, I grabbed my coat and rushed out. There was no sign of chummy, but in the narrow, dog-legging Lanes that was no surprise. Choice of direction boiled down to a fifty-fifty guess.

I looked in through the window of Brimmers as much in hope as apprehension. Jenny had either seen nothing, in which case she couldn't help me, or she'd spectated at a pretty comprehensive balls-up, in which case . . .

Elegantly trouser-suited and severely unsmiling, brow furrowed in the only gesture of exasperation she could allow herself with customers present, she stared out at me along a narrow line of sight through the windowful of hats. I grimaced. And she inclined her head to the right.

I turned left, hurried round the next corner and headed on, scanning the shops and side turnings as I went. No glimpse of duffel rewarded my efforts and within a few minutes I was out in North Street, amidst traffic and noise and bustling passers-by.

Then, incredibly, I saw him, pacing up and down at a crowded bus stop on the other side of the road. He pushed his glasses up to the bridge of his nose with a stab of his middle finger and squinted expectantly in the direction from which a bus would come. A gathering of bags and folding of buggies amongst his companions at the stop signalled its imminent arrival even as I watched. I glanced to my left and saw a double-decker bearing down on them.

The bus had stopped and was loading by the time I managed to dodge across the road. I saw chummy stepping aboard and, peering through the window, spotted his desert boots as he took the stairs to the top deck. 'Where's this bus going?' I asked the harassed mother ahead of me and relayed her answer to the driver when I made it to the front of the queue. 'Patcham, please.' But there turned out to be a flat fare of a pound. My destination was entirely up to me.

Actually, of course, it was up to chummy. I sat about halfway back downstairs and awaited his descent. The bus lumbered round by the Royal Pavilion, took on more passengers and headed north.

Ten minutes slow going took us up London Road to within sight of the Duke of York's Cinema. Several people got up as we approached a stop. Then the desert boots appeared round the corner of the stairs. Chummy was on the move. I rose discreetly behind a broad-backed youth and was last but one off the bus.

Chummy was walking north by then, towards the traffic lights at the junction ahead. I followed at what I judged to be a safe distance, lingering in a shop doorway as he reached the lights and waited for them to change, then hurrying after him as he crossed.

He was heading east now, along Viaduct Road, where heavy traffic roared past dingy Victorian terraces. He plodded along, head bowed, displaying not the slightest interest in his surroundings, nor any inclination to glance over his shoulder. It seemed to me that if he'd left the Rendezvous so abruptly because I'd aroused his suspicion, he should have been warier. I concluded that he'd more probably left because he was ready to; as simple as that – I was irrelevant.

I saw him dig a bunch of keys out of his pocket a few seconds before he stopped by the door of a house dingier even than most of its neighbours and let himself in. I heard the door clunk shut as I approached. I carried on walking, noting the number as I passed: 77. Then I stopped and doubled back at a slower pace for a second, more lingering look.

Number 77 was a standard two-up, two-down Victorian working-class dwelling, rendered in a shade of blue darkened by grime and neglect. Paint was peeling from the sash window frames. The front door was not original, being plain and unpanelled, but it wasn't in much better condition than the rest of the house.

I'd slowed nearly to a halt, my brain struggling with the problem of what to do next. I'd discovered where he lived. It was something. But it was a long way short of enough. Perhaps I should try the knocker, though if he answered I'd only have another problem to grapple with: how to explain myself.

Then the door suddenly opened. And chummy stared out at me. 'Do you want to come in, Mr Flood?' he asked.

'Well, I . . .'

'You may as well, seeing as you've come this far.'

There was logic in that. There was also a hint of menace. But that could merely have been a symptom of guilt on my part. I felt more than a little foolish. 'You know who I am?'

'Yes.'

'You have me at a disadvantage, in that case.'

'My name's Derek Oswin.' He pushed his glasses up on his nose again. 'Are you coming in?'

'All right. Thanks.'

I stepped past him into a cramped hallway. Steep, narrow stairs straight ahead led to the upper floor. To my right was a sitting room, with a kitchen at the end of the hall. The sitting room looked to be anciently furnished, but tidy. The condition of the exterior had prepared me for a scene of squalor, but what met my eyes was the complete reverse.

The front door closed behind me. 'Can I take your coat?' Oswin asked.

'Er . . . Thanks.' I took it off and he hung it next to his duffel-coat on one of three wall-mounted hooks. The hall wallpaper was some kind of anaglypta, in a pattern I seemed vaguely to recognize. It's the sort of thing one of my great aunts would have chosen and very possibly did.

'Would you like a cup of tea?' Oswin enquired.

'OK. Thanks.'

'I'll turn the kettle on. Go through.' He flapped a hand towards the open door behind me. I turned and stepped into the sitting room while he padded off to the kitchen.

The room was small and spotlessly clean, dominated by a sage-green three-piece suite. There was a television and video player in one corner and a bookcase in another, either side of a tiny tile-flanked fireplace. The walls were papered in the same pattern of anaglypta as the hall. Derek Oswin's parents – or maybe his grandparents – had obviously decided to keep it simple.

'I'm afraid I've run out of biscuits,' my host announced, reappearing in the doorway.

'Don't worry about it.'

'I expect you're wondering . . . how I know who you are.'

'And why you pretended not to back at the Rendezvous.'

'Yes.' He grinned nervously. 'Quite.' Then the kettle began to whistle. 'Excuse me.'

He vanished again and I took another look around the room, spotting the video of *Dead Against* lying on top of the bookcase. It turned out to be just the plastic cover, how- ever. The video itself had been removed. The picture on the front of the cover showed Nina Bronsky in her black leather hit-woman's gear. I'd only been given a head-and-shoulders shot on the back.

'Here we are,' said Oswin, reappearing once more, this time with a teapot, two mugs and a bottle of milk on a tray. He set the tray down on the small coffee-table next to the sofa. 'I hope you don't want sugar. I . . . never touch it.'

'Just milk is fine.' I held up the video. 'One of my questions is answered.'

'Not really.'

'No?'

'I didn't need that to recognize you, Mr Flood. I remember you as Hereward the Wake.'

This was a genuine surprise. My TV début a quarter of a century ago in a studio-bound series about the legendary leader of resistance to the Norman Conquest is a vague memory even for me.

'I've always been a fan of yours.' Oswin broke off to pour the tea. 'Won't you sit down?' He lowered himself into an armchair. I took one end of the sofa and added some milk to my mug. It was a Charles and Di wedding souvenir mug, I noticed, as was Oswin's. 'I bought a dozen,' he explained, seeming to sense that he needed to. 'As an investment.'

'You shouldn't use them, in that case.'

'Don't worry. It was a very poor investment.'

I sipped some tea. 'What's this all about, Mr Oswin?'

'Call me Derek. Please.'

'OK. Derek. Why are you bothering my wife?' It seemed pointless now to pretend Jenny hadn't put me onto him. It seemed indeed that 'Derek' had foreseen everything that had happened.

'Are you two still married, then? I thought, with her living in Mr Colborn's house . . .'

'Our divorce hasn't been finalized yet,' I said through gritted teeth.

'Oh, I see.' Derek eyed me over the rim of his mug. 'That's interesting.' He pronounced 'interesting' as four distinct syllables. He was, I realized, a strange mixture of maladroit-ness and precision, insecurity and perceptiveness.

'Interesting in what sense, Derek?'

'I'm sorry about the . . . charade . . . earlier. I suppose I . . . enjoyed stringing you along. Besides, I thought we could . . . speak more freely here.'

'So, speak.'

'I didn't mean to worry' – he smiled – 'Mrs Flood.'

'She seems to feel you've gone out of your way to worry her.'

'I can see how she might think that. But it isn't true. I just couldn't come up with any other way of engineering a meeting with you.'

'You've been harassing her in the hope that I'd come and ask you to lay off?'

'Yes.' He grimaced sheepishly. 'I suppose I have. Sorry.'

I should have felt angrier than I did. But Oswin's meek air of vulnerability somehow drained all hostility out of me. Besides, I was perversely grateful to him for another meeting he'd engineered, albeit indirectly. 'That wasn't a very clever thing to do, Derek.'

'Not very nice, I admit. I really am sorry if I've worried Mrs Flood. But clever? Well, I think it *was* that, as a matter of fact. Because it worked, didn't it? As soon as the Theatre Royal announced you were coming, I knew I'd have to try and meet you. But how could I be sure you'd *agree* to meet me? That was the problem.'

'Your solution seems to have been pretty hit and miss to me.'

'True. But I have time on my hands, Mr Flood. Lots of it. So it was worth trying.'

'How did you know my wife owns Brimmers?'

'She gave an interview to the *Argus* when the shop opened. There was only one tiny reference to you. But I spotted it.'

I bet he did. Derek Oswin was some kind of nutter, that was clear. Eccentric, if you wanted to be generous. Obsessive and possibly manic, if you didn't. But was he dangerous? I sensed not. Still, the acid test was yet to come. 'Why were you so anxious to meet me, Derek?'

'Because I've always wanted to. Ever since you played Hereward. You're my hero, Mr Flood. I've seen everything you've ever done. Even *Lodger in the Throat*. I travelled up to Guildford for a matinée in its opening week.'

'What did you think of it?'

'Marvellous. Absolutely marvellous.'

'That's not been the general reaction, I'm afraid.'

'No, well, it wouldn't be, would it? Most people are too stupid to get the point. The plot's wasted on them. They just laugh at the jokes.'

'If only they did.'

'Orton pretended to be crude and cruel, but actually he was sensitive and soft-hearted. I've been reading his *Diaries* and that's what I've come to understand. Look at the way he couldn't bring himself to abandon Halliwell, even when Halliwell started to become violent. He paid for that with his life.'

'I'm glad you enjoyed the play, Derek.'

'Oh, I did, Mr Flood, I did. You know, the set reminded me of . . . well, of this house.'

Glancing around, I saw what he meant. The set for *Lodger in the Throat* is the shabby sitting room of a small and neglected lower-middle-class family dwelling in an unnamed Midlands town. When the play opens, the three Elliott siblings, along with the wife of one of them, have gathered there following their mother's funeral. I play James Elliott, the oldest of the three. Jocasta Haysman is my wife, Fiona. Martin Donohue plays Tom, my resentful younger brother. And Elsa Houghton is our sister, Maureen. Mother's death, following Father's disappearance fifteen years previously, has freed us to sell the house and share the proceeds, which we're eager to do as soon as we can rid ourselves of Mother's disagreeable lodger and suspected lover, Stanley Kedge, the part Jimmy Maidment was ideal for but Fred Durrance somehow isn't. The property boom should have given this aspect of the plot added piquancy, but that's been lost along with a lot else during the tour. 'Actually,' I said, 'this is all far too spick-and-span to be mistaken for the set.'

'Thank you.'

'How long have you lived here?'

'All my life.'

'Your parents?'

'Both dead.'

'Any brothers or sisters?'

'No. I was an only child.'

'So, no resemblance to the Elliotts.'

'No. None at all.' He laughed – a soft, whinnying sound. 'I really like Orton's depiction of the family, though. And the way you play it. You think you can get shot of Kedge very easily, but then he starts to undermine you, one by one, to expose your guilty secrets. The state of your and Fiona's marriage. Tom's redundancy. Maureen's lesbianism. I was sorry, in a way, that Orton introduced so much farce into the plot rather than just letting Kedge pick you apart, a step at a time.'

'That would be more Chekhov than Orton.' I didn't care for the way Derek had referred to me in the second person when talking about James Elliott. The identification was – and is – a little too close for comfort. Still, I couldn't deny his analysis of the play was acute. After needling away at the Elliotts to no great effect, Kedge plays his decidedly un-Chekhovian trump halfway through the first act. Father did not just disappear fifteen years ago. Mother murdered him. '*Stuck him with the carving knife like an underdone Sunday joint*', as Kedge puts it. He shows them the bloodstains on the floorboards under the carpet and recounts how he buried the body in the garden. They can't sell now, can they, for fear that the new owner will discover the corpse and the police conclude that they knew all about it? But maybe they can, if they're desperate enough to take the risk. Except that at the end of the first act a Water Board official, Morrison, turns up to report that a leak in the locality has been traced to the stretch of main beneath their garden. It's going to have to be dug up. '*But don't worry*,' says Morrison. '*We'll put everything back as we found it.*'

'I saw you once in Chekhov,' said Derek. '*Uncle Vanya*. At Chichester.'

'You think I should play James Elliott as more of a tortured soul than a greedy prig?'

'Perhaps. I mean . . . none of you seem to miss your mother . . . or your father. There's no . . . love.'

'Do you miss your mother and father, Derek?'

'Oh yes.' He looked away. 'All the time.'

'Sorry. I didn't mean to—'

'It's all right.' He gave a crumpled smile. 'It's nice of you . . . to ask.'

'You'll have to blame Orton for the lack of love in the play.' And us for failing to draw any out, I reflected. At the beginning of the second act, James stumbles into the sitting room at dawn the following day and wakes Tom, who has spent the night there on a Z-bed. It suddenly occurred to me that I could delay waking him and look round the room at the pictures and ornaments, at all the reminders of our childhood, that I could, in a few telling moments, inject some real feeling – some love – into the part, before the farce resumes. Derek Oswin had somehow succeeded in making me want to improve my performance. Even though, by any logical analysis, it wasn't worth the effort.

'I suppose so. Although you could argue . . . that it ends on a loving note.'

'You could, yes.' Panic mounts among the Elliotts as the second act unfolds. It's Saturday and the Water Board are due in with their digger on Monday. There is an argument about whether to attempt to remove the body in the interim, assuming Kedge can be persuaded to reveal exactly where it's buried. But Kedge has an alternative to propose. He has a hold of some kind over Morrison – by implication, sexual. If the Elliotts let him stay on, he will ensure that the garden remains unexcavated. To this they reluctantly agree. Then, just as they're about to leave, an old man turns up, claiming to be a long-lost relative, as indeed he is – their father. His return from the supposed dead exposes Kedge's fraud, to which Morrison was party, and the tables seem utterly turned, until Father points out that the house is now his and he has no intention of selling, or evicting Kedge. They are, it seems, former lovers, free to admit as much and live together now Mother is no longer able to come between them.

'But Mr Durrance doesn't carry it off very well, does he?'

'No, Derek. He doesn't.'

'Was Mr Maidment better?'

'A lot.'

'I thought so.'

'He was one of the reasons I took the part.'

'And then he died.'

'Yes.'

'Which changed everything.'

'Well, death does, doesn't it?'

'You're thinking about your son?'

I stared at Derek in amazement. It was true. Peter had come into my mind, as he often does, peering uncertainly round the corner of a door my thoughts have nudged ajar. I should have realized Derek Oswin would know about him. But somehow I'd failed to.

'Now it's my turn to apologize.'

'No need.' I drained my mug. 'I must be going anyway.'

'You have a busy afternoon ahead of you.'

'Quite busy, yes.' I stood up. 'I'd like to be able to tell my wife you'll stop hanging around the shop.'

'I will. I promise. There'd be no point. Now we've met.'

'Thank you.'

'I hope the play goes well this week.'

'Are you coming to see it?'

'I wasn't . . . planning to. I haven't got a ticket.'

'I could get you one.'

'Well . . . that's very generous. Thank you.'

'What night would suit you best?'

Derek thought for a moment. 'Wednesday?'

'Wednesday it is. The ticket will be waiting for you at the box office.'

'OK. I'll look forward to that.' He rose and extended his hand. 'It's been an honour meeting you, Mr Flood.' We shook.

'Next time, approach me direct.'

'Will there be a next time?'

'I don't see why not.' He wore such a look of puppy-dog eagerness that I added, before I could stop myself, 'You could join us after the show on Wednesday. We'll make up a little party and have a meal somewhere.'

'Are you serious?'

I smiled to reassure him. 'Yes.'

'Gosh. That really is generous. Thanks a lot.'

'Until Wednesday, then.'

'Until Wednesday. Meanwhile' – he grinned – 'I'll try out some other cafés.'

'You do that.'

'Apologize to Mrs Flood for me, will you?'

I nodded. 'I'll be sure to.'

For a man as thoroughly duped as I'd initially been by Derek Oswin, I felt surprisingly pleased with myself as I headed south down London Road. I'd solved Jenny's problem for her and reckoned I could capitalize on her gratitude. Roger Colborn's absence on unspecified business I counted as a distinct advantage. True, I hadn't turned up anything to his discredit, as I'd hoped I might, but there was still every reason to suppose I could manoeuvre Jenny into seeing me again. I cut through the Open Market to reach The Level, buying a juicy Cox's Orange Pippin on the way, which I munched sitting on a bench near the playground. Then I rang her.

'Hi.'

'Jenny, it's me.'

'I hope you've got better news than I think you have.'

'As a matter of fact, I have.'

'Really?'

'I've spoken to him, Jenny. His name's Derek Oswin. He's harmless. A bit weird, like you said, but basically OK. And he's going to stop bothering you. I have his word on that.'

'What's that worth?'

'You won't have any more trouble with him. You have my word as well as his.'

'Are you sure?'

'Positive.'

'Well . . .' Her tone softened. 'Thanks, Toby. Thanks a lot.'

'My pleasure.'

'Derek Oswin, you say? I don't know the name.'

'You wouldn't.'

'Why's he been doing this?'

'It's a long story. Which I'd be happy to share with you. We could go into it over lunch.'

'Lunch?'

'Why not? You still eat, don't you?'

There was a lengthy pause. Then she said, 'I'm not sure meeting again is a good idea.'

'When does Roger get back from his business trip?'

'Tomorrow night. But—'

'Let's have lunch tomorrow, then. While you've time on your hands. I'd suggest today, but I'm due to meet the press at two thirty and it would be a rush.'

'Oh God.' The tone of her voice suggested exasperation, but there was a faint, residual fondness thrumbling away beneath it. She wasn't going to turn me down. She didn't have the heart to. Besides, lunch was the least she owed me. 'I suppose . . .'

'Just an hour or so, Jenny. There's no hidden agenda. A friendly little lunch. That's all.'

She sighed. 'All right.'

'Great.'

'I'll pick you up from the Sea Air at twelve thirty.'

'I'll be waiting.'

'OK. I'll see you then. But, Toby—'

'Yes?'

'Don't try to make something of this, will you?'

'No,' I lied. 'Of course I won't.'

I snatched a pub lunch on my way to the theatre, but nobly refrained from alcohol. Upon arrival, I was looking, it seemed to me, a good deal brighter than either Jocasta or Fred, the other two cast members regularly wheeled out to meet the press. (I'd taken steps early in the tour to block Donohue appearing on such occasions.) It was the last time we'd have to do this, but no end-of-term jollity crept into our exchanges with the less than dynamic representatives of the local media whom Brian Sallis shepherded into the auditorium.

Fred cracked his usual jokes. This he does more or less on autopilot, dreaming the while, no doubt, of a TV sitcom contract. Jocasta put on a brave face – and there are none braver – to describe what a pleasure it was to return to Brighton. I recall her saying much the same about Guildford, Plymouth, Bath, Malvern, Nottingham, Norwich, Sheffield, Newcastle and Poole. They were evidently both a little surprised when I embarked on an unprecedented considera-tion of whether the Elliotts' fractured relationships were a reflection of Orton's own family history. I have my doubts whether any of it will make it into print, but what the hell? Strangely, I felt it needed saying.

'Popped in to see your shrink yesterday, did you, Toby?' Fred enquired afterwards over a cup of tea. 'It's a bit late to come over all Freudian.'

'Just trying to ring the changes,' I replied.

'Ringing tills are the only thing that would have stopped Leo closing us down. And they didn't happen. So there's no point arty-farting round the script now.'

'I can't help myself,' I said with a shrug. 'I'm an artist.' To which Fred's only response was a peal of laughter.

While I was trading insults with Fred, a note was pressed into my hand. I didn't bother to read it until I popped into my dressing room to use the loo before the technical rehearsal got under way. The contents of the note were, to say the least, a surprise. *Please phone Jenny. Urgent.* I rang her straight away.

'Hi.' Even in that one minute monosyllable there was detectable tension.

'Jenny, it's me.'

'What in God's name are you playing at, Toby?'

50

'What do you mean?'

'You said you'd got . . . Oswin, or whatever he calls himself . . . off my back.'

'So I have.'

'No. You haven't. He's still there. Still monopolizing a stool at the Rendezvous and staring across at us. At *me*.'

'He can't be.'

'But he is. He's been there all afternoon.'

'That's impossible. He assured me—'

'He's *there*, Toby. Take my word for it. Like I took yours. For all the good it did me.'

For a moment, I was dumbstruck. What was Derek Oswin's game? In promising me that he'd leave Jenny alone, he'd sounded utterly sincere. And breaking his promise so swiftly was doubly perverse.

'What do I do now?' Jenny snapped.

'Leave it with me. I'll—'

'*Leave it with you?*'

'The technical starts in a quarter of an hour. I can't get away until after that. I'll go back to his house. Find out what the problem is.'

'I thought you already had.'

'Obviously not. But he won't pull the wool over my eyes a second time. You can count on that.'

'Can I?'

'Yes, Jenny, you can.' I grimaced at myself in the mirror above the dressing table. 'I won't let you down.'

The technical rehearsal is a blurred memory. My thoughts were vainly devoted to unravelling Derek Oswin's devious motives. Staging practicalities suddenly counted for nothing. Martin Donohue made some crack about me having late improvements to suggest, Fred having presumably tipped him off about my comments to the press, but they were far from my mind. I had nothing whatsoever to suggest, except that we finish as soon as possible. And for that there was no lack of consensus. We were done in less than an hour.

I headed straight for the stage door afterwards, debating whether I should check the Rendezvous before trying Oswin's house. But the debate was resolved before it had properly begun. A letter had been left for me with the doorman during the rehearsal. 'By some bloke in a duffel-coat.' Oswin was still at least one step ahead of me.

I stepped out into Bond Street, tore the envelope open and read the note inside, written in ballpoint in a small, precise hand.

Dear Mr Flood,
I am sorry I misled you earlier. I did not expect you to contact me so soon. I was not properly prepared. I did not tell you the whole truth. I think now I should. It concerns Mr Colborn. So, if you want to know what it is, meet me by the Hollingdean Road railway bridge at 8 o'clock this evening. I realize that is a very inconvenient time for you, but I think I must ask a small sacrifice of you as an earnest of your good intentions. I will be there. I hope you will be too. It would be best if you were. I will not give you another chance of learning what this is all about. And you will regret spurning that chance, believe me. I shall look forward to seeing you later.
  Respectfully,
  Derek Oswin

Yesterday afternoon, I knew nothing of Derek Oswin. This morning, I was still unaware of his name. Now, within six hours of our first meeting, he had me dangling on a string. I cursed him roundly under my breath as I walked through the crowds along North Street in the approximate direction of the Sea Air, wrestling in my mind with the conundrum of how to respond to his message.

He wouldn't be at the Rendezvous, of course, even if it was still open. He wouldn't be at home either. He'd make sure I had no chance of speaking to him until the time he'd chosen:

8 p.m. And to speak to him then, with curtain up at 7.45, I'd have to pull out of the evening's show. Such, in his own quaint phraseology, was the earnest of my good intentions he'd decided upon. Common sense said I should scorn his summons. Pride in my own professionalism rammed the point home. But there was the definite hint of a threat in his closing sentences. There'd be a penalty to pay for standing him up. That was certain. And only he knew what it was.

I didn't get as far as the Sea Air after all. I doubled back to Bond Street and skulked about on the opposite side from the stage door. When I'd left, Brian had been putting the understudies through their paces, but I didn't reckon that would take long. The last week of a Londonless run is no time for doing more than the minimum. Sure enough, I'd not been there above ten minutes when Denis Maple and Glenys Williams emerged into the lamplight.

I dashed across the road and caught up with them before they'd reached the corner. They looked understandably surprised to see me.

'Hello, Toby,' said Glenys. 'What's wrong?'

'Nothing,' I replied. 'Could we have a word, Denis?'

'Sure,' said Denis, frowning at me.

'I can take a hint,' said Glenys. 'See you both later.'

She beetled obligingly off, leaving Denis with the frown still fixed on his face. 'Shall we go back in?' he asked, nodding towards the stage door.

'No. What about a quick drink somewhere?'

'Do you think that's a good idea?'

'Oh yes.' In ordinary circumstances, drinking so close to a performance would have been a very bad idea. But the circumstances weren't ordinary. Not by a long way. 'Definitely.'

I piloted a bemused Denis to a youth-oriented pub in the North Laine, where anonymity for a pair of middle-aged actors was virtually guaranteed. Denis is easing his way back into the theatre after heart trouble and I was well aware he didn't need the stress I was about to inflict on him. The least I could do was give him a chance to get used to the idea that tonight wasn't going to be quite like every other night on tour.

I ordered a scotch and persuaded him to join me, then we plonked ourselves down as far as possible – which wasn't very – from the nearest rock-blaring loudspeaker.

'Something on your mind, Toby?' Denis prompted.

'Yes.' I took a swallow of whisky and came straight to the point. 'You'll be playing James Elliott this evening.'

'What?'

'You'll be standing in for me, Denis.'

'What do you mean?'

'Just what I say. I won't be there.'

'But . . . there's nothing wrong with you.'

'I have to be somewhere else.' I would have lowered my voice as I ploughed on, but the wall of sound meant our conversation had to be conducted at a bellow. 'It can't be helped.'

'You're baling out?'

'Just for tonight. Normal service resumes tomorrow.'

'You're joking.'

'No. I'm serious, Denis. You're on.'

He stared at me for a moment, then said, 'Bloody hell,' and gulped down most of his whisky.

'Want another?'

'Better not, if I'm performing tonight.' He thought about the prospect, then added, 'On reflection, perhaps I better *had*,' and held out his glass.

By the time I'd fetched our refills, his shock had lessened enough for puzzlement to show through. 'Not like you to let the side down, Toby.'

'No choice.'

'Care to elaborate?'

'Can't.'

'Are you planning to phone in sick?'

'No. Brian would be round to the Sea Air quicker than you

54

can pour a Lemsip. And I wouldn't be there. So, I wondered if . . .'

'You want *me* to tell them?'

'Would you?'

'Bloody hell.' Denis made a pained face. 'What am I supposed to say?'

'Exactly what's happened.'

'It won't go down well.'

'I imagine not.'

'Leo will get to hear.'

'Of course.'

'It'll be a black mark against you.'

'Not the first.'

'Even so . . .' Denis worked with me on several episodes of *Long Odds*. We know each other well enough for much to be left unsaid. The consequences of my no-show were sure to be uncomfortable, but, given the severely limited future of *Lodger in the Throat,* no worse than that. A little local difficulty was all either of us had cause to anticipate. 'You do know what you're doing, don't you, Toby?'

'I think so. Besides . . .' I smiled. 'You'll wow them, Denis.'

There was well over an hour to go till I was due to meet Derek Oswin when Denis and I parted. I walked down to the front and stared out to sea. I could still have changed my mind then. In fact, I *did* change my mind, several times, as I contemplated the fall-out from what I was about to do. Leo would play the heavy producer with a will. And I could hardly complain. Walking out on the show, albeit for one night only, was gross dereliction of an actor's duty. Part of me was appalled that I was even considering it.

But, in the final analysis, what did it really matter? They can say what they like. They can even dock my salary if they want to. The play's going nowhere. We all know that. Whereas my rendezvous with Derek Oswin . . .

I suddenly decided that maybe I didn't have to choose after all. I ran most of the way up to the taxi-rank in East Street and jumped breathlessly into a cab. We were in Viaduct Road ten minutes later. Telling the driver to wait, I dashed to the door of number 77 and hammered at it with the knocker.

No response, of course, and no light showing. That was as I'd expected, really, but it had been worth a try in case I caught Oswin on the premises. My guess was that he was already lying in wait for me at the meeting-place he'd nominated. I leapt back into the cab and named it as our next port of call.

Hollingdean Road is one of the limbs of the 'Vogue Gyratory', as the driver called the confused meeting-point of thoroughfares near the Sainsbury's superstore out on the Lewes Road. He stopped just short of the railway bridge, in the gateway of a used-car pound, where I told him to wait again. The cuboid roofline of a modern industrial estate loomed above me as I got out, next to the older brick ramparts of the bridge. You think Brighton is all pier and theatricals and in my game you don't have to question the thought, but Oswin was drawing me into a duller, grimmer Brighton altogether. I just had to hope I could draw myself out again in double quick time.

I hurried under the bridge, checking my watch as I went. It was gone seven now. The point of no return was approaching more rapidly than I'd allowed for. The road curved sharply right on the other side, while an access lane led straight on into a dimly lit sprawl of depots and factories. Two stark blocks of flats reared above them to the west. I looked around. There was no sign of Oswin.

A minute passed. And part of another. Then I knew. Oswin wasn't going to show up early. I wasn't going to catch him out. The terms he'd set were all or nothing. I started back to the cab.

'Where now?' the driver asked, as I opened the door and slumped into the passenger seat.

I looked at my watch again. It was 7.05. I could still be at the theatre by 7.10, the latest acceptable arrival time for the cast, or at least very shortly after. It was what I should do, professionally, prudentially. It was crazy to let Oswin mess me around. I didn't need to. I simply wasn't willing to. And yet . . . *'I will not give you another chance of learning what this is all about.'*

'Back into the centre?' the driver prompted.

'Yes,' I answered in an undertone. 'Back into the centre.'

He pulled out into the road, then reversed into the gateway, preparatory to heading back the way we'd come. I thought of Jenny and the true nature of the chance Oswin might be offering me.

'No,' I said suddenly. 'I've changed my mind. I'm staying here.'

By 7.20, Denis must have broken the news. Jocasta and Elsa would probably be worried about me. Fred's reaction would veer more towards the sarcastic, Brian's the disbelievingly dumbstruck. But he *would* have to believe it. As for what Donohue might say . . .

By 7.40, after fruitless attempts to raise me on my mobile as well as at the Sea Air, Brian would authorize the announce-ment to the audience. *'In this evening's performance, the part of James Elliott will be played by Denis Maple.'*

At 7.45, as the curtain went up, I was standing under the Hollingdean Road railway bridge, watching and waiting. I silently wished Denis luck – and myself some too.

'Mr Flood?' I heard Oswin's call before I saw him, slipping out of the shadows along the access lane. 'I'm over here.' It had just turned eight o'clock.

I moved forward to meet him. His face was a sallow mask in the sodium lamplight. I didn't have much doubt in that instant that I was dealing with a madman. But I already knew his was a very strange kind of madness. Almost more of an alternative sanity.

'Thanks for coming,' he said.

'You didn't leave me much choice.'

'You could have honoured your contract with Leo S. Gauntlett Productions. Just as I could have honoured my promise to leave Mrs Flood alone.'

'So, why the bloody hell didn't you?'

'I explained in the letter. You took me by surprise. I . . . panicked.'

'Still feeling panicky?'

'A little. I thought you might be . . . angry.'

'I will be.' I stepped closer and stared straight at him. 'If you don't tell me now what this is really all about.'

'Oh, I will. Of course, Mr Flood. Everything.'

'For a start, what are we doing here?'

'I used to work round here. Like my father. And his father before him. We all worked for the Colborns in our time.'

'Doing what?'

'What we were told. I'll show you the site.' He led the way up the gently sloping land and I fell in beside him. 'That's the wholesale meat market,' he said, indicating the long, low building to our right, above which we were steadily rising. 'And this is the City Council's technical services depot.' He pointed to the drab, straggling structure to our left. 'Up here used to be the entrance to Colbonite Limited.'

What in God's name, I wondered, was the point of all this? We'd reached a padlocked wire-mesh gate, blocking access to a compound of slant-roofed shacks, decrepit workshops and debris-strewn yards. I gazed past Oswin into the dark and dismal middle distance, perceiving nothing of the slightest significance.

'It covered the whole area between here and the railway line,' he went on. 'There used to be a siding serving one of the warehouses. It was disused by the time I started, in nineteen seventy-six, straight from school. My A levels weren't much use at Colbonite, but Dad reckoned I should be . . . contributing.'

'What did Colbonite do?'

'Made things, Mr Flood. Anything and everything in plastic. Kitchenware. Garden furniture. Radio and television casings.

58

And boxes. Lots and lots of boxes. Mr Colborn's great-grandfather founded the business in eighteen eighty-three. And his father wound it up one hundred and six years later. I haven't had a steady job since. Thirteen years there. And thirteen years away.'

'Well, I . . . '

'Not much to look at, is it?'

'No, but—'

'Why should it be? That's what you're thinking. Companies come and companies go. Livelihoods with them. So what? Who cares?'

'Apparently you do, Derek.'

He looked round at me in the darkness. I couldn't tell what sort of an expression he had on his face, couldn't tell if there was any expression at all. The traffic rumbled under the bridge behind us. A dog barked somewhere. The wind rattled a corrugated roof on the other side of what had once been the premises of Colbonite Ltd.

'How about coming to the point?' I said, trying to squeeze the impatience out of my voice.

'Yes. Sorry. Of course. Mind if we walk on?'

'Where are we going now?'

'Back towards Viaduct Road. My route home every working day for thirteen years.'

The lane curved sharply to the left ahead of us and climbed between a high wall to one side and the Colbonite site to the other. There wasn't a soul to be seen. What exactly did I think I was doing prowling around such an area with a borderline head case for company, when I was supposed to be on stage at the Theatre Royal? So far, I'd gained nothing but unsought and unwanted information about Derek Oswin's one and only spell of regular employment. He'd worked for the Colborns. He no longer did. As he himself had said: so what?

'Since my parents died,' he went on, 'I've had a lot of time to myself. Too much, I expect. Living on your own, you get . . . set in your ways.'

That was undeniable. But there are ways . . . and then there are Derek Oswin's ways. 'You said you were going to come to the point.'

'I am, Mr Flood, I am. Colbonite *is* the point. I've studied its history, you see. I've become an expert on it.'

'Have you really?'

'I probably know more about it than Mr Colborn does himself. Do you want me to tell you about Mr Colborn? Young Mr Colborn, I mean. I imagine you do. Is he worthy of Mrs Flood? The question must have crossed your mind.'

'What would you say?'

'I'd say not. He has . . . a treacherous character.'

'But it was his father who closed down the business.'

'Under pressure from his son. Roger Colborn wanted to close us down from the moment he first became involved. Colbonite held a valuable patent on a dyeing technique. He reckoned it was more profitable to sell that than keep us going. He was probably right.'

'You call that treacherous?'

'I do, yes. The workforce didn't get a slice of what the Colborns sold the patent for. All they got . . . was redundancy.'

'Even so—'

'And there was more to it than that. A lot more. So, I decided to put my excess of spare time to some use. I compiled a detailed history of Colbonite. I wrote the whole story. From start . . . to finish.'

The lane had turned another bend by now and brought us out onto a busy road leading down into the city. A brightly lit tanker was visible in the far distance, cruising across a wedge of darkness that was the sea. We started down the hill towards it.

'This is Ditchling Road,' said Derek. 'It's a straight line of sight from here down to St Peter's Church and out to the Palace Pier. It always was a lovely view to walk home with.'

'I'm sure it was, but—'

'I want the history to be published, Mr Flood. That's the thing. I can't bear to think I've gone to all that trouble for nothing. I asked Mr Colborn for help. He'd know the right people to approach. Or he could finance publication himself. He can well afford to. But he refused even to consider the idea. Of course, not everything in it is . . . to his credit . . . but it *is* the truth. Isn't that what matters?'

'It should be, Derek.'

'Not the whole truth, of course. I can't claim that. There are things I know – things Mr Colborn knows – that aren't in it. He'd realize that if he read it.'

'But he hasn't read it?'

'I don't think so. I've sent him a copy. More than one, actually. I thought the first might have gone astray. He doesn't respond to my messages. That's why I've been trying other ways to get his attention.'

I'd found Roger Colborn out in a lie. He knows Derek Oswin. I suspect he knows him only too well. It's not much of a lie, of course. Why trouble your fiancée with such a tale? A half-cracked ex-employee with a no doubt unreadable company history he wants you to usher into the literary world is someone any of us could be forgiven for airbrushing out of our acquaintance. As for closing down Colbonite and flogging off a patent, some would construe that as good business practice. Hard-headed, yes, but not especially hard-hearted.

'It's become clear to me that I'm wasting my efforts where Mr Colborn is concerned,' said Derek.

'You may well be.'

'I have higher hopes of you, Mr Flood.'

'Really?'

'Your agent, Moira Jennings, represents writers as well as actors.'

'How do you know who my agent is?'

'It wasn't difficult to find out. It's not difficult to find out lots of things, if you have the time.'

'You want me to get your history of Colbonite published?'

'It's called *The Plastic Men*. What do you think of the title?'

'Not bad. But—'

'Anyway, I don't expect you to work miracles, Mr Flood. I just want the book . . . seriously considered. If it's not deemed marketable, I shall accept that.'

'You will?' Derek's sudden ascent into realism had taken me aback.

'I'll have to.'

'Well, er, yes, you—'

'Would you be willing to ask Miss Jennings to take a look at it?'

'I might.' I pulled up. Derek carried on for a few steps, then turned to look at me. 'On one condition.'

'I promise to stop bothering Mrs Flood.'

'You promised before.'

'Yes. I'm sorry. I won't break my word again.'

'How can I be sure?'

'Because I broke my promise – and obliged you to miss tonight's performance – for a very specific reason. It was to help you.'

'Help *me*?'

'Certainly.'

'How in God's name do you reckon you've done that?'

'Can't you guess?'

'No, Derek. I can't.'

'I'd better explain, then.'

'Yes. You had.'

'It's a little . . . delicate.'

'I'm sure I can cope.'

'What I mean is . . . why don't we go back to my house and discuss it? I could . . . make some cocoa.'

Some offers are too good to refuse. Cocoa with Derek Oswin isn't one of them. But soon enough there we were, in his neat, tidy sitting room, two mugs of steaming unsugared cocoa and a plate of digestive biscuits between us. He'd obviously stocked up since my earlier visit. I eyed him expectantly across the coffee-table.

'This had better be good, Derek.'

'Don't worry, Mr Flood. It's Cadbury's cocoa. Not some supermarket brand.'

The man makes jokes. Not good jokes. And not often. But any humour's better than none, I suppose. Mine was veering towards the rueful, given that they'd be into the interval at the Theatre Royal by now.

'I didn't time our appointment to test your seriousness,' he continued through a taut smile. 'I didn't doubt that you meant to do all you could to help your wife.'

'Why, then?'

'Well, what happened when I put in an appearance at the Rendezvous this afternoon?'

'She called me.'

'And what will happen now we've met again?'

'That remains to be seen.'

'You'll surely let her know the outcome, though?'

'Yes,' I cautiously agreed.

'To achieve which you'll have let down your fellow actors and aroused the ire of Mr Leo S. Gauntlett.'

'I'm glad you appreciate that.'

'I do. And so will Mrs Flood, won't she?' His smile relaxed. 'Don't you see? I've increased her obligation to you. I've put her further in your debt. I've made it easier for you to . . . win her back.'

'I don't believe it,' I said. But I did believe it. Derek Oswin, Brighton's least likely matchmaker, had decided to punish Roger Colborn for scorning his manuscript – punish him in every way that he could devise.

'I mean your wife no harm, Mr Flood. None at all. But . . . if you want to let her think I might . . . in the interests of spending more time with her . . .' He pursed his lips and gazed benignly at me. 'That's fine by me.'

I sighed and took a sip of cocoa. It was easy to get angry with this man, but hard to stay that way. 'Broken marriages aren't so easy to put back together, Derek. They really aren't.'

'You don't know till you try.'

63

'OK. But look – ' I pointed a finger at him. 'From now on, you let me try – or not – as I see fit. Understood?'

'Absolutely.'

'You do *not* interfere.'

'Mrs Flood won't see me again unless we pass by chance in the street. I won't go to the Rendezvous. I won't even walk past Brimmers.'

'I'll hold you to that.'

'Of course.'

'I can get my agent to consider your book. I can also get her to *un*consider it.'

'I do understand, Mr Flood.'

'All right. You'd better hand it over.'

He jumped up, suddenly eager. 'I ran off a copy for you this afternoon. Hold on while I fetch it.'

He went out and up the stairs. I took another sip of cocoa, then turned round in my chair to inspect the contents of the bookcase, which was just behind me. I recognized my host's Tintin books by their phalanx of narrow red spines. He looked to have the full set. I pulled one out at random – *The Calculus Affair* – and opened it at the title page, where, next to a picture of the aforesaid professor pottering down a country lane, a fountain-penned inscription read, *To our darling Derek, from Mummy and Daddy, Christmas 1967*.

'Are you a Tintin fan?' The question came from the doorway. I turned to find Derek, photocopied manuscript in hand, staring quizzically at me.

'No. Just . . .' I closed *The Calculus Affair* and slid it back amongst the others. 'Looking.'

'That's all right.' But it didn't sound all right. There was a tightness in his voice. He was still staring, past me now, at the row of books. He plonked the manuscript down on the table, circled round behind my chair and carefully removed *The Calculus Affair* from the shelf. Then, his tongue protruding through his teeth in concentration, he fingered aside two other books and pushed it into the space between them. 'You put it back out of sequence, Mr Flood,' he explained. '*The Calculus Affair* is number eighteen.'

'Right. I see.'

'Order matters, don't you think?'

'Yes. I suppose so. Up to a point.'

'But where does the point properly lie? That's the question.'

'And what's the answer?'

'We must each find it for ourselves.' He stood upright and retraced his steps. 'And then we must preserve it. Or, if endangered, defend it.'

'So, this is *The Plastic Men*,' I said, leaning forward to inspect the manuscript, happy indeed to change the subject, given how hard I'd have found it to say what the previous subject really was.

'Yes. That's it.'

The manuscript didn't look as bulky as I'd feared it might. No thousand-page epic, then, for which I was grateful, if only on Moira's behalf. But handwritten, to judge by the top sheet, which bore the words, *THE PLASTIC MEN, a History of Colbonite Ltd and its Workforce, by Derek Oswin.* There were traces of line markings in a rectangle in the centre of the page. As I leafed through the sheets, I saw each one was the same. Derek had written his book on feint-line A5, so that photocopying it onto A4 had isolated the words within wide, white margins. Not exactly conventional presentation.

'Will you read it yourself, Mr Flood, or just send it straight off to your agent?'

'I imagine you'd like a swift response.'

'Well, I would, yes.'

'Best send it straight off, then.' Neatly handled, I reckoned. Let Moira get somebody to flog through it. She's paid to do that sort of thing. 'This way, you'll probably hear something before Christmas.'

'Oh, good. That would be nice.'

'I can only ask her to give you an honest opinion, Derek. You know what that means, don't you?'

'She may turn it down. Oh yes. That's clear enough. And fair enough. It's all I'm asking for.'

'If she says no, I don't want to hear that you've reappeared at the Rendezvous.'

'You won't.'

'I'd better not, Derek. Believe me.'

'I do, Mr Flood. I do.' He looked so contrite that my heart went out to him, sentimental fool that I am.

'I know you thought you were acting for the best this afternoon and I'm grateful for your concern. It was still a stupid thing to do, though. Nothing of the kind must happen again.'

'It won't.' He smiled, presumably in an attempt to reassure me. 'I guarantee.'

'Good.'

'Although . . .'

'What?'

'I just wondered . . .'

'*Yes?*'

'Well, when do you next intend . . . to speak to your wife?'

'That's none of your business.'

'No. Of course not. But if I can help . . .' His wobbly smile reshaped itself. 'Mr Colborn's away at the moment, you know.'

'I do know. But how do *you* know?' Stupid question, really. How does he come by any of his copious store of information?

'I, er, keep my ear to the ground. Anyway, it occurred to me . . . you might want to . . . visit Wickhurst Manor. While Mr Colborn's not in residence.'

'That doesn't sound like a very good idea.'

'No? Well, it's up to you, Mr Flood, entirely up to you.'

'So it is.'

'Marlinspike Hall, I call it.' There came a snatch of his whinnying laugh. 'Of course, if you're not a Tintin fan . . .'

'It's where Tintin lives in the books. I know that much, Derek.'

'Yes. Well done. Actually, Captain Haddock owns the house and Tintin and Professor Calculus also live there. But they didn't always. It originally belonged to Max Bird, the corrupt antiques dealer. In *The Secret of the Unicorn*—' He broke off and blushed. 'Sorry. You're not interested in all that. Though there's an odd coincidence. Mr Colborn runs his business from Wickhurst Manor. Just as Max Bird ran his from Marlinspike Hall. And they both have a habit of over-looking what's right under their noses.'

This struck me as no coincidence at all, even if it was all true, but I nobly refrained from saying so. I made to rise. 'Well, I think I'd better be—'

'Do you want to see a photograph of the house?'

'Of Wickhurst Manor?'

'Yes.'

I should have declined the offer. Instead, I heard myself saying, 'All right.'

'I won't be a tick.' He was off again, out through the door and up the stairs.

I gazed at Derek's treasured manuscript. A history of a defunct plastics company. Ye gods! I turned the title page over. Derek, to my surprise, had contrived an epigraph of sorts for his *magnum opus*, a skit on the start of T. S. Eliot's poem 'The Hollow Men'.

> *We are the plastic men*
> *We are the moulded men*
> *Leaning together*
> *Headpiece filled with polymer.*

Yes, I reckoned, Moira was really going to love this.

Then Derek was back, a wallet of photographs in his hand. He sat down and carefully laid the contents out on the table next to the manuscript. *A* photograph, he'd said, but he'd actually used an entire roll of 24 on assorted middle-distance views of Wickhurst Manor.

A red-brick neo-Georgian residence of considerable size

and style, the place is, viewed from any angle, absurdly large for two people to live in. Two matching pedimented bays with tall sash windows flank the central block, which boasts a four-columned portico to the entrance reached across a paved and pot-planted terrace. There are wings to the rear, one connected to a single-storey extension that doubles back on itself to enclose what looks like a kitchen garden. There's a large lawn to the rear, bordered by trees, a smaller one to the front, bisected by a curving drive. At the opposite end of the house from the kitchen garden there's a car park, occupied in most of the pictures by ten or twelve vehicles.

The trees are in full leaf. Sunlight gleams on the car roofs and picks out the white curls of croquet hoops on the rear lawn. This was Wickhurst Manor in high summer. When the photographer, I reflected, would find camouflage easiest to come by.

'I took most of them from the public right of way,' said Derek. I noted his delicate use of the word 'most'. 'The house was built in nineteen twenty-eight by Mr Colborn's grandfather, on the ruins of the medieval manor. The family had lived in Brighton until then, in one of the villas along Preston Park Avenue. Business was obviously booming, though Colbonite's wage rates were still rock bottom at the time.'

'What business is Colborn in now?'

'General investment. Moving his money around to make the most out of it, day to day. And advising other people on how to do the same. Hence the staff. It's an intensive operation. Mr Colborn believes in capitalizing on any advantage, however slight.'

'Perhaps he needs to, to maintain this place.'

'Perhaps so.'

'Handy for you, the right of way.'

'Rights of way are meant to be handy. I believe in using them.'

'I'm sure you do.'

'The path leads down from Devil's Dyke, crosses the

68

Fulking road, cuts through the woods near Wickhurst and heads north-west towards Henfield.'

'Sounds like you're giving me directions, Derek.'

'Well, if you need directions—'

'I'll ask.' I stood up. 'Now, I'd better be going.'

'Right.' Derek gathered the photographs and replaced them in the wallet. 'By the way . . .' He looked at me uncertainly. 'Does your offer of a ticket for Wednesday night still stand?'

I smiled. 'Of course. Unless the stunt you've pulled today goads the management into withdrawing my privileges.'

'Gosh.' His eyes widened in horror, causing his glasses to slide halfway down his nose. 'Do you think it might?'

'On balance . . .' I affected indifference. 'Probably not.'

I left *chez* Oswin with *The Plastic Men* in a Sainsbury's carrier bag and the dregs of the evening ahead of me. The theatre would be turning out shortly. Brian Sallis had probably left a dozen messages on my mobile, none of which I wanted to hear. Nor was I eager to return to the Sea Air – where doubtless more messages awaited me – any sooner than I had to. I dropped into a pub halfway down London Road and weighed my options over a scotch. *'When do you next intend to speak to your wife?'* Derek had asked. It was a good question, given that I knew she'd want to be told what I'd accomplished as soon as possible. And there was only one answer. I finished the scotch in one and headed for the taxi rank at the railway station.

Half an hour later, I was out in the colder, darker world beyond the downs, pressing a button next to an intercom grille set in one of the pillars supporting the high black-railed gates at the head of the drive leading to Wickhurst Manor.

There was a crackle. Then I heard Jenny's voice, nervously pitched. 'Yes?'

'It's me, Jenny.'

'Toby?'

'Yes.'

'What are you doing here?'

'Can I come in?'

'Why didn't you phone?'

'I thought you'd want to hear what I have to say in person.'

'Oh God.' There was a pause. Then she said, 'Well, since you're here now . . .' Then there was a buzz. The gates began to swing open.

I stepped back to pay off the taxi driver, then hurried in through the gates and started along the drive.

The noise of the taxi's engine faded into the distance. All I could hear after that was the hiss of the wind in the trees and my own footfalls on the tarmac of the drive. I rounded a screen of shrubs and saw light from the house spilling across the lawn. Then I saw the house itself. There was a figure standing in the brightly lit porch, waiting for me.

Jenny was dressed in jeans and a sweatshirt, a stark contrast with the outfit I'd glimpsed her in at Brimmers. But her expression, I realized as I drew closer, was much the same. She wasn't smiling. Then a dog barked and appeared at her side – a reassuringly placid-looking Labrador.

'Yours or Roger's?' I asked, nodding to the dog, who padded out across the terrace to meet me.

'Roger's father's originally,' said Jenny. 'Here, Chester.' Chester obediently retreated. 'You'd better come in.'

'Thanks.' I followed the pair of them into a wide hall, panelled in light wood and scattered with thick, vividly patterned rugs.

'You shouldn't have come here, Toby,' said Jenny, calmly but firmly. 'I asked you not to.'

'Did you?'

'It was understood between us.'

'But we haven't always understood one another properly, have we, Jenny?'

She sighed. 'Why did you come?'

'To tell you what's happened.' I held up the bag. 'This is

part of the price I've paid for getting Derek Oswin off your back. For good, this time.'

'Are you sure I've seen the last of him?'

'Nothing's certain, I suppose. But I'm confident. Because of this.'

'What's in the bag?'

'I'm not sure you'll believe it.'

'Try me.'

'Why don't we . . . go in and sit down?'

'This was just an excuse, wasn't it, to nose around here?'

'Not *just*, no.'

'All right. Come up.' She led the way up the elegantly curved staircase. 'Roger uses the reception rooms on the ground floor for his office. We do most of our living on the first floor.'

The stairway and the landing were decorated with tasteful lavishness, modern abstracts jostling for space on the mellow-papered walls with landscapes and portraits from a more distant era. We entered a drawing room where logs were crackling in a broad fireplace, in front of which Chester had already stationed himself. The furnishings were like a cover shot for an interior-design magazine – throws, rugs, urns; fat-spined books on the table; thin-stemmed candlesticks on the mantelpiece. Jenny favouring to my certain knowledge a plainer style, I categorized it as stuff Colborn had probably had shipped in for him by a lifestyle consultant. Disliking him was already proving to be simplicity itself.

'Do you want a drink?' Jenny asked. She held up a bottle of Laphroaig.

'Thanks.'

She poured me some and handed me the glass.

'I'd have had Roger down as a Glenfiddich man.'

'You've never met Roger.' *And you're never going to*, her eyes added.

'Derek Oswin's met him. Many times.'

Any reaction Jenny might have displayed she artfully hid in the motion of sitting down. She waved towards an armchair opposite her and I lowered myself into it. Then she said, 'Just tell me, Toby.'

'All right. Oswin used to work for Colbonite. You know about the company?'

'Of course. Roger's father closed it down . . . years ago.'

'*Thirteen* years ago.'

'There you are, then. Ancient history. Roger wouldn't remember one employee out of . . . however many there were.'

'He'd remember this one. Odd you should mention history, actually, because that's what's in the bag. Oswin's history of Colbonite. He's been trying to persuade Roger to help him get it published. Roger hasn't wanted to know. But Oswin's not one to take no for an answer, so, in his very own crackpot fashion, he's tried to pressurize Roger into reconsidering . . . by harassing you. The fact that he's a fan of mine . . . is purely coincidental.'

Jenny looked relieved to hear this explanation. She even smiled. 'I see. So, Roger pretended not to recognize Oswin in order not to worry me. While I didn't mention Oswin in order not to worry *him*.'

'Probably,' I grudgingly agreed.

'Why have *you* got the manuscript?'

'It's part of the deal I struck with Oswin. I'll have Moira give it the once over. In return, he'll lay off you.'

'But surely it's unpublishable.'

'For certain, I should think. But he'll be content as long as it's given serious consideration. I reckon that was Roger's mistake. Refusing even to look at it.'

'More likely he knows Oswin of old as a waste of space.'

We exchanged an eloquent glance. Jenny's sympathy for the flotsam and jetsam of society used sometimes to annoy me. None of it was on show now, though. Was this new hardness, I wondered, one of the consequences of her relationship with Roger Colborn, the plastic man turned arbitrageur and landed gent?

'Will Oswin honour your . . . deal . . . if Moira turns the book down?'

'He says so.'

'And you believe him?'

'Yes. He knows there's nothing more he can do.'

Jenny looked less than wholly convinced. 'Well, at the very least, I suppose it'll be a breathing space. And I'm grateful for that. How did you manage to accomplish this so quickly?'

'I missed this evening's performance.'

'You did *what*?'

'It was the only time Oswin was willing to see me.'

'Why on earth did you allow someone like that to—'

The telephone was ringing. I stared at it and so did Jenny. I think we were both certain who was on the other end. Jenny leaned across the arm of her chair and plucked the receiver out of its cradle.

'Hello?' She smiled. 'Hello, darling . . . Yes . . . Yes, very quiet.' She was on the move now, slipping out through a communicating door into an adjoining room. The door closed behind her and her voice receded to a muffled murmur. Chester opened an eye, registered her absence and sank back into a torpor.

I cast a jaundiced glance round the room, wondering if I'd recognize any of the items she kept when we separated. But there was nothing, not a single familiar object, only more of the same impeccably composed contents of an idyllic country-house life. 'Is this really what you want?' I muttered, refraining from supplying the obvious answer.

Then I spotted a framed photograph on top of the cherry-wood hi-fi cabinet. I rose and went across for a gander. There was Jenny, carefree and happy, grinning at the camera as she wrapped an arm round the new man in her life. Her companion had to be Roger Colborn. They were leaning together by the tiller of a yacht, a triangle of sail visible above them, a sparkling chunk of sea behind. Colborn looked lean, muscular and nauseatingly handsome, with thick dark hair greying at the temples, blue eyes, a firm jaw and assorted indicators of rugged machismo. To make matters worse, he and Jenny

73

appeared to be very much in love. I sighed and turned away, only to confront a reflection of myself in the mirror above the mantelpiece. Hair thinner and greyer than Colborn's, waist-line looser, musculature less evident, I could do no more than shrug.

The door clicked open and Jenny stepped back into the room. 'Sorry about that,' she said. 'Roger always calls around now when he's away.'

'Thoughtful of him.'

'Look, Toby—'

'At a guess' – I tilted the photograph towards her – 'I'd say he's about my age.'

'Yes.' Jenny compressed her lips. 'He is.'

'But wearing better.'

'I don't want to play this game, Toby. I'm grateful for what you've done about Derek Oswin. But—'

'Mention him to Roger, did you?'

'No. Of course not.'

'I should, if I were you. Secrets at this stage of a relation-ship . . . can prove tricky.'

'I probably will discuss it with him when he gets back.' I sensed she wanted to tell me to mind my own business. But the favour I'd done her meant she couldn't take such a stance. 'You can leave that to me.'

'Yes. Of course. Sorry.' I smiled, daring her to smile back. 'It's hard to get out of the habit of offering you advice.' The same, I could have added, went for several other habits. Touching her, for instance. That's something I badly want to do – now I'm not allowed to.

'I *am* grateful, Toby.'

'Least I could do.'

'I'm sorry it led to you missing the show. Won't that get you into quite a lot of trouble?'

'I'll survive.'

'I'm sure you will.'

'Are we still on for lunch tomorrow?'

'Actually, no.' She gave an embarrassed little smile.

'Roger's coming back earlier than he expected. He suggested . . . picking me up for lunch.'

I found myself wondering, for no rational reason, whether Roger had somehow got wind of my contact with Jenny and decided he'd better hurry home and spike my guns. It was an absurd idea, of course, but in that instant strangely credible. 'We could make up a threesome,' I suggested, using sarcasm to shield my disappointment.

Jenny looked at me for several silent seconds, then said, 'I'd better drive you back into Brighton.'

Jenny's bought one of the new fish-eyed Minis. She's always liked Minis. I remember the one she had when we first met. Travelling in the modern souped-up version tonight revived more than a few memories for both of us. But we didn't share them. My mind wrestled with a slippery tangle of things I wanted to say and needed to say – but didn't. Time was suddenly short. And all I could do was watch it pass.

Eventually, oppressed by the thought that we may well not meet again before I leave Brighton and spotting the Duke of York's Cinema ahead as we approached Preston Circus, I said, 'Derek Oswin lives in Viaduct Road. Number seventy-seven.'

'Do I need to know that?' Jenny countered.

'You may do.'

'I hope not. If Oswin leaves me alone, I'll be happy to leave *him* alone.'

'When you mention him to Roger, will you also mention me?'

'What do you think, Toby?'

'I think not.'

'Really?'

'Yes. Really.'

'Well, there you are, then.'

'But am I right?'

Her answer took so long coming that I began to think it never would. She had to say something, though. 'I only asked you to approach Oswin because I genuinely believed you were the key to his interest in me. I'm grateful to you for proving that isn't the case. But now you have . . .'

'You want me to back off.'

Another wordless interval followed. We were past St Peter's Church by this time, heading south down Grand Parade. I watched Jenny clench and unclench her jaw muscles. Then she said, 'That's what separation means, Toby.' She glanced round at me. 'Let it go.'

Back here at the Sea Air, Eunice had gone to bed, leaving a note for me on the hall table.

> Brian Sallis called. Phone and in person. Seems
> you've been a naughty boy, Toby. I hope you know
> what you're doing. Well, there has to be a first time
> for everything, doesn't there?
>   E.

Even in my less than joyous condition, I raised a chuckle at Eunice's characteristically perky perspective on events. I'll have to do some fence-mending tomorrow, no question about it.

I came up here to my room, broached my emergency whisky supply and pondered Jenny's parting plea to me. '*Let it go.*' Rich, that, I reckon. She came to me for help and I obliged. Now she wants me as well as Derek Oswin off her back. Life isn't quite as simple as that, Jen, however sweet and easy lover boy's made it feel lately. I'm not letting this go. Not just yet. Tomorrow, I'll post *The Plastic Men* to Moira. Then . . . we'll see.

And what *about The Plastic Men*? I need something un-readable to lull me off to sleep. Let's take a late-night look at the little man's *chef d'oeuvre*. Let's get past the title page and the epigraph and see what we find.

An *Introduction*, no less.

The Oxford English Dictionary defines plastic as 'any of a large and varied class of wholly or partly synthetic substances which are organic in composition and polymeric in structure and may be given a permanent shape by moulding, extrusion or other means during manufacture or use'.

Most of us know what the word means without needing to understand the chemistry of polymerization. Acrylic. Alkathene. Araldite. Bakelite. Bandalasta. Beetleware. Celluloid. Cellophane. Ebonite. Ivoride. Jaxonite. Lycra. Melamine. Mouldensite. Nylon. Parkesine. Perspex. Plasticine. Polythene. Polystyrene. PVC. Rayon. Styron. Terylene. Tufnol. Tupperware. UPVC. Vinyl. Viscose. Vulcanite. Xylonite. We are all familiar with at least some of these.

The first semi-synthetic plastic, based on cellulose nitrate, was invented by Alexander Parkes during the 1850s. He named the substance Parkesine and displayed it at the International Exhibition of 1862. In 1866 he launched the Parkesine Company to market products made using the material. Parkes was a brilliant inventor but a poor businessman. In 1869 he was forced to sell his patent rights to the Xylonite Company. He did not give up, however. When those patents expired, he set up in business again, launching the London Celluloid Company in partnership with his brother Henry in 1881. This venture also failed.

The Parkes' works manager, Daniel Colborn, decided to carry on alone. He returned to his native Brighton and built a workshop in Dog Kennel Road (the original name for Hollingdean Road), where he began trading in 1883 as Colbonite Ltd.

The Colbonite workforce was at first very small. It soon began to increase, however, as the company prospered. Labour was in plentiful local supply. A large area of artisans' dwellings (later categorized as slums) existed to the south. By the outbreak of the First World War, Colbonite's workforce stood close to a hundred. One of those hundred was my grandfather, George Oswin, who took a job working 55½ hours per week in the Colbonite acid shop in 1910, at the age of fourteen, on a wage of 1½d. per hour. His descriptions to me of his working life are one of the principal sources of information I have drawn on in the compilation of this history, especially where the early period is concerned.

Before I enter into an account of working conditions at Colbonite during this period and the industrial processes applied there to plastics manufacture, I should try to set the scene.

Colbonite's premises filled a roughly triangular plot bounded by the Brighton to Lewes railway line, the municipal slaughterhouse and the Jewish cemetery in Florence Place. The slaughterhouse opened in 1894, replacing the Union Hunt kennels which had given Hollingdean Road its original name.

To the south lay the small and largely middle-class parish of St Saviour's. The next parish to the south was St Bartholomew's, where most of the Colbonite workforce lived in densely packed terraces.

Most of these houses were demolished in the slum clearance programmes of 1955–66. Only photographs and memories can tell us what the area looked like before then. St Bartholomew's Church, which has the highest nave of any parish church in England, was built in 1872–4 at the instigation of Father Arthur Wagner as an inspiration for its poverty-stricken parishioners. It soared to what must have been awesome effect above the narrow streets, just as it still soars above the car parks and vacant lots that have succeeded them.

My grandparents began their married life literally in the shadow of the church, at a house in St Peter's Street. My grandfather walked past St Bart's every workday morning at about 6.30 *en route* to Colbonite, where he was due to clock on at 7.00. In London Road he could catch a tram that took him most of the way, but he only did this in severe weather. Usually, he crossed London Road, cut through via Oxford Street to Ditchling Road and walked north uphill to Hollingdean Lane, which led round to the Colbonite site.

I imagine him – as I want you to imagine him – in the final stage of that walk, dawn breaking over Brighton on a chill March morning *circa* 1930, as he approaches his destination. He is familiar with his surroundings. There is the railway line behind him, emerging from a cutting. A train may be chugging east along the track, belching steam as it accelerates away from London Road Station. To his left is the ivy-clad brick wall enclosing the Jewish cemetery. Ahead, on lower ground, is the slaughterhouse, where at that moment doomed creatures are very possibly being unloaded from a line of trucks shunted onto the siding that also serves Colbonite. Behind the slaughterhouse, smoke is rising from the chimney of the corporation's so-called dust destructor, where the collected refuse of Brighton is daily reduced to ashes. It is not a pleasing vista, though no doubt any vista is pleasing to a man such as my grandfather, who survived four years on the Western Front during the First World War – the Great War, as he always called it. (He remained grateful to old Mr Colborn for keeping his job open for him during the hostilities.)

He looks to his right as he rounds the bend in the lane and sees Colbonite's brick-built workshops, roofed in corrugated iron. He turns in past the company sign – COLBONITE LTD, PLASTICS MANUFACTURER, EST. 1883. He nods to the gateman and proceeds across the yard towards the shed where his clogs and leggings are stored. He has arrived.

The first chapter of this history will attempt to recreate in detail the kind of experience an average working day for an average employee of Colbonite such as my grandfather would have been at this time. Later chapters will consider the company's efforts to keep pace with changes in the plastics industry worldwide and how these affected the workforce. The closing chapters will analyse the circumstances leading to the closure of the company in 1989 and the fate of those who found themselves out of work as a result.

Mmm. An 'average working day' for an 'average employee' of a defunct plastics company more than seventy years ago. I'm not sure I want to know about that. I'm not sure anyone does. I'm even less sure that Moira will be willing to try and sell it. Sorry, Derek. I don't think we're onto a winner here.

I'm suddenly weary. Wearier than I would have been if I'd done my stuff at the theatre this evening. It's been a long day. And a strange one. It's time to call it a night.

TUESDAY

Tired as I may have been last night, I woke early this morning, roused as much as anything by queasy anticipation of the recriminations that were bound to flow from my no-show. A strategy of sorts evolved as I showered and shaved. It amounted to pre-emptive grovelling.

First, I wanted *The Plastic Men* off my conscience, though. I scrawled an explanatory note to Moira (that was naturally less than comprehensive in its coverage of recent events) and reached the St James's Street post office just after it had opened. I bought a large jiffy bag, stuffed the note and the manuscript inside and despatched the lot to my esteemed agent by recorded delivery. She'll receive it by noon tomorrow.

The morning was dry but drearily overcast. Brighton needs sunshine to look even close to its best. In its continued absence, I plodded down to the sea front and struck west towards the Belgrave Hotel, where I knew Brian Sallis to be staying. (Along, theoretically, with Mandy Pringle, although in practice she was almost certainly tucked up with Donohue at the Metropole.) My plan was to catch Brian early, perhaps over breakfast, before he'd properly remembered how angry he was with me.

But his day turned out to be further advanced than I'd expected. As I neared the Belgrave, I spotted him ahead of me on the promenade, dressed in jogging kit and using the railings above the beach for a hamstring-stretching routine prior to reeling off a brisk few miles along the front. I hailed him.

His first reaction was surprise. Then came puzzlement. Followed shortly by exasperation. 'Good morning, Toby,' he said through a mock smile. 'And fuck you.'

'I'm sorry about last night, Brian,' I responded.

He stared at me, then cupped a hand round one ear. 'Is that the end of the speech?'

'What else can I say?'

'You could try telling me your absence was something I just dreamt; that your unexplained, unannounced, utterly in-excusable failure to do what we pay you to do – and pay very generously at that – was merely a figment of my imagination.'

''Fraid not.'

'Alternatively, you could offer what I personally suspect you're not going to be able to concoct: a decent excuse for letting us all down. Or, failing that, maybe you could just try the truth, Toby. Yes. On balance, I'd favour that.'

'It was a personal matter, Brian. A critical situation. I had no choice but to be somewhere else.'

'Are you going to tell me what this critical situation was?'

'No. But it's over now. Permanently resolved. You have my word on that.'

'A word from you is what I'd have welcomed yesterday afternoon, Toby. A word of warning that you were going to run out on us.'

'I warned Denis.'

'You don't work for Denis. You work for Leo. And as Leo's representative, I was entitled to an explanation.'

'Yes. Like I say, I'm sorry. I don't expect to be paid for last night's—'

'You won't be, believe me. In fact' – he tossed his head and gave the railing a thump with the heel of his hand – 'Leo was all for laying you off for the rest of the week. I talked him round in the end, not because I was anxious to go easy on you, quite the reverse, but—'

'Because you'd sell fewer tickets.'

'Yes,' Brian reluctantly agreed.

'Which Leo would have been quick enough to realize himself once he'd stopped spitting nails. I do understand. We're locked in a commercial embrace.' As grovelling went, this sounded defiant even to my own ears. I tried at once to soften the message. 'I'll give it a hundred per cent for the rest of the week.'

Brian sighed. 'That's something, I suppose.'

'It's the best I can do.'

'Just don't expect any offers from Leo in the near future.'

'I won't.'

Brian frowned at me. Good-hearted fellow that he basically is, he'd worked off his anger, leaving space in his mind for gentler thoughts. 'You're not in any kind of trouble, are you, Toby?'

'None you can help me with.'

'What's that supposed to mean?'

'I don't know.' I summoned a smile. 'Generalized mid-life crisis. Plus pending divorce from a woman I'd very much like to stay married to. Troubles enough, without pissing off one of the West End's leading impresarios for good measure.'

'You said it.' Brian pondered my litany of woes for a moment before continuing. 'Does this have anything to do with Jenny? I gather she lives in Brighton now.'

'So she does.'

'And?'

'And nothing. Tell me how the show went . . . without me.'

'Since you ask, Denis rose to the challenge magnificently. He turned in an excellent performance.'

'Maybe I did him a favour, then.'

'Maybe. But let's be clear. This was a one-off. Any repetition . . . and I couldn't answer for what Leo might do.'

'There'll be no repetition.'

'Officially, it was twenty-four-hour flu.'

'I've recovered ahead of schedule, then.'

'Just make sure there isn't a relapse. I'd like you at the theatre early tonight. Let's say six thirty.'

'Fair enough.'

'Until then . . .'

'Yes?'

'Stay out of critical situations.'

'I'll be sure to.'

'OK.' He began a tentative jog on the spot. 'You should take up running, Toby. It might help with those troubles.'

'I'll think about it.'

'See you later, then.' He turned and started off towards Hove.

'You will,' I shouted after him.

My evening performance as James Elliott was in truth the only certainty in the day that lay ahead of me. Last night, light-headed after whisky on an empty stomach and overtired to boot, I confidently asserted that I'd prise my way into Roger Colborn's secrets in the hope of finding some that would sour Jenny's relationship with him. Easier said than done, of course. Walking slowly in the direction Brian Sallis had run off in, I admitted to myself that I had no good reason to suppose such secrets existed, let alone any obvious method of penetrating them.

I stopped and leaned against the railings, staring out glumly at the grey, listless motion of the sea. It wasn't too late to talk Eunice into rustling up some breakfast. Nourishment might even prove inspiring. I decided to head back to the Sea Air.

My mobile rang before I could act on the decision. I guessed the call would be from Moira. I suspected word of my misdemeanour might already have reached her. But it wasn't from Moira. Nor from anyone else I'd have expected to hear from.

'Ah, Toby. Denis here.'

'Denis? What are you doing up? You should be sleeping the sleep of the just after standing in for me so valiantly – and so impressively, Brian tells me.'

86

'The play went all right, no question. It was good . . . being out there again.'

'Why do you sound so down in the mouth, then?'

'Could we meet . . . for a chat, Toby? Like . . . now?'

'All right. But . . . what's this about? I can assure you I'll make it on stage tonight.'

'It's nothing to do with the play.'

'What, then?'

'I'll tell you when we meet.'

I had to be satisfied with that and we agreed to meet at the Rendezvous in a quarter of an hour. Denis, of course, had no reason to think the choice of venue significant. I told myself it made sense to check that Derek Oswin really was laying off Jenny. But maybe the proximity to Jenny it offered was its real appeal.

I was the first to arrive and had guzzled a Danish by the time Denis put in an appearance. Happily, there was no sign of Derek. I stood Denis a coffee and we sat down at a corner table, where he lit up with ill-disguised urgency.

'I thought you'd given up,' I remarked with studied neutrality.

'So did I.'

'I hope this isn't a reaction to performing last night. I never intended to put any undue—'

'Forget the play, Toby. This is about what happened afterwards.'

'Afterwards?'

'I've been in two minds about whether to tell you. But I think . . . you really had better know.'

'Know what?'

'I'm ashamed of myself, to be honest. I should never have allowed the situation to develop. But . . . the evening had gone so well. I just thought it was getting better and better.' He shook his head. 'Stupid. Bloody stupid.'

'What are you on about, Denis?'

'All right. I'll get to the point.' He lowered his voice and leaned forward confidentially. 'Several of us went into the Blue Parrot for a drink after the show. You know the place? Just along from the theatre. Anyway, I'd not been there above five minutes when this girl – a real looker, she was – sidled up to me and congratulated me on my performance. She called me Toby and said what an honour it was to meet me. I assumed she'd missed the announcement about me standing in for you and, I don't know why, but I didn't . . . point out her mistake. Well, I do know why, of course. I was afraid it might put her off. I mean, she was just gorgeous and . . . she was giving me the eye and . . .'

'You thought you were onto a good thing.'

'Yeah.' Denis nodded in dismal agreement. 'That's about the size of it. She didn't speak very good English. She clearly *wasn't* English. I reckoned that accounted for the misunderstanding. But I wasn't bothered. Why would I be? It's not often I get luscious young lovelies coming onto me. She suggested going to some club she knew. I was half-cut and . . . pretty pleased with myself. So, I left the others to it and Olga – that was her name – and I went to some basement jazz joint this side of North Street. We weren't there long. I mean, she was all over me, Toby. Starstruck and . . . randy with it.'

'Why do I have the feeling this ended badly?'

'Because I wouldn't be telling you about it otherwise. Next stop after the jazz club was her flat. She lives in Embassy Court. Well, that's where she took me. You know it? Art Deco block on the sea front. Seen better days. A lot better, let me tell you. Outside it's just dilapidated. Inside . . . it's a rathole. I should have turned round and walked straight out.'

'But you didn't.'

'No. We made it to her flat. I was . . . pretty high by then. I reckon she must have spiked my drinks. I was . . . up for anything. And so was Olga. Before I knew what was happening, she started taking her clothes off. Well, I gave her a helping hand. Who wouldn't in the circumstances? It seemed like my lucky night. Turned out to be anything but. I'd just got her down to her G-string when a door from an adjoining room burst open and this big bloke – I mean, seriously big – was suddenly pulling us apart. He was frighteningly strong. And angry. But angrier with Olga than with me. "This is the wrong man," he shouted at her. "This isn't Toby Flood, you brainless tart." Then he threw me out. Literally threw. I'm lucky not to have some broken ribs to add to the bruises. I remember bouncing – yeah, actually bouncing – off the wall on the other side of the corridor and seeing the door of the flat slam shut behind me. I heard Olga screaming inside. I think . . . he was hitting her.' Denis's head drooped. 'I got the hell out.'

I couldn't find anything to say at first. The implication was clear. Somebody had put up the girl to lure me back to a flat in Embassy Court. Why? What exactly were they planning to spring on me? And who were they? More to the point, who were they working for?

'Perhaps I should have tried to fetch help,' Denis went on. 'I feel responsible for whatever man mountain did to Olga after I'd slunk away. I *did* mislead her, after all.'

'You also think she spiked your drinks, Denis. Remember that.'

'Even so . . .'

'And where would this help have come from? The police?'

Denis rolled his eyes. 'Seemed wiser to crawl back to my B and B and pretend it had never happened.'

'I'm sure it did.'

'Thought I'd better fill you in on it, though. Somebody targeted you, Toby. No question about it. Maybe Olga's under age. I mean, you just can't tell these days, can you? Specially when you're not thinking straight to start with. It could have turned nasty. Very nasty.' He smiled grimly at me through his cigarette smoke. 'Except you'd probably have had the good sense to give her the brush-off at the Blue Parrot.'

'I'd like to think so.'

'Did you see something like this coming? Is that why you didn't do the show last night?'

89

'Absolutely not. Believe me, Denis. I had – I have – no reason to think I'm being . . . targeted.'

'But you are, old son. Take my word for it.'

'I don't suppose Olga gave you her surname?'

'No. Nor her national insurance number. She's probably an illegal. And, before you ask, I didn't think to note the flat number. I can't even be sure which floor we were on. I wasn't at my most observant. Even if I had been, it'd probably do you no good. As for man mountain, I'd go a long way to avoid meeting him, if I were you.'

'Yes, but—' Interrupted by the trill of my mobile, I snatched it out of my pocket. Moira this time? Wrong again.

'Hello, Toby.'

'Jenny. Hi.'

'What are you doing over there?'

'Oh. You, er, spotted me, did you?' I craned for a view of Brimmers through the window, but could discern little beyond smoke, condensation and assorted passers-by. 'Well, I thought I ought to check that Derek Oswin's playing ball. And I'm glad to say he is.'

'So I see.'

'Don't worry. I'm not going to make a habit of it.'

'Is that Denis Maple with you?'

'Yes. Do you want a word?'

'No, no. But . . . give him my love.'

'OK.'

'Goodbye, Toby.'

The call ended. Denis raised an eyebrow at me. 'Jenny?'

'She lives in Brighton. Runs the hat shop opposite here, actually.'

'Really?' He peered towards Brimmers. 'Is that why you chose this place to meet?'

'In a sense. She sends her love, by the way.' A strange commodity, love, I thought. Ample to share among friends and acquaintances, yet it can't be dispensed, even on a token level, to an estranged spouse.

'You should never have let her go.'

'I'm well aware of that.'

'Is it too late to . . . repair the damage?'

'Probably.'

'But not definitely.'

'No. Not definitely.'

'You've got the rest of the week to work on it.'

'So I have.'

'Ah!' Denis seemed suddenly to have glimpsed the truth. 'Is that what you were up to last night?'

'Maybe.'

'Just as well Olga got the wrong man, then. Wouldn't have looked too good to Jen, would it, if the police had been after you for whatever was planned to happen in that flat?'

'No, Denis. I think we can safely say that it wouldn't.'

I left Denis to chill out as best he could after his experiences of the night before, walked back down to the front and made my way along to Embassy Court. I remembered it vaguely as a visually striking chunk of Thirties Art Deco: white-plastered balconies tiered like a sleek-lined wedding cake. But the only wedding cake it resembles now is Miss Havisham's. Lumps of plaster have fallen off. Some of the windows are boarded up. Rust is leaching through the balconies.

I stood by the Peace Statue on the seaward side of the road, looking up at the building, wondering if by any chance Olga was looking down at me. Perhaps it was just as well Denis couldn't remember which flat she took him to. There was no telling what might happen if I succeeded in tracking her down.

Someone had put her up to last night's mischief, though. That was obvious. Who stood to gain from blackening my name? I could only think of one candidate. But he wasn't supposed even to be in Brighton, let alone have any reason to believe I posed the slightest threat to him.

Then another thought struck me, as disturbing in its way as it was also weirdly comforting. Why had I missed the show? Because Derek Oswin had forced me to. As an earnest of my good intentions, so he'd said. But could he actually have lured me out to Hollingdean Road to ensure I came to no harm elsewhere? Was it possible that he'd appointed himself my guardian angel?

If so, it suggested he knew who was gunning for me. I hot-footed it up to Western Road and boarded the next number 5 bus to come along.

My mobile rang just as the bus was pulling away from the Royal Pavilion stop. At the third time of asking, it *was* Moira.

'A very good morning to you, Toby. How's the head?'

'Clear as a bell, Moira. Why shouldn't it be?'

'Not hung in shame, then? Nor topping off a spike outside the Theatre Royal?'

'Ah. Leo's been onto you, has he?'

'Yes. And I fully expect his lawyers to be onto me some time today as well.'

'No, no. He'll call off the dogs when he hears I'm back on board. The box office would take too big a hit without me. I'm in sackcloth and ashes. But I'm still in a job. You don't need to worry about your commission.'

'I'm actually more worried about you, darling. You've not previously been noted for an artistic temperament. What happened? Did everything get too much for you?'

'A personal crisis blew up. Now it's blown over. Simple as that.'

'Doesn't sound simple.'

'I'll tell you all about it next time we have lunch.'

'I'll hold you to that.'

'Meanwhile, I've, er, a favour to ask of you.'

'Apart from salvaging your professional reputation, you mean?'

'Yes, Moira. Apart from that.'

By the time I got off the bus near the top of London Road, Moira had agreed, albeit bemusedly, to have one of the agency's literary specialists give *The Plastic Men* prompt and serious attention as soon as she received it. She had also urged me to put in a *mea culpa* call verging on the obsequious to Leo Gauntlett, in the interests of papering over the cracks in his opinion of me. I reckoned I'd need a few stiff drinks before making such a call, which was one of several good reasons for postponing the task.

The chance of an illuminating chat with Derek Oswin was another. But no answer came the stern reply at 77 Viaduct Road. Whatever he was doing in lieu of camping out at the Rendezvous, it evidently didn't involve staying at home. Nor did I have a mobile number for him. In fact, I rather doubted he possessed a mobile. Even a land-line was touch and go. I'd not noticed a phone in the house. It would be entirely like him to be technologically incommunicado.

I found myself walking back into town along Ditchling Road, past the Open Market. Remembering Derek's account in his introduction to *The Plastic Men* of his grandfather's route to work, I cut through to London Road along Oxford Street. The vast, soaring flank of St Bartholomew's Church was dead ahead. I began trying to imagine the area in the old man's day. Trams, gas lamps and as many horse-drawn vehicles as petrol-driven. All the men in hats, all the women in skirts. It wasn't so very different. Not really.

Standing outside St Bart's, though, I realized that wasn't true. Where had all the houses gone? Where were the rows upon rows of 'artisans' dwellings'? Vanished. Swept away. Erased. Such is the reach of municipal dictate. But its reach isn't limitless. It can't alter the past. It can only rewrite the present. And pay lip service to the future.

Suddenly, I remembered Syd Porteous. *'Anything I can do for you while you're here – anything at all – just say the word.'* And for him I did have a mobile number. Why not tap his allegedly compendious local knowledge? Why not indeed? I tugged the beer mat with his number on it out of my coat pocket and gave him a call.

'Hullo?'

'Syd Porteous?'

'Hole in one. That sounds like . . . hold on, hold on, let

the grey matter work its magic . . . Toby Flood, the errant actor.'

'You're right.'

'But are *you* right, Tobe? That's the question. My contacts in the usheretting community tell me you let down the punters last night. I've got a ticket for tonight, you know. Should I be asking for my money back?'

'No, no. I'll be on tonight.'

'Great news. And I'm more than appreciative of this personal reassurance. Nice one, Tobe.'

'That's not . . . the only reason I rang.'

'No?'

'You said . . . if there was anything you could do for me . . .'

'Any assistance, small or large, a pleasure and a privilege. You know that.'

'I wondered if we could . . . meet up again. Run over a few things.'

'Absolutely-dootly. When did you have in mind?'

'As soon as possible. This lunchtime, perhaps?'

'Fine by me. The Cricketers again?'

'Why not?'

'Okey-dokey. Noon suit you?'

'Well, I . . .'

'Grrreat.' Whether Syd was genuinely trying to impersonate Tony the Tiger of Frosties fame I wasn't sure, but it certainly sounded like it. 'See you there and then.'

I had just over an hour to concoct a cover story for the questions I planned to run past Syd. I went into the church in search not so much of inspiration as of a quiet place to think and found myself in a vast and curiously empty space more like a Byzantine ruin than an Anglican church. Father Wagner had cleverly supplied the parishioners with as complete a contrast to their domestic circumstances as could be imagined. I wondered if little Derek had come here of a Sunday with his parents and grandparents. I wondered if he'd gazed up at the distant roof and dreamt of touching the sky. I decided then to abandon the cover story before I'd invented it. I decided to ply Syd with an approximation of the truth.

His Tuesday lunchtime gear was the same as his Sunday evening kit, but he'd swapped wine for beer and put one in for me as well. 'Unless,' he said with a wink, 'you go Methodist on play days.'

'Beer is fine,' I responded, just about catching his drift.

We retired to a fireside table with two pints of Harvey's. 'It's a real bonus seeing you again so soon, Tobe,' he said after a swallow of best bitter. I winced more than somewhat at 'Tobe', realizing that I really hadn't misheard on the phone, but knew I'd have to go with it. 'To what do I owe it?'

'Well, it's, er . . . a delicate problem.'

'Delicacy is my speciality.'

'My wife and I split up a few years ago.'

'Sorry to hear that. Occupational hazard, so they say.'

'It's pretty common in the acting profession, that's for certain. Anyway, our divorce hasn't come through yet, but—'

'Are we talking last-minute reconciliation here?'

'No, no. Jenny lives with a man. They plan to marry as soon as they can. I . . . well, they live near Brighton, as a matter of fact. The point is that Jenny and I parted amicably. I'm still . . . concerned about her. So, I'm anxious to assure myself that this bloke's not . . .'

'A wrong 'un?'

'Yes. Exactly. And he's local. So, thinking about what you said Sunday night, I wondered if . . . you might know anything about him.'

'Hoping to dig up some dirt, are you, Tobe? Something that would make Jenny think twice about marrying him?'

'If there's dirt to be dug, fine. If not, fine again.'

'Point taken.' Syd leaned as far across the table as his paunch allowed. 'Who is he?'

'Roger Colborn.'

Syd frowned thoughtfully. 'Colborn?'

'Know the name?'

'Maybe. What else have you got on him?'

'Some sort of businessman. Lives in a big house out near Fulking. Wickhurst Manor.'

'Thought so.' Syd grinned. 'Father in plastics.'

'Yes. Colbonite Limited.'

'That's it. Colbonite. Walter Colborn – Sir Walter, as he became – was Roger's old man. He had a younger brother, Roger's uncle, Gavin. Gav and I were in the same year at Brighton College.'

'You were?'

'No need to look so surprised. My dad had high hopes for me. His timing was spot-on, as it happens. He didn't go bust until the year after I left. But that's another story. Gav made senior prefect and went to Oxford, much good that it did him. Time's evened up the achievements score between us, I'd say. He's having to prop and cop these days, same as me, but he doesn't have the aptitude for it. Too old, too lazy and usually too drunk to make the effort. That about sums him up.'

'How well do you know him?'

'Middling to fair. We're not exactly close.'

'And the nephew?'

'I've met him a few times. Nothing more. Gav doesn't speak kindly of him. That I can tell you. Whether it damns the fellow . . . is trickier to say. Gav got nothing out of the family business, see. His father left it all to Wally, probably for a good reason. That's niggled away at Gav over the years. So, the nephew who inherited the lot isn't top of his pops.'

'I suppose that might make Gavin quite . . . forthcoming . . . where Roger's concerned.'

'Very possibly.'

'Any chance of . . .'

'Meeting for a chinwag? I think I might be able to arrange that, Tobe. Seeing as it's you who's asking.'

'It'd be great if you could.'

'Shouldn't be too difficult. Can I let him know scotching Roger's marriage plans could be a part of the equation?'

'If you think that'll make him happier to talk to me.'

'Sure to, I'd say.'

'I appreciate this, Syd. I really do.'

'Don't mention it. Leave *me* to mention it, when I need a favour in return.' Syd guffawed. 'Don't worry. I haven't got a starstruck niece trying to get into RADA by the back door. The odd complimentary ticket's about the most I'm likely to touch you for.'

'Any time.'

'Actually, though, now I come to think about it . . .' He looked almost sheepish as he turned an idea over in his mind.

'What?'

'Well, I, er, I'm . . . bringing a guest to the play tonight. A lady. To be as frank and open as you must already know I always am, Tobe, Audrey's not been that long widowed, so I'm treading carefully. Trying to register a few Brownie points. If you could see your way clear . . . to joining us for a bite of supper after the show . . . I reckon I might just zoom up in her estimation.'

In the circumstances, I could hardly refuse. Not for the first time, Syd had outmanoeuvred me, since it appeared that I'd be repaying a favour before it had actually been done. 'My pleasure, Syd.'

'Grrreat.' He beamed tigerishly at me. 'We're going on to the Latin in the Lane. Do you know it?'

'I think so, yes.'

'Maybe you could catch up with us there when you've got changed. You know, spring a surprise on her.'

'OK.'

'And by then . . .' He winked. 'I might have news of my old school chum.'

Supper with Syd Porteous and Audrey the eligible widow wouldn't have been my choice of late-night entertainment, but at least it sounded safe, which, with Denis's misadventures in mind, was an undeniably good thing. I excused myself from a prolonged session at the Cricketers on the excellent grounds that Syd would want me to be at my actorly best

97

come the evening and took myself off for a fish and chip lunch. Gavin Colborn promised to be a valuable contact, possibly *in*valuable: an embittered uncle to tell me the worst about his well-heeled, good-looking nephew. Or the best, depending on your point of view.

A couple of hours' zizz was what I needed to set me up for the evening. I headed for the Sea Air with that as my sole ambition for the afternoon. Halfway along Madeira Place, however, I was waylaid.

I noticed a sleekly glowing dark-blue Porsche parked on the other side of the road. One admiring glance was all I gave it. Then I heard the door slam and my name was called. 'Toby Flood?' I turned and looked.

And there was Roger Colborn in jeans, leather jacket and sweatshirt, leaning against the driver's door and gazing across at me. He smiled faintly, as if daring me to pretend I didn't know who he was.

'Can we have a chat?'

I crossed over to his side, elaborately checking for traffic to give my brain a chance to work out what he was up to. It failed. 'Roger Colborn,' I announced neutrally.

'Pleased to meet you, Toby.' He offered a hand. We shook. 'I've just been having lunch with Jenny.'

'Oh yes?'

'She told me about the help you've been giving her . . . with this little shit, Oswin.'

I nodded. 'Right.'

'I'm ahead of my schedule today. So, I thought I'd come over and thank you. In person.'

'There was no need.'

'When someone goes out of their way for me, I like to acknowledge the fact.'

'But I didn't . . . go out of my way for you.'

'For me. For Jenny. Same difference.' His smile broadened. 'Busy this afternoon?'

'Not really, no.'

98

'Then come for a drive with me. I reckon we ought to . . . get to know each other.'

'You do?'

'It'll avoid any . . . future misunderstandings. Come on. This beauty's been cooped up while I've been away. I need to give her a run. Why not come along? We can talk on the way. And let's face it, Toby, we do need to talk.'

Colborn had a point. He also had an edge of steel beneath the thin, silky affability. I could have argued the case for declining his invitation. But the case for gleaning whatever there was to be gleaned from his company was a good deal stronger.

We started north, the Porsche dawdling throatily along the city streets, then struck east towards the racecourse. Colborn's priority seemed to be to explain why he and Jenny had kept each other in the dark where Derek Oswin was concerned, although he must have realized I'd place my own construction on that, whatever he said.

'There's been a communications failure, Toby, in this case for the best of reasons. Neither of us wanted to worry the other. I know Oswin of old, of course. I've been ignoring him in the hope that he'll go away. It never occurred to me that he'd bother Jenny. Seeing him with a video of one of your old films naturally made her think his interest in her had something to do with you. There you have it.'

'I quite understand.'

'I'm glad you do. And, like I say, I'm also grateful. To be honest, I think it's a good thing we've met like this. You and Jenny were together quite a while. There's no sense trying to pretend your relationship with her never happened. It's part of her. We're adults, you and me. We know how it works. We should be able to deal with it.'

'I agree.'

'Great. So, what have you got lined up after this play?'

'Oh, there are several possibilities.' I had no intention of discussing the state of my career with Colborn, however adult and rational we were supposed to be. A change of subject was in order. 'I'm curious about Oswin. What can you tell me about him?'

'He used to work for my father's firm, Colbonite. I did myself, for a while. On a different level from the likes of Oswin, obviously. Christ knows what he's been up to since it folded.'

'Nothing, as far as gainful employment's concerned.'

'No surprise there. The guy's a loser.'

'But he's been in touch with you?'

'Sadly, yes. He's bombarded me with letters and phone calls about this history of Colbonite he's written. He's even sent me copies of the bloody thing.'

'Read it?'

'I'm a busy man, Toby. Ploughing through the rambling reminiscences of Derek Oswin isn't something I have either the time or the inclination to get around to. My father wound Colbonite up thirteen years ago. It was just a two-bit middling plastics company. One obscure victim of the slow death of British manufacturing. Who the hell cares?'

'Oswin said something about a valuable patent.'

'Did he?' Colborn's brow furrowed briefly at that, then he concentrated on the mirror as we joined the A27, heading east. A surge of acceleration took the Porsche into its pre-ferred cruising range. But its driver's discourse had stalled.

'Was it valuable?'

'Mmm?'

'The patent.'

'Oh, moderately. It was a formula to prevent discoloration by sunlight. One of the company's precious few assets. But selling it didn't make my father rich beyond the dreams of avarice, let me tell you.'

'Richer than the redundant workforce, though, I assume.'

'They were paid their dues. Oswin has nothing to complain about.'

'I'm not sure he *is* complaining. About that, anyway.'

'What will your agent do with the book?'

'Read and reject, I imagine.'

'Let's hope that satisfies Oswin.'

'I think it will.'

'And you think I should have arranged something similar before this got out of hand. Well, you think right.' Colborn glanced at me. 'Thanks for getting me out of a hole I dug for myself, Toby. You've done *me* a favour as well as Jenny. I won't forget that.'

How magnanimous of him. And of me. At this rate he'd soon have been inviting me to a round of golf at his club. We were two civilized men of the world, finessing our way round the compromises and contradictions of embodying both Jenny's past and her future.

Complete bullshit, of course. What Roger Colborn was really engaged in was risk assessment. Was I an irritant that would soon go away of its own accord? Or a challenge he had to face down?

Somewhere beyond Lewes, he turned off the main road and headed up a steep lane onto the downs. There was a parking area at the top and broad vistas in all directions: a quilt of fields and woodland to the north, a grey slab of sea to the south.

'Game for a walk, Toby?' he asked in the moment of silence after the engine had died. 'I find the open air helps clear my thoughts. And there's something I really do want to be clear about.'

I agreed, with little enthusiasm. We climbed out into a cold-edged wind. I gazed along the crest of the downs, where a couple of hikers were the only humans in sight. The going looked chill and muddy. I was persuaded to squeeze into a spare pair of wellingtons. We set off. And Colborn began to lay out his thoughts.

'Jenny's made me a better person, Toby. Maybe she did that for you as well. If so, losing her must have been a real blow. I certainly wouldn't want to go back to being what I was before I met her. It was the biggest stroke of luck in my life. I'll never do anything to hurt her. You have my word on that.

101

I love her. I honestly believe I always will. And I know I'll always protect her. She's safe with me. It's important you should understand that. I may not be quite as good for her as she is for me. That would be impossible. But I'm good enough. Plenty good enough.'

'I'm sure you are,' I lied.

'But what about you, Toby? Where are you going? According to Jenny, things aren't looking too bright for you. Tell me to mind my own business if you like, but, as I understand it, this play you're in has been, to put it bluntly, a flop.'

'It hasn't gone as well as we'd hoped.'

'And film work's pretty much dried up for you.'

'I wouldn't—'

'There's no need to be defensive about it.' He held up a hand to silence me. 'The point is that I have contacts in the film world. Not Hollywood, it's true, but in Europe. Co-production's the name of the game. I have a stake in several projects.'

'What are you trying to say?'

We stopped. He turned to look at me, the wind ruffling his hair. 'I'm saying I could get you into something. Back on the screen. In the relatively big time. Where you belong.'

He meant it. That was obvious. And whether you regarded it as the repayment of a favour or the removal of a stone from his shoe, the effect was the same: a problem solved for both of us. This, I suddenly realized, was what being a businessman meant. The making of attractive offers. The doing of productive deals. Cost-effectiveness. The profit margin. The bottom line.

'We don't have to like each other, Toby. Mutual respect is all it takes.'

'Why be a loser when you can be a winner? Is that what you mean?'

'Something like it.'

'I'd be a fool to turn you down, then.'

'So you would. But I come across plenty of fools. I'm used to having win-win propositions thrown back in my face.'

'I'm a jobbing actor, Roger. I can't afford to say no.'

'In that case, we'd better make sure there's something lucrative on hand soon for you to say yes to.'

'It'd be music to my agent's ears.'

Colborn smiled 'Don't you just love being pragmatic?'

'It's something of a novelty for me,' I coolly replied.

'You'll get used to it.' His smile broadened. 'I promise.'

We returned to the car and started back towards Brighton. Colborn elaborated briefly and pointedly on the nature of his profitably pragmatic business.

'It's all about timing, Toby. When to get into something. When to get out. And the key to timing is the same as the condition upon which God hath given liberty to man: eternal vigilance. That's what my staff do for me. Observe vigilantly. Freeing me to take time off. And to open my mind. I've learned to reject nothing without considering it. And to be willing to reject everything. It's worked well for me.'

'Do you have any relatives or dependants to support?'

'Ex-wives and children, you mean? None. Which helps, of course. It's easier to take risks when there's no-one else to worry about. Meeting Jenny's made me a little more risk-averse, I admit, even though she's quite capable of supporting herself, as the success she's made of Brimmers demonstrates. To be honest, I'd always avoided long-term relationships, partly because I knew they might turn me into a more cautious operator. But I've got to the stage where I can indulge a little caution. And Jenny's well worth any adjustments I've had to make to my life.'

It was all plausible enough, this slickly packaged version of himself Colborn was serving up. But it didn't convince me. And not just because I didn't want to be convinced. I'd spotted a flaw in his logic. What exactly was the ratio between the profits he'd turned on his shrewdly timed investments and the pile of cash he'd no doubt inherited from his father – the residue of that 'two-bit middling plastics company'? It wasn't so much about timing as editing. And when you edit a

103

story there's always a danger that you'll leave a few loose ends dangling. I decided to give one a tug.

'Where was your office before you inherited Wickhurst Manor, Roger?'

'I didn't . . . put the business on its current footing until after my father died, actually.' That was one up to me. And he knew it. His change of tack was swift and clumsy. Or maybe it was just meant to *seem* clumsy. 'I hope missing the play last night didn't get you into too much trouble, by the way.'

'I'm weathering it.'

'Good.' He judged a pause minutely before continuing. 'How did your stand-in cope?'

It was an unusual question to ask. Why should he care? Why should he even bother to enquire? The only answer that came to mind was a deeply disturbing one. It was bad enough to think Denis might have been the victim of a botched set-up meant for me and commissioned by the man who'd just made me an offer too good to refuse. But it was somehow worse, far worse, to suppose that the set-up hadn't been botched at all; that Denis's brush with calamity had been devised quite deliberately as a message to me: a demonstration of what might befall me if I were foolish enough to reject the offer.

'I trust he didn't do too good a job,' Colborn went on with a chuckle. 'You wouldn't want the idea to get around that you're . . . expendable.'

Soon enough we were back in Madeira Place. 'Thanks for the ride,' I said as I climbed out. 'My pleasure,' he responded. I closed the passenger door behind me and watched him pull away. The car sped the short distance to the end of the street. Its brake lights blinked. Then it swung onto Marine Parade and was gone.

I headed straight across the road, sleep out of the question now but some kind of rest definitely in order. A glance up at the ground-floor bay window of the Sea Air told me that too was to be denied me. The residents' lounge ought by rights to have been deserted, given that I'm the only resident. As a result, I thought for a fragment of a second that the face I saw peering down at me might be some kind of hallucination. But no. Melvyn Buckingham really was there, craning his neck round the wing-back of his chair for a view. Our celebrated director had paid me a call.

I encountered Eunice in the hall, bearing a tea-tray towards the lounge. She whispered an apology to me. 'I'm *really* sorry about this, Toby. I couldn't turn him away, could I? Not when he's come all this way.'

'You didn't have to bake him a cake,' I grumbled, catching the homemade aroma rising from a generous slice of Dundee.

'I baked it for *you*. Here.' She handed me the tray. 'Take it in while I get back to my chores.'

I scowled after her as she descended discontentedly to the basement, then took a deep breath and processed into the directorial presence.

Melvyn was kitted out in the squirely tweeds he favours despite his metropolitan lifestyle. His expression, which ranges swiftly from approving smirks to pained grimaces during rehearsals, was currently fixed in a frown that indicated either anger or perplexity.

I plonked the tray down and smiled at him. 'Brian didn't say you were thinking of coming down.'

'It was to be a surprise,' Melvyn responded. 'Ever since Leo told me he wasn't bringing the play in, I've been meaning to see for myself where you've gone wrong. I was in the Canaries last week, catching the sun, so this was the soonest I could manage. I mentioned the trip to Leo over lunch yesterday. As you can imagine, it's turned out to be rather more apposite than I'd anticipated. Leo called me at an ungodly hour this morning, asking – nay, insisting – that I read you the riot act on his behalf.'

'He's over-reacting. I missed one performance. That's all there is to it.'

'Very possibly. But he who overpays is entitled to over-react.'

'Do you want some tea?'

'I *want* a stiff gin, dear boy. But in its absence I suppose the soothing leaf will suffice.'

I poured and handed him his cup, adding, 'I recommend the cake,' in my most enticing tone.

'It does look good.' Melvyn's gluttony has always eclipsed his professional judgement. He was a goner. 'All right.'

I handed him that too and watched as he took a bite. He was still munching through a first mouthful to his evident satisfaction when Eunice flounced into the room, balanced a plate bearing another slice on the arm of my chair and flounced out again.

'Leo's anxious to ensure things don't go off the rails this week,' Melvyn spluttered through the sultanas.

'They won't.'

'Fortunately, the *Argus* didn't make a big thing of your . . . indisposition.' He nodded to a copy of the paper lying on the floor next to his chair. 'There's a lot of flu about.'

'But I'm over mine.'

'I certainly hope so.'

'There's nothing for Leo to worry about.'

'He doesn't seem to agree. I fear the letter spooked him.'

'What letter?'

'You didn't know about it?'

'I've no idea what you're referring to.'

'Oh.' He wiped some crumbs from his lips. 'You'd better take a look, then.' With an effort, he pulled a piece of paper from his jacket pocket and handed it over. 'It was delivered to Leo's office this morning.'

As soon as I unfolded the sheet, I recognized the handwriting. In one sense, the source was no surprise. In another . . .

77 Viaduct Road
Brighton
BN1 4ND

2nd December 2002

Dear Mr Gauntlett,
I do not want you to worry when you hear that Mr
Flood has missed this evening's performance of
Lodger in the Throat. As you may be aware, Mr
Flood's estranged wife lives here in Brighton. Since
Mr Flood arrived yesterday, I have been assisting
him as best I can in his endeavours to effect a
reconciliation with Mrs Flood. I feel sure you would
not want to stand in the way of such a development.
After all, it would make Mr Flood a more
contented man and therefore a more assured actor.
    As it happens, it is necessary for Mr Flood to be
somewhere other than the Theatre Royal this
evening. He will probably decline to explain his
absence, which is why I am writing to emphasize
that it is quite simply unavoidable if his future
wellbeing is to be secured. In the circumstances, I
am confident that you will be tolerant of the
inconvenience caused to your company.
    Incidentally, perhaps I could take this opportunity
of mentioning that the play's disappointing
performance on tour is largely attributable in my
opinion to the unsympathetic direction of Mr
Buckingham, who has insisted upon treating it as
some form of drawing-room comedy rather than
the merciless satire on family life that it actually is.
    Respectfully yours,
    Derek Oswin

The name Edna Welthorpe popped into my thoughts as
I finished the letter. She was the pseudonymous phantom

Joe Orton invented for the purpose of writing teasing and tendentious missives to institutions whose pomposity needed pricking (in his opinion). Sometimes she'd even fire off a prudish complaint to a newspaper about one of Orton's own plays, all publicity being good publicity. I felt instantly and instinctively certain that Derek had written to Leo in the spirit of Edna Welthorpe, calculating that I would see the joke – but that neither Leo nor Melvyn would. But, though I saw the joke, I was also the victim of it. Derek really was mad, in the Ortonian sense. There was no telling what he might do next. If I'd thought I was in control of the situation, this letter showed me to be deluding myself.

I handed it back to Melvyn. 'I seem to have a prankster by the tail,' I said through a simulated smile. 'This is rather embarrassing, isn't it?'

'You *are* acquainted with Mr Oswin, dear boy?'

'Yes. But he isn't acting as my go-between, or—'

'Then why did you miss the play?'

My smile became a stiff grin. 'You've got me there.'

'Who is he?'

'Nobody you need to bother about. In fact, that's exactly what he is. Nobody.'

'I wish Leo agreed with you. He seemed to think the ghastly little pipsqueak had a point.' Melvyn reddened. 'About my direction.'

'Oswin's just trying to get a rise out of us.'

'But *why* did you miss the play?'

'All right.' I held up my hands in surrender. 'It did have to do with Jenny . . . and my attempts to persuade her to . . . call off the divorce. But Oswin isn't . . . assisting me . . . in any way.'

'Then how does he know so much about it, pray?'

'Oh God.' I stood up and stared out through the window, a view of slowly falling dusk seeming preferable to holding Melvyn's gaze. 'There'll be no more Edna letters, I assure you.'

'Edna?'

108

'Never mind. Forget Derek Oswin. Please. Leave him to me.'

'I'd be glad to.'

'I'll sort him out.' I gave my dimly reflected self a confirmatory nod. 'Once and for all.'

I eventually persuaded Melvyn to leave on the grounds – to which he could hardly object – that I needed a rest before the performance. This was undoubtedly true. But lying on my bed, with the only light in the room a drizzle of amber from the nearest street lamp, I found rest hard to come by. What did Derek Oswin think he was playing at? The question would have been troubling enough to ponder without the added complication of Roger Colborn's brazen attempt to buy me off, backed up as it very possibly was by the threat of still cruder inducements. What in the name of sweet Jesus had I got myself into? And how, more to the point, was I to get myself out?

Not, I reasoned, by storming round to Viaduct Road and throttling the epistolarian of number 77, tempting though the idea was. Derek would probably claim he had written to Leo in the genuine hope of persuading him to go easy on me, just as he had supposedly manoeuvred me into missing the play in the first place solely for the purpose of making Jenny think well of me. It could even be true. I didn't know whether I was over- or under-estimating him. He'd sent the letter to Leo before knowing if I'd do his bidding, which suggested a supreme confidence in his tactics. But confidence and madness often go hand in hand.

Not in Roger Colborn's case, though. He's the ultimate rationalist. And confident to boot. It occurred to me that he and Derek are strangely alike, for all their apparent dissimilarity. They both think they have the measure of me. And they both might be right. *I* certainly don't have the measure of *them*. Yet.

*   *   *

Gavin Colborn may be my conduit to the truth. And I was relying on Syd Porteous to lead me to him. Until my post-show supper with Syd and his lady friend, therefore, I could make no headway. Derek would have to wait. Everything was on hold. Until I'd got back on stage and done my stuff. As some seemed to doubt I still could.

But I wasn't one of them. In fact, tonight's performance of *Lodger in the Throat* was a liberation for me. I could stop thinking about the complexities of the Jenny–Roger–Derek triangle and enjoy myself as James Elliott, the middle-aged middle-class man of repute who suddenly senses that his carefully managed life is falling apart around him. I stopped straining for effects and played it like I saw it was. For the first time, I found myself believing in the person I was supposed to be. Orton hadn't written a comedy with a serious undercurrent, I realized. He'd written a tragedy so bleak you had to laugh at it.

And *how* they laughed. A Brighton audience was bound to be at the sophisticated end of the spectrum of those we'd played to, but their responsiveness none the less took me by surprise. If it had been like this earlier in the tour, we'd all be looking forward to a New Year in the West End. We'd hit our stride too late.

That we'd found it at all was attributed by an over-excited and over-lubricated Melvyn Buckingham to my more asser-tive projection of the character of James Elliott. And this, he told anyone who was willing to listen as drinks and hangers-on circulated afterwards round the star's and co-star's dressing rooms, was the result of an intensive examination of the role we'd conducted earlier.

'It's strange,' I smilingly whispered to Jocasta. 'I don't seem to have any memory of that.'

'Something galvanized you, Toby,' she said. 'Even if it wasn't Melvyn.'

'More likely to have been the widespread reports of how well Denis did last night.'

110

'He did do well. But he's still not in the same league as you, not when you're really on form, anyway. That bit at the start of act two, where you delayed waking Tom and took a sort of poignant tour of the set – where did that come from?'

'Not sure. It just . . . came.'

I was sure, of course. Derek Oswin of all unlikely people had turned me into a better James Elliott. I didn't know whether to welcome his influence or resent it. Either way, he was hardly a conventional source of artistic advice. In fact, however you looked at it, he was a thoroughly disturbing one.

Melvyn was evidently set on making his night in Brighton memorable. I extricated myself with some difficulty from the party he was getting together and headed for the Latin in the Lane.

The restaurant was three-quarters full, bubbling and bustling in best late-night Italian tradition. Judging by the numerous glances and murmurs I attracted on my way through, many of the diners had adjourned there from the Theatre Royal. Among those was Syd Porteous, who'd added a tie to his standard clobber. It looked worn and thin enough to be of the old-school variety. He greeted me as if we'd known each other for years (which in some strange way it felt as if we had) and introduced me to his suitably surprised companion.

'Sydney, you dark horse,' she exclaimed. 'You never said it was Mr Toby Flood we were meeting.'

'An evening with me is a venture into the unexpected,' Syd responded with a roll of the eyes. 'Tobe, this lovely lady is Audrey Spencer.'

Audrey *was* lovely, despite an outfit that might have flattered her fifteen years ago but now verged on the affectionately sarcastic. There was a lot of bosom and a lacy fringe of bra on display. And the pink trousers – I couldn't avoid noticing when she set off for the loo later – were stretched round a bottom that needed camouflage rather than emphasis. What age couldn't either wither or expand, though,

111

was the sparkle in her eyes, her mischievously crooked grin and her effervescently winning personality.

'I haven't enjoyed myself at the theatre as much in I don't know how long,' she enthused. 'That Orton was a one, wasn't he? Not that the words would count for a lot if you didn't deliver them so well, Toby. Sydney tells me he actually met Orton once. Has he mentioned that to you?'

'He has, yes,' I replied, glancing at Syd.

'I had no idea he moved in such exalted circles, you know. I'm beginning to realize he's a man of mystery. Just as well I like a good mystery, isn't it?'

At which Syd fingered his tie and tried to give his self-satisfied smirk a mysterious edge.

Such banter continued as we ordered our meals and made steady inroads into the Piedmont end of the wine list. Syd wasn't one to stint ladies *or* actors. Feeling more than somewhat pleased with myself following what had to count as our best yet rendering of *Lodger in the Throat*, I was happy to indulge my host, especially in view of the pay-off I was hoping for.

This was delivered during the first of Audrey's nose-powdering expeditions. Syd lowered his voice to a hoarse growl, leaned towards me and announced, 'I've been in touch with Gav Colborn as promised, Tobe. He's happy to meet. The Cricketers at noon tomorrow suit you? Same time, same place, like? May as well keep it simple.'

'I'll be there.'

'Perfecto. Although, as it happens, you don't have to wait until then for some interesting gen on the Colborn clan.'

'I don't?'

'No. Wait till Aud gets back. She can spring it on you.'

'Audrey can?'

I had to be content with one of Syd's ludicrously choreographed winks by way of an answer. Within a few minutes, though, Audrey rejoined us, whereupon Syd asked her to tell me all about something they'd discussed earlier.

'Oh, *that*.' Audrey cast a sympathetic glance in my direction. 'Are you sure Toby wants to hear about it, Sydney? It's really not very exciting. Or jolly. And we're supposed to be having fun.'

'I hope you are, darling,' said Syd, using 'darling' for the first time I could recall. 'Tobe *will* be interested, I promise.'

'All right, then.' She turned towards me. 'Sydney asked me if I'd heard of a plastics company called Colbonite, though why he should think I might have done . . .'

'He that asketh receiveth,' murmured Syd.

'Well,' Audrey went on, 'it's a strange thing, but I do know the name. I'm secretary to one of the consultants at the Royal Sussex. He's a cancer specialist. Over the years, he's treated quite a lot of people who worked for Colbonite. The thing is—'

The trill of my mobile was a sound I didn't want to hear. With a gabbled apology, I plucked it out of my pocket, intending to dispose of the caller in short order. Melvyn in his cups was my bet, urging me to join the party. But it wasn't Melvyn.

'Toby, this is Denis. Where are you?'

'A restaurant in the Lanes.'

'Is there any chance . . . you could meet me . . . sort of right now?'

'I'm in the middle of a meal, Denis.'

'I wouldn't ask if I wasn't . . . pretty desperate.' And it was true to say he did sound desperate. There was a quiver of anxiety in his voice.

'What's wrong?'

'The man mountain who threw me out of Embassy Court has shown up at my digs. They're after me, Toby. Christ knows why. But I'm frightened, I don't mind admitting it. I don't know what to do.'

'Where are you now?'

'I'm at a bus stop in North Street, with a load of students waiting for a midnight run back to the University. I figure there's safety in numbers. But there won't be any numbers to be safe in when the bus turns up.'

I struggled to suppress my irritation, knowing that if Denis was in trouble, it was probably on my account. 'OK, OK,' I said. 'I'll be with you as soon as I can get there.'

I rang off and smiled ruefully at my bemused companions. 'I'm *really* sorry about this. A friend of mine is . . . in difficulties. I'm going to have to go and find out what the problem is.'

'You're leaving us, Tobe?' Syd looked positively distraught. 'Don't say that.'

'I've no choice, I'm afraid.'

'We understand, Toby,' said Audrey. 'What are friends for but to help out in an emergency?'

'True enough,' Syd reluctantly agreed.

'Do you have time for me to finish telling you about Colbonite?' Audrey asked. 'There isn't a lot to it, in all honesty.'

'Well . . .' I glanced at my watch. It was approaching a quarter to midnight, which meant Denis was safe enough for the present. 'I can stay for a few minutes.' And I did want to hear about Colbonite. Oh yes. 'Your boss treated a lot of workers from Colbonite, you said. For cancer?'

'Yes. Of the bladder, mostly. I don't know about "a lot", though. More like a steady trickle. Terminal cases, usually, I'm afraid.'

'And this has gone on . . . since the company closed?'

'Yes. Well, cancer often develops a long time after exposure . . . to whatever causes it.'

'And what does cause it . . . in these cases?'

'I don't know.'

'But Gav might,' put in Syd.

'Yes. I suppose he might.' I looked back at Audrey. 'How many cases are we talking about?'

'I couldn't say.'

'Go on. Just a guesstimate. I won't quote you on it.'

'Well . . .' She thought for a moment, then said, 'Several dozen at least.' And then she thought for another moment. 'Maybe more.'

I must have left the Latin in the Lane later than I'd thought. By the time I reached North Street it was five past midnight. The city centre's main thoroughfare was cold and empty. There was no knot of raucous students waiting for transport back to the campus. And no sign of Denis.

I retrieved his mobile number from my phone and rang it. No answer. I tried again. Still no answer.

I stood at one of the deserted bus stops, wondering what to do next. Denis might have got on the student bus, I supposed, although a trip out to Falmer would only leave him with the problem of how to get back. Or he might have pulled himself together and returned to his lodgings. But there we came to a gaping lack of information. I didn't know where he was staying.

Unable to think of any other recourse, I rang Brian Sallis. There was a slur to his voice when he answered and a blurred hubbub in the background. I imagined he was in a restaurant somewhere, with Melvyn and most of the cast. And I imagined they were having a good time – unlike me.

'Toby? Where are you?'

'A bus stop in North Street, since you ask.'

'*What*? Get yourself down here. We're at the King and I in Ship Street. Great squid, let me tell you.'

'Nice idea, Brian, but I have to find Denis Maple. Do you know where he's staying?'

'He's probably tucked up in bed by now.'

'I don't think so. And this is urgent. *Where is he staying?*'

'No need to shout, old chap. Anyway, I haven't got that info on me, Toby. Somewhere in Kemp Town, I think. Hold on. I'll ask.' But asking did no good. No-one's memory was working too well. I cut Brian off in the middle of further urgings for me to join them and rang Denis's mobile again.

Still there was no answer. 'Where are you, Denis?' I said aloud. 'Where in hell are you?'

Could he have headed for the Sea Air? It was one possibility I could check fairly easily. And it was in the same

115

general direction as his lodgings, so there was some frail kind of logic to it. I started walking. Fast.

Within minutes, I'd reached the Old Steine. Traffic was thin and buses there were none. The stops to left and right were all empty. I started across towards St James's Street, redialling on my mobile as I went. Yet again, there was no answer.

But then, just as I was about to give up, I heard a bleeping, joining the ringing tone in a weird stereo. I was halfway along the pavement that runs past the northern side of the gardens around the Victoria Fountain. I stopped dead and listened for a second, hardly able to believe what I was hearing. The phone stopped ringing and the message service cut in. I cancelled the call and redialled. The phone started up again. I turned to my right, towards the fountain.

There was a figure lying on the ground near the base of the fountain, readily mistakable for one of the many deep shadows cast by shrubs, bench-ends and cast-iron dolphins. I knew it was Denis before I reached him. He was lying on his side, legs drawn up. As I stooped and rolled him over onto his back, his mobile fell out of his hand.

'Denis? Denis, are you all right?' But he was as far from all right as you can get. His mouth was open. But he wasn't breathing. His eyes stared sightlessly up at me, a shaft of lamplight catching the whites. I felt beneath his ear for a pulse, then at his wrist. Nothing. I jabbed at the 9 button on my mobile. A chasm of time opened around me in the dark-ness and the silence. At last, there was an answer. I demanded an ambulance. I gabbled out our location. 'He's not breath-ing,' I shouted. 'I think his heart's stopped. I need you here *now.*'

It's a straight run from the hospital. The streets were empty. The ambulance was probably there within five minutes. It felt infinitely longer, of course. I dredged some first-aid principles out of my memory and tried to kick-start Denis back to life with mouth-to-mouth and chest compressions. But it's more than likely my technique was too faulty for any good to have

116

come of it. I felt stupid and helpless and desperate. And responsible. Yes. I felt that as well.

Death's the biggest absolute of all. Strange, then, that we can be so vague about the moment of its arrival. The heart stops beating. The body stops moving. Later, eventually and reluctantly, the brain closes down. When exactly that happened to Denis Maple – at what precise minute he finally blinked out of existence – is a matter for futile debate. Was it before I found him? Or while I was manhandling him to no effect? Or during the ambulance ride? Or later still, at the hospital? I don't know. I never will.

The pronouncement, though: I can be clear about that. A nurse came to me in the hospital waiting area. 'I'm afraid it was too late,' she said. 'We couldn't save him.' Denis was dead, a heart attack the preliminary verdict. I'd mentioned his heart trouble, so it must have seemed a straightforward case to the doctors. Something like this was always on the cards for a man in his fragile state of health. Alcohol; stress; over-exertion: anything could have brought it on. He was just unlucky to be alone when it happened.

Unlucky? Yes, Denis was certainly that. Maybe his biggest misfortune was to be a friend of mine. I put him up for the understudy job. He needed something undemanding to ease his way back into acting. And he needed the money. So, I helped him out.

Of this world, it now transpires. The strain of performing last night. The strife he ran into afterwards. And the events of tonight, which I can never ask him to relate or explain. I brought those down on his head. And his heart.

I must have phoned Brian. Or else I must have asked the nurse to do it for me. I can't remember exactly how it happened. But at some point he was there at the hospital, along with Melvyn and Jocasta and Mandy. They were all there. And so was I.

But Denis wasn't. He was nowhere.

*   *   *

117

'What happened?' they asked me. And I tried to tell them. But I didn't really know. And what I did know can have made little sense. A garbled call. A search. A discovery. A death. You could squeeze the context and meaning out of it if you were so minded and all you'd be left with is a medical fact. Denis's heart stopped. And so did he.

They delivered me back to the Sea Air, concerned that I was in shock and shouldn't be left alone. I roused myself sufficiently to persuade them that I'd be all right. Eventually, they left.

In the morning, Brian will notify the rest of the cast and company. Then he'll contact Denis's next of kin. 'A tragic misfortune' is probably how he'll describe it. Not like Jimmy Maidment's suicide. There's no cause to think this is a jinxed production. As for the rest of us . . . life goes on. And so must the play. Let's see it in proportion. Denis wasn't well. A game guy, but an ailing one. Even understudying was too much for him. It's sad it had to happen. What else is there to say?

I sit here in my room, with my whisky and my tape recorder, trying to piece together in my mind what must have happened. After the second act got under way, Denis probably went for a meal with Glenys. (I can check that with her in the morning.) Then what? A few drinks on his own somewhere? (Glenys is no night owl.) A film, maybe? If I'd looked, I might have found an Odeon ticket stub in his pocket. It's a trivial detail in itself, of course. The fact is that around eleven o'clock Denis must have got back to his lodgings and found the man mountain from Embassy Court waiting for him. Or spotted him waiting and beaten a retreat. Maybe he was followed. That would explain him taking refuge in a bus queue. Maybe he just *thought* he was followed. Same difference, really. So, he phoned me. The only one who'd take him seriously. But the bus arrived before I showed up. He didn't get on. He waited for me. Not for long, though. Maybe he saw man mountain again. Maybe he just panicked. Same difference again? I don't think so. I was only five minutes late. Surely he'd have hung on that long. My guess is that he left because he had to. He was followed. Or chased. Was he running when the pain hit him? He must have known what it was. He headed for the benches by the fountain to rest. Or to hide. He took out his phone to make a call. For an ambulance, maybe. Or to me. Whichever it was, he never got as far as dialling the number. He went down. And stayed there. His pursuer melted away into the night. Precious minutes slipped by. Too many minutes. Until I found him.

What do I do now? They were getting at Denis to warn me off, to show me what they were capable of. They can't have meant to kill him. They can't have known he had a weak heart. But he did. And now he's dead because of it. And because of *them*. And because of *me*. Somebody should pay for that. Yes. Somebody really should.

WEDNESDAY

I woke this morning to the fleeting delusion that Denis Maple's death was just a dream. Reality soon had me back in its grip, however. I'd slept for seven solid hours, but didn't feel more than superficially refreshed. It was gone ten o'clock. I was due to meet Gavin Colborn at noon. And there was someone else I needed to see first.

Already, my day was barely under control. My days on tour had previously been slow, short and empty. But that had changed now I'd come to Brighton.

I showered, shaved and dressed hurriedly. Then I called Jenny. She didn't sound pleased to hear from me. And she didn't want me to come round to Brimmers; I could say what I wanted over the phone. But I couldn't. In the end, I think she understood that. We settled on the Rendezvous at 11.15.

Heavy rain was falling from an ashen sky, the rain driven diagonally up Madeira Place by the wind beating in off the sea. The weather made the route I took to the Rendezvous, along the storm-lashed front and up Black Lion Street, a crazy choice. But I wasn't ready to cross the Steine yet and to pass the spot near the fountain where I'd found Denis. I wasn't just looking for answers. I was avoiding some as well.

I wondered if the staff of the Rendezvous had begun to notice Derek Oswin's absence, or to recognize me as a regular. They gave no sign of either as I bought a coffee and joined Jenny at her table.

She was looking stern and impatient. I think she'd been debating with herself whether I was in danger of becoming as much of a nuisance as Derek. Clearly, she had no idea what I was about to tell her.

'Denis Maple's dead.'

'Oh God.' Shock silenced her for a moment. Then she asked, 'What happened?'

'Heart attack.'

'That's dreadful. I'm sorry, Toby. You and he got on so well. It must be a blow. To the company as well. I mean, coming after Jimmy Maidment . . . When did this happen?'

'Just after midnight.'

'And when did you hear about it?'

'I was there when he died, Jenny. Or just after. He'd phoned me. He was worried, you see. Worried and frightened. Somebody was following him. *Chasing* him.'

'Surely not.'

'Surely yes. You know why he and I met here yesterday morning? Because Denis wanted to tell me something. Something he reckoned I *had* to be told about.'

'What?'

I studied Jenny's face as I related Denis's story and the events of last night. I blurred the context, of course. I said nothing about Syd Porteous or the meeting with her fiancé's uncle he was setting up for me. Nor did I mention said fiancé's virtual offer to me of a film part. The rain sluiced down the window behind me. Steam rose from the *espresso* machine. And skittering there, in the faintest twitches of Jenny's mouth and the flickers of her gaze, I read the beginnings of doubt. She wasn't sure – she wasn't absolutely certain – that all this amounted to nothing.

'I'm sorry Denis is dead,' she said, breaking the silence that fell after I'd finished. 'He was a lovely man.'

'Yes. Which would be tragic enough. But he didn't need to die. That makes it worse than a tragedy.'

'You don't know what happened after you spoke to him. You can't know. He may have . . . imagined the man at his lodgings.'

'No. Denis was as level-headed as they come.'

'He was also a sick man. For all you know, sicker than he was letting on.'

'I'll give you that. It's possible, entirely possible. But something more than his own imagination tipped him over the edge. And that something comes back to me.'

'What are you suggesting?'

'I'm *deducing* exactly what I'm supposed to deduce, Jenny: that paying attention to Derek Oswin isn't a good idea. That I should lay off. That I should leave well alone.'

'Denis was drunk by his own admission on Monday night and probably drugged too. You can't draw any conclusions from what he *thought* happened to him at Embassy Court.'

'I think I can.'

'Well, you *can't*.' She glared at me. 'It's absurd.'

'Reckon I've got it all wrong, do you?'

'Yes. I do. Why in God's name should anyone want to stop you speaking to Derek Oswin?'

'Presumably they're afraid of what he might tell me.'

'What *can* he tell you, Toby? He worked for a plastics company, not MI5. For Christ's sake, pull yourself together.' She blushed and looked around, suddenly aware that she'd been speaking too loudly. She hunched forward and dropped her voice. 'Listen to me. You're upset about Denis. You're getting this out of proportion. There's no conspiracy going on. There's just . . . life . . . and death.'

'I suppose a heart attack's better than cancer.'

'What's that supposed to mean?'

'A lot of Colbonite's staff died of cancer. Did you know that?'

She didn't answer. Maybe she couldn't answer. She stared at me, blinking rapidly, struggling to decide there and then whether the things I'd said reflected any more than my desire to believe the worst of Roger Colborn. She wanted to believe

125

the best of him, naturally. Neither of us was exactly unbiased. Which made the truth hard for us to come by – or to recognize when we did.

'I may have given Roger the impression yesterday that I could be bought off. Could you put him right on that for me, Jenny? There's no deal.'

Now she was angry. I'd taken a step too far. I'd lost her. 'Nobody's trying to buy you off, Toby.' She pushed her chair back, the feet squealing against the floor, and stood up. 'I'm not going to listen to any more of this. It's—' She steadied herself, holding up both hands and closing her eyes as she took a deep breath. Then she opened them and looked down at me.

'Jenny, I—'

'*No.*' She looked at me a second longer. 'Not another word.' She turned and headed for the door.

Leaving me to stare into my coffee and begin the all too easy task of calculating how I could have handled our conversation so much better. The waitress came over to clear Jenny's cup. As she did so, the spoon fell out of the saucer and clattered down onto the table.

'Sorry,' she said.

'Me too,' I murmured.

I was still slumped over the dregs of my coffee some minutes later when my mobile rang.

'Toby, it's Brian Sallis. How are you feeling this morning?'

'Much the same as last night, Brian. How are you?'

'Rather shook up, actually. But I, er . . . just wanted to . . . check you were OK.'

'I'll be on stage tonight. You don't need to worry.'

'I didn't mean that. I meant . . . generally.'

'Generally? On the grim side of OK, I suppose.'

'This has knocked the wind out of everyone's sails, Toby. I've been . . . notifying people all morning. There's a lot of . . . distress.'

'Denis was a popular guy.'

'So he was. Look, on that subject, could you do me a favour?'

'Try me.'

'I spoke to Denis's brother earlier. Ian Maple. He's coming down here today. He wants to know what happened and, well, you know more than anyone.'

'You want me to talk to him?'

'I'm meeting him off the train and taking him round to the undertaker's. After that, I'm not sure what he'll want to do. Could I ring you this afternoon and fix something up?'

'Sure.'

'Thanks. I appreciate it. It's shaping up into a pretty bloody day, to be honest, with the press to handle and . . . everything else. Melvyn's gone back to London, by the way. I mean, that was the plan all along, but—'

'We wouldn't want Melvyn to have to change his plans.'

'No.' Ordinarily, Brian would have sprung to our director's defence, but he didn't seem disposed to make the effort this time. 'Thanks again, Toby. I'll be in touch later.'

It was close to noon when I left the Rendezvous, dashing from shelter to shelter through the rain to the Cricketers, where the foul weather had kept custom to a minimum.

Rain or shine made little difference to Syd Porteous, however. He was already installed with a pint and a crumpled newspaper. He greeted me with a frown of concern and a solicitous pat on the shoulder.

'Sorry to hear you've lost one of the company, Tobe. Bit of a facer, that.'

I looked at him in some dismay, unprepared as I was for the news to have spread so fast. 'How did you know?'

'It was on the local news this morning.'

'What did they say?'

'Nothing much. Denis Maple was his name, right? Understudy. Heart attack, apparently.'

I nodded. 'So it was.'

'The name rang a bell. Tell me to mind my own if you

like, Tobe, but was it him you had to rush off and meet last night?'

'Yes.' I had no choice but to admit it.

'So . . . what happened?'

It was a fair question. I couldn't have supplied a complete answer even if I'd wanted to. Syd already knew more about my affairs than was good for him. Far more than I knew about his. Some judicious pruning of the facts was called for. 'Denis was obviously upset when I spoke to him. He was probably already feeling unwell. He'd keeled over by the time I got to him. There was nothing I could do.'

'He was the bookie in *Long Odds*, wasn't he?' Syd asked.

'You have a good memory.'

'Names and faces.' He tapped his forehead. 'They've always stuck. Aud and I were sorry you had to dash off like that. If we'd—' He broke off as the door opened behind me. 'Watch out. Here's Gav.' Then he added, in a hasty whisper, 'Best not mention the untimely to him, hey? Might jangle his nerves.'

I was still puzzling over Syd's reasoning when he commenced a grinning introduction. Gavin Colborn failed to reciprocate with a grin of his own, my impression being that he'd need lessons before attempting one. His narrow, bony face was set in sombre lines beneath a jutting brow. He was as thin as a rail and slightly stooped, dressed in a frayed grey suit and black rollneck beneath the sort of raincoat Harold Wilson used to wear. He'd lost most of his hair and the only similarity to his nephew was to be found in the bizarrely beautiful sapphire blue of his deep-socketed eyes. The idea that we needed to worry about making him nervous seemed utterly absurd.

'Great to see you, Gav,' Syd enthused irrepressibly between the practicalities of ordering drinks. 'It's been too long. Far too long.'

'I don't get out so much these days,' said Colborn, a gust of sour whisky reaching me on his breath.

'You'll have seen Tobe's face on the poster at the Royal.'

'I've not passed that way recently. I'm no theatregoer, Mr Flood.'

'It's not everyone's cup of tea,' I responded, speculating idly on what Gavin Colborn's cup of tea could possibly be.

'I gather you want to discuss my nephew.'

'Small talk's never been Gav's speciality,' said Syd as we carried our drinks to the fireside table that was rapidly becoming our regular berth. 'I've told him it's the key to success with the ladies, but he takes no notice.'

'I assume you're a busy man, Mr Flood,' said Colborn, lighting up a cigarette. 'I don't want to bore you.'

If this remark was meant as a put-down, it signally failed. 'We're on first names here, Gav,' said Syd. 'Isn't that right, Tobe?'

'Yes, Syd,' I said with self-conscious emphasis.

'Well, then . . . *Toby*,' said Colborn, 'let me see if I understand the situation. Syd tells me you're seeking to assess my nephew Roger's suitability as a husband for your ex-wife, about whose welfare you're still . . . concerned.'

'That's right.'

'You've met him?'

'Yes.'

'How did he strike you?'

'They didn't come to blows, Gav,' put in Syd.

Colborn said nothing, letting his question hang in the air while Syd got a chortle out of his system. 'He's obviously intelligent,' I eventually replied. 'And charming. Attractive to women, as well, I imagine.'

'Yes,' said Colborn deliberatively. 'He's certainly all of those things.'

'But is he honest?'

'That's the essence of your inquiry, is it . . . Toby?' (He still didn't seem at ease with my Christian name.) 'Is Roger an honourable man?'

'Well, is he?'

'What do you think?'

'I'm . . . inclined to doubt it.'

129

'So you should.'

'Any . . . particular reason?'

'Several. But I must declare an interest. Or rather a grievance. I have Roger to thank for my present situation. Penury's a miserable experience and it grows more miserable with age. You can be poor, happy and young. So they tell me, anyway. But poor, happy and old? That you cannot be.'

'You should have backed more of my tips over the years, Gav,' said Syd. 'You've got to speculate to accumulate.'

'I wouldn't need to if Roger hadn't shafted me.' There was bitterness in Colborn's voice now. He was no doting uncle.

'How did he do that?'

'By manipulating his father – my elder brother, Walter – who took over the running of the family firm, Colbonite, when our father stepped down. He thought he could do a better job without me on board. I was . . . eased out.' A rough calculation suggested that Roger could only have been a child at the time Gavin was describing and in no position to manipulate anyone, but I didn't contest the point. Soon enough, I sensed, we'd come on to meatier stuff. 'I had some company shares, held in trust during our father's lifetime and subsequently mine to do with as I pleased. The same arrangement was made for our sister, Delia. They weren't worth a lot. Or so I thought. Roger went straight into Colbonite from university. In the mid-Eighties, he . . . persuaded me to sell him my shares. He chose his moment well. I was . . . going through a bad patch. I needed the money. I found out later he'd pulled the same trick with Delia. What neither of us knew was that he'd already started encouraging Walter to wind up the business. Closing Colbonite down freed them to sell the company's most valuable asset – a dyeing patent. That set Roger up very nicely. Having bought Delia's shares as well as mine, his slice of the pie was that much bigger. And Delia and I got no slice at all. Do you know what he said when I confronted him? "It was nothing personal, Uncle," he said. "It was just a matter of business." A matter of business? The bastard. It was a matter of *two and a half million pounds*.'

130

'Christ!' Syd choked on his beer. 'I never knew it was that much.'

'You know now.'

'No wonder you were seriously dischuffed.'

'I had no legal claim, you understand, Toby,' Colborn went on. 'I could only ask for what Roger described as a hand-out. I could only . . . beg. Which I did. To no avail. He wouldn't pay me a penny.'

'What about your brother?'

'Walter said it was up to Roger. After all, it was Roger who'd bought my shares. So, Walter settled into a comfortable retirement at Wickhurst Manor, Roger slid off to Jersey to dodge the taxman and I . . . got by as best I could.'

'Delia too, presumably.'

'No. Delia got lucky. She met a rich man and married him. It was wine and roses for her too. I was the only one on bread and water. Still am.'

'Roger more or less admitted he hadn't been above a bit of sharp practice in the past,' I said. 'He claims to be a reformed character since meeting Jenny.'

'The love of a good woman can work miracles,' said Syd with a sickly smile.

'Believe that if you want to,' Gavin retorted. 'Roger will certainly want you to. He was an evil child. And he's grown into a devious, self-serving man.'

'We're into leopard-and-spots territory here, are we, Gav?' Syd enquired.

'Put it this way.' Gavin's voice dropped to a sandpapery rasp. 'If Roger's suddenly developed a soft centre, how come he's failed to put right any of the strokes he's pulled? A hand-out to his impecunious uncle wouldn't go amiss, considering how he ripped me off sixteen years ago, but there's been bugger-all sign of it. And what about all those poor sods who've had their lives shortened by working for Colbonite? What's he done for them, eh?' Gavin made a circle with his thumb and forefinger. 'That's what.'

'Are you talking about . . . the cancer victims, Gavin?' I tentatively asked.

'You're better informed than I thought,' he replied, treating me to a meaningful stare.

'I mentioned them,' said Syd.

'I wasn't aware you knew either.' Gavin's stare swivelled round to his old school chum in a less than chummy fashion.

'I keep my ear to the ground and my nose to the wind. It's amazing what you pick up.' (Especially if your girlfriend's secretary to an oncology consultant, I reflected.)

'Is there a definite connection between these cancer cases and Colbonite?' I asked.

'Not as a scientifically proven certainty, no. Walter and Roger hired a chemistry boffin at the University to tie the argument up in knots. Most of the people affected are dead now anyway. There'd be their next of kin, of course. If they could make the case stick, they'd be entitled to compensation.'

'Stacking up to more than two and a half mill?' put in Syd.

'No doubt a lot more. As I understand it, the carcinogen was a curing agent used in a dyeing process. The patented method required its use in a dangerously unstable form. Inhalation of the fumes over a period of years . . . was a death sentence.'

'Did Roger and your brother know that?' I asked.

'I suspect so, yes. Not at the beginning. But before the end. They sold the patent and closed the company down not because it was unprofitable but because they were afraid the cancer scare would slash its value. Technically, Colbonite didn't go into liquidation. It was sold to a shell company that was wound up shortly afterwards. Roger's idea, I'm sure of it.'

'You're going to have to explain that ploy to us high-finance duds, Gav,' said Syd.

'It means that even if a case for compensation was made out, Roger couldn't be billed for it, because the responsible party, Colbonite, last belonged to somebody else.'

'So he's in the clear?' I asked.

'Not quite. If he knew about the risk and failed to disclose it to the purchaser of the patent, he's guilty of fraud.'

'And who was the purchaser?'

'A South Korean conglomerate.'

'Who'd be just as anxious to dodge compensation.'

'That's true.'

'So they're hardly likely to sue Roger.'

'No. But a criminal case could be brought against him in this country.'

'Theoretically.'

'I admit it's . . . improbable.'

'Looks like you'll just have to dream on, Gav,' said Syd.

'Indeed. But that's hardly the point you're interested in, is it . . . Toby? You wanted to know the moral calibre of the man. Now you do.'

'Think this'll put the missus off him, Tobe?' Syd asked.

'If she believes it, yes.'

'Then I hope you can convince her,' said Gavin.

I looked enquiringly at him. 'Some proof would help.' Then I remembered *The Plastic Men*. And Roger's stubborn refusal to read it. Maybe there *was* proof, in the least expected quarter.

Gavin, of course, knew nothing of Derek Oswin and his painstaking history of Colbonite. But that didn't mean there weren't any pointers he could put my way. 'I don't know what kind of evidence is likely to sway your wife. Roger has a gift for deceiving people, as I've learned to my cost. She probably wouldn't believe anything I said. You could ask Delia to speak to her, I suppose. One woman to another. But Delia's grasp of the facts is . . . limited.'

'How could I contact her?'

'I'll give you her telephone number.' He reached for Syd's newspaper, tore an edge off the front page and wrote a name and number on it, then handed the scrap to me. 'If you do speak to her, send her . . . my regards.'

The Colborn family was clearly no warm and harmonious unit. Syd raised an eyebrow at me as I pocketed the note. A brief silence fell.

Then Gavin said, 'There's something else you could mention to your wife. Walter's death . . . left a lot of unanswered questions.'

'Car smash, wasn't it?' Syd asked with a frown.

'Walter was hit by a car while walking along a lane near Wickhurst Manor. The driver was charged with manslaughter.'

'I never knew that,' said Syd. 'I thought it was just . . . an accident. But . . . *manslaughter*?'

'The case never came to court. The driver died while awaiting trial.'

'How does that help me convince Jenny that Roger covered up the cancer connection?' I asked.

'The driver died of cancer,' Gavin replied. 'He was a former employee of Colbonite. And he was terminally ill when he drove Walter down. If you want my opinion, he held Walter responsible for his illness.'

'You mean . . . he murdered your brother?'

'In effect, yes.'

'Good God.'

'I can't say I blame him.'

'Maybe not. But . . . when did this happen?'

'November, nineteen ninety-five.'

'Was their . . . working relationship . . . reported at the time?'

'I don't recall. I knew of it. As did others. Whether it made the pages of the *Argus* . . .' Gavin shrugged. 'Roger's a great puller of strings.'

'You could check that, though, Tobe,' said Syd. 'They'll have the *Argus* back to eighteen hundred and God-knows-when up at the Library.'

'Yes,' I mused. 'So they will.'

'I hope I've been of some help,' said Gavin.

'You have. Yes. Thanks.' My mind drifted to the contents of Derek's book. How had the introduction concluded? '*The closing chapters will analyse the circumstances leading to the closure of the company in 1989 and the fate of those who found*

134

themselves out of work as a result.' The word 'fate' took on a sharper meaning in the light of Gavin's revelations. Derek had to know about the cancer. He couldn't very well have avoided writing about it. His history of Colbonite amounted to a charge sheet against Sir Walter and Roger Colborn. No wonder Roger didn't want to help him get it published. I could only wish in that moment that I hadn't sent it off unread to Moira. I could get it back from her, of course. And even sooner I could speak to the author himself.

'Did Colbonite have a pension scheme?' Syd suddenly asked.

'I don't know,' Gavin replied brusquely. 'What does it matter?'

'I was just thinking it could have been a bargain operation for Sir Walt and Roger the compensation dodger. Half the staff claimed by the big C before they could make any in-roads into the fund? Sounds like one long contributions holiday.'

'It has to be said, Gavin,' I remarked, 'that your brother doesn't seem to have been any more scrupulous than your nephew.'

'Walter didn't cheat me out of my shares.'

'No. But he cheated a lot of his workers out of a long and healthy retirement.'

'Under Roger's influence. He thought the boy could do no wrong. He never saw his true nature. Besides . . .' Gavin took a long pull on his cigarette. 'Walter didn't have a long and healthy retirement himself, did he? He was made to pay for what he'd done.'

'Unlike Roger.'

'Yes. Unlike Roger.' Gavin stared morosely into his glass, then looked up at me. 'So far.'

Inventing an appointment at the theatre in order to extricate myself, I left Syd and Gavin to chew over old times if they had a mind to and headed for the taxi rank in East Street. A cab was soon speeding me north to a tower block beyond the station, a lower floor of which houses Brighton Central Library.

Where I discovered, to my chagrin, that my taxi driver wasn't a regular patron of the library service. Either that or he was singularly bloody-minded. Because, after paying him off and mounting the steps, I found the door firmly locked. Brighton Central Library is closed on Wednesdays.

I sheltered in the porch, cursing the bureaucrat responsible for such a stupefyingly inconvenient arrangement. Then I noticed the soaring roofline of St Bartholomew's Church to the south and realized just how close I was to Viaduct Road. Maybe, I thought, this wasn't a wasted journey after all.

There was no immediate response to my knock at the door of number 77. But the top sash of the ground-floor window was open by several inches. Derek surely wouldn't have gone out leaving it like that. I knocked again, more firmly.

I thought I heard Derek's voice from the other side of the door. But a lorry thundered by, drowning out every other sound for several seconds. I knocked once more. Then I *did* hear his voice, pitched at a panicky falsetto.

'Go away. Leave me alone.'

'Derek,' I shouted. 'It's me. Toby Flood.'

There was a silence. Then: 'Mr Flood?' Panic seemed to be subsiding.

'Please let me in, Derek. It's wet out here.'

'Are you . . . alone?'

'Just me and fifty cars a minute.'

The door opened and Derek peered out at me like a water vole apprehensively observing a river in spate. 'Sorry, Mr Flood,' he said. 'I didn't . . . well, I thought . . . he might have come back.'

'Who?'

Derek ushered me hurriedly in and closed the door. He pushed firmly against the latch to make sure it had fully engaged, then pointed me towards the sitting room, my question having apparently escaped his attention.

136

'Who did you think might have returned, Derek?'

'Mr . . . C-Colborn.'

'Roger Colborn's been here?'

'Y-yes.' The stress of a visit from his former boss had evidently introduced a stammer into Derek's already hesitant delivery.

'What did he want?'

'Please . . . go through.' He was still pointing to the sitting room.

I went in and nodded towards the lowered window. 'If you're worried about a return visit, shouldn't you close that?'

'Oh God, yes.' He moved past me, yanked the window shut and turned to me with a wavering smile. 'Sorry. I'm a l-l-little . . . on edge.'

'So I see.'

'Mr Colborn shouted at me. I don't like . . . shouting.'

'I'm not going to shout.'

'No. Of course not. Please . . . sit down.' For the moment at least, the stammer had subsided. We sat down either side of the fireplace. Derek kneaded his hands together, frowning down at them. Then he looked across at me and said, 'Is it true . . . that Mr Maple's dead?'

The question was oddly phrased. He could either not know or be in no doubt on the point. 'Yes,' I replied cautiously.

'Oh. God. I am . . . sorry.'

'You say that as if it's your fault.'

'P-perhaps . . . it is.'

'He died of a heart attack, Derek. It was nobody's fault.'

'I'm not sure.'

'Why not?'

'The way . . . Mr Colborn talked about it.'

'What way was that?'

'He, er, mentioned it . . . and said . . .'

'What did he say, Derek?'

Derek took a deep breath to steady himself. Then he said, 'He came here and told me to stop causing trouble for him. To forget my history of Colbonite. To leave his . . . your

137

wife . . . alone. And to leave you alone too. He said I should go away for a few days. Until *Lodger in the Throat* had finished its run. I told him I didn't want to go anywhere. That's when he mentioned Mr Maple's . . . death. He said it was an example of what happened when people got out of their depth. He said . . . it should be a warning to me.'

'A warning?'

'Yes. How did . . . Mr Maple die, Mr Flood?'

'I'm not sure. I think he was being chased when his heart gave out. He wasn't a well man. After Monday night's show, he met someone who seemed to think he was actually me. They didn't realize he was the stand-in. I think they had something nasty planned for me. When they realized their mistake, they sent Denis packing. But last night, according to a phone call he made to me, they came after him again.'

'Do you think . . . they were working for Mr Colborn?'

'What do you think?'

'I don't know.'

'Tell me, Derek, did you manoeuvre me into missing Monday night's performance to save me from whatever was planned?'

He looked at me blankly and shook his head. 'No. I had no idea . . . *anything* was planned.'

'That letter you wrote to Leo Gauntlett . . .'

'Did it help?' he asked eagerly.

'Not exactly.'

'I wanted him to understand that you weren't being irresponsible.'

'Really? Wasn't it just a little . . . tongue-in-cheek?'

'Well . . .' Derek flushed coyly. 'Maybe . . .'

'It reminded me of an Edna Welthorpe missive.'

At that he beamed. 'They're gems, Mr Flood. Absolute gems. Do you remember her exchange of correspondence with Littlewoods?'

'You aren't going to write to any more of my associates, are you?' I'd have been sterner with him, but so fragile was the state Colborn had left him in that I felt I couldn't risk even hardening the tone of my voice. 'It's got to stop, Derek.'

'Yes. Of course.' He hung his head like a guilty schoolboy. 'I'm sorry.'

'No more tricks. No more stunts. Clear?'

'No more.' He gazed at me earnestly. 'I promise.'

'Good.'

'Is that why you came? Because of the letter?'

'Partly. I . . . found myself in the area.'

'Not on your way to the Library, were you?'

'What makes you ask?'

'It's just that . . . when we met at the Rendezvous on Monday, you asked me for directions to the public library.'

'So I did. And you told me it was in New England Street.'

'That's right. But actually . . . it's closed on Wednesdays.'

'I know. I've just come from there.'

'Oh dear. That must have been annoying for you. What were you trying to find out? If I can help . . .'

'I wanted to look at back copies of the *Argus*.'

'Ah. Actually, the *Argus* isn't archived at New England Street. You need the Local Studies Library in Church Street for that.'

'Also closed on Wednesdays?'

'I'm afraid so. You'll have to wait until tomorrow.'

'Not necessarily. You see, I think you *can* help, Derek. In fact, I'm sure of it. I wanted to read what the *Argus* had to say about the death of Sir Walter Colborn.'

'Oh. That.'

'Yes. *That*. I understand he was knocked down by a car, driven by a former employee of Colbonite, who was terminally ill with cancer at the time.'

'Sounds like . . . you already know all about it.'

'Is it true a lot of Colbonite workers contracted cancer of the bladder after handling a carcinogenic curing agent used in a dyeing process?'

'Yes.' Derek's reply was almost a whisper. 'One of the chloro-anilines. Nasty stuff.'

'No doubt you mention this in *The Plastic Men*.'

'Oh yes, Mr Flood. It's all there. Chapter and verse.' He smiled weakly. 'There was a sign on the door of the dyeing shop. Somebody spray-painted over the E in dyeing on one occasion. A pretty black sort of joke.'

'Did you work with this stuff?'

'Good Lord, no. I was a filing clerk.'

'But those who did are mostly dead now?'

'Yes. I checked on them all. They're listed in an appendix to *The Plastic Men*. Names. Ages. Cause of death.'

'Which one of them murdered Sir Walter?'

'He was only charged with manslaughter.'

'Who was he, Derek?'

'Kenneth Oswin.' Derek stared at me. 'My father.'

It was as obvious now as it should have been before. He didn't blame Roger Colborn for closing Colbonite down. At least, not only for that. There was something far worse to lay at his door. 'Why didn't you tell me?'

'I thought it might . . . put you off.'

'Because there's a feud between your families? Well, it certainly skews the perspective, that's for sure.'

'There's no . . . feud.'

'In your book, do you accuse the Colborns of knowing how dangerous the curing agent was?'

'I don't exactly . . . accuse them. But . . .'

'You lay it on the line.'

'I suppose I do. Yes.'

'That's libel.'

'He could sue me. I wouldn't mind.'

'You asked Colborn to help you get the book published. Why? You must have known he'd move heaven and earth to *stop it* being published.'

'I just wanted to . . . get a reaction.'

'Well, you got one, didn't you? More of one than you bargained for, if the state you were in when I arrived is anything to go by.'

Derek squirmed in his chair. 'I just don't see why he should get away with it.'

'Take after your father in that, do you? He obviously decided Sir Walter shouldn't get away with it either.'

'It wasn't like that.'

'What was it like?'

'Dad went out to Wickhurst that day to plead with Sir Walter to help out the families of the men who'd died and those, like him, who were already terminally ill. He'd gone down with cancer shortly after Colbonite closed, but he'd recovered. Then it came back. He'd been a shop steward in his day. He . . . felt responsible. He thought he could talk Sir Walter round. He'd only bought the car a few years previously, so Mum could drive him back and forth to the hospital. Anyway, he told me later what happened when he got to Wickhurst Manor. Sir Walter refused to discuss the matter. Ordered him off his property. Then stalked off to take his dog for a walk. Dad sat in his car for a while, fuming, then decided to go after Sir Walter and make a last effort to talk him round. He'd seen him set off along the lane that leads north from Wickhurst towards Stonestaples Wood, so that's the way he went. He was going too fast. And he was never a good driver, anyway. He was in a lot of pain by then as well. He went round a sharp bend and saw Sir Walter too late to stop or swerve aside. It was an accident, Mr Flood. That's what it was. Just an accident.'

'The police obviously didn't think so.'

'Well, Dad said some things . . . about his illness. He wanted them to charge him with manslaughter, you see, or better still murder. He wanted a high-profile trial. The chance to say what Sir Walter had done to his workers. The truth is, though, it *was* an accident.'

'Does Roger believe that?'

'I don't know what he believes. I'm sure he had the trial delayed, though. He has a lot of friends; a lot of influence. Thanks to him, Dad never had his day in court.'

'I'm sorry for your loss, Derek.'

'Thanks, Mr Flood.'

'When did your mother . . .'

'Not long after Dad. Looking after him put a huge strain on her. After he passed away, she just . . . faded.'

'Leaving you alone, to think about Roger Colborn and how to get back at him.'

'I'm not after revenge.'

'No? Well, he won't give you a day in court any more than he gave your father one, Derek. That's the truth. You've more or less admitted the book's libellous. No publisher will touch it. The only way you can get anywhere with this is to prove the case – scientifically. And even then . . .' I hesitated. If Derek didn't know about the sale of Colbonite to a shell company and the consequences of the move, I wasn't sure I wanted to be the one to tell him.

'Mr Colborn has taken precautions against every contingency, I know. He's been very clever.'

'You're not the only one bearing a grudge against him, if it's any consolation. I met his uncle. Gavin Colborn. He told me all about Sir Walter's death. Except that he never mentioned your father was the car driver.'

'He's probably forgotten the name. There's no reason why he should remember it. We've never met. I saw him a few times, at Colbonite. But I was . . . beneath his notice.'

'You have something in common, though. A desire to put a spoke in Roger Colborn's wheel.'

'It would be nice . . . to do something.'

'Yes. And I'm the spoke, aren't I? If I could win Jenny back . . .'

'Mr Colborn would be seriously put out.'

'It's not exactly justice. But it's better than nothing. The only problem is, I'm not sure I can pull it off.'

'Surely, if Mrs Flood understands what Mr Colborn did to people like my father . . .'

'*If* she understands, Derek. Oh yes. She couldn't stomach that. But how do I prove it to her? How do I convince her I'm not levelling an unfounded accusation in order to split them up? Where's the hard, incontrovertible evidence?'

Derek pursed his lips, rocking back and forth slightly in his chair as he pondered our shared difficulty. Then he said, with a meek acceptance of the unalterable, 'There isn't any.'

'You see?'

Suddenly, Derek stopped rocking. He pondered a little longer, then said, 'No evidence as such. Only witnesses.'

'The tainted kind, if you mean the likes of you and Uncle Gavin. He suggested his sister, Delia, but seemed to doubt she knew enough to sway Jenny.'

'I feel he's almost certainly right there. As far as knowledge is concerned, I could only suggest Dr Kilner.'

'Who?'

'The biochemist Colbonite "consulted" over the risks posed by the curing agent. Dr Maurice Kilner. He was a head of department at the University of Sussex.'

'*Was?*'

'Since retired.'

'With a handsome pay-off from the Colborns, presumably.'

'I'm not sure. If Mr Colborn has a weakness, it's parsimony. I saw Dr Kilner in Waitrose a few months ago. He didn't look as if he was living in the lap of luxury.'

'No?'

Derek shook his head, smiling faintly at the notion he'd planted in my mind without needing to put it into words. 'No.'

'I'm surprised you haven't spoken to him about this.'

'I don't think he'd be willing to discuss anything with a former employee of Colbonite. He'd be fearful of the consequences.'

'What about somebody who'd never worked for Colbonite?'

'It might be different.'

'There's only one way to find out.'

'Yes, Mr Flood. There is.' Derek cleared his throat. 'Would you like to know where Dr Kilner lives?'

*   *   *

143

I left Derek in a much calmer state than I'd found him in. *The Plastic Men* was going nowhere. He understood and accepted that. But our campaign against Roger Colborn – if it *was* a campaign and if it *was* ours – *that* might yet have legs. It was agreed I'd try to contact Dr Kilner and would tell Derek what I'd accomplished, if anything, after tonight's show.

The rain had stopped. I walked down London Road through the drying grey early afternoon, wondering just what kind of an ally I'd saddled myself with in Derek Oswin. He can be relied on in some things, but not in others. And he's frightened of Roger Colborn – understandably. Perhaps I should be as well. But other imperatives have blanked out fear. I can't let Jenny marry this man, even if I fail to win her back. And I can't ignore what happened to Denis.

The Great Eastern in Trafalgar Street was still serving food. I sat in a cosily gloomy corner and worked my way through a late lunch while mulling over my next move. I had an address for Dr Kilner, but no telephone number. I borrowed a directory from behind the bar, but he wasn't listed, so there was no other way to approach him but on the doorstep. I swapped the directory for a Brighton *A–Z* and found Pennsylvania Court in Cromwell Road, Hove, just behind the county cricket ground. There was nothing to be gained by delay, unless I wanted to give myself the chance to change my mind. And that I didn't. Resisting the lure of a second drink, I headed for the taxi rank up at the station.

The cab was most of the way to my destination when fate intervened, in the form of Brian Sallis on my mobile.

'I'm with Ian Maple, Toby. We're at Denis's lodgings in Egremont Place. Can you join us here?'

Dr Kilner, it was apparent, would have to wait.

Thanks to already being in a taxi when Brian called, I was at Egremont Place in no more than ten minutes. Brian was waiting for me outside number 65, a narrow-fronted, bay-windowed house near the northern end. Ian Maple, he explained, was inside, sorting through his brother's possessions.

'He's pretty cut up, Toby, as you can imagine, and looking for answers.'

'Answers to what?'

'Questions raised by a message he had from Denis last night. Look, he knows you found Denis and that the two of you went back a long way. Can I leave you to . . . go through what happened?'

'You're not coming in?'

'I have to get back to the theatre. Just tell the poor chap as much as you can. Mrs Dunn will let you in. She's expecting you.'

As promised, Mrs Dunn *was* expecting me. She'd put Denis up more than once over the years and was clearly upset. 'It's a terrible thing, Mr Flood. He was too young to go and do this on me.'

'I know.'

'His brother's upstairs. Second floor, front. Will you tell him what we talked about earlier is fine by me?'

'Sure.'

I climbed the stairs and found the door to Denis's room ajar. A younger, balder, bulkier version of my late friend and colleague was sitting on the edge of the bed, staring into space. He was wearing blue jeans and a grey fleece over a sweatshirt. He looked like a tough guy who at the moment wasn't feeling very tough at all.

It took several seconds for my presence to register with him. Then he stood up slowly, the bed springs creakily extending themselves, and fixed me with a clear-eyed gaze.

'Toby Flood?'

'Yes. Pleased to meet you.' We shook hands, his grip large and powerful. 'Though sorry, of course, about the circumstances.'

'Yeah.'

'Mrs Dunn asked me to tell you . . . something you discussed earlier . . . is fine by her.'

'I asked if she could put me up for a couple of days.'

'You're stopping over?'

'Till I find out what Denis had got himself into. Brian Sallis reckoned you might know.'

Thanks, Brian, I thought; I owe you one. 'He said you'd had a message from Denis.'

'Yeah. On my answerphone.' He pulled a small tape recorder out of his pocket and stood it on the bedside cabinet. 'Want to hear it?'

'If you don't mind.'

He pressed the PLAY button. An electronic voice announced, *'Next new message. Received today at eleven fifty-three p.m.'* Then Denis was speaking to us, his voice hushed and fuzzy. *'Hi, Ian. Big brother here. Sorry not to have caught you. I've run into some trouble. Not sure how serious. Could be very. I might need some help. I have a bad feeling and . . . Send Mum and Dad my love, will you? It's too late to call them. Hope all's well with you. 'Bye.'*

Ian Maple rewound the tape, then switched the machine off. 'What's it all about, Toby?' he asked.

'Hard to say.' I sat down on the only chair in the room, playing for time to little purpose. My instincts told me not to involve this man I hardly knew in my dealings with Roger Colborn. Yet I couldn't simply deny all knowledge. I should have checked the events of the previous evening with Glenys. I should have prepared myself. I'd done neither. Playing a part without any kind of rehearsal is playing with fire. But it's what I had to do. 'Denis phoned me shortly before he left that message for you. He said someone was . . . chasing him. He wasn't very specific. He was at a bus stop in North Street. I agreed to meet him there at midnight. When I got there, he'd gone. I walked towards my lodgings, thinking he might have headed in that direction. That's how I came to find him, by the fountain on the Steine.'

'Already dead?'

'I'm afraid so.'

Ian sat back down on the bed, to another squeal from the springs. 'Do you think someone *was* after him?'

'He said so.'

'Did you believe him?'

'Yes.' I couldn't write Denis off as a fantasist, however evasive I was being. 'I believed him.'

'Who was it?'

'I don't know.' (True enough.)

'No idea at all?'

'None.' (Not true enough.)

'I mean to find out.'

'I wish you luck. It's going to be difficult.'

'I won't let that stop me. Having me as a kid brother wasn't always a cakewalk. I owe it to Denis to try.'

'How are your parents taking this?'

'It's knocked them for six. Me too, I don't mind admitting. Another heart attack was always on the cards. You just don't think it'll happen, though, do you?'

'No. You don't.'

'When did you last speak to Denis? Face to face, I mean.'

'We had coffee together yesterday morning.'

'How did he seem then?'

'Chirpy as ever.'

'Sallis said Denis stood in for you the night before.'

'Yes. I had flu.'

'That a fact?' There was a hint of scepticism in his tone. His gaze was disconcertingly direct. I was already certain that he suspected me of holding something back. 'If you remember anything, Toby, however minor, however . . . apparently trivial, that could help me . . .'

'I'll let you know straight away.'

'Denis said you fixed him up with this job.'

'I put a word in, nothing more. It was the least I could do. Denis was one of the best.'

147

'Yeah. He was. That's why it's such a crying bloody shame it had to end like this.'

I couldn't disagree with that last sentiment. But nor could I share everything I knew with Denis's brother and aspiring avenger. Derek was in a fragile enough state as it was without having Ian Maple cross-questioning him. As for Roger Colborn, I didn't rate Ian a match for him. And one favour I did owe Denis was to avoid dragging another member of his family into my troubles. If I could.

The light was already failing as I trailed back towards the Sea Air. I'd just about concluded that there wasn't enough time to have another go at Dr Kilner, when I reached St James's Street and spotted a bus bound for Hove bearing down on me. A sprint to the next stop got me aboard with just enough breath to ask the driver if he was going along Cromwell Road. And since he was . . . I paid my fare and sat down.

As soon as I'd got my breath back, I phoned Brian.
   'How'd it go with Ian Maple, Toby?'
   'As well as could be expected, given that you'd told him I knew what Denis was mixed up in.'
   'I didn't have much choice once I'd listened to the tape. Besides, you do know, don't you? That's the vibe I'm getting.'
   'Ian's going to get himself mixed up in it as well if he has his way. I'd like to prevent that.'
   'Can't help you there, Toby. The guy's entitled to ask who he likes what he likes. This is really no legitimate concern of Leo S. Gauntlett Productions.'
   'Great.'
   'Sorry, but there it is.'
   'Yeah. Of course. Look—' I was going to ask him for Glenys's mobile number, but suddenly changed my mind. What was the point now of finding out what Denis did or didn't say to her last night? I could hardly expect her to keep Ian Maple in the dark on my account. The cards would

148

simply have to lie as they fell. 'Never mind. See you later, Brian.'

The phone was hardly back in my pocket when it rang again. My first thought was that Brian was back on to check I hadn't taken umbrage on a disastrous scale. I had no stand-in now, after all. But it wasn't Brian.

'Hi-de-hi, Tobe. Syd squeaking. Anxious to confirm you got as much as you wanted out of my old school chum, Gav of the omnipresent smile.'

'Meeting him was a big help, Syd. Thanks for setting it up.'

'You thinking of paying his sister a call?'

'Maybe.'

'Only, if you are, I suspect the encounter might go more smoothly with me riding shotgun for you. Delia and I have what you might call history.'

'Do you really?'

'It's just a thought, Tobe. Could make all the difference.'

'I'll certainly bear it in mind.'

'Just give me a bell whenever.'

'Will do.' (Or, far more likely, will not do.)

'One other thing.'

'Yes.'

'Aud's suggestion, actually. But I'm all for it, natch. When are you planning to leave Brighton?'

'Sunday.'

'Fancy a spot of lunch before you go? Aud roasts an awesome joint, let me tell you. I could motor you over to her place and deliver you to the station afterwards. Send you off well fed and watered. Know what I mean? Chance to catch up with how the week went.'

Sunday suddenly felt an impossibly long way off. How will the week have gone? For the moment, I couldn't have hazarded the remotest of guesses. There seemed, however, no point in arguing. I can easily pull out nearer the time. 'OK, Syd. You're on.'

'Grrreat.'

*　　*　　*

Pennsylvania Court: a bland red-brick five-floor apartment block on the cusp of well-to-do and down-at-heel. I rang the bell for flat 28 and put the odds on a response at eighty-twenty. Where else would a retired academic be on a winter's late afternoon but at home? I was right.

'Hello?'

'Dr Kilner?'

'Yes.'

'I wonder if we could have a word. My name's Flood.' How to talk my way in was a problem I'd failed to devise a cast-iron solution to. 'The thing is—'

'Toby Flood, the actor?'

'Well, yes. I—'

'Come on up.'

The door-lock release buzzed. Obediently, I pushed and entered.

Maurice Kilner was a short, stocky, beetle-browed man with greased hair and unfashionably thick-framed glasses. His rumpled cardigan and baggy trousers were hardly *homme à la mode* either. He ushered me in with a welcoming smile that never made it to his watery grey eyes. The flat was comfortable in a senior-common-room kind of way, but the furniture was generally as threadbare as its owner. There was presumably a good view of the cricket ground, though. And two shelves full of *Wisden*s in one of the several bookcases suggested that was a feature Kilner might well appreciate.

Much less apparent was why he'd so readily admitted me. A fan, perhaps? Somehow, I didn't think so.

'Roger Colborn warned me to expect a visit from you, Mr Flood.'

'Did he?' (Clever old Roger.)

'This is sooner than I anticipated, though. Do you want a drink? Scotch, perhaps?'

'No, thanks.'

'Keeping a clear head for this evening's performance? Very wise. You don't mind if I have one, do you?'

'Not at all.'

He poured himself a large Johnnie Walker. I wondered if he was bolstering his nerves, but reckoned it more likely to be a bachelor's early-evening habit. 'When do you have to be at the theatre?' He sat down and waved me into another chair.

'Shortly after seven.'

'I'd better not hold you up, then. You've obviously come to talk to me about Colbonite.'

'Yes. I have.'

'What have you heard?'

'That just about anyone who had the bad luck to work in their dyeing shop went down with bladder cancer on account of a carcinogenic curing agent. And that Roger Colborn and his father did nothing to prevent it.'

'I was merely engaged by Colbonite to do some research for them.'

'I know.'

'I'm glad you do. Because that's all it was. Research. Carried out rigorously and diligently.'

'Research into what?'

'The mechanics of carcinogenesis arising from exposure to aromatic amines, specifically methylated chloro-aniline – the infamous curing agent.'

'Which you gave a clean bill of heath?'

'Of course not. It was identified as a carcinogen nearly forty years ago.'

'Then why were Colbonite using it?'

'Because there are no ready substitutes. It's still in regular use today, Mr Flood. The issue is the scale of risk. Based on the quantities involved and the working practices put in place, my findings suggested that Colbonite were not exposing their staff to unacceptable levels.'

'How come they all wound up dead, then?'

' "All" is an exaggeration. And a certain proportion of any

151

cohort is bound to develop cancer. For the rest, I'd be inclined to suspect wilful disregard of safety procedures as the cause. People working in dangerous industries are often their own worst enemies, you know. You must have seen road menders operating pneumatic drills without bothering to wear ear defenders.'

'It was their own fault, then?'

'It's one possibility. Another is that Colbonite were routinely using larger quantities of the substance than they declared to me. But I think that unlikely. Sir Walter Colborn was an ethical and responsible employer.'

'What about his son?'

'I'd say the same of him.'

'Perhaps your research was flawed.'

'Even more unlikely.' Kilner smiled. 'Approximation may pass muster in your profession, Mr Flood. Not in mine.'

'Let me get this straight. Colbonite's workers weren't in any danger other than of their own making?'

'I didn't say that. I advanced their inattention to proper safety procedures as a hypothetical explanation for any disproportionate incidence of bladder cancer that medical practitioners may have detected. I say *may* because it's certainly never been brought officially to my attention. Mr Colborn has explained to me your interest in this matter. It can hardly be described as dispassionate, now can it?'

'Can yours?'

'By definition.'

'How much did they pay you? How much is Roger Colborn *still* paying you?'

'I was paid an appropriate fee at the time. That's all.'

'You don't expect me to believe that.'

'I can only state the facts as I know them to be.'

'Don't you care about the men who died?'

'They didn't die through any negligence on my part.'

'You have a clear conscience, then?'

'I do, yes.'

'Or maybe no conscience at all.'

Kilner sipped his whisky and smiled tolerantly at me, as if I were a student at a seminar making provocative remarks that he had no intention of being provoked by. 'Roger Colborn is a businessman, Mr Flood,' he said softly. 'I recommend you do business with him.'

I walked down to the sea front after leaving Pennsylvania Court, then headed east towards Brighton and the Sea Air. The evening was turning cold and I was grateful: I needed the chill and the darkness after my encounter with Maurice Kilner. What kind of a deal he'd done with Roger Colborn hardly mattered. He'd done one that suited him and he advised others to follow his example. Derek had suggested he might be a weak spot in Colborn's defences, but in reality he was rock solid. And all the more contemptible because of it. I wondered if Derek had known exactly what I would find, if he had chosen Kilner as an example to me of the moral bankruptcy to which a man could be led by bargaining with the ever-eager-to-bargain Roger Colborn. It seemed all too likely. Derek had promised to give up his trickery. But maybe he didn't regard this as trickery. Maybe this was just what came naturally.

The show must go on. Like so many clichés, it's horribly true. Denis was such an amiable and popular man that every-body involved with *Lodger in the Throat* was depressed this evening. Badinage was absent, leaving an empty space to be filled with doleful exchanges and soulful looks. Fred's supply of wry one-liners had dried up. Jocasta was puffy-eyed and virtually mute. Even Donohue's egotism had failed him. But we were present and correct. We were ready to perform.

Just after the quarter-hour call, I had a visitor to my dressing room: Glenys Williams.

'I'm really sorry to interrupt, Toby, but I feel I ought to let you know that Ian Maple wants to see me this evening, to discuss . . . Denis's state of mind last night.'

'Did you have supper with Denis?'

'Yes.'

'How was he?'

'Fine, I thought. But, looking back, I suppose he was rather on edge. He mentioned – well, implied, really – that standing in for you the night before had . . . got him into some trouble. He wouldn't elaborate. But he did say . . . you knew all about it.'

'I see.'

'Yet his brother said to me on the phone this afternoon that you'd been unable to help him. So, I'm guessing you'd prefer me not to mention Denis's remark to him.'

'I would, yes.'

'But doesn't Ian have a right to know?'

'Yes. And I'll make sure he does know eventually. I can't ask you to lie, Glenys, but . . . just for the moment . . .'

'You want me to cover for you.'

I nodded. 'How about it?'

She gave me a grim little smile. 'Denis always said you were hard to say no to.'

We performed, everyone agreed, very well, though without scaling last night's heights. I was often distracted and fractionally slow to respond. It wasn't so much that I couldn't concentrate as that my concentration was elsewhere. The audience was entertained without being entranced.

At the interval, some instinct, some impression I'd picked up, made me call the box office from my dressing room to check that Derek had collected his complimentary ticket. But no. He hadn't.

The second act was even more of a blur than the first, as I tried and failed to stop myself wondering between other people's lines why he hadn't shown up. He'd said he would be there. He'd claimed to be looking forward to it. What could have prevented him?

The box office confirmed after I got off stage that his ticket was still lying unclaimed in its envelope. There were no messages for me. There was no word from Derek Oswin. He hadn't come. He wasn't going to.

I'd arranged to meet him at the stage door twenty minutes after the curtain fell. I waited there until half an hour was up, refusing repeated invitations to adjourn with the rest of the cast to a restaurant. Then I called a taxi and headed for Viaduct Road.

It was a quieter place late at night. The traffic still came in pulses, regulated by the lights at Preston Circus, but there was less of it. Most of the houses were in darkness. Pedestrians there were none.

To my surprise, a light was showing at number 77, in the hall. I could see the glimmer of it through the open curtains of the sitting room. The room itself looked to be empty. I knocked at the door and waited. There was no response. Then I put the knocker to longer, heavier duty use. If Derek was asleep in bed, I didn't mean him to stay that way.

Still no answer. I stooped and took a squint through the letterbox. It gave me a view of the hall, the lower half of the stairs and the doorway into the unlit kitchen. Then I noticed the bulky hem of Derek's duffel-coat hanging on its hook. He wouldn't have gone out without it. He had to be at home.

But then I noticed something else. Two of the balusters on the staircase were broken, their snapped halves protruding at forty-five degrees, as if they'd been kicked by somebody standing on the stairs. The same somebody, perhaps, who'd rucked up the hall rug. You couldn't have walked across it without tripping.

'*Derek!*' I shouted through the letterbox. But nothing stirred. I moved to the sitting-room window and peered in. Nothing appeared out of place, as far as I could tell, although the fact that the curtains, including the nets, were open was odd in itself. The nets had been open when Derek had slammed the window shut earlier, I remembered. Perhaps—

He hadn't flicked the snib back into place. I must have

distracted him. And then he must have forgotten about it. The window was unlocked.

I glanced about. There was no-one within sight. I waited for a wave of traffic to pass, then pushed up the sash. The squeal of the wood sounded loud to me, but was probably nothing unusual. After another glance along the street, I hoisted one leg over the sill and scrambled in, then closed the window behind me.

The distinctive, indefinable scent of somebody else's home met me, in a general silence that amplified the ponderous tick of a clock in the kitchen. My eyes adjusted to the half-light as I stood there. Then I saw Derek's books, strewn on the floor beneath the bookcase. Nothing else in the room had been disturbed. But it didn't need to have been. I knew Derek wouldn't have done even that. He wouldn't have creased a single page of his Tintin collection, let alone have them lying higgledy-piggledy on the floor.

I went out into the hall and looked up the stairs. There were muddy shoe-prints on several of the treads. Derek's? I didn't think so. I climbed to the landing, where the light was also on. There was a bathroom and two bedrooms, the front one containing a double bed and dressing-table. I guessed it had been where Derek's parents slept, kept by him as they'd left it. His room was to the rear, the door half-closed, a light on within.

I pushed the door fully open. The bed hadn't been slept in. There was a desk by the window, an ink-spotted blotter neatly positioned dead centre, between an anglepoise lamp and a globe. The drawers of the desk had been pulled open. In the centre of the room a wooden chest lay on its back, the lid open on the floor, the contents spread across the rug in front of the fireplace: a photograph album, old children's annuals, an ancient much-loved teddy-bear and a slew of paper.

I stood in the room, staring down at Derek's scattered keepsakes, trying to reconstruct the events that had left these clues behind. I went back out onto the landing and looked down the stairs. The broken balusters; the rumpled rug: what

156

did they mean? I imagined Derek answering the door to threatening strangers, retreating up the stairs, being over-hauled and dragged back down, struggling and kicking. Then I saw a glint of metal on the doormat below me. I padded down the stairs for a closer look.

It was one of Derek's Tintin brooches, lying face down. I turned it over and Captain Haddock grinned up at me through his bushy tar-black beard. I stood up with the brooch in my hand and noted the tear in Derek's duffel-coat where it had obviously been ripped free. The hall was narrow. It had probably happened without anyone noticing, not even Derek.

There'd been a brief but focused search. That was clear. The bookcase and the bedroom chest and desk had been the targets. Maybe they'd found what they'd been looking for in one of them. *The Plastic Men* was my guess. The manuscript – and any related documents. That had to be the answer. I looked back at one of the shoe-prints on the stairs. A small, muddy oak-leaf had been trodden into the carpet. Where, I wondered, was the nearest oak tree to Viaduct Road? I didn't know, of course. I hadn't a clue. But there were oaks out at Wickhurst. I was sure of that.

What had happened after they'd got what they came for? Why wasn't Derek here, traumatized and trembling? Because they'd taken him with them, that's why. They'd probably called a van round from wherever its driver was waiting, bundled Derek in and driven off. It wasn't just the book they'd come for. It was the author.

Would I see matching shoe-prints outside on the pavement, maybe skid marks where the van had sped away? I edged the front door open for a look.

The latch slipped from my grasp as the door was suddenly thrust wide open, striking me in the chest and throwing me back against the wall. A bulky figure moved in and past me, slamming the door shut behind him.

'Hi,' said Ian Maple, staring at me beadily from close quarters.

'You,' was all the response I could manage.

'Yeah. That's right. Me. I followed you from the theatre. Glenys Williams isn't a good liar. And you're not a much better one. So . . . how about telling me what the fuck's going on?'

It seemed I had no choice. We sat in Derek Oswin's armchairs, as the kitchen clock counted the continuing seconds and minutes and hours of his absence. And I told Ian Maple everything that had led to his brother's death. There was no point holding any of it back. Like Glenys had said, he had a right to know. And now he'd asserted that right.

'Denis was caught in the crossfire between you and Roger Colborn,' he accurately and bleakly concluded. 'There's no other way to look at it.'
    'No,' I had to agree. 'There isn't.'
    'And now Colborn's grabbed this Oswin guy.'
    'Looks like it. Though not in person, I imagine.'
    'No. His goons will have done that for him. The same goons who went after Denis.'
    'Probably, yes.'
    'Not a very nice man, Colborn, is he? Except in your wife's opinion.'
    'She knows nothing about this.'
    'Perhaps it's time she was told.'
    'She won't believe me.'
    'Maybe she'll believe *me*.'
    'Maybe.'
    'What do you want to do about Oswin?'
    'I'm not sure. Call the police?'
    Ian looked at me sceptically. 'You haven't a shred of evidence against Colborn. Even if the police believe Oswin's been abducted, they won't go looking for him at Wickhurst Manor. And they wouldn't find anything if they did. From what you tell me, Colborn will have been sure to cover his tracks. As things stand, the police would be more likely to arrest us than anyone else. Besides, my guess is that Colborn

158

just wants to put the fear of God into Oswin. He'll have him back here by morning.' He shrugged. 'If not, I'll pay him a call. And find out just how tough he really is.'

And so it was agreed, however reluctantly on my part: we'd await Derek's return, find out what had happened to him and decide how to react then. Ian was confident he'd be back. I was less certain. Colborn's no fool, I told myself. Doing Derek serious harm would be asking for trouble. And yet . . .

I found a key to the front door in one of the kitchen drawers and pocketed it when we left. We walked south through the chill, star-spattered Brighton night. Little was said. We'd talked ourselves out back at Derek's house. And neither of us quite trusted the other.

We parted by the Law Courts in Edward Street. 'I'll go back to Viaduct Road mid-morning,' I said. 'I'll let you know whether Derek's there or not. And, if he is, what state he's in.'

'I'll be waiting on your call.'

My call, yes. But watching him walk briskly away along the street without a backward glance, his broad shoulders hunched against the cold, I had the distinct feeling that what happened next would be his call, not mine.

But that's been the way of it ever since I arrived on Sunday. First Jenny, then Derek, now Ian Maple. Plus Roger Colborn, of course. They've all dictated my agenda, in their different ways. They've all decreed what's best for me. Or worst, depending how you look at it.

There's a matinée tomorrow. From lunchtime onwards I should be thinking about nothing beyond the dramatic and comedic challenges of *Lodger in the Throat*. As it is, acting is likely to be just about the last thing on my mind.

I'm so tired I can't sort the questions I should be asking myself into any logical order. Did I interpret the scene at 77 Viaduct Road correctly? Is Derek Oswin really being held somewhere against his will? Fraud and corruption you might expect of a certain ruthless type of businessman. But abduction and possibly worse? I thought Colborn was too clever for that, too subtle, too confident that less overt measures would always serve him better. Maybe I thought wrong.

If so, it's not just Derek I should be worried about. There's Jenny to consider as well. What kind of a man has she become involved with? She's normally a good judge of character. She must know what he's really like. He can't have deceived her so completely. Can he?

I don't know. I'm not sure. About that or anything else. I have a feeling akin to seeing something out of the corner of my eye that isn't there whenever I look directly at it. Something's going on, beyond Colborn's dirty tricks and dirtier dealings. I've been told so many different and conflicting stories that I can be certain of only one thing: I haven't come close to the truth; I haven't even glimpsed it.

But I will.

THURSDAY

It had to happen eventually. The sun was shining, low and cold in a cloudless sky, when I left the Sea Air this morning after one of Eunice's hearty breakfasts that somehow hadn't heartened me. I walked north up Grand Parade, chilled by a biting east wind and a gnawing anxiety about what I'd find.

Near the Open Market I fell in with the imagined footsteps of Derek Oswin's grandfather as he traced his daily route to work seventy or eighty years ago. But they kept on climbing the hill towards Colbonite, while I turned into Viaduct Road and made my way to the door of number 77.

There was no answer to my knock. It was as I'd feared, then. Derek had not returned. I let myself in and was met by the unaltered silence of last night; by Derek's duffel-coat hanging on its hook, the broken balusters sagging from the stair-rail, the books strewn across the sitting-room floor.

I glanced into the kitchen, then headed up to the bedroom. Nothing had changed there either. Nor, in Derek's continued absence, was it likely to. I sat down on the bed and rang Ian Maple.

'Yuh?' His answer was gruffly matter-of-fact.

'Toby Flood here, Ian. I've done as we agreed. There's no sign of him.'

'Understood.'

'What do you mean to do now?'

'Pay our friend a visit.'

163

'Be careful.'

'I'll call you later.' And with no assurance as to carefulness, he rang off.

Ian hadn't asked what my plans for the day were. I think he assumed I'd be busy at the theatre, leaving him free to probe the affairs of Roger Colborn in whatever way suited him best. But I had four hours at my disposal before I had to report for the matinée and I intended to put them to good use.

I picked up the photograph album from among the scattered contents of the chest and opened its stiff leather cover. The pages were black card, the captions beneath the photographs written in white ink in a copperplate hand. The Oswins' camera-caught memories kicked off with Kenneth and Valerie's wedding at St Bart's in July 1955. Kenneth was a thin, hollow-chested man with curly hair and a toothy grin, Valerie even thinner, fine-boned and graceful, surprisingly beautiful. (Why that surprised me I couldn't say, but it did.) The best man and bridesmaids were also snapped and identified and the best man cropped up in other pictures as I leafed on through. Burlier than Kenneth Oswin, with slicked-down hair and a stern gaze, Ray Braddock, or 'Uncle Ray' as later captions referred to him, was some sort of close family friend or relative to judge by the frequency of his appearances. He was to be seen standing by the pram when baby Derek made his début in front of the lens in the summer of 1958. Grandfather Oswin was a rarer subject, an older version of Kenneth who cropped up sporadically and never with Grandmother; she'd presumably died some time before 1955. Valerie's parents and siblings were rarer still. Perhaps they lived some distance away. Certainly the Oswins didn't travel far with their camera. Beachy Head was just about the most exotic locale. Brighton sea front, Preston Park and the back yard of 77 Viaduct Road were the commonest settings. Around 1972 the captions started being written in a different hand, which I recognized as Derek's. That was also when Grandfather Oswin died, if his abrupt disappearance

164

from the album was anything to go by. But Uncle Ray was still on the scene and remained there until the photographs fizzled out in the early Eighties, with several pages still unused. Never the most prolific of snappers, the Oswins appeared to have given up altogether.

By then Kenneth, Valerie and Uncle Ray had moved from their twenties into stolid middle age and Derek had grown from infancy to a mop-haired young man of uncertain bearing. He'd changed little in the years since, while his parents had both died, leaving him alone in this house of his childhood, a family home become both his refuge and his prison. As for Uncle Ray . . .

I phoned directory enquiries and they confirmed that there was a Braddock, R., listed in the Brighton area. They even gave me his address: 9 Buttermere Avenue, Peacehaven. I tried the number. No reply. And no answerphone either. Well, I could easily try later.

Next I conducted a search of all the obvious places where Derek might have stored or hidden the original of *The Plastic Men*. On top of the wardrobe and behind it. Under the bed. Beneath the stairs. In the kitchen cupboards. I didn't expect to find it, of course. I was as certain as could be that it had left with him. Sure enough, I found nothing.

Then I put a call in to Moira, crossing my fingers that I'd catch her in an obliging mood.

'What can I do for you, Toby?' Her tone left the issue of her mood tantalizingly undecided.

'You received the manuscript yesterday?'

'Yes. But if you think I've already got a response to it for you, then—'

'No, no. It's not that. I have another favour to ask of you.'

'The news about Denis was dreadful,' she said, apparently failing to register my last remark. 'I'll really miss him, you know, even though I hardly ever saw him. He was always so chirpy.' It was only then that I remembered Denis had been a client of hers, albeit not one of her most famous. 'Brian Sallis said you found him. Is that right?'

165

'Yes. It is.'

'If there's anything I can do . . .'

'There is, actually. It concerns the manuscript.'

'What's that to do with Denis?'

'Long story, Moira, which I'll be happy to go into another time. The point is, I need it back.'

'The manuscript?'

'Yes.'

'But you've only just sent it to me.'

'I know. And now I need it back. Urgently.'

'Why?'

'It's too complicated to explain. But it's important, believe me.'

'You're not making any sense, Toby. First you send me this, this . . . what is it, plastic something? . . . demanding an instant evaluation, then you demand it back again.'

'I'm well aware that it must sound crazy, Moira. You'll just have to trust me when I say there's a very good reason.'

'I know you and Denis were friends from way back. You must be upset. But—'

'*I need to see the manuscript.*'

'All right. All right. Calm down. If you want it, you must have it, I suppose.'

'Thank you.'

'I'll have it posted to you this afternoon. What's your address in Brighton?'

'Actually, Moira . . .'

'What?'

'I was hoping someone could bring it down to me. Today.'

'Are you joking?'

'No. You have umpteen juniors at your beck and call. You wouldn't miss one of them for a few hours. I'd rather not rely on the post. And it really is *very* urgent.'

'May I remind you that the bloody thing's only up here because you sent it to me, Toby?'

'I realize that. But—'

'Can't you ask the author to run you off another copy?'

166

'Impossible.'

'Any point my asking why?'

'Not really. Just lump all my credit points together and offset this favour against them.'

'What credit points?'

'Be reasonable, Moira. I'm asking you to help me out of a deep hole here.'

'Of whose digging, may I ask?' She paused, though not long enough for me to devise an answer, then resumed, her voice suddenly gentler. 'Sorry. You've been under a lot of strain, I know. Probably *more* than I know. All right.' During the next pause I heard her take a long draw on her cigarette. 'Tell you what, Toby. I really can't spare anyone today. Tomorrow, though, I'm supposed to be working at home. I'll substitute a day trip to Brighton, manuscript in hand, and you can pour out your troubles to your aunty Moira over lunch. Good enough?'

Only *just* good enough, to be honest. I wanted *The Plastic Men* in my hands, there and then, to comb for clues to what had happened and evidence to use against Roger Colborn. Short of going up to London to get it, however, I was going to have to wait until Moira brought it to me. The matinée meant I couldn't leave Brighton. The consequences of another no-show by me, with no understudy on hand, didn't bear contemplation. I suspected Moira had volunteered to act as courier because she wanted to reassure herself as to my state of mind. She'd lost two clients in this run of *Lodger in the Throat* – Jimmy Maidment was one of hers as well – so maybe she was getting twitchy.

If so, it seemed she wasn't the only one. I let myself out of the house and headed round the corner into London Road to catch a bus back into the centre. While I was waiting at the stop, Brian Sallis rang me.

'Good morning, Toby. How are you?'

'You don't need to worry, Brian. I'll be at the theatre by two o'clock.'

'Oh, I didn't phone to check up on you. Please don't think that.'

'I'll try not to.'

'It's true. The thing is, well . . .'

'Spit it out, for God's sake.'

'All right. Sorry. Leo and Melvyn are coming down to see the matinée. I thought you ought to know.'

'The pair of them?'

'Yes.'

'Why?'

'Just to see how we're going, I suppose.'

'Don't give me that. We're two days from closure.'

'Ah, but are we?'

'What do you mean?'

'I have the impression Melvyn's report on Tuesday night's show may have made Leo think twice about taking us off.'

'You can't be serious.'

'I don't see any other way to read it. Play it this afternoon like you did Tuesday and . . . who knows? It could be very good news.'

Brian's definition of good news and mine were quite a way apart at that moment. I sat on the top deck of the number 5 as it rumbled south, bemused by the ironies of my situation. If Leo really was considering an eleventh-hour stay of execution for *Lodger in the Throat* and, by implication, a London transfer, I should be psyching myself up for a persuasive and possibly clinching star turn as James Elliott. The rest of the cast could be relied on to pull out all the stops. The chance was there to be seized.

But the chance was to me more of a burden. I couldn't spare much thought for acting as matters currently stood. In fact, I couldn't spare *any*. Reality doesn't often intrude into the life of an actor. Pretence is all, off stage as well as on. For me, though, that had changed. Utterly.

The only problem was explaining my predicament to other

168

people in a way that would make sense to them. And I knew it was a problem I couldn't hope to solve.

As if to underline the point, Brian was back on to me before I'd even got off the bus.

'I've just spoken to Melvyn, Toby. I'm having lunch with him and Leo at the Hôtel du Vin. It's in Ship Street. You know, where Henekeys used to be.'

'I'm sure you'll have a wonderful time.'

'Ah, but Leo's suggested you join us, you see. That's why I called. Not for the whole meal, obviously. Wouldn't want to put you off your stroke.' His laugh was not contagious. 'One o'clock OK for you? It's only a ten-minute walk from there to the theatre.'

I agreed, of course. I only had to think how rejecting a lunch invitation from our esteemed producer would go down with my fellow cast members, whose salaries he paid, to realize I had no choice. Buttering up Leo and Melvyn was something I had neither the wish nor the leisure to engage in, but come one o'clock I was going to be doing it none the less.

I hopped off the bus at the Steine and doubled back at an Olympic-style walk to the Local Studies Library in Church Street. I glimpsed a representative sample of library-going folk poring over microfilm-readers as I entered, but fortunately there were several vacant places. I just had to hope none of those using the machines were consulting November 1995 editions of the *Argus*.

As I peeled round to the enquiries desk, however, I came face to face with someone extremely unlikely to have come there in search of anything else.

'Toby,' said Jenny, shuffling together a sheaf of photo-copied pages, conspicuous by their having been printed white on black. 'What are you doing here?'

'*I could ask you the same question*' was such an obvious retort that I didn't utter it. I just looked at her, then down at the sheets of paper in her hand, recognizing at a glance the

169

headlines and columns of a newspaper page and deciphering a date at the top of one: *Friday, November 17, 1995*. Then I looked back up at her and said simply, 'Snap.'

A few minutes later, we were standing in the grounds of the Royal Pavilion, near the entrance to the Museum. It was cold enough to ensure we were in no danger of being overheard. A dusting of frost still clung to the grass where the sun hadn't reached. And Jenny's breath clouded faintly in the air as she spoke. Anger as well as a chill wind had reddened her cheeks.

'You set me up, didn't you? It was a test, to see which way I'd jump. Well, congratulations, Toby. You twitched the lead and I came running.'

'I don't know what you're talking about.'

'I should have realized you'd put Ian Maple up to it, of course.'

'Up to what?'

'Drop the pretence, Toby. It won't wash.'

'You've spoken to Ian Maple?'

'You know I have.'

'No. I don't. When was this?'

Jenny shifted her gaze and took a long, slow breath. The white-on-black photocopies were clutched tightly in her hand. I reached out and tugged gently at them. She let go.

'The print's come off on your fingers,' I remarked, irrelevantly. She shivered, tempting me for a moment to put a warming arm round her shoulders. But of course I didn't. 'Why don't we grab a coffee somewhere?'

'Tell me the truth, Toby.' She looked me in the eye. 'Did you send Ian Maple to see me?'

'No.'

'He came to the shop just after we opened.' Which meant *before* I phoned him from Viaduct Road, I realized; nice of him to mention the visit. 'He was very . . . insistent. And the things he said about Roger . . .' She shook her head. 'I don't believe any of it.'

'I told him you wouldn't.'

'So you did send him?'

'No.'

'But everything he knows . . .'

'He had from me, I admit.'

'Including this nonsense about Oswin being abducted?'

'Not nonsense, actually.'

'It must be.'

'If you're so sure, why did you look these up?' I fanned out the photocopies in my hand.

'To remind myself of the facts. Which Roger told me a long time ago, in case you're wondering.'

'And what *are* the facts, Jenny?'

She cocked an eyebrow at me. 'Perhaps you should read them for yourself.'

'Why don't you just tell me?'

'Because you might not believe me.'

'If we could agree on what the truth is, Jenny, we'd have no choice but to believe each other.'

Her mouth tightened. Her focus flicked cautiously around the middle distance. Then she said, 'All right. We'll talk. But you'll have to read the *Argus* reports first. Then we'll both know what we're talking *about*. There's a café in the Museum. I'll wait for you there.'

I sat down on a bench where the surrounding buildings screened me from the wind but not the sunshine and sorted the photocopied sheets into chronological order.

There were seven in all, the first five dating from November 1995. A short but prominent article, accompanied by an indistinct photograph of a car cordoned off behind police tape in a country lane, reported Sir Walter Colborn's death in the issue of 14 November. The headline reads, PROMINENT LOCAL BUSINESSMAN KILLED IN COLLISION WITH CAR. It goes on:

Sir Walter Colborn, former chairman and managing director of Brighton-based plastics company Colbonite Ltd, died yesterday after being struck by a car while walking along a lane close to his home, Wickhurst Manor, near Fulking. The incident occurred shortly after 3 p.m.

The driver of the car, a dark-blue Ford Fiesta, has not been named. He has been detained in custody and is assisting the police with their inquiries.

By the following day, the *Argus* was able to report SURPRISE MANSLAUGHTER CHARGE FOLLOWING DEATH OF SIR WALTER COLBORN:

Police yesterday charged a man in connection with the death on Monday of prominent local business-man and politician Sir Walter Colborn. Kenneth George Oswin, 63, from Brighton, has been charged with manslaughter and will appear before Lewes magistrates tomorrow.

Another page of the same issue carried a fulsome obituary of the eminent departed.

Walter Colborn was born in Brighton in 1921. He was the grandson of the founder of Colbonite Ltd, a plastics company based in Hollingdean Road, Brighton, which closed in 1989. Walter Colborn was educated at Brighton College and went up to Pembroke College, Oxford, after serving with distinction in the Army during the Second World War. He succeeded his father as chairman and managing director of Colbonite in 1955 and later served as a West Sussex County Councillor for many years, latterly as deputy leader of the Conservative group. He was also energetically involved in a host of charitable causes and was a prominent member of

172

the Brighton Society and an adviser to the West Pier Trust. He was knighted in 1987 in recognition of his distinguished record of public service. He married Ann Hopkinson in 1953. The couple had one son, Roger, who survives Sir Walter. Ann Colborn died in 1982.

Next day, Kenneth Oswin was remanded in custody by Lewes magistrates, according to a terse paragraph lodged obscurely near the bottom of a page. Someone had cottoned on to his connection with Colbonite by the day after, however, raising the profile of the case. MAN CHARGED WITH MANSLAUGHTER OF SIR WALTER COLBORN WAS FORMER EMPLOYEE ran the headline, above an article revealing how Roger Colborn had got in on the act.

Roger Colborn, son of the late Sir Walter Colborn, confirmed yesterday that Kenneth Oswin, the man charged with manslaughter following Sir Walter's death on Monday after he collided with a car being driven by Mr Oswin, was a former employee of Colbonite Ltd, the Brighton-based plastics company, founded by Sir Walter's grandfather, which closed in 1989. Mr Colborn, who assisted his father in the management of the company, said he knew of no reason why Mr Oswin should bear Sir Walter any ill will. Mr Oswin, he added, had been 'generously treated, like all the company's staff, at the time of its closure, a regrettable but unavoidable event brought about by increasingly intense foreign competition'.

How nice, how bland, how very reasonable Roger sounded. There was no mention of chloro-aniline or cancer or shell companies or deftly dodged compensation. The average un-informed reader probably concluded, if they concluded anything, that Kenneth Oswin was some kind of nutter with a grudge, the details of which would emerge at his trial.

But there was to be no trial, as a paragraph in the *Argus* for Wednesday, February 7, 1996, made clear.

> Kenneth George Oswin, 63, of Viaduct Road, Brighton, the man awaiting trial for the manslaughter of Sir Walter Colborn last November, died yesterday at the Royal Sussex County Hospital in Brighton, where he had recently been transferred from Lewes Prison. He had been suffering from cancer for some time.

That wasn't quite the end of the matter, however. An inquest followed two months later, skimming over the ground that a trial would doubtless have examined in depth. SIR WALTER COLBORN'S DEATH WAS UNLAWFUL KILLING, CORONER RULES, ran the *Argus* headline.

> An inquest heard yesterday that the prosecution would have argued at the trial of Kenneth Oswin for the manslaughter of Sir Walter Colborn that Mr Oswin intended to do Sir Walter serious and probably fatal harm when he drove a Ford Fiesta car into him on a quiet country lane near Sir Walter's home north of Brighton on the afternoon of November 13 last year.
>   Detective Inspector Terence Moore of Sussex Police told the coroner that the collision occurred on a stretch of the lane with good visibility and that examination of the car showed that Mr Oswin had first struck Sir Walter a glancing blow, knocking him to the ground, then reversed over him. A charge of manslaughter was only preferred to murder because of doubts about Mr Oswin's state of mind, which might well have justified a plea of diminished responsibility. Mr Oswin was suffering at the time from cancer, of which he later died while awaiting trial. Detective Inspector Moore added that Mr

174

Oswin consistently denied deliberately killing Sir Walter, but refused to give any account of what had occurred on the afternoon in question.

The coroner said in his summing-up that the outcome of Mr Oswin's trial could not and should not be taken for granted, but that a verdict of unlawful killing was clearly appropriate in the matter of Sir Walter's death. He added a personal tribute to the deceased, whom he described as a great loss to the community.

I went into the Museum and up to the café on the first floor. Jenny was waiting for me at a table overlooking the art gallery. She'd have been able to see me coming from there, though the intensity with which she was staring into the frothy remains of her *cappuccino* suggested she might easily have missed me. I bought a coffee for myself and joined her.

'OK. I'm up to speed on the facts,' I said quietly, laying the sheaf of photocopies on the table between us. 'Those the *Argus* printed, at any rate.'

'Kenneth Oswin murdered Roger's father,' said Jenny, leaning forward across the table and treating me to a lengthy, scrutinizing stare. 'You accept that?'

'Yes.' I had to. Derek's suggestion that the collision was accidental could only be wishful thinking at best. His version of the event was seriously at variance with the facts. 'But the question is: why?'

'Because he blamed Sir Walter for the cancer that was killing him.'

'With good cause.'

'Yes, Toby. With good cause.' She went on staring at me. 'You think Roger's answerable for his father's cavalier attitude to the health of the Colbonite workforce?'

'I think Roger aided and abetted his father in evading responsibility for the consequences, Jenny. By which I mean *financial* consequences. I also think Roger may have taken extreme steps to silence Derek Oswin on the point.'

175

'Rubbish. I don't believe for a moment Roger's even been to see Oswin.'

'Where's Derek gone, then?'

'How should I know?'

'You say Roger told you about all this a long time ago?'

'Yes.'

'How come you didn't recognize Derek's surname when I mentioned it to you, then?'

'Roger never actually told me the name of the man who killed his father, as far as I can remember. If he had, I might well have forgotten. I didn't think it mattered. I still don't.'

'What about the cancer cases, Jenny? Not a penny paid in compensation. How does Roger square that with his conscience? How do you?'

'Sir Walter resorted to undeniably shady tactics when he wound the company up. Roger makes no secret of that. He protested against them at the time and fell out with his father as a result.'

'We only have Roger's word for that, presumably.'

'I believe him.'

'Naturally. And let's suppose it's true. Just for the sake of argument. Suppose Roger really did advocate coming clean about the chloro-anilines but was overruled by his old man. Why didn't he do something about it when Sir Walter died and he inherited the wherewithal to pay out some long over-due compensation?'

'He considered the idea. He took advice.'

'Oh yeah?'

'To pay out in one case would mean paying out in all. It would have bankrupted him.'

'Well, we couldn't have that, could we?'

'As a matter of fact . . .'

'What?'

'He has . . . helped . . . in a few of the more desperate cases. With hospice fees and the like. He's had to be . . . discreet about it.'

'To avoid admitting general liability?'

'Yes. So, is that what you're accusing him of, Toby? Trying to repair some of the damage his father did without ruining himself in the process?'

'No. That's your gloss on what I suspect he's really been up to. And I'm not the only one who suspects it.'

'Ian Maple said you'd spoken to Roger's uncle.'

'Yes. Informative fellow, Gavin. See a lot of him, do you?'

'I've never met him. But I know his version of events can't be trusted.'

'And how do you know that? Because Roger told you so, perhaps?'

'His sister Delia says the same.'

'Does she?'

'Yes. And I can arrange for her to say it to you as well if that's what it'll take to make you call off this . . . ludicrous campaign.'

'Denis is dead, Jenny. And Derek Oswin is missing. I'm not making any of that up. I think Roger is a dangerous man to know.'

'Ah. So, you're trying to protect me.'

'Why wouldn't I?'

'Why indeed?' She sat back and shook her head at me. 'Surely you can see you're deluding yourself, Toby? Denis died of a heart attack. It's sad, but it could have happened at any time. As for Derek Oswin, so what if he's gone walkabout and left his house in a mess? You can't blame Roger for that.'

'Can't I?'

'You're not going to believe anything I tell you, are you?'

'Are you going to believe anything *I* tell *you*?'

Jenny sighed. 'For God's sake . . .'

'It cuts both ways, you know. You think I'm deluding myself. Well, that's exactly what I think you're doing.'

'Yes.' She almost smiled then, some of her old exasperated fondness for me bobbing briefly to the surface. 'I suppose you do.'

'Tell me what you'd accept as proof.'

'Proof?' She thought for a moment, then leaned forward

again. 'All right. Delia has no axe to grind. Certainly not in Roger's favour, anyway. He bought her Colbonite shares as well as Gavin's and ultimately netted a substantial profit on them. So, she should resent him on that account. Agreed?'

'Yes,' I responded, suddenly cautious. Gavin had portrayed his sister as a fellow victim of Roger's machinations. He'd even suggested I ask her to corroborate his story. But Jenny seemed oddly confident Delia would back up Roger's version of events. If she did, I wouldn't have proved my case. In fact, I'd have gone a long way towards *dis*proving it.

'Come and see her with me. She knows the history of all of this. And she's an honest person. I can assure you of that. If she sides with you . . . I'll have to take it seriously.'

'And if not?'

'*You'll* have to take it seriously.'

'How do I know this isn't a set-up?'

'You have to trust me, Toby. That's how.'

I drank some coffee, studying Jenny's face over the rim of the cup. She was right, of course. I had to trust her. If I didn't, I was lost. But she'd misunderstood me, anyway. It wasn't her I suspected of setting me up. Not that it mattered, really. I'd left myself without an escape route. 'All right. Let's do it.'

'When?'

'You tell me. There's a matinée today, so I'm pushed for time, but I'll fit it in.'

'I'll have to give Delia some notice. How about this afternoon – between performances? She lives in Powis Villas. It's a short walk from the theatre.'

'I know where she lives. Gavin gave me her address.'

'All right. I'll phone her and explain.'

'Why not phone her right now?'

'Why not?' Jenny smiled at me defiantly, took out her mobile and dialled the number. A few moments passed; then she started speaking. But only to leave a message asking Delia to call her urgently. She rang off. 'I'll let you know what I fix up. It may have to be tomorrow, of course. I can't speak for Delia's availability. I'd better be going now. I've left Sophie in charge long enough.' She stood up and reached out for the photocopies, then changed her mind. 'You can keep those.'

'Thanks. It'll spare you the effort of hiding them from Roger.' I regretted the remark instantly. But there was no taking it back.

Jenny looked down at me with a kind of baffled pity. 'You really don't understand, Toby, do you?'

'Don't I?'

'No. And it seems, God help me, that I'm going to have to prove that to you.'

I tried Ray Braddock again after Jenny had gone. Still no answer. I had his address, of course, but there was no point going there if he wasn't in. I walked back out into the cold, clear, late-morning air, where the shadows were long, but sharply etched. I looked across at the minarets and onion domes of the Royal Pavilion and spared a sympathetic thought for sad old fat George IV. All he'd really wanted to do was enjoy some cosy domesticity with Mrs Fitzherbert, who happened, after all, by every seemly definition to be his wife. Yet they were forced to live apart. Their separation was in many ways George's own fault, just as losing Jenny was mine. But culpability doesn't make such miscarriages of life easier to bear. Quite the reverse, actually.

It was just gone noon and there was little I could usefully do before joining the three musketeers for lunch. Why I gravitated to the Cricketers I'm not sure, except that it had become something of a midday habit. What I hadn't realized was that it was also a midday habit for my self-appointed friend Sydney Porteous.

'Great to see you, Tobe. Couldn't keep away, hey?'

'Something like that.'

'Allow me the distinct pleasure of buying you a drink. Pint of Harvey's best?'

179

'I'll plump for tomato juice, thanks. There's a matinée this afternoon.'

'So there is. Very wise.' He ordered a Virgin Mary and a top-up for his own pint. 'Shall we huddle by the fire? It's brass monkeys out there today.'

Drinks in hand, we went and sat down. Syd smacked his lips at another swallow of beer, while I sipped my under-Worcestered tomato juice and glanced wincingly around at the ever tinselier auguries of Christmas.

'Wrecks the whole month, doesn't it?' said Syd, evidently reading my thoughts. 'Piped carols and office parties. Who needs them, hey? Not pagans with no office to go to, that's for sure.'

'Quite.'

'Still, my Christmas is shaping up to be a little less throat-slittingly depressing now Aud's on the scene. She's really looking forward to seeing you on Sunday, by the way.'

'Sunday?'

'She's cooking you lunch, remember?'

Now I did remember. Yes, of course. Sunday lunch with Syd and Aud. How had I ever agreed to that? It was a good question. But the rhetorical alternative I actually posed was, 'How could I forget?'

'You've got a lot on your mind, Tobe. A spot of forgetfulness is only to be expected.' He lowered his voice confidentially. 'How goes the campaign?'

It struck me as odd that he'd used the same word as Jenny to describe my activities. What made it odder still was how unlike a campaign they felt to me. 'I'm making steady progress.'

'Excellent. Decided yet whether you'll need me to ride shotgun for you when you drop in on the fragrant Delia?'

'I won't need to impose on you, Syd.'

'It'd be no imposition.'

'Even so . . .'

'Your call, Tobe. Entirely your call.'

'I appreciate the offer, but . . .'

180

'You'd rather go it alone. Understood. I suppose I was just angling for an excuse to renew our acquaintance.'

'How *were* you acquainted?'

'Oh, well, Gav invited me out to Wickhurst Manor a few times during our schooldays. Delia's a couple of years older than us. I remember her first as a Roedean sixth-former. Awesomely ladylike. She taught there for quite a few years, you know, after finishing school and Oxford – or Cambridge, I can't honestly recall which. I always fancied her and there was a period in my late twenties and her early thirties when . . .' He spread his hands. 'Well, I blew my chance, that's what it comes down to. But I don't reckon I ever had much of one. I wasn't really in her league. As I've not an itty-bitty doubt her sister-in-law made crystal clear to her. Ann Colborn was always down on me. And she and Delia were like that.' Syd wrapped his index and second fingers together.

'Ann Colborn died young, didn't she?'

'Fairly.'

I waited for Syd to expand on the remark, but he didn't. Such reticence was uncharacteristic. 'I looked up Sir Walter's obituary in the *Argus*, Syd,' I said by way of a prompt.

'Ah. So you know, then?'

'That his wife died in nineteen eighty-two, yes. When she can't have been much more than fifty, judging by Sir Walter's age.'

'Didn't it mention . . . how she died?'

'No.'

'So you *don't* know.'

'Know what?'

'Suicide, Tobe. Ann Colborn took her own life. Drove her car off Beachy Head. Nice car, too. Jaguar two point four.'

'She killed herself?'

'Well, it definitely wasn't murder.'

'Why did she do it?'

'Depression, I think they said. You know, "while the balance of her mind was disturbed". Let's face it, it'd have to be disturbed for her to take the Jag with her. Mind you, it's a classier exit than going under the wheels of a Ford Fiesta.'

I've thought about that last comment of Syd's since. Yesterday, he claimed not to know that the driver of the car that killed Sir Walter was charged with manslaughter. Strange, then, that he should none the less remember the model of car involved. When he dropped it into our conversation at the Cricketers, I made nothing of it, still dismayed by the realization that Roger Colborn's mother had committed suicide. Looking back, however, I see it as proof of what I've begun to suspect: that Syd's garrulous manner conceals rather more than it reveals; that he knows rather more than he's so far chosen to disclose.

'I think Delia was still living at Wickhurst Manor then. Ann's death must have been a real blow to her. She's married since, of course. And married well, according to Gav. So, if reasons are what you're looking for, you could ask her, I suppose. She's had twenty years to get used to what happened.' Syd thought for a moment, then went on. 'Say, you don't think Ann Colborn topping herself is . . . connected with all this, do you?'

'No. Do you, Syd?'

He shrugged. 'No way to tell. Doesn't seem likely, does it? I certainly wouldn't put a lot of money on it. But, then again . . .' He grinned. 'I might risk a fiver.'

I reached the Hôtel du Vin ten minutes late thanks to my brain-picking session with Syd. My mind was still focused on the distant mysteries of the Colborn family. I was in no mood and poor condition to make up a foursome with Brian Sallis, Melvyn Buckingham and the demigod of the West End himself, Leo Simmons Gauntlett.

They were already at their table in the large and busy restaurant when I arrived. Melvyn was all smiles and 'dear boys' after several pre-prandial gins, but Leo looked as if his ulcer was playing him up again. A man of notably untheatrical appearance – more accountant than impresario – he can

182

charm and schmooze and fly kites with the best of them when he has to. His natural temperament veers more towards the plain and practical, however, and sometimes the downright pessimistic. It was immediately apparent to me that he hadn't arrived in Brighton with the highest of hopes. But, canny financier that he is, he doesn't like to give up on any investment unless he absolutely has to. This was my chance to persuade him that in this case he might not have to. Unfortunately, not only did I feel unequal to the challenge, I also felt signally indifferent to the outcome.

'Melvyn thought he saw something new in the show Tuesday night,' he said over his doctor's-orders salad after I'd ordered a starter and a mineral water to keep them company. 'Did it feel like there was something new in it to you, Toby?'

'Not sure.'

'Not sure's a bit bloody weak this late in the day.'

'It's the best I can do.'

'Denis's death has knocked us all sideways, Leo,' put in Brian.

'Ah yes,' said Melvyn, slurping some wine. 'Death – the great leveller.'

'I don't know about death,' said Leo. 'What concerns me is whether there's any life in *Lodger in the Throat*.'

'There always has been,' I said. 'We just haven't been very successful at finding it.'

'Hah. Sounds like you agree with your friend Unwin. It's all down to unsympathetic direction.'

Melvyn choked and spluttered on another mouthful of wine. 'Am I never to hear the last of that ghastly fellow and his impertinent letters?'

'Actually, Leo, his name's Oswin,' I pointed out. 'Not Unwin.' Then Melvyn's use of the plural registered in my mind. 'Did you say letters?'

'Oh yes,' Melvyn replied. 'Another one arrived this morning.'

'I suppose you get used to your fan mail containing a

certain percentage of crackpot material,' said Leo. 'It's come as an eye-opener to me, though.'

'What did the letter say?'

'See for yourself.' Leo flourished a sheet of paper from inside his jacket and handed it to me. 'Keep it if you like.'

It was Derek's distinctive handwriting, no question about it. He'd sent a second letter, after promising me he wouldn't. Or had he? He probably posted it yesterday morning, *before* he undertook to end the correspondence. Technically, he hadn't broken his promise. But nor had he warned me that a second missive was already on its way. Not for the first time, he'd been economical with the facts. It seemed to be something of a local custom. Why, I wondered, had Derek seen fit to write to Leo again?

77 Viaduct Road
Brighton
BN1 4ND

4th December 2002

Dear Mr Gauntlett,
Further to my previous letter, I realize that I
omitted to say something very important about Mr
Flood. As someone to some degree responsible for
the advancement of his career, you should be aware
that it is not only for his considerable acting
abilities that Mr Flood is to be cherished. He is
also, you see, an honourable and generous man,
as I know from my personal experience. He has
tried to help me just as I have tried to help him. I
find it hard to imagine that any other person of
Mr Flood's eminence would spare me so much
attention. It is a reflection of the nobility of his
character and I wish to pay tribute to that. I only
hope it does not redound to his disadvantage.
Should it do so, however, I call upon you to do

184

everything you can to assist him. He would richly
deserve any kindness you could render him, since
there may come a time when he is not the best
judge of his own interests.

Respectfully yours,
Derek Oswin

'You assured me he wouldn't write again, dear boy,' said
Melvyn as I folded the letter and slid it into my pocket. 'Is it
to become a regular event?'

'No. Definitely not.'

'First he questions Melvyn's direction,' said Leo. 'Now
your judgement, Toby. A bit bloody presumptuous, isn't
he?'

'I'm afraid he is, yes. But you've heard the last of him.'

'Really?'

'You reserved a ticket for him last night, Toby,' said Brian.
'It wasn't taken up.'

'I believe he's left town.'

'Good riddance,' mumbled Melvyn.

In some ways, I wanted to echo the sentiment. If Derek
was in trouble, as I believed he was – big trouble – then it was
of his own making. But I wasn't trying to get him out of it
just in order to win Jenny back. I was also trying to help
Derek for his own infuriating sake, as he in his oddly acute
fashion seemed to understand. In the opinion of some, the
time has already come when I'm not the best judge of my own
interests. And in the opinion of others, I never have been.
But, as it happens, I'm the only judge who counts.

Not as far as the future of *Lodger in the Throat* is concerned, though. That's down to Leo S. Gauntlett.

'I hope I haven't had a wasted journey,' he grumbled,
spearing a cherry tomato.

'Don't worry, Leo,' I said, dredging up some bravado and
beaming at my companions like the versatile actor I am. 'I'll
ensure you go back to London with a spring in your step and a
song in your heart.'

Leo regarded me acidly for a moment, then said, 'You're not going to try and turn it into a bloody musical, are you?'

Brian and I left Leo and Melvyn to their coffees (and brandy, in Melvyn's case) in order to be at the theatre by two o'clock. We were threading through the crowds of Christmas shoppers in North Street when Jenny rang me.

'I've spoken to Delia, Toby. She can meet us late afternoon. When will you be free?'

'We'll finish about five fifteen. I could be at Powis Villas by . . . a quarter to six.'

'All right. I'll be there when you arrive. It's number fifteen.'

'I know. Fine. But look . . .' I edged into a doorway, waving Brian to go on ahead, which he did, though only far enough to put himself out of earshot. 'Jenny, there's something that's bound to crop up when I speak to Delia and I'm not sure if you know . . . about it.'

'Oh yes. What's that?'

'Roger's mother. Ann Colborn.'

'Yes?'

'She killed herself, Jenny. She and Delia were pretty close, apparently. I . . . well, I didn't want . . . to spring it on you.'

There was the briefest of delays before Jenny responded, but it was a delay that told a tale of its own. 'Of course I know about Roger's mother, Toby. It's not a secret.'

'Good.' *I've just done you a big favour, Jenny*, I thought to myself. *Do you realize that? You can clear this up with Delia before I arrive now. Thanks to me.* 'I just . . . wanted to check.'

'Well, now you have.'

'Yeah, OK. See you later.'

I caught up with Brian and explained to him that I'd have to leave the theatre straight after the show. There'd be no time for a debriefing session with Leo and Melvyn. He was clearly put out by this, since they wouldn't be staying for the evening performance, but, as I said to him, 'Leo will decide what's best for business, Brian, you know that. With or without encouragement from me.'

I was glad to reach the haven of my dressing room and relieved, in some ways, to be about to go on stage. The adrenalin doesn't course through my system during live performances the way it used to, but I was confident there'd be enough of it pumping around to put the tangled complexities of my involvement with the Colborn and Oswin families past and present out of my mind for a couple of hours.

I changed into my costume, applied a little make-up and sat quietly, trying to will myself into the thoughts as well as the persona of James Elliott. The quarter-hour was called, then the five minutes. And then my mobile, which normally I'd have switched off, trilled into life. In the interests of my preparation routine, I should have ignored it. Naturally, I didn't.
    'Yes?'
    'Ian Maple here, Toby. We need to meet.'
    'I'm due on stage in a few minutes.'
    'Things have taken . . . an unexpected turn.'
    'This will have to wait, Ian.'
    'It can't.'
    'But it has to.'
    'When can we meet? It's got to be this afternoon.'
    'All right. Come to the theatre an hour from now. Use the stage door. I'll leave word you're to be shown to my dressing room. We'll talk during the interval.'
    'Understood.'
    He rang off and I headed for the door.

My mind lost all focus during the first act. That's not as bad as it sounds. Sometimes I'm at my best when I just surrender control and let it happen. The down side is that I'm in no position to analyse such a performance. It is what it is, good *or* bad. The rest of the cast were probably on their mettle, knowing Leo and Melvyn were in the audience, but how they thought it went, or more importantly how they thought Leo thought it went, I have no idea.

Ian Maple was waiting in my dressing room, as agreed. He looked sombre, but, surprisingly, more relaxed than last night. He remained where he was on the couch when I entered. On the floor at his feet was a long, narrow object wrapped in a carrier bag bearing the name Dockerills, an ironmongery shop in Church Street I'd passed several times.

'Thanks for telling me you'd already dropped in on my wife when we spoke this morning,' I said by way of an opener, turning the dressing-table chair round and sitting down to face him.

'You've seen her?'

'Yes.'

'Ah.' He rubbed his unshaven chin. 'I didn't know you were planning to.'

'I wasn't.'

'But I was. I told you that.'

'All right. Let's not waste time.' It was true to say we couldn't afford to. And recriminations were clearly not going to make any impression on Ian. He meant business. 'What's happened since? Have you met Colborn?'

'Not exactly. I've seen him.'

'Seen as in "observed"?'

'As in "followed". I hired a car and drove out to Wickhurst. Spotted Colborn leaving in his Porsche as I was cruising towards the entrance, so I just fell in behind and let him take me where he was going.'

'And where was that?'

'Car park up on Devil's Dyke. Where a bloke was waiting for him in a Ford Transit. A big bloke. Fucking huge.'

'Denis's man mountain.'

'That's what I figured. Colborn pulled in next to the van. They talked for a few minutes. Colborn handed him an envelope. Then they went their separate ways. I followed man mountain.'

188

'Are you sure they didn't spot you?'

'It's a nice day. There were quite a few cars up on the Dyke. Dog-walkers and such. I blended in. I'm good at doing that.'

'OK. So, where did man mountain take you?'

'Fishersgate. Part of the sprawl between here and Worthing. A mix of housing and factories. There's a small, down-at-heel industrial estate next to Fishersgate railway station. He drove in there and went into one of the units. There was no-one waiting for him that I saw. Unless they stayed inside, of course. The main shutter-door was down. He let himself in by a wicket-door. Came out about ten minutes later and drove away. I kept following. He headed into the centre of Brighton. Stowed the van in a lock-up garage in Little Western Street, then took off on foot. By the time I'd parked the car, I'd lost him. So, I went back to Fishersgate and took a closer look at the warehouse he'd gone into. No signs of life. No trace of ownership. Bloke in the welding outfit next door knew zilch.'

'What do you reckon, then?'

'I reckon it's where they're holding Oswin.'

'Based on what?'

'Based on man mountain going there to check on something after a confab with Colborn. And it's a guess I mean to back up.'

'How?'

'We're going in tonight.' He toed open the bag on the floor to reveal the jaws of a stout pair of bolt-cutters. 'These'll get us through the perimeter fence and the padlock on the wicket-door.'

'You're serious?'

'The best way to nail Colborn is to spring Oswin. There's no sense in holding off. But . . .'

'What?'

'I'll need you to watch my back and, maybe more importantly, explain to Oswin that I'm one of the good guys.'

'This sounds risky.'

'Of course it's risky. What did you expect? A stroll on the beach?'

'It's just . . . I'm an actor for God's sake. I'd be a liability.'

'I can't do it on my own. And there's no-one else I can ask to help. Now . . . are you in or out?' He stared at me levelly, defying me to pass up the chance I undeniably craved to pin something on Roger Colborn. Nor was that the only consideration, as Ian was well aware. 'Delaying won't help Oswin, you know. The longer someone like him is in the hands of man mountain's kind, the worse it'll be for him, believe me.'

'I do believe you.'

'Well, then?'

'All right. Let's do it.'

'I'll pick you up from the bottom of Madeira Place at midnight. OK?'

I nodded. 'OK.' There really was, it seemed, nothing else for it.

The second act sped past, my mind autopiloting me through to the close. The applause sounded less than wholeheartedly enthusiastic, but midweek matinées attract an undemonstrative lot. In a fragmentary conversation afterwards, Jocasta struck a hopeful note. 'I think we've given Leo something to think about.'

Well, she might have been right. But, even if she was, it was nothing like as much as I had to think about. Two performances of *Lodger in the Throat* and a spot of breaking and entering constituted a distinctly challenging workload.

'If I were you,' I said to my reflection in the dressing-room mirror as I changed out of my James Elliott kit, 'I wouldn't do it.'

Night had fallen by the time I left the theatre. Gift-laden shoppers were trailing along North Street. The air was cold and the spirit Christmassy, as a gust of piped 'Jingle Bells' from a shop near the stage door forcibly reminded me. I hurried along Church Street past the fuming crawl of traffic and cut across Dyke Road to Clifton Terrace, where a chill, quiet serenity prevailed, then round the corner into Powis Villas, a sloping street of semi-detached residences sporting stylish verandahs and expensive cars in the driveways.

Jenny answered the door at number 15 and showed me into a high-windowed drawing room furnished and decorated with tasteful restraint. A log fire blazed invitingly beneath a gilt-framed oil, the subject of which I instantly recognized as Wickhurst Manor.

Delia Sheringham rose from a fireside chair to greet me. Tall, slim and fine-boned, dressed plainly but elegantly, she was grey-haired yet younger in appearance than her probable age had prepared me for. Her eyes were a softer, more forget-me-not shade of blue than her brother's and nephew's. Her smile was softer too, her voice altogether gentler. But her self-control was palpable. There was no way to tell whether she had just been recounting the circumstances of her sister-in-law's suicide or the state of her preparations for Christmas.

'Would you like a drink, Mr Flood?' she enquired. 'Jenny and I are having tea.'

'Tea would be fine, thanks.'

Jenny poured me a cup. We all sat down. I sipped some tea.

'My husband and I have tickets for your play on Saturday night,' said Delia. 'I'm sure we'll enjoy it.'

'We aim to please.' Whether Orton's scatological humour would appeal to her I privately doubted. The state of mind of the lead actor come Saturday night was also questionable. Delia was facing a less certain prospect than she knew.

'Jenny's explained your . . . difficulty, Toby. May I call you Toby? I dare say you find people tend towards overfamiliarity because of your profession. It must be a bore for you.'

'Not at all. And certainly not in your case.'

'Very well, Toby. You should understand that I'm not in the habit of discussing my family's affairs with outsiders. Indeed, I'm hardly in the habit of discussing them with other

191

members of my family.' She smiled thinly. 'The Colborns do not wear their hearts on their sleeves. But that doesn't mean they don't have hearts. Or consciences. The illness that affected so many Colbonite employees has weighed on Roger's conscience, I know, as it should have. I believe Jenny has told you of his efforts to help some of them.'

'Yes.' I glanced across at Jenny. 'She's told me.'

'No doubt you think those efforts inadequate. Well, you may be right. He is constrained, however. You should be aware of that. I've done a little for some of them myself. Again, no doubt, too little. I played absolutely no part in the management of Colbonite, of course. I had no idea what . . . corners . . . Walter might have been cutting to sustain the business at a time when others were going to the wall in the face of foreign competition. They *were* Walter's decisions, however. No-one else's. Certainly not Roger's. I believe he did his best to improve safety practices after joining the company. As for his purchase of the shares Gavin and I held, I regarded that as an expression of his confidence that he could make a success of it. I was happy to sell. So was Gavin. Roger took a risk and profited from it. Why should I resent that? I know Gavin resents it, but I fear he's blaming Roger for his own mistakes. You've met Gavin. You know the kind of man he is.'

'He sends his regards.'

My remark drew a sharp look from Jenny, but Delia smiled tolerantly, as if she'd been the subject of a justified rebuke. 'Ours would be called a dysfunctional family in the current jargon. Gavin's character is flawed by self-indulgence. A refusal to accept responsibility for his own actions is the greatest self-indulgence of all.'

'He seems to think he was cheated out of his inheritance.'

'You can't be cheated out of something you haven't earned, Toby. Gavin has never understood that. But I don't want to be too hard on him. His elder brother was not without flaws himself. They were flaws of a rather different order, however. Walter wasn't a self-made man. How could he be as the third

192

generation to run Colbonite? But he'd have liked to be, you see, and probably would have been in other circumstances. The company could easily have collapsed in the nineteen fifties. Walter sustained it virtually single-handedly. Father's contribution was negligible by then. Thanks to Walter, the Colbonite workforce probably had an extra twenty to thirty years of employment. He saw that as a genuine achievement.'

'But there was a price to pay, Delia, wasn't there?'

'Yes. It's clear now there was. Which brings me to Walter's greatest failing: his absolute inability to admit a mistake when he'd made one. Gavin's tactic is to blame others. Walter's was denial. I don't believe he went to such lengths to evade liability for the cancer cases simply because of the huge amount of money that might have been involved. I believe he did it because he couldn't convince himself that he *was* liable. It would have meant he was wrong to have done the things he did to keep Colbonite in profit, which, by his definition, he couldn't have been. There was his reputation to consider as well. He feared public disgrace far more than bankruptcy. He was a stubborn and dogmatic man. I say that though I loved him dearly. He could not, *would not*, admit to error, in large things or in small. He could be infuriating. Sometimes worse than infuriating.'

'Is that what drove his wife to suicide?'

Delia didn't flinch at the mention of her late sister-in-law. She'd been prepared for it, after all. But her face did quiver slightly. It was a tender subject, even after twenty years. 'Ann wasn't a strong person. That wasn't Walter's fault, of course. But he ignored the warning signs. He didn't take enough care of her. He was too busy. With Colbonite. With his politics and good causes. It shouldn't have happened. But it did.' Delia diverted her gaze towards the fire and fell silent. It seemed she'd said as much as she could bear to about Ann Colborn's fatal plunge from Beachy Head.

'I'm sorry for putting you through this, Delia,' said Jenny, with a glare in my direction. 'Toby insisted on hearing the whole story.'

'With good reason, I've no doubt,' Delia responded. She looked across at me then, her expression fractionally but significantly altered from the placid earnestness of earlier. Jenny couldn't have seen the strange, fleeting hint of ambiguity in her eyes. It was reserved for me. There was more she could have said, it lightly implied, more she could have divulged. But not more of the same. I'd been given the authorized version. And I wasn't going to be given any other.

Jenny showed me to the door, transparently keen on a private word before I left.

'It wasn't easy for Delia to go into all that, you know,' she whispered to me as we stood in the porch, the front door half-open. 'I hope you're satisfied.'

'You think I should be?'

'Of course.'

'Well, that's settled, then.'

'I'd like you to say it as if you mean it.'

'And I will. When I do.'

'You have to give this up, Toby.'

'Tell you what, Jen. If I find Roger has nothing to do with Derek Oswin's disappearance and the poor bloke duly reappears unharmed . . . then I'll give it up.'

'You promised to abide by what Delia said.'

'No. I promised to take it seriously. And that's exactly what I'm going to do. What I want *you* to do is take care. I meant what I said earlier about Roger being dangerous. Hard as you may find it to believe, that's why I'm being such a pain.'

'Not hard to believe, Toby.' She opened the door wide. 'Just impossible. As you always are.'

When I left Powis Villas, I had barely half an hour at my disposal before I was due back at the theatre. Tomato juice and a bag of nuts in a nondescript pub halfway between the two made for a frugal pit stop. I turned my mobile back on to check for messages and found one waiting for me from Moira. Fearing she'd changed her mind about delivering *The Plastic*

Men in person tomorrow and wondering how the bloody hell I was going to get hold of it in that case, I listened in.

'*Toby, this is Moira. What exactly is going on? I thought we'd agreed I'd bring this wretched manuscript down to you tomorrow. If that wasn't good enough, you should have said. Anyway, is lunch still on or not? Perhaps you'd be so kind as to let me know.*'

What in God's name was the woman on about? I called her at the office, but only got the answering machine. It was the same story on her home number. I left messages on both to the exasperated effect that as far as I was concerned our plans were unaltered and I'd be expecting to meet her off the 12.27 train, *The Plastic Men* wedged firmly under her arm. She's always adroitly managed to avoid giving me her mobile number and now I was left wondering why I can be contacted more easily by my agent than she can be by me.

The time for wondering was not long, however. I was soon on my way down Bond Street to the stage door of the Theatre Royal. Brian greeted me with the news that Leo and Melvyn had departed for London well pleased with what they'd seen. I fancied he was just trying to put me and the rest of the cast in a good mood, but others seemed wholly convinced that a West End transfer had been snatched from the jaws of a provincial fizzle-out. Donohue was looking even more pleased with himself than usual, for instance, though Fred suggested to me in passing that Mandy Pringle was more likely to be responsible for that than Leo S. Gauntlett. 'That's Brighton for you,' he said with a wink. 'So they tell me.'

This evening's performance is an even hazier memory for me than this afternoon's. I've been James Elliott for *Lodger in the Throat*'s two and a half hours of running time on seventy-seven occasions since we opened in Guildford ten weeks ago, so it's hardly surprising that most of those are part of one vague and messily merged recollection. None of them faded faster into that *mélange* than tonight's, however. It ended only a few hours ago, but it could as easily be several days, or even weeks. Those few hours have made sure of that.

The others must be getting used to me opting out of communal supper parties after the show. No-one made more than a desultory effort to talk me into joining them. Perhaps they realized I wasn't likely to be good company.

I walked down to the pier after leaving the theatre, bought a portion of fish and chips and ate them in the biting cold night air, staring out across the sea that could be heard more than seen in the inky darkness, wondering with oddly detached curiosity whether I really was going to go through with what Ian Maple had planned. I still didn't really know, when the time came, which way I'd jump.

I got back to the Sea Air just before 11.30. That was past Eunice's normal bedtime, so it was a surprise to see her light still on and even more of a surprise to be met by her in the hall, looking flustered and far from sleepy.

'Thank goodness,' she breathlessly greeted me. 'I was beginning to think you'd be out till the small hours.'

'Would it have mattered if I was?'

'Ordinarily, no. Of course not. But . . . after what's happened . . .'

'What *has* happened?' My first thought was that Binky had met with an accident. What else could disrupt Eunice's domestic routine as dramatically as something clearly had?

'I didn't like to phone you at the theatre. I knew you'd need to concentrate on your performance. But it's been such a worry for me, not knowing what to make of it.'

'Make of *what*, Eunice?' I piloted her into the residents' lounge, switching on the lights as we entered.

'It's been such a to-do. My nerves are all a-jangle.'

'Sit down and tell me all about it.'

'Yes. Of course. You must be wondering why I'm making such a fuss.' We settled in opposite armchairs in front of the

196

gas fire. 'Turn that on, will you, Toby? It's as cold as the grave in here.'

'Sure.' I flicked the fire into life and returned to my chair. 'So, what, er . . .'

'It was while I was out shopping this afternoon. You were at the theatre for the matinée, of course, which meant the house was empty. It's almost as if they knew it would be. The policeman who came reckoned it was what he called . . . an opportunist. Looking for money to buy drugs, like as not, and just gave up and went away when they couldn't find any. I'm not so sure though.'

'Are we talking about a burglary, Eunice?' (If so, the policeman sounded spot-on to me.)

'I suppose we would be if anything had been taken. But that's the point. Nothing was. They smashed a pane in one of my windows and forced the latch. The basement's out of sight unless you're right outside on the pavement, of course. Upset my Busy Lizzie, climbing in, they did. But nothing else was touched downstairs, as far as I can tell. If they were looking for money, they didn't look very hard. Walked straight past my Chivas Regal. There must be a good few quid in there all told. The policeman reckoned notes were what they had in mind, but, like I told him, if they're so desperate, why would they be so choosy?'

A dimly recalled glimpse in Eunice's kitchen of an old Chivas Regal bottle, used as a repository for small change, mostly of the copper variety, was all that enabled me to follow this account. Once again, I had to side with the policeman. But I sensed that wasn't what Eunice wanted to hear.

'Till the glazier's been tomorrow, I shan't feel safe. And there's you to consider, Toby. They'd have gone through the house, wouldn't they? Stands to reason. Was there any money in your room? The policeman asked me to check with you. Nothing looked to have been disturbed up there, but how can I say for sure?'

'The only cash I've got is in my pocket, Eunice. Nothing to worry about there.' Then it struck me that maybe there *was* something to worry about. 'Hold on, though. There's my chequebook.'

'Oh, my.'

'I'd better go up and see if it's still there. You stay here. And relax. There's not much you can do with a chequebook these days without the plastic to back it up.'

When I reached my room, I saw at once that Eunice was right. It had a distinctly and reassuringly undisturbed look. I pulled open the drawer of the bedside cabinet and there was my chequebook, lying just where I'd left it. All was well.

Except that it wasn't. As I turned round from the cabinet, my glance fell on the small table next to the armchair. The dictaphone was also where I'd left it, on the table. But the hatch of the cassette compartment was open. As I moved towards it, I knew what I'd see. The cassette was missing. Trembling now, I went back to the cabinet and reopened the drawer, wider than before. The previous cassette was also missing.

Everything I disclosed to this machine, secretly and con-fidentially, yesterday and Tuesday and Monday and Sunday, had gone. Everything I said and guessed and hoped and suspected could be heard by another. How to put your enemy several steps ahead of you in one easy lesson: tell them what you've done and what you're going to do; then make them a gift of the whole lot.

The unused tapes in their plastic outers had been left behind, as if to assure me that the burglars had known exactly what they were doing. No-one could have known I was making these recordings. To that extent, their theft was opportunistic. The break-in was a fishing expedition. And the catch must have surpassed expectation.

It was five minutes to midnight by my alarm clock. Ian Maple might already be waiting for me at the end of the street. The risks he'd proposed to run were surely doubled now. Whoever had the tapes could listen to them and judge what we were likely to do. They didn't know Ian had trailed man mountain to the warehouse, it was true, but they knew we'd be looking for Derek. They knew we weren't going to stand idly by.

Time was nearly up. I headed downstairs.

Eunice had fallen asleep, her anxiety lessened, I supposed, now I was on the premises. I turned off the fire and nudged her awake.

'Oh. Toby. There you are. I must have . . . Is everything OK?'

'It's fine, Eunice. Nothing touched. Chequebook intact.'

'Well, that's a blessing, though—'

'You should get to bed.'

'Yes. Yes, I should.' She rose stiffly from the chair and I saw her out into the hall. 'I'm glad you haven't lost anything, Toby. But to my mind that only makes it more mystifying.'

'These druggies don't necessarily do things that make sense. It could have turned out a whole lot worse.'

'Well, yes, that's true.'

'I'll say goodnight, then. Try not to worry. You need some sleep. We both do.'

That last point was undeniable. But I wasn't going to have the chance of any shut-eye for some time yet. I watched Eunice toddle off downstairs and waited for a minute or so after the basement door had closed behind her in case she came back. Then I headed out.

Ian Maple had parked his hire car at the end of the street. He flashed his headlights as I stepped out from the porch of the Sea Air. In the thirty yards or so of pavement I covered to reach him, I rehearsed the ways I could convince him that we shouldn't go ahead. The hardest thing of all to explain was how I'd failed to realize what a hostage to fortune the tapes represented. I should have taken better care of them, or better still never recorded my thoughts and experiences in the first place. That's what he'd say. It's certainly what he'd think. How could I have been so stupid? Just how big a liability was I?

But he never said or thought anything of the kind. Because, when I opened the door and slipped into the passenger seat, I knew, with the shock of sudden self-awareness, that I wasn't going to tell him. I wasn't going to breathe a word.

'All set?' he asked, glancing round at me.

'All set.'

We drove west along Kingsway through the chill and empty night. The Regency terraces of Hove gave way to the redbrick semis of Portslade. Ian kept assiduously to the speed limit. Nothing was said. The journey stretched into the darkness beyond the amber coronas of the street lamps.

Some time after the road veered away from the shore, he turned off into the drab hinterland of Fishersgate. We went under a railway bridge and turned west again along a residential side street, ending in the closed gates of a small industrial estate.

'Here we are,' he announced, pulling in some way short of the gates.

The jumble of brick-built warehouses and workshops within was deserted, the run-down look of most of them suggesting they contained no riches to make breaking in worthwhile. The close proximity of housing and the height of the fence were powerful deterrents as well.

'You're not going in here, are you?' I asked. 'It only takes one insomniac to look out of the window . . .'

'Follow me,' said Ian, opening his door. 'You'll see.'

We set off on foot, Ian carrying on one shoulder an old rucksack, which I assumed held the bolt-cutters and any other tools he reckoned we might need. An ill-lit path led off beside the garden wall of the last house before the gates to a foot-bridge over the railway line, with steps down from the bridge onto the empty eastbound platform of Fishersgate station, a small unmanned halt. I lagged behind as Ian started down the steps from the bridge. The platform below us was fenced off

200

from a strip of no-man's-land between it and the perimeter fence of the industrial estate. But there was nothing to prevent Ian scrambling over the railings near the bottom of the steps and dropping down into the strip. He signalled for me to follow, which I did, so much less adroitly that he had to give me a hand. We were trespassing now. And we'd soon be doing a lot worse than that.

The fence round the industrial estate was topped with razor-wire. There could be no question of climbing over it. We crouched at its base in deep shadow, listening and watching, just in case. But nothing stirred. There were no insomniacs, no late-night prowlers – other than us. Ian pointed to the warehouse whose side wall was facing us and whispered, 'That's it.' The shuttered entrance was no more than twenty rubbish-strewn yards away. He slid the bolt-cutters out of the rucksack.

That's when I heard the rumble of an approaching train. Ian heard it in the same moment and crouched lower, pulling me down with him. There was a spark from the conductor rail somewhere behind us, then the train was rushing past through the station, its thinly peopled carriages brightly lit. And then it was gone again, surging on towards Worthing.

'Don't worry,' said Ian as we cautiously raised our heads. 'No-one will have seen us. And even if they did . . .'

He left the thought unfinished and started at the fence with the bolt-cutters. The wire yielded easily and within a couple of minutes he'd cut a large semicircle in the mesh. He pulled it back and held it there for me to crawl through, then scrambled after me.

We picked our way between a rusting skip and a pile of old car tyres to the front of man mountain's warehouse. There we paused again, ears and eyes straining in the darkness. But there was nothing to hear or see. The premises around us hardly warranted guard-dog patrols. And we were out of sight of the nearby houses. I began to feel fractionally less anxious. There was clearly no-one about. Maybe man mountain hadn't thought we might try something like this. Or maybe, it occurred to me, the warehouse was a deliberate blind.

There was only one way to find out. Ian flicked on his torch and trained the beam on the padlocked hasp securing the wicket-door, then handed the torch to me and fastened the jaws of the bolt-cutters round the U-bar of the padlock. It put up stiffer resistance than the fence wire. Ian's forearms shook as he strained to pierce the steel, his breath steaming in the torchlight.

Suddenly, the steel gave. The U-bar snapped, the padlock fell to the ground and the hasp flopped forward. Ian shoved the bolt-cutters into his rucksack, flicked the hasp fully back and cautiously tried the handle below it. The door opened. He took the torch from me and stepped through. I followed, pushing the door shut behind me.

The torch beam moved around the interior. Quite what I'd expected I couldn't have said, but there was certainly no sign of Derek. The place looked like it had once been used for car repairs. I glimpsed an inspection ramp and a rack half-filled with tyres. Towards the rear was a small, partitioned-off office. But Derek's face did not pop into view at the window.

The torch beam moved back to the door. There was a panel of switches beside it. 'Try them,' said Ian. 'Let's see what we've got.'

I pushed one of the switches down. It controlled a fluorescent light fitted to one of the beams above us. The tube flickered and hummed into action. I pushed another switch, activating a second light. The shadows retreated.

But no secrets were revealed. The warehouse was bare and dusty, ancient car-repair equipment abandoned in its corners. We stood where we were for a moment, gazing about us in search of something, anything, that might suggest we were on the right track. But there was nothing to see. And nothing to hear either. If Derek was really being held there, even bound and gagged, he'd surely have made some noise. Yet there was none.

We moved past the office to an open door at the rear of the

warehouse. Ian stepped through with the torch and almost immediately retreated, shaking his head to me. I went back to check the office, even though I could see through the window that it was empty, save for one broken-backed swivel chair. There was nothing else.

'Looks like we've drawn a blank,' I murmured to Ian as I joined him in the centre of the warehouse.

'I don't believe it.'

'You can see for yourself.'

'He's here. I know it.'

'There's no-one here except us.'

'There has to be.'

'But there isn't.'

'Hold on. What about those?' Ian pointed to a row of four steel plates, set in the concrete floor. 'Covers for an inspection pit, do you reckon?'

'Must be, I suppose.' I caught his gaze. 'What are you thinking?'

'I'm thinking we should take a look at what's under them.'

He moved to the rectangle covered by the plates and prised up the ring handle countersunk in the one farthest from the entrance. A gentle tug didn't achieve anything. The plate was evidently heavier than it looked. Ian braced himself and pulled harder.

For a shard of a second I thought some creature – a mouse maybe – had raced out from under the plate and sped towards the wall. Something certainly flew faster than my eye could follow in that direction, then straight up the wall. There was a loud cracking noise above us. I looked up and saw the descending shadow of something large and heavy. I opened my mouth to shout a warning to Ian, who was standing directly beneath it. But he'd already seen it coming and was throwing himself clear.

Too late. With a deafening crash, a pear-shaped lump of concrete large enough to be used as a wrecking ball slammed into the floor. Ian screamed and fell, his trailing leg caught beneath it. The rope that had held the ball aloft wound down after it into the cloud of dust raised by the impact. The ball wobbled and rolled clear of Ian, then threatened to roll back again. I rushed forward and held it off him, then looked down into his white and grimacing face.

'Jesus Christ,' he hissed through gritted teeth. 'Jesus fucking Christ.'

My gaze moved to his right leg. The curvature of the ball meant his foot and knee had escaped injury, but his ankle and lower shin were a bloody pulp. The angle of his foot and the jagged spike of bone protruding through a blood-darkened rent in his jeans told their own story. 'I can't hold this for long,' I shouted down to him. 'Can you move?'

'Not . . .' He dragged himself a short distance across the floor, shuddering with the effort. 'Not . . . far.'

But it was far enough. I let the ball roll back into position and knelt beside him. There was sweat beading on his forehead. He was shivering, his breaths coming fast and shallow.

'Some sort of trap,' he said, forcing the words out. 'Very . . . fucking clever.'

'Your leg's a mess. Broken . . . and then some.'

He nodded, absorbing the information. 'Is there . . . much bleeding?'

'Not so very much, no.'

'Let me see.' Pushing himself up on his elbows, he squinted down at his leg. 'Christ. That doesn't look good.' He slowly lowered his head to the floor. 'Raising the cover . . . released a rope. I saw it. But not . . . quickly enough.'

'Me too.'

'Safe . . . if you tie it off on the wall first. Otherwise . . .' He shook his head, willing himself to concentrate. 'What's in the pit?'

For a moment, I'd forgotten that was what we were supposed to be finding out. I kicked the loosened cover aside and peered in. Neatly stacked plastic bags of white powder met my gaze. I pulled up the other covers to reveal more of the same. 'It's a drugs cache,' I said. 'There's a lot here.'

'Fuck,' was all Ian managed by way of reaction.

I knelt back down beside him. 'I'm going to call an ambulance,' I said, pulling out my mobile and glancing at the wound in his leg. 'There's nothing else for it.'

'Don't.' He grabbed my arm. 'We'll both be arrested.'

'We have no choice. You can't stand up, let alone walk out of here.'

'No. But . . . you can.'

'I'm not leaving you in this state.'

'You have to.' He coughed, wincing from the pain that must have been increasing all the time. '*I'll* call the ambulance.' He thrust his free hand into the pocket of his fleece and pulled out his own mobile. 'And I'll tell the police the truth. Except . . . I'll say I came here tonight . . . alone. I'll say . . . I didn't tell you . . . what I was planning to do.'

'You think they'll believe you?'

'I don't know. But . . . they're likelier to . . . than if they have us both down . . . as burglars . . . or worse . . . trying to talk our way out of trouble . . . aren't they?'

'I'm not sure. There has to be—'

'I don't have the strength to debate it. It's what we're going to do. You'll back up . . . my story . . . when the police . . . question you . . . won't you?'

'Of course. But—'

'That's good enough.' He pressed the button on his phone three times and stared up at me. 'You'd better get moving.'

The fact that leaving Ian to wait for the emergency services to show up made sense didn't make it easy to do. He was in a lot of pain and his condition wasn't going to improve until he got the medical attention he badly needed. But he was right. By staying, I'd only be asking for trouble. Whatever I could do to redeem the situation couldn't be done from a police cell.

The sirens were yowling closer through the still air when I scrambled back through the fence and hauled myself up onto the steps of the railway station footbridge. I stood at the top of the steps for several minutes as they drew closer still. The flashing lights of police car and ambulance began to strobe through the darkness beyond the rooftops of the nearby houses. They were almost there. I walked to the other end of the bridge and down the steps into the next street, dialling Ian's number on my mobile as I went.

'Yuh?' He sounded gruff and breathless, but alert.

'The cavalry's arrived.'

'So I hear.'

'How are you feeling?'

'I'll make it, Toby. Don't worry. And don't phone again . . . or do anything stupid . . . like contacting . . . the hospital. OK?'

'OK.'

'Be seeing you.' With that, he rang off. And I hurried on into the night.

It was a long, cold walk from Fishersgate station to the Sea Air. I had time to think, time to put what had happened into some kind of logical framework. Ian Maple would be all right, or as all right as somebody could be facing a long stay in hospital and interrogation by the police. Their first thought was bound to be that he was involved in drugs trafficking. I could talk them out of that, of course, as I intended to. But they only had our word for it that man mountain was associated with Roger Colborn. Drugs and prostitution could be seen as the beginning and the end of it. We hadn't found Derek Oswin, after all. We couldn't even prove he needed to be found. And we certainly couldn't prove Colborn was responsible for his disappearance. But we could put some pressure on him. We could oblige the police to ask him a few awkward questions. It wasn't much. But it was better than nothing. Colborn had been using man mountain to do his dirty work. That was clear to me, even if it wouldn't necessarily be clear to the police. What we'd stumbled on at the warehouse was likely to put man mountain behind bars, however, and therefore out of action. Colborn wouldn't be able to call on him any longer. He was going to be on his own. And I was betting he wouldn't like it.

I trudged up Madeira Place more than an hour after leaving Fishersgate station, chilled and weary, as barely able to put one foot in front of the other as I was to piece together the consequences of our bungled night's work. I slid my key into the door of the Sea Air and pushed it open, eager to reach the sanctuary of my room.

Then I stopped. There was an envelope lying on the door-mat in front of me. It hadn't been there earlier. I picked it up, carried it to the hall table and switched on the light. There was no name or address on the plain brown manilla envelope, no clue as to who might have dropped it through the letter-box. The contents were bulky, sharp-edged and solid to the touch. I tore the flap open and slid them out.

Three dictaphone microcassettes, held together by a rubber band. Not two, the number stolen earlier, but *three*. I snapped the band off and looked at them. They were all the same brand. There was no way to tell which two were mine and which the odd one out. Except that two had been rewound to the start of the tape. I hadn't done that. It was as simple a message as could be devised. They'd been listened to and then discarded. Returned to me, almost scornfully.

The third had tape wound onto the right-hand spool. Not much, but some. This was another kind of message.

I hurried up to my room, slid the cassette into the machine and pressed the rewind button. Within seconds, the tape was back to the start. Then I pressed the play button. And heard Derek Oswin's voice.

'Hello, Mr Flood. Sorry . . . about all this. I've got us both . . . into a l-lot of t-trouble. The thing is, well . . . I've been told . . . to say this to you. Drop it. Everything. S-s-stop asking questions. L-leave it alone.' He gulped audibly. 'If you d-do that . . . and go quietly back to London on Sunday . . . they'll let me go . . . unharmed. And there'll be no danger . . . to Mrs Flood. That's all you have to do, Mr Flood. Nothing . . . at all. Otherwise—'

*　　*　　*

I poured myself some whisky and listened to the tape again. Derek sounded strained and nervous, as well he might. I didn't feel too good myself. The glass trembled in my grasp and the whisky burned in my throat. Colborn was determined to stop me digging out the truth, because the truth had the power to destroy him. I was close to the answer, too close for his comfort. Listening to the tapes must have confirmed his worst fears, hence the change of tactics. Trying to buy me off hadn't worked, so now he meant to scare me off. And, just in case I didn't care what he did to Derek, there was an additional threat he could be certain I'd take seriously. To Jenny. So much for his claim to be genuinely in love with her, to be a better man because of her. Maybe he was bluffing. But he knew I'd never call his bluff. Because I *do* love her. I would never do anything to endanger her.

Some time tomorrow, the police will come to me and ask me to corroborate Ian Maple's story. How can I do that without effectively rejecting Colborn's ultimatum? Calling off the search for the truth is almost as difficult as going on with it. And judging what's best is more difficult again. But I'll go on making these recordings. That's one decision I have made. I'll have to take better care of them, of course. I'll have to carry them with me to make sure they don't fall into the wrong hands a second time. In one way, they're a liability. But they're also a true and accurate record of events. I may have need of that when this is all over. Colborn thinks he can force me to do his bidding. Maybe he's right. We'll see. But, even if he is, that may not be enough. We may have passed the point of no return. If so, doing nothing won't be an option. For either of us.

FRIDAY

I was roused this morning by Eunice knocking at the door of my room and calling my name. The sleep I came out of was so deep it left me confused and woolly-headed. Memories of the day and night before reassembled themselves scrappily in my mind. I'd lain awake till God knows when, debating with myself what I should and shouldn't have done. Then, at some point I couldn't recall, a trapdoor had opened, plunging me into oblivion.

'Toby, Toby,' came Eunice's voice. 'Are you awake?'

'I am now,' I muttered, scrabbling for a sight of the alarm clock. The time apparently, was eight minutes to ten. I felt like I could have slept till noon. 'What is it?' I shouted, gravel-throated.

'There's a couple of policemen downstairs. They want to speak to you. It's urgent, they say.'

They'd come, as I'd known they would, come with their battery of questions, to which I had no better or safer answers after sleepless hours of reflection than I had before. 'What's it about?' I asked, sitting up woozily and silently congratulating myself on my disingenuousness.

'They wouldn't tell me. Just insisted they had to speak to you.'

'All right. I'll come down. But . . . it'll take me ten minutes or so to wash and dress.'

'I'll tell them.'

*　　*　　*

My thoughts were only marginally clearer fifteen minutes later when I made a gingerly descent to the residents' lounge. I was unshaven and I'd strained a muscle in my thigh, probably while climbing up onto the footbridge at Fishersgate station. I was neither looking nor feeling at my best.

The same may have been true of Detective Inspector Addis and Detective Sergeant Spooner, as they introduced themselves. Their suits were rumpled, their faces set in glum folds. Both were paunchy, liverish-looking men, unhealthily accustomed to late nights and canteen fry-ups. Addis, the shorter and balder of the two, had distractingly exophthalmic eyes, a gum-chewing habit and a subdued Black Country accent. Spooner sounded local, but didn't seem any friendlier on account of it.

'Sorry to disturb you so early, Mr Flood,' said Addis, with light sarcasm.

'I don't generally get to bed till the small hours after a performance, Inspector,' I said, already sensing that I needed to be on the defensive.

'Late nights are an occupational hazard in our game as well as yours, sir,' said Spooner. 'We haven't had much sleep ourselves.'

'No? Well, I'm sorry to have kept you waiting. But I'm here now.'

'Your landlady kept us occupied, sir, with her colourful observations on the shortcomings of our uniform division.'

'Yeah,' said Addis. 'Gather you had a break-in here yesterday.'

'There was a break-in, yes. Eunice was very upset about it.'

'But nothing was taken.'

'Apparently not.'

'And not much of a mess made.'

'That's unusual,' put in Spooner, with an exaggerated nod of deliberation.

'But I don't suppose it's why you called.'

212

'No, sir, it isn't,' said Addis. 'Though what's brought us here is also . . . unusual.'

'Are you acquainted with a Mr Ian Maple, sir?' asked Spooner.

'Yes. He's the brother of a recently deceased fellow actor, Denis Maple. Denis died earlier this week of a heart attack. Ian came down here a couple of days ago to, er . . .'

'Find out what had happened,' said Addis. 'Yeah. So he tells us.'

'Look, Inspector, what exactly is this all about?' I tried to look genuinely mystified.

'Mr Maple's under arrest, sir. Well, he will be when he wakes up from the anaesthetic. They're operating on him now up at the Royal Sussex.'

'Operating?'

'Badly broken right leg, sir,' said Spooner. 'He was in a bit of a mess when we got to him. Any idea why he might have been breaking into a warehouse out at Fishersgate last night?'

'What?'

'The large quantity of hard drugs stored on the premises seems the obvious explanation,' said Addis; they were warming up their double act now, alternating their lines in a practised routine. 'But Mr Maple tells it differently.'

'When did you last see him, sir?' asked Spooner.

'Er . . . yesterday afternoon. He came to see me at the theatre during the matinée interval.'

'To discuss . . . what, sir?'

'Well, he'd, er, been trying to track down a man Denis said had . . . threatened him. It seemed likely . . . to both of us . . . that the encounter had put a lot of stress on Denis, leading to his attack.'

'Who is this man, sir?'

'I don't know. I never met him.'

'But Denis Maple mentioned him to you?'

'Yes.'

'And you mentioned him to Ian Maple?'

213

'Yes.'

'Did you also tell him you thought this guy had mistaken Denis Maple for you?'

'I said Denis thought that.'

'But you don't?'

'I've no reason to.'

'No reason, sir?' put in Addis.

'That's right, Inspector.'

'Really?'

'Look, I—'

'Are you acquainted with a Mr Derek Oswin, sir?' asked Spooner.

'Yes.'

'Also a Mr Roger Colborn?'

'Yes.'

'What about a Mr Michael Sobotka?'

'Who? No, I—'

'Big fellow,' said Addis. 'Very big. Polish extraction. Known to us. Suspected pimp, pusher, God knows what. Mr Maple's description of the man his brother had some sort of run-in with fits Sobotka to a T. Mr Maple claims the drugs in the warehouse belong to him.'

'Is that so?'

'We don't yet know, sir,' Spooner answered. 'We're still checking.'

'Well, I . . . wish you luck.'

'Do you know of a connection between Oswin, Colborn and Sobotka?' asked Addis, his tone suddenly hardening.

'No.' The lie was told. 'I don't.'

'Do you have any reason to believe Mr Oswin may have been abducted?'

'No.'

'Or that Sobotka may have carried out that abduction, acting on behalf of Mr Colborn?'

'No.'

'Do you know of any reason why Mr Colborn should wish to have Mr Oswin abducted?'

'No.'

'Or why Mr Maple should believe he had a reason?'

'No.'

'Strange.' Addis gave me a long, cold stare. 'Mr Maple seemed sure you would.'

'We called on Mr Oswin before coming here,' said Spooner. 'There was no-one at home.'

'Maybe he's gone away.'

'When did you last see Mr Oswin?' asked Addis.

'Er . . . Wednesday afternoon.'

'Did he say he was thinking of going away?' asked Spooner.

'Not that I recall. But . . . I wouldn't have expected him to. We're not exactly close.'

'How are you acquainted with him, sir?'

'He's a fan.'

'Really?' put in Addis.

'Yes.'

'Do you pay house calls on many of your fans?'

'They don't generally invite me.'

'But Mr Oswin did?'

'Yes.'

'What did you discuss with him?'

'My . . . career.'

'Your *career*?'

'Is it true that Mr Oswin's been bothering your ex-wife, sir?' asked Spooner. He consulted a notebook. 'Jennifer Flood, proprietress of a hat shop in the Lanes?'

God, the sheer mental agility required to carry off a lie is so exhausting. I could only hope by this stage that my acting technique was compensating for any obvious deficiencies in the logic of my account. 'She's not my ex-wife yet, Sergeant,' I said wearily. 'Technically, we're still married.'

'But separated?'

'Yes.'

'Mrs Flood is currently living with Mr Colborn, in fact?'

'Yes.'

'So, has Mr Oswin been bothering Mrs Flood?'

215

'He wanted her to arrange for him to meet me. I agreed . . . in order to get him off her back.'

'Sounds like the answer's yes,' commented Addis.

'Have you been to Mr Oswin's house since Wednesday afternoon, sir?' asked Spooner.

The key to successful lying is to avoid as many subsidiary lies as possible. It's a principle I clung to then, tempted though I was to abandon it. 'Yes,' I said. 'Yesterday morning. First thing. He wasn't in.'

'Snap,' said Addis. 'I can see why you think he may have gone away.'

'Anything strike you as amiss at the house, sir?' asked Spooner.

'No.'

'Didn't take a squinny through the letterbox, then?' Addis put in.

'No.' I was clearly meant to infer they had.

'Why did you go there?' asked Spooner.

'He didn't use a ticket for the Wednesday evening performance I'd had put back for him. I wanted to find out why. I suppose a spur-of-the-moment trip away is the likeliest explanation.'

'You're not worried about him?'

'No. Why should I be?'

'Why, indeed, sir?' Addis responded.

'About Mr Maple . . .'

'Yeah?'

'Are you really intending to charge him?'

'The circumstances don't leave us much choice. We've got him bang to rights. We'll be investigating every aspect of the case, of course. Unless the Drugs Squad take it over. It was a big haul, I can tell you that. Unless you can back up Mr Maple's version of events . . . it looks bad for him.'

'I'm sure whatever he did last night was motivated by a genuine concern for his late brother. There'll have been no criminal intent.'

'That's your opinion, is it, sir?'

216

'Yes.'

'But you can't actually confirm this Oswin–Colborn–Sobotka connection?'

'No.'

'That's our problem, you see.' Addis interrupted his gum-chewing long enough for a fleeting smile. 'Well, it's more Mr Maple's problem, actually.'

After they'd gone, I cadged a mug of coffee off Eunice, assured her I wasn't about to be carted off to the police station and stumbled upstairs for a shower and a shave. I kept telling myself I'd done the only thing I could in the circumstances. Letting Ian Maple down was redeemable. Defying Roger Colborn might not be. But I wasn't sure it was true. Exonerating Ian would mean daring Colborn to do his worst, this week *or* next. And that threatened Jenny, who mattered far more to me than Ian Maple or Derek Oswin. Colborn's ultimatum was even more effective than he could have hoped.

My first thought when I heard Eunice's by now familiar knock at the bathroom door was that Addis and Spooner had come back, a sufficiently disturbing possibility for me to tighten my grasp on the razor and nick my chin as a result.

'I'm sorry to disturb you again, Toby,' Eunice called. 'There's someone else to see you.'

'Who the hell is it this time?' I shouted, wrenching off a length of loo paper to mop up the blood.

'A Mr Braddock. Elderly gentleman. Most insistent. He says he won't leave till he's spoken to you.'

Ray Braddock, come to my door, rather than me to his. I felt sick as I confronted my reflection in the mirror above the basin. This didn't sound good. 'All right,' I called back. 'I'll be right down.'

A few minutes later, I was back in the residents' lounge, struggling to assemble another and subtly different version of events for the benefit of my latest visitor.

Ray Braddock was a man of seventy or so, big-limbed and broad-shouldered, but bent and hollowed out by age and labour, white hair cut squaddy-short, as if to emphasize the hearing aid looped round one of his spectacularly large ears. His face was raw-boned and weather-worn. His rheumy eyes gazed out at me from beneath a hooded brow. The raincoat and flat cap I'd spotted hanging in the hall clearly belonged to him. They were of a piece with the baggy tweed jacket, patched jeans and slack-collared shirt. His solitary and taciturn nature was palpable. There was no Mrs Braddock waiting at home, nor had there ever been. He was a man reliant on his own devices.

He rose from his chair and shook my hand, his grip carrying with it a memory of faded strength. 'Good of you to see me, Mr Flood,' he said in a rumbling voice.

'You're a friend of the Oswin family, I believe, Mr Braddock. Derek mentioned your name.'

'He mentioned yours to me and all, Mr Flood. That's what brought me here.'

'Oh yes?'

'I'm worried about the boy, see.'

'Let's sit down.' I pulled up a chair for myself close to his, into which he stiffly lowered himself. 'Why are you worried?'

'The police were at the house in Viaduct Road this morning, seemingly. I had a call from the boy's neighbour, Mrs Lumb. They'd been asking her what she'd seen of Derek lately. Well, she's not had sight of him since Wednesday. And it was Wednesday afternoon he came to see me. He was in a . . . peculiar mood. That's when he mentioned you. You're helping him with his book, apparently.'

'Well, I . . . sent it to my agent, certainly. To see what she thinks of it.'

The frown permanently fixed to Braddock's face deepened at that. 'Read it, have you?'

'I glanced at the first few pages, nothing more. I . . . wasn't sure what to make of it.'

'I'll tell you what I make of it. A temptation to fate, that's what. Bloody Colbonite. Why can't he leave it alone?'

'I don't know.'

'No.' He stared at me in silence for a moment, then said, 'Reckon you wouldn't.'

'Did Mrs Lumb say why the police are looking for Derek?'

'They didn't let on. Now then, Mr Flood, have you seen Derek since Wednesday?'

'Not as it happens, no.'

'I was afraid you'd say that.'

'Perhaps he's gone away.'

'Where to?'

'I wouldn't know.'

'No. And you wouldn't suggest it if you knew the boy as well as I do. He'd not go far. Unless he was forced to. Mrs Lumb heard some sort of a commotion Wednesday night. She couldn't make out what was going on. Anyhow, she's not seen Derek since. She *thinks* she saw a strange man leaving the house yesterday morning, but she's not sure. He might have been just turning away from the door. She didn't catch a clear sight of him, worse luck.'

Au contraire, I thought to myself: it was *my* very good luck. 'We are sure he's not at home, are we? I mean, perhaps he's just . . . lying low.'

Braddock shook his head. 'I have a spare key, Mr Flood. I let myself in. I was afraid . . . well, you never know, do you, with someone like Derek? He hasn't the strongest of temperaments. Anyhow, he's not there, but there's been some damage done. Things turned over and such. I can't help but be worried about him. He's my godson, see. With his mother and father gone, I feel . . . responsible.'

'I wish I could help.'

'From what Derek told me, he'd made a nuisance of himself to you. Hanging around your wife's shop. To be honest, it occurred to me you might have set the police on him. I couldn't blame you. The boy's his own worst enemy.'

219

'But essentially good-natured. There's no harm in him. I made no complaint to the police, I assure you.'

'You felt sorry for him, I take it. Well, that's to your credit. A man in your position doesn't need to truck with Derek's sort. I know that. Mind, he did, er, mention your wife's . . . association . . . with Roger Colborn.'

'Ah. Did he?'

'None of my business, of course. None of Derek's either, if it comes to it. But Colborn's not to be trifled with, any more than his father was. I don't say that lightly, Mr Flood. If Colborn was seriously rattled by this blasted book of Derek's, he'd not be above . . .' Braddock's jaw muscles champed away during the wordless interlude into which the thought drifted. Then he said, 'The boy's out of his depth. That's what it amounts to. If he'd only leave it alone . . .'

'I know all about Colbonite, Mr Braddock. And about the part Derek's father played in the death of Sir Walter Colborn. I do understand . . . your concern.'

'Do you, though?'

'I'm glad to see you looking so well.'

'For an old Colbonite hand, you mean?' Braddock grunted. 'I got out early. Soon as I started to notice my skin turning yellow. Oh yes. It was as bad as that. I took a lower-paid job with the Co-op. I tried to talk Ken into leaving as well, but he said he needed the money, with Val and Derek to support. He reckoned Colbonite was the only place he could find a job for the boy. Well, he was probably right, at that. And there were other reasons. I see that now. Ken played his cards close to his chest, even with me.'

'Derek seems to think Sir Walter's death was an accident,' I said, aware that I shouldn't in strict prudence be encouraging the old man's ruminations, but still eager, despite myself, to penetrate to the heart of the mystery.

'It was no accident,' said Braddock, compressing his lips.

'You and Kenneth Oswin were close friends.'

'We were. Since boyhood.'

'Were you surprised . . . when he took such drastic action?'

'I was. I'd not have said he was the vengeful sort. Mind, he denied to me later that he'd done it for revenge.'

'Why, then?'

'He wouldn't say. Except that it was for Val and Derek's sake.'

'How could that be?'

Braddock shrugged. 'He was a dying man. I've never been sure he knew himself why he'd done such a thing. There was no way Val and Derek could gain by it. He must have been . . . rambling.'

'Do you think Sir Walter got what was coming to him, though, whatever the motive?'

Braddock weighed the question in his mind, then nodded. 'You can't deny the natural justice of it. A lot of good men died young to line the Colborns' pockets. But that's the way of the world. You can't fight it.'

'Maybe Kenneth Oswin was determined to try.'

'Maybe. But that's for him to account for to the Almighty. What bothers me now is the thought that Derek might have tried his hand at the same game.'

'What do you mean to do about it?'

'Nothing I can do. If I go to the police, it might only make things worse for the boy.'

'Yes,' I said, affecting reluctant agreement. 'It might.' It might also alert Addis and Spooner to how economical I'd been with the facts during our discussion. All in all, I had a lot of compelling reasons to steer Braddock away from the forces of law and order, at least for the moment. 'But aren't they likely to come to you?'

'Only if someone points them in my direction. Mrs Lumb knows better than to do that. She and I don't make trouble for each other.' He cleared his throat. 'I'm hoping you might . . . agree to watch what you say . . . if they come a-calling on you.'

It was just as well, I reflected, that Braddock hadn't arrived an hour earlier – for both of us. 'You can rely on me,' I said. 'I'm sure Derek will turn up soon, with no harm done.'

'I wish I was sure.'

'If I hear from him, I'll let you know straight away.'

'I'd take that as a kindness, Mr Flood. My number's in the book.'

'Right.'

'Well, I've taken up enough of your time. I'd best be on my way.' He stood up, but made no move towards the door. It was apparent that he still had something to say. I rose and looked at him promptingly. Several seconds passed during which he seemed to ponder the wisdom of his words. Then, in a gruff undertone, he finally unburdened himself. 'Derek's the nearest to family I have left. I must do what I can for him.'

It was nearly noon by the time Ray Braddock made his plodding exit, leaving me with less than half an hour to get up to the station and meet Moira off the 12.27. I flung on a coat and hurried out into a cold, grey, mizzly midday. A glazier's van was parked outside and I could hear Eunice in conversation with its driver down in the basement area. He was one visitor to the Sea Air I didn't need to worry about.

On my way to the taxi rank in East Street, a thought suddenly came to me. It would have occurred to me sooner, but my own need to avoid the police was so well served by Braddock's similar reluctance that I hadn't bothered to question it. Yet the question was a good one. Why *was* the old man so leery of the boys in blue? What did he have to be frightened of? Like more or less everyone else mixed up in the misadventures of Derek Oswin, he was hiding something. But what? And why?

My brain was obviously suffering from anxiety overload, because it was only when I was halfway to the station in the back of a taxi that I remembered Moira's bizarre message of yesterday afternoon. I turned on my mobile and checked for further word from her, but there was none. My various tart responses had presumably dispelled the muddle she'd some-how got herself into. Ordinarily, I'd have looked forward to a boozy lunch with the gossipy guzzler herself, but, the circumstances being about as far from ordinary as conceivably possible, the prospect had lost its lustre. Even the opportunity to lay my hands on the manuscript of *The Plastic Men* had turned sour on me. If I couldn't use any ammunition it provided me with against Roger Colborn, maybe, I reflected, I was better off not knowing what that ammunition might be.

This reflection was about to recoil on me, however. The 12.27 arrived only a couple of minutes late and Moira was one of the first passengers through the barrier. Loud, red-haired and generously proportioned, she's never faded into any background I've ever seen. The *faux* leopard-skin coat and purple beret made sure the concourse of Brighton railway station on a dull December day hadn't a chance of being an exception. What I noticed, however, even before the mandatory hug and triple kiss, was that she was carrying nothing apart from her handbag.

'Where's the manuscript, Moira?' I asked, as soon as we'd disentangled ourselves.

'You don't have it, do you?' she responded bafflingly. 'I was afraid of that.'

'You were supposed to bring it with you.'

'I was hoping your messages didn't mean what they seemed to.'

'What the hell's going on?'

'That, Toby, is a very good question.'

It was a question I only got some sort of an answer to once we were installed in a taxi, heading for La Fourchette in Western Road, Moira's choice of lunch venue.

'I had to go out shortly after you called yesterday morning,' she began. 'I didn't get back to the office till after lunch. That's when I found out what had happened.'

'Which was?' I prompted impatiently.

'Well, I'd asked Lorraine to retrieve the manuscript from Ursula because you wanted it back in a hurry, but I hadn't told her I was planning to bring it down here today, so, when this guy showed up—'

'What guy?'

'He said you'd sent him to fetch the manuscript. Naturally, Lorraine thought you'd told me you'd send someone round for it and I'd forgotten to mention it to her. Simple as that. So—'

'She handed it over?'

'I'm afraid so.'

'Catch this guy's name, did she?'

'Er, no.'

'What did he look like?'

'Unremarkable. Medium height, medium build. She probably did no more than glance at him. After all—'

'Why should she bother to take reasonable care of something I'd entrusted to you? Good question, Moira. And I can't think of an answer. Mr Nobody swans in off the street, tickles Lorraine under the chin and walks out with a manuscript he had no claim to. Most natural thing in the world. Perfectly understandable. Happens every day.'

'Look, Toby, I'm sorry. It's very . . . unfortunate.'

'*Unfortunate?*'

'I shall have a serious word with Lorraine. You can be certain of that. But what's the big deal? Surely you can get another copy from the author as I suggested to you yesterday.'

'The original's gone missing.'

'What?'

'Along with the author, as a matter of fact.'

Moira stared at me in amazement. 'Missing?'

'As in "vanished without trace".'

'But that means . . .' Her brow furrowed in agently concern. 'What have you got yourself mixed up in, Toby?'

The answer was more than I had any intention of divulging to Moira. Colborn must have learned of the copy of *The Plastic Men* I'd sent to her from Derek. He'd had the original – along with any other copies – removed from 77 Viaduct Road. An artful sortie to the Soho offices of the Moira Jennings Agency had now completed the collection. There was no other way to read it. Roger Colborn's opportunistic instincts had prevailed yet again.

'You're not going to tell me what this is all about, are you, Toby?' Moira demanded after we'd ordered our lunch and started on a bottle of Montagny, her insistence that she had a right to know only enhanced by the embarrassment she felt at losing the manuscript. 'You're putting me in an impossible position.'

'Actually, I'm not. It's telling you that would do that.'

'Does this have something to do with Denis?'

'I can't discuss it, Moira. Sorry. My hands are tied.'

'But that bloke who tricked Lorraine was part of some . . . conspiracy. Is that what you're saying?'

'I'm saying I can't discuss it.'

'And Jenny. Is she involved? I know she lives down here. Brian Sallis implied your no-show on Monday night was on her account.'

'When did he imply that?'

'When I spoke to him yesterday afternoon, after trying to speak to you.'

'I see.'

'Do you? Do you *really*? As your agent, Toby, I have to look at the big picture, which at the moment isn't a very attractive one where you're concerned.'

'What's that supposed to mean?'

'It means you need to be careful. There's a chance Leo may decide to bring *Lodger in the Throat* into London after all.'

'Well, that's good news, isn't it?'

'It is . . .' She paused, apparently unconvinced. Then she added, '*If* you're still in the cast.'

I bridled instantly. 'Why the bloody hell shouldn't I be?'

'Because, Toby,' she replied, lowering her voice, 'Leo may calculate that the only viable way of bringing it in is by economizing on the salaries. And thanks to my negotiating skills your salary's the biggest by quite a margin.'

'He wouldn't do that.'

'Wouldn't he?' Moira looked at me over the rim of her glass, one eyebrow cocked. 'I dare say Martin Donohue would be willing to take over your part at a cut-price rate just for the career leg-up it would give him.'

There was no denying that. In fact, the harder I thought about the possibility Moira had raised, the more horribly plausible it became. I'd seen little of my fellow actors off-stage in recent days. I'd opted out of all their post-show suppers. I'd made myself remote and semi-detached. If there were whispers going round, they were unlikely to have reached my ears.

'Leading the cast of an unsuccessful production is plain bad luck,' said Moira. 'Getting sacked from that role in a pro-duction just about to redeem itself, on the other hand . . . is something you can't afford to let happen, Toby. Trust your aunty Moira on this one. It's an absolute no-no.'

Our meals arrived. Moira tucked into hers with relish, while I picked listlessly at mine and reflected on the truly sickening prospect she'd conjured up for me. Martin Donohue replacing me as James Elliott? His name, *and not mine*, up in lights outside a West End theatre? The week was just getting worse and worse.

Perhaps my pitiful expression penetrated Moira's defences. Or perhaps sating her hunger allowed the sympathy in her soul to take flight. She ordered a second bottle of wine, which I'd refrained from suggesting for fear of being thought even more unprofessional than she already had me down as. She lit a cigarette and reached across the table to give my hand a consoling squeeze.

'It probably won't happen, Toby. I just want you to be aware of the vulnerability of your position. Besides, acting's only a job. There *are* more important things to think about. Your marriage to Jenny, for instance.'

'It ends next month, Moira. Decree absolute.'

'Does it have to?'

'I can't think of any way to stop it.'

'You could try telling her you still love her.'

'She knows that. The problem is that *she* no longer loves *me*.'

'I bet she does.'

'Your cheer-up act lacks subtlety, Moira. You haven't seen Jenny in over a year. How would you know what she feels?'

'You two belong together. It's as simple as that.' Our plates were removed. She leaned back and observed me with narrow-eyed acuity through a curl of cigarette smoke. 'If you hadn't lost Peter, you'd never have lost each other. You know that better than I do.'

My mouth dried. My self-control faltered. It's strange how, despite the passage of time, the grief I never properly shared with Jenny remains no more than a stray word away. 'There's nothing to be gained by dwelling on what can't be altered,' I said stiffly.

'Have you seen much of Jenny since you came to Brighton?'

'Not as much as I'd like. And not exactly in favourable circumstances, either.'

'But you *have* seen her?'

'Yes. Several times.'

'At whose instigation?'

'Well, initially . . . Jenny's.'

Moira smiled. 'Doesn't that tell you something?'

'She simply wanted me to do her a favour.'

'Really?'

'Yes. Really.'

'As your agent, friend and counsellor on female psychology, Toby, I have to say that sometimes you can be mind-numbingly obtuse. Don't you get it?'

'Get what?'

'The message.' Moira stubbed out her cigarette and leaned across the table again. 'No woman eagerly counting the days to the legal finalization of her divorce asks her soon-to-be-ex-husband for anything, however minor, however trivial, or contacts him for any reason whatsoever, unless, in some secret part of her mind, she's come to doubt whether she genuinely wants to lead the rest of her life without him. She's not going to admit that, of course. She's going to deny it vehemently, in fact, even to herself. But it's the truth. My experience of divorce is, let's face it, considerable, so you'll have to acknowledge me as an authority on the subject. Jenny *was* asking you to do her a favour. But it wasn't the one she spelt out. Forget the pretext, Toby. Concentrate on the subtext. Do *yourself* a favour.'

Men mismanaging their love lives was a subject that evidently appealed to Moira. When we left La Fourchette, well fed and altogether too well wined, she announced her intention to tour the Royal Pavilion before returning to London. 'High time I saw inside the old sot's lair.' I walked her through the Christmas shoppers to the Pavilion entrance, but declined to accompany her further. We parted outside, Moira fudging a climactic apology for losing the manuscript of *The Plastic Men* by advising me to forget whatever *l'affaire* Oswin amounted to and devote my remaining leisure time in Brighton to winning back Jenny. Then, in a tipsy swirl of leopard-skin, she was gone.

I walked down to the pier and out along it, remembering my meeting there with Jenny last Sunday. Could Moira be right? Was Jenny as reluctant in her own way to let go as I was in mine? The afternoon was cold and murky, the pier all but empty. The sea was a heaving, foam-flecked mass, greyer than the sky. A fine drizzle blurred the illuminated signs. I stopped and stared back towards the shore. Colborn had been too quick and too clever for me. He had me where he wanted me. He was in control. But not of Jenny. She was his weak spot. And my chink of light.

*   *   *

Ten minutes later, I pushed open the door of Brimmers and entered the shop for the first time. Two customers were debating the merits of a fluffy pink cloche with a thin, bright-eyed, blonde-haired young woman I took to be Jenny's assistant, Sophie. Of Jenny herself there was no sign. I headed towards the door at the rear marked PRIVATE. But Sophie cut me off.

'Excuse me, sir,' she said, starting with surprise as she either recognized me or deduced who I was. 'Oh,' she added, her mouth holding the shape of the word as she stared at me.

'I'm looking for Jenny.'

'She's . . . not here . . . at the moment.'

'When are you expecting her back?'

'I'm not, actually.' Sophie cast a nervous sidelong glance at the pair with the cloche and dropped her voice. 'Mr Flood, I—'

'Where is she?'

'I . . . don't know.' Reading the scepticism in my face, she lowered her voice still further, to the level of a whisper. 'She's gone away.'

'She said nothing about this yesterday.'

'It was arranged at short notice. She phoned me this morning. An urgent family matter, apparently. She won't be back until after the weekend.'

I'd done it again. I'd underestimated Colborn. Jenny was gone, whisked away, placed beyond my reach. I said no more. I couldn't bear to. I brushed past Sophie and hurried out of the shop.

From a window-seat in the Rendezvous, I rang Jenny's mobile. It didn't come as any great surprise to find it was switched off. I left no message. Sipping my *espresso*, I wondered if there really could have been a family crisis. It seemed wildly improbable. But a tactical retreat to her parents' house in Huntingdon or her sister's in Hemel Hempstead wasn't. I had both numbers back at the Sea Air, but ringing them was pointless. Either she hadn't gone to them or they'd be under instruction to tell me she hadn't. Besides, there was another possibility I *could* check, personally. And at that moment I badly wanted to do more than log up futile phone calls.

The taxi dropped me a hundred yards or so short of the entrance to Wickhurst Manor, at the end of the lane leading north towards Stonestaples Wood, the lane where Sir Walter Colborn met his end seven years ago and from which his killer's son, Derek Oswin, took those covert photographs of the house he'd shown me. I'd bought an Ordnance Survey map of the area before leaving Brighton, but the light was failing so fast it wasn't going to be useful for long. A chill, damp winter's evening was encroaching rapidly as the taxi pulled away and I started up the lane.

Derek had mentioned a right of way skirting Wickhurst Manor. The dotted green line shown on the map diverging from the lane about a quarter of a mile ahead had to be it. I stepped up my pace, racing against the twilight.

If the path hadn't been marked by a fingerpost, I might easily have missed it. The route meandered off muddily through the trees flanking the lane. The going was slow and slippery, thorns dragging at my coat and trousers as I diverted round the deeper puddles. But I pressed on, confident that the boundary of the manor couldn't be far.

Nor was it. Through the tangled undergrowth I spotted the perimeter wall ahead, creeper-hung flint patched in places with brick. It was no more than five feet high and I could see the trunk of a fallen tree propped against it that looked the likeliest means of climbing over.

The theory was fine, its execution clumsy. The tree trunk was slimy and soft with decay. I scrambled up onto it and immediately slipped straight off, further jarring my already twanging thigh muscle, an unwelcome reminder that I was neither young nor fit enough for such antics. But needs must. I scrambled up again, stretched precariously to a foothold on

230

top of the wall and crouched there, squinting for a view of the ground on the other side.

The shadows were too deep, however. It was a question of trusting to luck. I lowered myself cautiously down, clutching onto a flint-edge and a branch of the tree, and ended up knee-deep in a patch of nettles. Blundering clear, I found myself on the fern- and thorn-strewn fringe of a plantation of fir trees. Their serried ranks opened up tunnels of sight through the deepening dusk to open ground beyond. Wincing from sundry nettle stings and thorn slashes, I headed along one of the diagonals, the going easy under the conifers through rustling drifts of needles.

I caught my first sight of the house as I emerged from the plantation on its far side. A barbed-wire fence separated me from a hummocked stretch of parkland. Beyond, the chimneys and roof of Wickhurst Manor were silhouetted, black against the grey-black sky. There were lights on in several of the ground-floor windows and a couple on the first floor as well. As I watched, a car came into view, moving down the drive away from the house, its headlamps tracking round the leafless branches of the trees as it followed the curving route to the gates.

I snagged my coat on a barb as I squeezed between two wires of the fence, but tugged it clear and set off across the park. Fifty yards or so took me to another fence. Beyond this and a narrow lawn lay the single-storey wing of the house enclosing the kitchen garden. I was on the opposite side of the house to Colborn's office quarters. It was quiet here. There was no-one about. But, then, why would there be? It was nearly dark and growing colder by the minute. The drizzle was thickening into rain.

I crawled under the bottom wire of the fence, crossed the lawn and took a squint through the nearest window. This wing had originally been the servants' domain, I supposed. It looked now to be used for the storage of gardening equipment. I headed round the angle of the building in search of a door.

The first one I came to was locked. I went on, down to the rear lawn, moving away from the house so that I could see into the room at the far end, from which light was spilling onto shrubbery, without being seen.

It was one of the offices. A young woman in a regulation black trouser suit sat at a desk, talking on the telephone as she tapped at a computer keyboard. I stood where I was, watching and waiting. Two or three minutes passed. The telephone call ended. She continued to sit at her desk. Then the door of her office opened and Roger Colborn walked in. He was more casually dressed, in open-necked shirt, jacket and jeans. They exchanged smiles and a few words. Then he was gone again.

Another minute later, so was I, back across the lawn to the unlit part of the house. Logic and architectural tradition suggested there should be a rear entrance about halfway along the wall, facing the lawn. Its outlines clarified themselves as I approached. With the building occupied, it wasn't likely to be locked. But I braced myself none the less, half-expecting to trigger some dazzling security light with every step.

Nothing happened. I reached the door, sheltered by a porch. I tried the handle. The door opened, without so much as a creak. I stepped inside, closing it carefully behind me.

What to do now? The question imposed itself upon me as I stood in the shadow-filled hallway, listening to the distant sounds of office life. A telephone rang. A printer whirred. A filing-cabinet drawer clunked shut. I was trespassing on Roger Colborn's private property – playing into his hands, for all I knew. My first and only thought since hearing that Jenny had gone away was that she hadn't really gone away at all; that Roger was either holding her here against her will or had, more probably, persuaded her to lie low until I left Brighton. But what if I was wrong? What if she'd lost patience with both of us and gone away to think? If so, the most I could accomplish by coming here was to make a fool of myself.

Yet there are worse things to be than a fool, I reflected. I'd come too far to turn back. I tiptoed along the hall to the corner, where it opened out between the stairs and the front door. The lights were on here and, glancing up the stairs, I could see lights on above as well. The double doors leading to the office quarters could open at any minute, of course. I couldn't afford to linger. I swung round the newel post and started up the stairs two at a time, treading lightly.

About halfway up, I remembered the dog. Where was Chester? Docile or not, he was quite capable of barking. But he was Roger's dog, not Jenny's. With any luck, he had a basket in the office and was dozing in it right now. I pressed on.

There were lamps on in the drawing room and the door was open. I stepped into the room half-expecting to see Jenny sitting by the fire, reading a magazine and sipping tea, perhaps with Chester flaked out on the hearthrug. But the grate was empty. Jenny wasn't there. And nor was Chester.

The door into the adjoining room, where Jenny had gone to speak to Roger on the telephone during my previous visit, was ajar, a light shining within. I took a look inside. There was no-one there. I doubled back to the landing and tried one of the other doors at random. It led to a darkened bedroom. I retreated, my confidence in my own reasoning ebbing with each blank I drew.

Then I heard a noise above me – the creak of a floorboard. I stood stock still, my ears straining. There it was again, quite distinctly. Someone was up there.

The main stairs ended at the first-floor landing. There had to be a set of back stairs leading to the second floor. I hurried along the passage to the door at its far end and opened it. Sure enough, a narrow staircase led up from here as well as down – the servants' route, in times gone by. I started climbing.

A door at the top led to a passage running the width of the house, its ceiling angled to accommodate the slope of the roof. A couple of dormer windows admitted enough light from the lamps round the main entrance below them for me to see by. There were doors off to the right at intervals, but none was open. Nor was a glimmer of light visible beneath any of them.

I walked stealthily past, pausing by each to listen. There was no sound either. Yet there *had* been a sound. Floorboards don't creak of their own accord.

I was nearly at the end of the passage when the lights came on. I heard the flick of the switch behind me. A split-second later I was blinking and flinching in a sudden flood of brilliance.

'Turn round.' It was Roger Colborn's voice, raised and peremptory.

I obeyed, but slowly, playing for the time my eyes needed to adjust.

He was standing at the other end of the passage, having either followed me up the stairs or, more likely, stepped silently out of the first room I'd passed. The creaking floorboard had been a calculated effect, designed to lure me up there. That was obvious to me as soon as I saw what he was holding in his hand.

'It's a gun, Toby,' he said. 'As an actor, you should be used to handling some pretty good imitations of the real thing. But this *is* the real thing. And I know how to use it. I'm not a bad target-shooter, if I say so myself. And you're quite a tempting target, believe me.'

It occurred to me that he might really intend to shoot. Fear coursed through me, followed almost immediately by a strange, calming fatalism. Then logic kicked in. 'Murder, with a house full of witnesses?' My voice was quavering slightly. I could only hope it wasn't apparent. 'Is that a good idea, Roger?'

'The odds are I'd get away with it.' Roger smiled. 'We're two floors up from the offices. Nobody down there would hear the shot. I'd make sure your body was found many miles from here, of course. I can arrange that. And I will, if I have to. I don't want to kill you, Toby. But if you force my hand, I won't hesitate. Is that clear?'

'Crystal.' A little bravado goes a long way, I reasoned. I had to show I was afraid of the gun, not of him.

'Why did you come here?'

'I was looking for Jenny.'

'She's gone away.'

'So the girl at Brimmers said. But—'

'You thought she might be hiding from you here. Or that *I* might be hiding her?'

I shrugged. 'Something like that.'

'And you thought you could just walk in and rescue her? You're a bigger fool than I took you for. She isn't here. She really has gone away. As for walking in, you ought to know that a security camera was tracking you from the moment you got within twenty yards of the house. I saw you coming, Toby. Actually as well as metaphorically.'

'Where's Jenny gone?'

'That's none of your business.'

'And why has she gone?'

'The same applies. None – of – your – business.'

'What about Derek Oswin, then? What have you done with him?'

'Oswin?' Anger flared in Roger's eyes. He began to advance towards me. 'How many more times am I going to be asked to explain myself where that little shit's concerned? You've managed to plant some suspicion – some madness – in Jenny's mind. Don't try to persuade me that you believe any of it, though. *Just don't.*' He stopped about ten yards from me, the gun still rock-steady in his hand, still pointing straight at me. 'You aren't going to steal her from me, Toby. I'm not going to let you.'

'It's not up to you *or* me, Roger. It's up to her.'

'We'll see about that.'

'Yes. We—'

'*Shut up.*' His raised voice echoed in the passage. A muscle tightened in his cheek. I couldn't tell what his intentions were. I could only cling to the thought that killing me was about the surest way imaginable for him to lose Jenny. 'Take your mobile phone out of your pocket.'

'My phone?'

'*Just do it.*'

'OK, OK.' I slid the mobile out from inside my coat and held it up for him to see.

'Drop it on the floor.'

I bent forward, tossed the mobile aside and slowly straightened up.

'Now, open the door to your left.'

I stretched out my hand, turned the knob and pushed the door open. The light from the passage revealed nothing beyond a bare, linoleumed floor.

'Step inside.'

A couple of strides took me over the threshold. By the time I'd turned back round, Roger had moved to cover the doorway. We were closer than ever now. But I couldn't see the faintest trembling in his grip on the gun. Whether he could see the trembling I sensed in my own limbs was another matter.

'Turn on the light.'

There was no switch on the wall in the obvious place. I stared at where it should be, then noticed the cord hanging from the ceiling. I tugged at it and a fluorescent light flickered into life above and behind me.

'It's an old darkroom,' said Roger. 'My father was an enthusiastic photographer. He fitted this out to work in. No window. And a stout, lockable door.'

'You can't keep me here.'

'Close the door, Toby.'

'I'm due on stage this evening. The theatre management know where I am. They'll come looking for me.'

'Bullshit. You wouldn't have told anybody what you were planning. Close the door.'

'No.'

'I'm prepared to kill you, Toby. I'd almost be glad if you forced me into it, to be honest with you. It's your choice.'

We stared at each other for a long, slow second. I wasn't convinced he'd go ahead and shoot if I made a lunge at him. But Roger Colborn was capable of killing me. Of that I was convinced.

'Close the door.'

'You're making a big mistake.'

'I won't tell you again.' He raised his other hand to strengthen his grasp on the butt of the gun. I noticed the taut whiteness of his knuckle where his forefinger was curled round the trigger. His gaze was cold and intense.

'All right,' I said. 'Have it your way.' I closed the door.

A second later, I heard a key turn in the lock. Then nothing.

The room was about twelve feet square. There were work-benches round two sides and half of a third, with photographic equipment scattered across them – driers, trimmers, mounters, light boxes, processing trays and suchlike. A stool stood next to a sink set in one of the benches. There was a drying cabinet as well and an exhaust fan high on the far wall to provide ventilation. Sir Walter had done the thing properly. That much was obvious. And his thoroughness had extended to security. The door was solid. I've barged through a good few matchwood mock-ups in my time. Shoulder-charging the genuine article is a far cry from that. This door felt as if it wouldn't yield to anything short of a six-man battering-ram.

I opened the cabinet and checked the cupboards beneath the benches. Empty. What I could see was all there was. I sat down on the stool next to the sink and bleakly contemplated the folly of what I'd done. Jenny wasn't hiding *or* being held at Wickhurst Manor. I reckoned I believed Roger on that point. But *I* was being held, for how long and for what purpose I had no idea. The most disturbing reason that occurred to me was so that Roger could come back and deal with me after his staff had all gone home. Somewhat less disturbing, though depressing enough in its way, was the possibility that he meant to humiliate me by ensuring I missed tonight's performance of *Lodger in the Throat*. If so, his tactics were cruelly ironic. Only a few hours previously, Moira had urged me to avoid antagonizing Leo at all costs. Absenting myself from the theatre without explanation was, in the circumstances, just about the worst thing I could do. And Roger had it in his power to ensure that I did it.

I ran some water from the tap and douched my face, then massaged my forehead in the absurd hope that I could somehow force my brain to devise an escape route from the trap I'd fallen into. No bright idea, nor even a dullish one, came obligingly to mind. Roger was right: I was a bigger fool than he'd taken me for.

And then, quite suddenly, just as I'd abandoned the effort, perhaps *because* I'd abandoned it, an idea did present itself. *The sink*. My best chance of escape was while the staff were still on the premises. Roger couldn't afford to let them know he was holding me captive. But how could I take advantage of that fact? A flood was the answer, an emergency bound to attract the attention of everybody in the house.

I shoved the plug into the hole and turned both taps full on. The hot emitted nothing but a few dry-throated splutters, but no matter: the cold flowed healthily. The sink began to fill. I sat up on the bench opposite and awaited the inevitable.

Then the flow diminished. Within a few seconds, it had become a trickle. Within another few, it had stopped altogether. I stared at the tap in dismay. The water already in the sink was merely what the pipe this side of the stopcock had held. Roger had turned off the supply, guessing I might try just such a ploy. He was one step ahead of me yet again.

I held my head in my hands and uttered a mantra of curses. What was I to do? What in God's name was I to do?

Then the light went out.

It was 4.38 p.m., according to the luminous dial of my wrist-watch – the only source of light in the room – when I took my coat off, rolled it into a pillow and lay down on the floor. Being locked in a room you can't break out of is frightening, even if you're not prone to claustrophobia. There's the fear you can't reason away that you'll never be released, that this is the room you'll die in. I guess every prisoner must sometimes have the same nightmare: that the gaolers will vanish

238

overnight, that the door will never reopen. Freedom isn't the greatest loss, I realized, there, alone in the darkness and the silence. It's the control of your own destiny, however partial, that you miss the most, suddenly and savagely.

Time, meanwhile, becomes an instrument of torture. You don't know how much of it you have. Your future is no longer yours to determine. And there's no way out, unless your captor deigns to provide one. There is no escape. Turn the problem over in your mind as long and hard as you like: there is no solution.

But there is sleep. I can't have appreciated just how tired I was. At some point, fatigue overcame anxiety. And I slept.

I was woken by the flashing of the fluorescent light before it fully engaged. Then I was bathed in cold, white brilliance, the faint hum of the tube confirming that power had been restored. I blinked and winced from the ache in my neck, rolled over onto my side and squinted at my watch. It was 9.43 p.m. I'd slept for five hours. *Lodger in the Throat* was into the second act of its Friday night run, *sans* Toby Flood.

'Shit,' I murmured, struggling to my feet. The panic and chaos my absence must have caused burst into my thoughts. Letting the others down again was bad enough. But there'd been no stand-in this time. I'd left them comprehensively in the lurch. 'Shit, shit, shit.'

Then I heard the key turn in the door-lock. I stared at the knob, expecting to see it revolve, to see the door open. But nothing happened. There wasn't so much as the creak of a floorboard from the passage.

I reached out, grasped the knob, turned and pulled. The door opened.

There was no-one waiting on the other side. I stepped into the passage and, in the same instant, the door at the far end, leading to the stairs, clicked shut.

'Colborn?' I shouted.

There was no answer, no response of any kind. I went back

239

for my coat, then started walking along the passage, hesitantly at first, but faster with every stride.

There was no-one on the staircase. I headed down to the first floor and along the passage to the landing at the top of the main stairs. The door to the drawing room stood open. The fire had been lit within. I could hear the crackle of burning logs.

'In here, Toby,' came Roger Colborn's syrupy, summoning voice.

I stepped into the room. Roger was sitting in a fireside armchair, smiling in my direction. The chair opposite him was dwarfed by its occupant: a huge, broad-shouldered man dressed in black leathers, a mane of greying hair tied back in a ponytail to reveal a pitted face from which dark, deep-set eyes stared neutrally towards me. He tossed the cigarette he'd been smoking into the fire and stood up slowly, the leathers creaking faintly as he did so. He must have been six foot seven or eight and my immediate impression was that he'd have been able to break down the darkroom door without greatly exerting himself. He was Michael Sobotka, of course. But I wasn't supposed to know that.

Roger stood up too. 'Glad you could join us, Toby,' he said.

Sobotka was fast as well as big. He was next to me in two strides, grabbing my shoulders and hauling me across to the couch, where he plonked me unceremoniously down as if I were no more than a recalcitrant child.

'What do you want?' I demanded, trying not to sound as powerless as I felt.

'Just a little more of your time, Toby,' said Roger. 'That's all, I promise.'

'Who is this guy?'

'He's someone your late friend Denis Maple ran into earlier this week. Considering how Maple ended up, you'd be well advised to watch your step. My friend here is remarkably even-tempered, but brutal by nature. Isn't that so?'

This last question was directed at Sobotka, whose only

240

reaction was to throw a fleeting glance at Roger while he busied himself with putting on a pair of tight leather gloves. The gloves worried me more than his sullen, menacing demeanour. A lot more.

'If you'd done your stuff Monday night and fallen for the honey-trap,' Roger continued, 'I wouldn't have had to dip deep into my well of generosity and offer to buy you out. But you didn't have the common sense to take advantage of your good fortune, or even to lay off Jenny, which as her future husband I was entitled to expect you to. You've inconvenienced me, Toby. You've strained my tolerance. In fact, you've forced me into this. Remember that. You've left me no choice. Here.' He tossed something to Sobotka, who caught it nimbly in a gloved hand. It was a wineglass, wrapped in a clear plastic bag.

'What the hell's going on?'

'You'll see soon enough.'

Sobotka took the glass out of the bag, grabbed my right hand with vicelike force and squeezed my fingers and thumb against the bowl of the glass, rotating it as he did so. The surface felt greasy to the touch. After several seconds or so of this, Sobotka held the glass up to the light, nodded with evident satisfaction, replaced it in the bag and tossed it back to Roger, who stood it on the mantelpiece.

'You entered this house covertly this afternoon,' said Roger. 'I have the CCTV footage to prove that. You hid until the staff had gone home. Then you emerged – and attacked me.'

'What?'

'You took me by surprise. It was a vicious and unprovoked assault.'

'You're mad. Nobody's going to believe that.'

'I think they are, actually.' He nodded to Sobotka. 'I'm ready.'

Sobotka moved back to where Colborn was standing and, to my astonishment, punched him in the face. The blow, landing near his left eyebrow, sent Colborn reeling, but he steadied himself and stood upright again. A second punch took him somewhere between the jaw and cheekbone. He yelped, staggered, shook his head, then held up his hand in a signal of surrender and sank slowly into his chair.

Blood was oozing from the side of his mouth. He dabbed at it with a handkerchief and raised his other hand to the already reddening and swelling mark above his eye, wincing as his fingertips made contact. 'I reckon a spectacular black eye's guaranteed,' he said, lisping slightly. 'And there's a tooth loose as well. The split lip should look very impressive. Jenny's going to think you've seriously lost it, Toby. And she'll be right. You *have* lost.'

I stared at him, unable for the moment to speak. The man was mad. He had to be. Mad and *very* dangerous. If he was willing to have this done to him, what was he prepared to do to me?

'Let me sketch out your evening for you, Toby. After leaving me here to nurse my wounds, you went back to Brighton and killed a few hours getting seriously stoned. You didn't show up at the theatre, or even bother to warn them you weren't going to. Then you hooked up with a prostitute and went back to her place. Something went badly wrong there. Maybe you couldn't get it up after all that booze. Anyway, you got angry and stuck a wineglass in her face. Nasty. Very nasty. And very stupid too. She'd recognized you from the poster outside the theatre. And you didn't take the broken glass with you when you left. Fingerprints all over it, I'm afraid. *Your* fingerprints.'

'You won't get away with this,' I protested.

'Jenny's going to want to have nothing to do with you after she learns what you're capable of, Toby. It's not going to do a lot for your career either, is it? They won't send you down for long. First offence, previous good character, etcetera, etcetera. You might even get away with a suspended sentence. But acting? Forget it. I've been in touch with your boss, Leo Gauntlett. I've offered to put some money into *Lodger in the Throat*. Enough to give it a chance in the West End. I've

242

suggested he recast James Elliott, though. Bring in someone more reliable. Maybe you got to hear about that. Maybe that's why you came here this afternoon. To have it out with me. If so, all you've done is make certain he'll take up my suggestion.'

'You bastard.' Anger finally won out over shock and fear. I launched myself at him. But Sobotka stepped between us and grabbed me, doubling one arm up behind my back, sending a lance of pain through my shoulder.

'Let's get him out of here,' said Colborn. 'We're done.'

Pinning both of my arms behind me with such ease that I sensed the slightest resistance on my part could lead to a dislocation or worse, Sobotka frogmarched me out of the room and down the stairs. He paused at the bottom long enough for Colborn to overtake and open the front door. Then Colborn led the way across the terrace to where a Ford Transit had been backed up in position at the edge of the drive. He swung one of the rear doors open and turned to face me.

'You'll be dropped on the edge of town. What you do then is up to you. It won't make any difference. You could try getting your story in with the police first, but they'll see through it fast enough. The evidence is all one way. Denials and counter-accusations will count against you in the long run. You could make a run for it, of course. That's another option. Gatwick's only half an hour away by train. You might be able to get on a plane bound for somewhere exotic before they raise the alarm. Or you could just sit tight at the Sea Air and wait for them to come for you. They're all losing bets, believe me. I've fixed the odds.'

'What if I offered to leave Brighton now, tonight, for good?' The plea must have sounded as desperate as it truly was. 'I could save you the bother of setting me up.'

Colborn chuckled. 'It's too late for that.'

'You don't need to do this.'

'Oh, but I do. You pushed me too far, Toby. It's as simple as that.'

243

'What about Derek Oswin? What are you going to do with him?'

'Don't worry about Oswin. Worry about yourself.' He nodded to Sobotka. 'Get going.'

Sobotka levered me backwards, raising my feet off the ground until they were above the level of the floor of the van, then rammed me in through the doorway, giving a final shove that sent me on a bruising roll against a boxed-in wheel arch. The door slammed shut behind me. The lock clunked into position.

I sat up and felt my way forwards until I reached the plywood screen blocking off the cab. The back of the van was empty. I was the only cargo.

The van sagged to one side as Sobotka climbed into the driving seat. He started the engine, then paused to light a cigarette. I heard the click of the lighter through the screen. There were two thumps on the side of the van – a signal from Colborn. Sobotka ground the engine into gear and started away.

Sobotka's priority clearly wasn't the comfort of his passenger. The journey into Brighton was a bone-jarring purgatory. All I could do was cling to one of the wheel-arch boxes and wait for it to end.

I had no idea where we were when the van slowed, bumped up onto a verge and came to a halt. The engine was still running as Sobotka climbed out of the cab. A few seconds later, one of the rear doors opened. Sobotka's gigantic shadow loomed before me.

'Out,' he said. It was the first word he'd spoken to me. And the last.

I made a stooping progress to the door. He stepped back as I clambered out. Then he moved swiftly past me, slamming the door as he went.

I heard the driver's door slam a few seconds later. The gearbox grated. The van lurched down onto the roadway and accelerated away. I stared after it as an awareness of my surroundings seeped into me. I was at the edge of an unlit single-carriageway road. Ahead of me was a roundabout, bathed in sodium light. The van crossed it, moving fast, as I watched.

Then a dark-blue saloon car completed a slow revolution of the roundabout and took the same exit as the van. There was no other traffic in any direction. It was a strange, hypnotic scene. The van. Then the car. I didn't know what to make of it. And my mind was too beset by other matters for me to dwell on it.

I started walking towards the roundabout.

Sobotka had dropped me just short of an interchange on the Brighton bypass. There was a roundabout either side of the dual-carriageway cutting. I glanced down at the surging traffic as I trudged across the bridge above it towards the amber dome of the city.

I was on Dyke Road Avenue, heading south through empty suburbia, destination uncertain, determination undone. The choices Colborn had so generously set before me were each as poisonous as the other. If I went to the police, I'd lose the small amount of room for manoeuvre I had left. It wasn't as if there was anything I could do to help the prostitute I was going to be framed for assaulting – Olga, presumably. The police were on to Sobotka, of course, which set me wondering again about the car on the roundabout. But that didn't mean they'd believe me, given that to have any hope of convincing them I'd have to admit to lying when Addis and Spooner questioned me this morning. Making a run for it was crazy, though undeniably tempting. Yet where would I run *to*? *What* would I run to? I had to prove to Jenny that I was telling the truth. But how could I convince her? And how was I to survive until I got the chance?

I walked for what must have been at least two miles past silent houses, to any one of which theatre-goers might soon be

245

returning, complaining as they came about the last-minute change of cast in *Lodger in the Throat*.

It was well gone eleven o'clock by now. The Dyke Tavern was chucking out. I passed Dyke Road Park and the Sixth-Form College. I had my bearings in one sense, but in another not at all. I'd more or less come to the conclusion that going back to the Sea Air was about the best way to demonstrate my innocence. I might phone the police from there. I wasn't sure, though. I wasn't sure about anything.

At Seven Dials, I took a squint at the timetable displayed on one of the bus stops, according to which there was an 11.50 service to the Old Steine. Cold, footsore and limping on account of my strained thigh, I decided to wait there.

Fishing in my pocket for the pound fare, I winced as something sharp pricked my finger. I pulled out the offending article: Derek Oswin's Captain Haddock brooch. I'd jabbed myself with the pin.

I stared at the enamel face of the cartoon captain in the amber light of the nearby street lamp. I'd forgotten till then that I'd picked it up from the doormat at 77 Viaduct Road on Wednesday night. I must have dropped it into my pocket without thinking.

Another memory floated back to me then, of Derek confiding in me that he'd nicknamed Wickhurst Manor Marlinspike Hall. He'd made a point of telling me that though Tintin lived at Marlinspike in Hergé's books, Captain Haddock was the owner of the house. And there was some kind of coincidental connection with Roger Colborn's ownership of Wickhurst Manor. I couldn't remember exactly what it was – couldn't be sure Derek had even told me – but he'd certainly mentioned one. Emphasized its existence, indeed.

I imagined the scene as Derek was dragged down the stairs and out through the door of number 77, presumably by Sobotka. How had the Haddock brooch ended up on the floor? Had it simply been ripped off as they passed? Or had Derek deliberately torn it from his coat . . . and dropped it there . . . in the hope that I would find it? Was Captain Haddock his typically bizarre choice of messenger to me?

The idea was absurd, yet irresistible. I was clutching at a straw. But, as a drowning man, what else was I to do? I had Derek's keys. I could go to Viaduct Road easily enough and check whether there really was something I'd missed, some clue Derek had contrived to point me towards that would unlock the mystery. Besides, no-one would guess I'd gone there. As a hiding-place, it would take some beating. And, arguably, I did need a hiding-place.

I left the bus stop and headed north-east from Seven Dials, downhill towards Preston Circus and . . . Derek Oswin's home.

Nothing had changed at 77 Viaduct Road, except for the arrival of an electricity bill. I moved it off the doormat and pinned the Haddock brooch back onto Derek's abandoned duffel-coat, covering the tear. Then I went into the kitchen, hoping against hope that I might find something alcoholic to drink. I certainly needed something a lot stronger than cocoa.

A search of the cupboards turned up a half-empty bottle of sweet sherry. Valerie Oswin's tipple, perhaps. Or maybe Derek was a trifle addict. But I couldn't afford to be choosy. I poured some into a tumbler and took it with me into the sitting room.

The Secret of the Unicorn was the book in which his heroes finally moved to Marlinspike Hall. I dug it out of the slew of Tintin books on the floor and sat down to look at it. The blurb on the back referred to a sequel, *Red Rackham's Treasure*. I dug that one out as well.

The Tintin characters were vaguely familiar to me, but the stories hadn't left the faintest trace in my memory, though I'd read a good few in my childhood. I began to flick through *The Secret of the Unicorn*, gleaning the plot that underpinned the visual game-playing as I went. It didn't take long. Soon, I was able to move on to *Red Rackham's Treasure*. The story, as the titles imply, amounts to a treasure hunt, at the end of which

Tintin and Captain Haddock are able to move from their humble lodgings to Haddock's ancestral home, Marlinspike Hall. A voyage to the Caribbean in search of the buried riches of the pirate Red Rackham draws a blank and Haddock is actually only able to buy Marlinspike thanks to some money his friend Professor Calculus comes into by selling a valuable patent. Not until after taking possession of the house do Tintin and Haddock finally discover the treasure, hidden in a marble globe in the cellars.

I sat back and took several sips of sherry, though, like Haddock, I'd much have preferred whisky. A sense of futility, and, worse, stupidity, swept over me. What in the name of reason and sanity was I doing poring over Derek Oswin's childhood reading matter while my life was unravelling around me? Poor Olga had probably already had her cheek slashed to bolster the case against me, while Leo had doubt-less decided to sack me from the production of *Lodger in the Throat* and never employ me again. I was staring scandal and disgrace none too steadily in the face. Maybe I should have taken Colborn's offer when it was on the table. I didn't like to think what had happened to Derek because of my refusal. I liked even less to think what was going to happen to *me*.

The worst was that there was nothing I could do to prevent it. The idea that the Haddock brooch was some kind of message from Derek had been born of sheer bloody desper-ation. There was no message, no clue, no key, no hope, no globe waiting to spring open to my touch, revealing—

'Bugger me,' I said aloud, sitting suddenly upright. 'The globe.'

It stood on the desk in Derek's bedroom, in front of the window: a one-foot-diameter mounted globe, presumably given to him by his parents during his schooldays. Certainly the USSR hadn't yet dissolved into its constituent republics in this representation. I revolved the globe slowly, wonder-ing whether I really was on to something, or had just been suckered by meaningless coincidence.

248

The Oswins hadn't stinted their son. That was clear. The globe was an illuminated version. I noticed the wire trailing down to the plug behind the desk. I stooped to the socket and switched it on, but nothing happened. Then I spotted the rocker switch on the wire itself and tried that. Still nothing. The bulb inside the globe must have blown. Derek hadn't bothered to replace it.

But that, I knew, wasn't Derek's style. He bothered. He would have replaced it. Unless, of course, it hadn't blown. Unless, that is, he'd removed it. For a reason. For a very good reason. Red Rackham's treasure had been hidden inside a globe.

I picked the globe up and shook it gently. Something inside was sliding to and fro. I noticed a catch of some kind on the spindle at the north pole. I prised at it, releasing a pin inside the spindle and allowing the globe to be lifted off its base. As I manoeuvred the globe out of its sickle-shaped mount, something fell through the hole at the south pole and landed on the desk.

It was a microcassette, identical to those I've been using. But on this one there was a small paper label stuck to the front, with a date written on it in spidery ballpoint: *7/10/95*. Whatever was on the tape had been recorded a month or so before the death of Sir Walter Colborn in the autumn of 1995.

Where there was a cassette, there had to be a machine to play it on. That stood to reason. I checked the drawers of the desk. And there it was, at the back of the bottom drawer: a machine somewhat larger and probably a good few years older than the one I'd left at the Sea Air, but doubtless still working. The take-up spindle whizzed into action when I pressed the play button. There was plenty of charge left in the batteries.

I loaded the cassette, stood the machine on the bedside cabinet and sat down on the bed. Then I pressed the play button again.

There were two voices: a man and woman talking to each

other. The man sounded old, gruff and querulous, the woman younger, softer-toned, more distant. At first, I couldn't tell who they were. Then, as their identities became apparent, ignorance turned to disbelief. These two people couldn't be conversing in October 1995. It just wasn't possible, and yet they were. I could hear them. I could hear every word.

MAN: *Ann?*

WOMAN: *Yes?*

MAN: *Is that really you, Ann?*

ANN: *Yes, Walter. It's really me.*

WALTER: *It doesn't . . . sound like you.*

ANN: *I'm speaking through another. Besides, it's been a long time for me as well as you. Well, not* time *exactly. But long. Yes, it's been that. And I've changed. I'm Ann. But not the Ann you remember. Not quite. Although, of course . . .*

WALTER: *What?*

ANN: *I never was. Not really. Not the Ann you chose to believe I was. You know that, if you're honest with yourself. As I hope you are. As I hope . . . contacting me like this . . . proves you are.*

WALTER: *How can I be sure it's you?*

ANN (chuckling): *Still one for certainty, aren't you, Walter? Plain and unvarnished facts. You can live by them. But you can't die by them.*

WALTER: *I just want . . . to be absolutely—*

ANN: *I remember the look on your face when you came into my room at the maternity hospital and saw Roger bundled up in my arms. I remember it exactly. Do you?*

WALTER (after a pause): *Yes. Of course.*

ANN: *What do you want of me, Walter?*

WALTER (after another pause): *The truth, I . . . suppose.*

ANN: *The truth?*

WALTER: *Yes.*

ANN: *But you already know it.*

WALTER: *No. I don't.*

ANN: *You mean you don't wish to.*

WALTER: *You left no note. No . . . explanation.*

ANN: *A note would have become . . . public property. Studied by the coroner. Entered on the record. Would you really have preferred that?*

WALTER: *All these years, I've wondered.*

ANN: *What have you wondered?*

WALTER: Why?

ANN: *I couldn't stand the pretence any longer, Walter. It's as simple as that. It became . . . unendurable. It didn't have to be. You made it so.*

WALTER: Me?

ANN: *It doesn't matter. I forgive you. I forgave you even as I drove the car over the edge. It wasn't all your fault. I was partly to blame. You could say I started it. Yes, you could, Walter. In fact, why don't you? Why don't you call me some of the names you used to, when you were drunk and . . . burning with the shame of it?*

WALTER: *I didn't really mean . . . any of that.*

ANN: *Yes, you did. I don't blame you. It was a hard blow for a proud man to bear. And you've always been . . . so very proud.*

WALTER: *Not any more.*

ANN: *When did you change?*

WALTER: *It started . . . when you left. And lately, as I've grown older . . .*

ANN: *You've thought about death.*

WALTER: *Yes.*

ANN: *Face it with a clear conscience, Walter. I advise you, I implore you, free yourself of guilt. I ran away from my guilt. Don't make the same mistake.*

WALTER: *You didn't have so very much to feel guilty about, Ann.*

ANN: *Oh, but I did. I helped make you an unkinder man than you might have been.*

WALTER (after a bitter laugh): *Roger's taken after me in so many ways. There's irony for you. You made him . . . a likeness of me. You have no idea how unkind we've both been. A lot of people . . . have suffered.*

ANN: *I'm here for you only, Walter. It's impossible to explain. I feel nothing. But I understand everything. Whatever wrongs you've done, it's not too late to put them right.*

WALTER: *I'm afraid it is. In most cases, far too late.*

ANN: *But not in all cases?*

WALTER: *No. Not all.*

ANN: *Then attend to those. Without delay.*

WALTER: *Like you always urged me to?*

ANN: *You weren't listening then.*

WALTER: *I'm listening now.*

ANN: *I loved you once. But you drove love out. And all the ills of my life and yours rushed in to take its place.*

WALTER: *What am I to do?*

ANN: *Love again. That's all. Make peace with the world.*

WALTER: *I'll try. I truly will. But . . . there's something else. Roger. Oh God.* (A cough.) *Did you tell him, Ann? Did you . . . before you . . . ? Does he know? We've never spoken of it, he and I. And I've always wondered . . . whether he might have guessed, or . . . I just need to be certain, Ann?*

ANN (in a whisper): *He knows.*

The recording ended there, with the last word cut off so abruptly that it was easy to believe there was more to be heard in some other, fuller version of this strangest of exchanges. Sir Walter Colborn, talking to his dead wife, barely a month before his own death. It had to be a séance of some kind. Sir Walter had said Ann didn't sound like herself. That was because she'd spoken through a medium. He'd gone to someone who could call up her ghost, her spirit, her . . . whatever he believed it was. I'd have said Sir Walter Colborn was the last person to fall for that sort of thing. But what would I really know about him? Or about his relationship with Ann? Or about Ann herself, come to that?

I listened to the recording again. If the medium was a

charlatan, as I had every spiritualist down as, she was a smart one, no question. Sir Walter was convinced he was talking to Ann for the first time in thirteen years. You could hear the certainty of that growing in his voice. The reference to something no-one but she would be able to remember clinched it for him. And it lured him into discussion of some secret they'd long shared, about . . . Roger. '*Did you tell him, Ann? Does he know?*' Yes. Ultimately, he had her word for that. And so did I. '*He knows.*'

But what does he know? What is it that he and his father never spoke of, but both knew, without knowing that the other knew? And did anyone else know? Was anyone else in on the secret?

'What about you, Derek?' I said aloud. 'Is this what you've been getting at all along?'

I lay down across the bed, my head resting against the wall, and stared up at the shadow-vaulted ceiling. A dog was barking somewhere not far off, the sound echoing in some backyard similar to the ones I'd see if I opened the window and looked out. Then a police or ambulance siren challenged the noise and swamped it as it drew closer.

I sat up, suddenly and irrationally certain that they were coming for me. But no. They were taking some other route, bound for some other destination. The wail of the siren receded. The dog continued to bark. I was safe here, for the moment. But that was all. *For the moment.* The rest of tonight. Part of tomorrow. That was as much of a chance as I could carve out for myself of bringing Roger Colborn's world tumbling down around him. And the tape, hidden by Derek Oswin in a place where just about nobody – except me – might find it, was my only hope of doing so.

But what did it tell me? What was its *real* message? What was the secret?

If Derek knew, how, I asked myself, could he have come into possession of such knowledge? What connected him with the late Ann Colborn? Colbonite, obviously, if indirectly. But that applied to the whole workforce. And I had no reason to

253

suppose Ann ever went near the place anyway. There had to be something else. There had to be something *more*.

Ann had lived far from the tight, dull little circles Derek moved in. There was no point of intersection between their lives apart from the factory owned by *her* husband and *his* employer. And even that only applied to the six years between Derek going to work there in 1976 and Ann's suicide in 1982. There was nothing else. I thought of the Colbonite site in Hollingdean Lane, squeezed between the railway line and the municipal abattoir. Then I thought of the high white cliff top of Beachy Head, the blue of the sea below, the green of the turf above. And then—

I fell to my knees and grabbed the photograph album from where I'd left it yesterday, amidst the scattered contents of the wooden chest in the middle of the room. I flicked hurriedly through the pages, looking for the pictures I remembered. 1955. 1958. 1965. *Yes.*

Beachy Head, July 1968. There were two photographs of Derek as a ten-year-old, in striped T-shirt and short trousers with turn-ups, sitting on a picnic rug in one, taking guard with a cricket bat in another. Only the caption confirmed the location. The background could have been any fold of Sussex downland. There was no way to tell how close to the cliff the Oswins had chosen to picnic. I flicked on through the pages and soon came to another Beachy Head shot. August, 1976. The year, quite possibly the month, Derek had started at Colbonite. He was standing with his father in this picture. They were posed and smiling. Behind them, the ground fell, then rose again, exposing a white flank of cliff to the camera and the candy-striped lighthouse out to sea that fixed their location as exactly as a grid reference. The road described a long curve towards and then away from the edge of the cliff behind them. There were two or three cars parked in a lay-by just beyond the road's closest approach to the edge. Was one of them the Oswins'? I wondered. No. It couldn't be. Surely Derek had said his father had bought the car in which he killed Sir Walter only after he'd become ill, as if, prior to that, they'd had no car at all. I imagined they could easily have travelled to Beachy Head by bus. They wouldn't have needed—

My thoughts froze as my eye seized on the distinctive profile of one of the cars in the lay-by. The sleek line of boot and roof and bonnet, sunlight gleaming on polished paint-work. It was a Jaguar 2.4. And I had absolutely no doubt who it belonged to. Nor, come to that, as my mind dwelt for a second on the implications of what I was seeing, who had taken the photograph, who Kenneth and Derek Oswin were smiling at so warmly in the summer sunshine all those years ago, *who* I was *really* meant to see.

SATURDAY

Circumstances are subtler conspirators than humans. They decree stranger alignments and juxtapositions than any we can devise. I spent last night lying on Derek Oswin's bed in the house he was born in forty-four years ago, staring into a darkness familiar and congenial to him, but novel and threatening to me. I'd used *his* dictation machine to record *my* experiences. My own machine was out of bounds at the Sea Air, where I couldn't safely return. The police would be on my trail, I felt sure, chasing the dangerous man Roger Colborn had arranged for them to believe I was. That made my inexcusably unexplained no-show at the Theatre Royal a trivial problem by comparison. But it was made to seem trivial in its turn by my discovery of the truth about the Oswins' connection with the Colborns; the truth – and all the other truths it beckoned me towards.

But so far those truths were only suspicions. What I needed – what I had to lay my hands on before the police laid hands on me – was proof.

It was barely light when I left 77 Viaduct Road, unobserved, as far as I could tell, by Mrs Lumb at number 76. The morning was chill and damp, a fine drizzle fuzzying the still glowing street lamps. I headed down Ditchling Road to The Level, then cut across to St Bart's, following in the long-ago footsteps of Derek Oswin's grandfather, on his way home from a

259

ten-hour shift at Colbonite. His day would have been ending. Mine was only beginning.

I got into a taxi at the railway station and asked to be taken to Ray Braddock's address in Peacehaven: 9 Buttermere Avenue. The driver gave a couple of meaningful glances in the rear-view mirror as he started away and my heart jolted in alarm. Maybe the police had told the local radio station they were looking for me. But, when he spoke, he only did so along the 'Don't I know you from somewhere?' line I'd heard hundreds of times before.

'No,' I replied, forcing a smile. 'I just have one of those faces.'

Buttermere Avenue, Peacehaven, a long, straight road of cloned semi-detached pebble-dash bungalows, was as silent as the grave many of its residents were no doubt close to. Number 9 had an immaculately kept garden that made the house itself look shabbier than it really was. The sunburst gate creaked so loudly when I opened it that I seriously wondered if Braddock deliberately refrained from oiling it in order to be forewarned of visitors. The NO HAWKERS, NO CIRCULARS sign certainly didn't suggest he welcomed casual callers.

There was a light showing through the dimpled glass of the front door and I could hear the faint burble of a radio within. I pressed the bell, long and hard. There was no way to go about this but head-on. The burble was cut off at once.

A blurred and growing shape disclosed itself through the glass and the door was pulled abruptly open. Braddock, unshaven and swaddled in threadbare sweater *and* cardigan, glared out at me. Then, seeing who his visitor was, he softened his expression.

'Mr Flood. Have you heard from Derek?'

'No. But I've heard news of him.'

'You'd best come in.'

He led me down a narrow hall into a kitchen at the back of the house. The scent of fried bacon hung in the air. An

260

egg-smeared plate and a breadboard thick with crumbs stood beside the sink. On the table in the middle of the room was a teapot and a half-filled mug, steam whorling up from the rim. Plonked next to it was an open copy of the weekend edition of the *Argus*. I could only hope it had gone to press too early to report the mysterious absence of the star of the show from last night's performance of *Lodger in the Throat*.

'There's tea in the pot if you want some,' said Braddock.

'No thanks,' I responded.

'What's this about Derek, then?'

I took the photograph I'd brought with me out of my pocket and laid it on the table.

Braddock sat down, fumbled in his cardigan for a pair of heavy-framed glasses, put them on and squinted at the picture. After a moment's scrutiny, he frowned suspiciously up at me. 'Where'd you get this?'

'It was in the album at Viaduct Road.'

'Yeah, but—'

'I have a key.'

His frown deepened. 'You never told me that.'

'There are things you never told me, either.'

'I don't know what you mean.'

'Look at the picture.'

'I have done.'

'What do you see?'

'Ken and Derek at Beachy Head. A good long while ago.'

'Twenty-six years ago, to be precise. August, nineteen seventy-six.'

'If you say so.'

'What else do you see, apart from your old friend and your godson?'

He made a show of re-examining the photograph, then shrugged. 'Nothing.'

'There are cars in the lay-by.'

'Be odd if there weren't.'

'One of them's a Jaguar two point four.'

'Maybe.'

261

'Ann Colborn's car.'

'It could be anybody's.'

'No. It's hers. You know that.'

'I don't.'

'She took the photograph.'

'*What?*'

I sat down beside him. 'There's no point acting dumb, Ray. I've worked it out. With a little help from Derek. Your friend Ken Oswin and your boss's wife, Ann Colborn, were lovers, weren't they?'

He looked as if the suggestion had angered him. But shocked? No. He didn't look that. 'Are you trying to make fun of me, Mr Flood?'

'Certainly not. I'm just asking you to confirm what I'm sure you've known for many years. Roger Colborn is Ann's son by Ken, not Walter. Which makes him Derek's half-brother. He knows too. They both do.'

Braddock rubbed his chin thoughtfully, patently debating with himself whether to opt for denial or admission. His instinct was to damn me for a liar. But in the end his anxiety about what had happened to Derek swung the contest. 'How did you find out?' he said eventually.

'Does it matter?'

'There's no proof. There can't be.'

'There can be these days, actually. But Roger's hardly likely to submit to a DNA test, so we're left with strong suspicions and firm beliefs. Ann, Walter and Ken were in no doubt. Nor are you. Are you?'

'Ken never . . . came out and said it to me in so many words.'

'But . . .'

'Look, only Ann Colborn would know for sure, wouldn't she? Maybe not even her. And what difference does it make, anyway? There was something between her and Ken once, that's true. Maybe he was Roger Colborn's natural father. *Maybe.* But Roger's still Walter's boy in the eyes of the law. What the hell does it matter now, when all three of them are dead and gone?' He glared at me defiantly, but we both recognized the hollowness of his words. It mattered. It definitely mattered. 'Are you sure Derek knows?' he murmured.

'Yes.'

'And Roger knows and all?'

I nodded in answer.

'Dear Christ.'

'What about Derek's mother? Was she in on it?'

'No. I'm sure of that. Val wasn't . . . the inquisitive type. It happened before they were married. And it didn't last long.'

'It lasted till she died, Ray. The photograph proves as much.'

'I meant . . .' Braddock chewed his lip. 'I meant . . . they weren't lovers for long. But I don't suppose they forgot in a hurry, not if Roger . . .' He gave a helpless shrug.

'Beachy Head a regular rendezvous, was it?'

'How should I know?'

'Are you saying you don't?'

'Well . . .' He cleared his throat. 'Val never went there. She couldn't abide heights. But Ken and Derek liked a walk. Summer Sundays, they often used to take the train to Seaford, walk round the cliffs to Eastbourne and catch another train back from there. I suppose Ann Colborn . . . might have known that.'

'All this sheds new light on Sir Walter Colborn's death, don't you think?'

He bridled. 'I don't see how.'

'Maybe Ken blamed Sir Walter for Ann's suicide.'

'If he did, he never said so to me. And he waited a hell of a time to do something about it, didn't he?'

'He waited until he was dying. Until he no longer had anything to lose.'

'I don't believe it.'

'That's your prerogative. Anyway, it doesn't matter. What matters is whether Derek believes it.'

'If he's gone and stirred all that up . . .' Braddock shook

his head. 'Whoever told him about it has a lot to answer for.'

'Maybe no-one told him. Maybe he just worked it out.'

'Did he put this in his damn book, do you think?'

'Reckon so. Along with the explanation for the high death-toll among Colbonite workers. Not a palatable combination if you're Roger Colborn.'

'What's this man done to Derek?'

'I don't know. Let's hope nothing.' I was holding out on the old man, of course, shamelessly so. But I knew if I played him Derek's message he'd urge me to comply with Colborn's demands and go quietly – which I was no longer in any position to do. For me, it was all or nothing. And though Braddock had confirmed what I suspected, he hadn't given me what I needed: proof. Indeed, he'd made it clear he didn't believe any proof existed. But I didn't go along with that. I couldn't afford to. 'Who else knew about this, Ray? Who else knew for a fact?'

'No-one. Like I said, how could they, anyway? For a fact, I mean.'

'Think, man, think.' I'd grabbed his forearm without realizing it, I suddenly noticed. He seemed to have been as unaware of this as I was. Sheepishly, I let go. 'I have to nail this down.'

'Why?'

'For Derek's sake.'

'You reckon the boy's in danger?'

'I do, yes.'

'Well . . .' He licked his lips hesitantly.

'What?'

'There's Delia Sheringham, I suppose.'

'Delia?'

'Walter's sister.'

'I know who she is,' I snapped, realizing as I did so that Braddock might well have supposed I didn't. In the same instant, I remembered how close Syd Porteous had said the two of them were. 'What about her?'

'I bumped into her at the hospital once when I was visiting

Ken. It was only a couple of weeks before he died. They'd let him out of prison on bail by then, knowing the state he was in. Delia was coming out of the ward as I went in. She didn't recognize me. Well, I wouldn't have expected her to. But *I* recognized *her*. Pulled me up short, seeing her there. Why was she paying a call on the bloke supposed to have done her brother in?'

'Did you ask him?'

'No need. Ken told me straight off. He seemed to think it was funny. I mean, he was chuckling about it when I got to his bed. "What do you reckon, Ray?" he said. "Sir Walter died without leaving a will. His sister's just been in to tell me. Reckoned I ought to know." That seemed to tickle him. Which was some achievement, seeing how much pain he was in. I pretended not to understand, but it was plain as the nose on your face what he meant. Sir Walter didn't make a will because he no more had a wife living to leave his money to than he had—'

'A son.'

Braddock stared at me, then slowly nodded. 'That's how I read it.'

'And Delia wanted to make sure Ken knew about Sir Walter's intestacy?'

'Apparently. I don't know why. After all, it made no difference, did it? Roger inherited the lot, will or no will.'

'But it proves she knew.'

'That it does.'

I thought for a moment, then said, 'Can I use your phone? I need a taxi.'

'Where do you want to go?'

'Back into Brighton. In a hurry.'

'Going to see Delia, are you?'

'Yes.'

'I'll take you in my car, if you like.'

'All right. Thanks.'

*   *   *

Ten minutes later, we were heading west along the south coast road towards Brighton in Braddock's patched-up old Metro. The first couple of miles passed in silence. We both had plenty to think about, complicated in Braddock's case by a continual struggle to keep the windscreen clear of condensation.

By the time we were out of Saltdean and into the open country between there and Black Rock, the significance of Sir Walter Colborn's intestacy had begun to expand in my mind. It went beyond underlining his awareness that Roger wasn't his biological son, well beyond. Braddock had set the ball rolling for me by saying it made no difference. But it did. Potentially, it made all the difference in the world.

'That's it,' I suddenly said aloud.

'That's what?' asked Braddock, glancing round at me.

'Don't you see? Roger inherited as Sir Walter's son under the rules of intestacy. If it had been shown at the time that he wasn't his son, he wouldn't have inherited. The estate would have gone . . . to Gavin and Delia, presumably. Still would now, come to that. Gavin would press his claim even if Delia refrained. He'd have Roger by the short and curlies.'

'Are you sure about this?'

'I'm no lawyer. Maybe Gavin would have a case, maybe not. What I am sure of is that Roger wouldn't want to be tied up in the courts for years finding out.'

'You mean Derek's been a bigger threat to him than we reckoned?'

'Looks like it.'

'Then what do we do?'

'*You* do nothing. Leave it to me. I think I see a way to cut the ground from beneath Roger Colborn's feet. And it's going to be a pleasure.'

I had Braddock drop me in Clifton Terrace, just round the corner from Powis Villas. He was clearly still struggling to catch up with my thinking, preoccupied as he was with a question other concerns kept pushing to the back of my mind: where was his godson?

'I don't care if Roger Colborn comes out of this smelling of roses or horse manure, Mr Flood, just so long as Derek comes to no harm.'

'I reckon Derek's lying low,' I lied. 'Waiting – wisely – for the trouble he's caused to blow over.'

'And when will it blow over?'

'If I have anything to do with it . . .' I gave him what I intended to be a reassuring smile. 'Today.'

It wasn't till I reached the door of 15 Powis Villas that I realized just how hollow that reassurance was. I couldn't force Delia to tell me anything. Her husband was an unknown quantity. And they might both simply be out.

That last was my dismal conclusion when several lengthy prods at the doorbell went unanswered. I stepped back for a view of the drawing room through the front bay window. The room was empty.

Suddenly, I was aware of a movement behind me, dimly reflected in the window. I turned to find Delia Sheringham regarding me quizzically from the pavement. She was dressed for the weather, in raincoat, gloves, scarf and hat. The well-stuffed Waitrose carrier bags in either hand made it unnecessary to wonder where she'd been.

'Toby,' she said. 'This is a surprise.' She marched up the drive to where I was standing. 'And a relief.'

'In what way a relief?'

'I overheard two women in the queue for the checkout talking about *Lodger in the Throat*. One of them went last night.'

'Unlike me.'

'Exactly. But I see you've recovered from . . . whatever was wrong.'

'Hardly.'

'You'll be on tonight, though, I'm sure. Did I mention that John and I have tickets?'

'You did. But I wouldn't count on seeing me on stage. Or of feeling in the mood for a night at the theatre.'

'Why on earth not?'

'I've something to tell you.'

'Do you want to come inside?'

'I should think you'd want me to. It's the sort of thing best discussed behind closed doors.'

'You're being very mysterious, Toby.'

'Case of having to be.'

She sighed and bustled past me to the door.

Once we were inside, she led the way down the hall past the dining room to a large kitchen at the rear, instructing me over her shoulder to bring along the post that was lying on the mat. The kitchen windows looked out over a small, high-walled garden. I dropped the post onto the table as she stowed a few perishables in the wardrobe-sized fridge. Then she took off her coat, hat and scarf and filled the kettle.

'Coffee?'

'Thanks.'

'John's playing golf. It's something of a Saturday morning ritual, come rain or shine. He'll be sorry to have missed you.'

'I doubt it.'

She looked at me sharply. 'Why do you say that?'

'Because I doubt you'll tell him I've been here.'

She went on looking at me, saying nothing. I held her gaze. Then the kettle came to the boil. She spooned coffee into cups. 'How do you like it?'

'Black. No sugar.'

'Same as me.' She handed me my cup, took a sip from hers and flicked through the post.

Suddenly impatient, I took the photograph out of my pocket and dropped it onto the sheaf of letters. She stopped flicking.

'What's this?'

'I found it in an album at the Oswins' house. That's Derek.

And his father. At Beachy Head, in the summer of nineteen seventy-six.'

'Really? I don't quite see—'

'And that's your sister-in-law's car.' I stabbed at the image of the Jaguar in the lay-by. 'She took the picture.'

'That seems singularly improbable.' Delia sat down at the table and sipped some more coffee. 'I don't believe Ann knew the family.'

'She and Kenneth Oswin were lovers.'

'Don't be absurd.' She glanced reprovingly up at me.

'I won't if you won't.' I sat down opposite her. 'I've worked it out, Delia. I understand. I *know*.'

'What do you know?'

'That Roger is Kenneth Oswin's son, not Walter's.'

'This is utterly preposterous.' She took yet another sip of coffee. 'I think it might be best if you left.'

'I can prove it.'

She frowned at me. 'I don't think so.'

I took out Derek's pocket dictation machine and stood it on the table. 'I have a tape I want you to listen to. When you've heard it, you'll have to change your tune. You may as well do so now.' The only response I got to that was a toss of her head. 'You know it's true, Delia. You've always known. Ann confided in you. Gavin doesn't know obviously, otherwise—' I broke off. 'Why don't I just play it?'

'If you feel you must.'

'Oh yes. I do feel I must.' I pressed the PLAY button. And leant back in the chair.

Delia recognized Walter's voice at once. Her considerable powers of self-control couldn't suppress a flinch of surprise. She looked at me with a mixture of outrage and amazement, in which there was also a trace of fascination. Then, as the exchanges between her long-dead brother and her still-longer-dead sister-in-law proceeded, her gaze shifted to the machine itself and stayed there, fixed and focused, as if the tape inside was more than just a recording device, as if it held the souls and secrets of those two dead people she still loved.

269

The recording ended with Ann's whispered words, '*He knows.*' I leant forward, pressed STOP, then REWIND. 'You want to hear it again?'

Delia licked her lips. 'No.'

'There's a date on the label. Seventh October, nineteen ninety-five.'

'May I see?'

'Sure.' I ejected the cassette and showed it to her.

'I don't recognize the writing.'

'Nor do I. The medium's, perhaps.'

'You think what we've heard . . . was a séance?'

'Nothing else it could have been. And hardly shock news to you, Delia. I could tell from your expression that you understood the context straight off. My guess is Walter told you he was going to a psychic in the hope of contacting Ann.'

'Very well.' She drew herself up. 'As far as that's concerned, you're correct. Walter became interested in spiritualism in the last year or so of his life. He told me of his intention to consult a medium who'd been recommended to him and he asked my opinion.'

'Which was?'

'That such people are charlatans trading on the gullibility of grieving people.'

'You evidently didn't convince him.'

'That was clear to me at the time. Where did this tape come from?'

'Same place as the photograph.'

'How can Derek Oswin have come by it?'

'He's been preparing his case against Roger for years. Presumably, the tape originated with the medium. How Derek got hold of it I don't know. I'd be happy to ask him. *If* I could find him.'

'I fail to see how this . . . recording of a con trick . . . damages Roger.' She looked as if she believed her own words. But I knew she didn't. She *couldn't.*

'The medium mentions the look on Walter's face at the

maternity hospital. That's what convinced Walter he was really talking to Ann. Doesn't it convince you?'

Delia shrugged and said nothing. Her mouth tightened.

'They as good as come out and admit it. Roger wasn't their child. It's implied in more or less everything that's said.'

'Is it?'

'You know it is. Even if the medium is just acting a part, Walter isn't. "*Does Roger know?*" he asks. "*Did you tell him?*" What's he referring to, Delia? What's he so anxious about?'

'I really can't—'

'Yes, you can, God damn it.' I thumped the table as I spoke, rattling the cups in their saucers. Delia started back in her chair. 'Walter died intestate. He made no provision for Roger. He left no will naming him as his son. Irresponsible bordering on incomprehensible for a well-organized businessman with a large estate, wouldn't you say?'

'It was . . . an unfortunate oversight.'

'Bullshit. It was a tacit acknowledgement of the truth. Unlike your visit to Kenneth Oswin in hospital to tell him about Walter's intestacy. There was nothing remotely tacit about that.'

I'd wrong-footed her at last. She looked confused, weakened by a surfeit of contradictions and evasions. Braddock was right. She hadn't recognized him.

'You were seen, by an old friend of Ken's from Colbonite.'

'They must have . . . made a mistake.'

'Ken told him why you'd been there. He laughed about it.'

Delia closed her eyes for a moment and drew a long breath. Then she looked at me with much of her placidity and deliberation restored. 'Why are you doing all this, Toby?'

'Does it matter?'

'I believe it does. Your motive is actually transparent. To win back Jenny. As simple as that.'

'And pretty reasonable, given the kind of man – the kind of family – she's got herself mixed up with.'

'And what kind is that?'

271

'You tell me, Delia.'

'There have been tensions. Difficulties. I don't deny it. Since you insist upon pressing the point, I'll admit you're correct about Roger's parentage. Ann formed an attachment with Kenneth Oswin the summer before Roger was born. Walter was often away on business. Kenneth was shop steward at Colbonite and Ann fancied herself as some kind of socialist. She and Walter were going through a rough patch. He was . . . neglecting her, I suppose. And she was always . . . attracted to risk. Her pregnancy was a slap in the face for Walter. The doctors had already told him by then, you see, that he couldn't father children of his own. So . . .' Delia spread her hands eloquently. 'You may judge for yourself the anguish it caused. Ann told me the whole sordid story. She seemed in some strange way proud of herself. She delivered the son Walter craved. Our parents were delighted. They had no idea the baby wasn't really their grandson at all.'

'What about Gavin? He definitely didn't know?'

'I was the only member of the family in on the secret. Walter was deeply hurt, of course, but he doted on Ann quite pitifully. He couldn't bear the thought of losing her. He even agreed not to sack Kenneth Oswin because Ann threatened to leave him if he did. And he raised Roger as a loving father would. He never took out on him any of the pain he must have felt. In a sense . . .' Her voice drifted into silence. She smiled weakly. Then she resumed. 'I think that was his revenge. To make Roger so much like himself. To steal him from Ann. And he became more ruthless, of course. The Colbonite workforce – including Kenneth Oswin – suffered for that.'

'Why did Ann kill herself?'

'Self-destructiveness was part of her nature. As for the immediate cause, I can only guess. Shortly before her death, she confided in me that she'd decided to tell Roger the truth. He may not have reacted as she'd expected.'

'Meaning?'

'I think she wanted him to forgive her for betraying Walter.

I think she wanted to . . . reclaim him. To have his blessing, as it were.'

'Which wasn't forthcoming?'

'Perhaps not. I don't know. Roger and I have never discussed it. I don't even know for a fact that she went ahead and told him.'

'You heard the tape.'

'And you heard my opinion of mediums.'

'Is that why you visited Kenneth Oswin in hospital? To find out if Roger had told him he knew he was his son?'

There came another weak smile and a faint nod of her head. 'How very perceptive of you, Toby. Yes. It had long troubled me. With Walter gone, I felt I could safely ask the question.'

'What answer did you get?'

'An unsatisfactory one. Kenneth told me Roger had said nothing to him on the subject. Ever. And yet . . . I wasn't sure I believed him.'

'Why should he lie?'

'Ah. Clearly there are limits to your perceptiveness. But, as I said earlier, your motive is a narrow one. You seek only a reconciliation with Jenny. Have the decency to admit it, since you've obliged me to be so painfully honest. If she walked into this room now and said she wanted to revive your marriage, you'd happily forget Derek Oswin and Roger's alleged character flaws.'

'They're more than character flaws. Do you know why I missed the performance last night? Because *your nephew* held me prisoner and set in motion a plan to have me arrested for assaulting a prostitute.' The outburst had carried me too far. But it was too late to back out. 'Roger's scared, Delia. Do you know why? Not because he's afraid I'll steal Jenny from him. But because he's afraid Gavin will steal his inherited wealth from him, along with Wickhurst Manor, if he can prove Walter *wasn't* Roger's father and Roger therefore *wasn't* his rightful heir.'

'Nonsense.'

'You know it isn't.'

'On the contrary. I know it *is*. Listen to me carefully, Toby. You clearly have no understanding of the law. Even if Gavin could prove Kenneth Oswin fathered Roger, which would be next to impossible, he'd have no hope of persuading a court to overturn the settlement of Walter's estate on him, since Roger was born in wedlock and acknowledged by Walter as his son.'

Now *she* had wrong-footed *me*. 'Are you certain?' I mumbled.

'I made it my business to find out. As I'm sure Roger has. He has nothing to fear on that score.'

'But—'

'Which means he has no reason to engage in risky and illegal actions designed to prevent either you or Derek Oswin publicizing matters that can at worst merely embarrass him.'

'He held me in a locked room at Wickhurst Manor last night. And he instructed a drug dealer he knows called Sobotka to set me up on an assault charge. The police are probably already looking for me.'

'Really?' Her expression was suitably sceptical.

'Really. And truly.'

'It doesn't seem very likely.'

'But it happened.'

'So you say. But—' The ring of the wall-mounted telephone, modulated by the burbles and rings of various extensions elsewhere in the house, silenced Delia. She frowned, then rose smartly from her chair, marched across to it and picked up the receiver. 'Hello? . . . Oh, hello, darling. Still at the club?' The caller was clearly her husband. My attention drifted.

If Delia was right about the legal position, as I didn't seriously doubt she was, the tape and the photograph amounted to nothing but proof of a long-ago infidelity that posed no threat to Roger Colborn. But something did. That much I knew for certain. Something more than my love for Jenny and any affection she still harboured for me. But what could it be? What—

'Are you sure about this?' A note of urgency had entered Delia's voice.

When I looked towards her, I saw concern and puzzlement etched on her forehead. 'What can they possibly have been looking for? . . . Surely not. It's unthinkable . . . I've heard nothing from him . . . Of course . . . All right, darling . . . Yes . . . See you then. 'Bye.'

She put the telephone back on the hook and stared at me, her frown fading only slowly. She raised a hand to her mouth.

'What's wrong?' I prompted.

'The strangest thing,' she murmured.

'*What?*'

'John met somebody at the golf club this morning who lives at Fulking. Just down the road from Wickhurst Manor. He mentioned . . . well, it seems . . .' She moved slowly back across the room, but didn't sit down. She stood beside her chair, gazing out into the garden, collecting her thoughts, composing her words. 'It seems the police were at Wickhurst Manor last night. In force. It was described . . . as a raid.'

I remembered the dark-blue saloon car following Sobotka's van into Brighton after he dropped me near the bypass and felt a surge of relief. Maybe the police had picked up Sobotka before he could do his worst. Maybe I was in the clear after all. And maybe Roger wasn't. 'Did they make any arrests?'

'Apparently not. But they were there for some hours. John wondered if I'd heard from Roger. Or from our solicitor. He's Roger's solicitor too.'

'They're trying to link him with Sobotka, Delia. They were looking for drugs and any other evidence they could unearth.'

'I don't believe it.'

'I think you'll have to.'

'No. There has to be—'

The peremptory buzz of the doorbell cut her off. She glanced round, then down at me. The frown was back, in earnest.

'That could be them now,' I said softly. And it *was* a distinct possibility, one I faintly welcomed, whereas, before the phone call— The bell rang again. 'Are you going to answer it?'

'Wait here,' came the tight-lipped instruction. Then she was off down the hall, out of my sight, heels clacking on the wood-block floor. She reached the door just as the bell rang for a third time. It stopped in the instant that she turned the handle and pulled the door open.

It wasn't the police. I knew that before Delia said a word. I knew it by the nature of the brief silence that followed. 'Roger,' she said in quiet surprise. 'What brings you here?'

'Can I come in?'

'Of course. Please.'

I heard the door close and Roger clear his throat. There was another silence, as telling as it was fleeting. I didn't move a muscle. I may even have held my breath.

'Goodness,' said Delia. 'What happened to your eye?'

'I was attacked,' Roger replied, lisping slightly. 'By Toby Flood.'

'That's dreadful. Why would—'

'Jealousy. Pure and simple. The man's out of control. Which is why I have to contact Jenny. Urgently.'

'Don't you know where she is?'

'She went away for the weekend. To think, she said. She didn't want to be disturbed. After all the lies and innuendo Flood's filled her head with, I didn't blame her. But things have changed. Her mobile's switched off, so I have to find out where she's gone. I've tried her parents and her sister. No luck.'

'I don't see how I can help.'

'I thought she might have told you where she was going. In case of emergencies.'

'Well, I . . .'

'I'm right, aren't I? You do know where she is.'

'It's difficult. I . . . promised not to put you or Toby Flood in touch with her unless . . . well, unless . . .'

'Where is she?'

'I'm not sure I can—'

'*Where is she?*'

'Roger, let go. You're hurting me.'

'*Colborn,*' I shouted, jumping from my chair and striding to the door into the hall.

They were at the far end, near the foot of the stairs. Colborn had grabbed Delia by the wrist. He held on as he turned and looked towards me. He was gaunt and unshaven, dressed in black, his left eye haloed by a purple bruise.

'Let your aunt go,' I said, emphasizing each word. Slowly, with a half-smile, he released her. 'Of course,' I went on, suddenly eager to goad him, 'I use the word *aunt* advisedly. You're no blood relation to each other. Are you?'

'There's no need for this,' said Delia, flashing a look of irritation at me.

'What have you told him?' Roger demanded.

'Nothing,' I answered in her place. 'I'd already worked it out.'

'The hell you had.'

'Toby brought me a tape he wanted me to hear,' said Delia. 'Maybe you should hear it too.'

'What tape?' Colborn strode towards me along the hall and Delia followed him. I moved back to the table and, as they entered the room, pressed the PLAY button on the dictaphone.

The voices of Sir Walter and the medium Sir Walter clearly believed had contacted the spirit of his dead wife stopped Roger Colborn in his tracks. But only for a minute or so. Halfway through Ann's recollection of the expression on her husband's face at the maternity hospital, Roger moved to the table and stabbed the STOP button. He looked at me, then round at Delia. His thoughts were unreadable, his intentions unguessable. Did he have the gun on him? I wondered. It was hard to say if there was anything that heavy weighing down a pocket of his long, loose overcoat.

'I don't need to hear it again,' he said quietly.

'Did Derek send you a copy?' I asked, backing a sudden hunch.

'Somebody did,' Colborn answered levelly.

277

'You sent Sobotka to find the original at Viaduct Road, didn't you? But he didn't search thoroughly enough.'

'I don't know anyone called Sobotka.'

'I'm sure that's what you told the police, but the line's wasted on us. Probably on them too. They must have arrested Sobotka last night, before he could fit me up. Lucky for me. Unlucky for you. They'd already followed him to and from Wickhurst, I'm afraid, tying you in with his cache of drugs out at Fishersgate. Did they find anything incriminating when they turned the house over? We know about that as well, you see. Gossip on the nineteenth hole.'

'It's true,' said Delia, catching Roger's glance. 'John phoned from the clubhouse a few minutes ago. Alan Richards mentioned to him that the police . . . had been to see you.'

'Sorry I didn't tell you they had Sobotka's number, Roger,' I said. 'It must have slipped my mind.'

He pressed the EJECT button on the machine and took out the cassette.

'My guess would be that Derek made several copies. He's a belt-and-braces sort of guy. Whatever he may have told you, that's almost certainly not the original.'

'He's told me nothing.'

'You *have* spoken to him, then?'

'I didn't say that.'

'Where are you holding him?'

'I don't know what you're talking about.'

'Maybe you've released him now the police have started breathing down your neck. That would have been the sensible thing to do. But being sensible isn't always easy, is it?'

'Did you prevent Toby appearing at the theatre last night, Roger?'

Roger looked round at her. 'Is that what he's told you?'

'*Did you?*'

'Of course not.'

'But you do know this man . . . Sobotka?'

Roger sighed synthetically. 'All right. Yes. I know Sobotka. I used him for some . . . building work at Wickhurst. He's a bit of a rough diamond. I suppose it shouldn't come as a total surprise to learn he peddles drugs on the side. He was at the house yesterday. The police were obviously tailing him. They seemed to think – wrongly – that I'm the Mr Big in his operation. It may take me a little time to convince them I have nothing to do with it. In some ways, I'm sorry they didn't show up at the house earlier. They might have stopped Flood giving me a black eye.'

Looking at Delia, it was possible to conclude she actually believed Roger's version of events. I spread my hands. 'For God's sake.'

'Do you have anything to do with Derek Oswin's disappearance?' Delia persisted.

'I don't know where he is and I don't care,' Roger replied with studied weariness. 'He's nothing to me.'

'He's your half-brother,' I corrected him.

Roger glared at me. 'Congratulations on digging up that nugget of dirt on my family, Flood. Yes. Kenneth Oswin was my natural father. Delia's known that a lot longer than I have, so bringing it to her hasn't got you very far. As for the tape, if my father – the man I always regarded and still do regard as my father – was credulous enough to pay some tea-leaf reader to fake a *conversazione* with the spirit world, well, you know what they say, don't you? There's no fool like an old fool.' He tossed the cassette onto the table. 'It gets you nowhere. Absolutely nowhere.'

He was right. The thought hit me like a blow to the face. My ignorance of the finer points of intestacy had left me where I was now: swaying in the wind.

'I need to speak to Jenny, Delia,' said Roger. 'I think this has to count as an emergency, don't you?'

'I . . . suppose so.'

'I take it you *don't* believe any of Flood's allegations?'

'Well, I—'

'She visited Ken Oswin in hospital shortly before he died,' I interrupted, grabbing the only chance I seemed to have left of coming between them. 'I bet she's never told you that.'

Roger frowned. 'Is that true?'

'Yes.' Delia sat down in her chair between us. I read the move as an attempt to win some allowance for her age and sex. But she certainly had good reason to feel unsteady on her feet. 'I couldn't ask you if you knew he was your real father in case you didn't. I thought it likely, however, that if you did know you'd have spoken to him about it at some point. So, I . . . went to him and asked.'

'I knew. Thanks to Mother,' said Roger. 'But I never spoke to Ken Oswin about it.'

Delia nodded. 'That's what he said.'

'But you didn't believe him,' I put in.

'I had . . . some doubts, it's true.'

'Why?' asked Roger.

'I'm not sure. Clearly, I misjudged him. His . . . evasiveness . . . may have had more to do with his responsibility for Walter's death than anything else. Meeting the sister of the man he'd killed . . . may have unnerved him.'

'I suppose that accounts for it,' said Roger.

'I believe it must.'

'He never breathed a word to me about his relationship with Mother.' Roger picked up the snapshot of the Oswins, father and son, and stared at it for a moment. 'In all the years. Not a single word.'

'It must have been difficult for you,' said Delia softly. 'I'm sorry I—'

'Forget it.' Roger dropped the photograph. 'Toby here isn't interested in hearing about *my* problems.'

'You're still hiding something,' I said, determined to show him mere lack of proof couldn't shut me up. 'And I mean to find out what it is.'

'Of course you do.' He cast me a weary glance. 'I'd expect nothing less.' With a swirl of his coat, he moved past me and sat down in my chair, facing Delia. 'I have to speak to Jenny. Will you tell me where she is?'

'The Spa Hotel, in Tunbridge Wells.'

'Not so very far away, then.'

'She just needed . . . a chance to think.'

'Thanks to Toby and me messing her about.' Incredibly, Roger sounded genuinely remorseful. 'Poor Jenny.'

'If I leave a message on her mobile, she'll phone me back.'

'No need. I have a better idea.' He looked up at me. 'It's not much more than thirty miles to Tunbridge Wells. We could be there in less than an hour. That's we as in "you and me", Toby. What about it? You can say your piece to Jenny and I can say mine. You can tell her all about my shady parentage and apparently criminal associations. You can pull out all the stops. Subject to my right of reply. And when we're done, you and I, we'll see which of us she trusts the more. Which of us she really loves.'

'I'm not sure that's wise,' Delia began. 'If—'

'Leave this to us.' Roger's voice was raised now, his tone dismissive. He hadn't taken his eyes off me. 'What do you say, Toby? It's a fair offer.'

So it was, in a way. The very fact that he was making it smacked of desperation, or of deviousness. He had some trick up his sleeve, I felt certain. But he was daring me to believe I could trump it.

'Let's get it all out in the open. Give Jenny the choice. You or me. Or neither, I suppose. I'll stand by her decision. Will you?'

I could hardly reject the challenge, as Roger had surely calculated. In a sense, I'd been pressing for something of the kind all week. I had to accept. He knew that.

Which meant he was confident of the outcome. It wasn't a fair offer. It couldn't be. In fact, it was bound to be anything but. Nevertheless . . . 'All right,' I said. 'I'll go with you.'

'Good.' Roger stood up. 'Let's get going.' He moved past me to the door, then stopped and looked back. 'Don't forget to bring the cassette and the player, Toby. I'm sure you'll want Jenny to hear what's on the tape.'

His sarcasm made it certain that whatever happened in Tunbridge Wells he'd devised some way of coming out on top. All I could do now was cling to the hope that Jenny would see through him at the last. I loaded the cassette back into the machine and put it in my pocket, along with the Beachy Head photograph. Delia glanced at me anxiously, but said nothing. I held her gaze for a moment, then murmured, 'We'll speak later,' and headed after Roger.

'Don't worry, Delia,' he called, as he led the way down the hall. 'This is for the best, believe me.'

She made no reply and Roger didn't seem to expect one. We reached the front door. He held it open for me and I stepped out. His Porsche was parked on the drive. The house door slammed behind me and Roger fired his remote at the car, which unlocked and flashed a welcome. He walked past me and round to the driver's side, opened the door and slid into the car. He made no comment as I climbed into the passenger seat, merely started the engine and reversed out into the street.

And there, unexpectedly, he stopped. The Porsche idled throatily at the kerbside for several seconds. Then he said, 'Hold on,' threw the door open and jumped out.

'Where are you—' The slam of the door cut me short. And the answer to my question was soon apparent. He marched back up the drive of number 15 and rang the bell. He didn't glance once in my direction as he waited for Delia to respond. Then I saw the door open. He stepped inside.

I sat where I was, staring ahead at the wedge of sea visible between the houses. What was he up to? What could I do to outmanoeuvre him? I bludgeoned my mind for answers.

Several minutes passed. It suddenly occurred to me that Roger must have wanted to say something to Delia in my absence, something that would swing her sympathies away from me and towards him. Foolishly, I'd left the field open for him. There was no time to lose. I had to intervene.

Too late. He was already hurrying back down the drive. 'What's going on?' I snapped as he flung himself in.

'I just wanted to make sure Delia will keep this morning's events to herself.'

'Worried about the trouble Gavin might give you if he found out you're not his brother's son, are you?'

'Not worried. Keen to avoid it. There's a difference.'

'And did Delia promise to help you out?'

'Her lips are sealed.' He slipped the car into gear and started away in a burst of acceleration that carried us round the corner and along Clifton Terrace to the junction with Dyke Road, where he turned left and headed north.

By the time we'd reached Seven Dials and turned east towards Preston Circus, the silence between us had become heavy with tension. I broke it as defiantly as I could. 'However you spin it, Jenny isn't going to believe you, Roger. Do you realize that?'

'You reckon not?'

'I've known her a lot longer than you have.'

'True. But have you known her better?'

'I love her. I've always loved her.'

'Tell me why.'

'What?'

'Tell me why you love her.' The traffic was moving slowly ahead of us, through the lights under the railway bridges behind Brighton station. 'I'd really like to know.'

'I . . . er . . .'

'Not a fluent start, is it, Toby? "I, er." I suppose you actors need lines to be written for you before you sound convincing. You see, I don't think you do love her. Not in the way I do. I think you only want her back to prove you haven't ruined the most important relationship in your life.'

'A man like you is incapable of understanding love,' I fired back at him. '*That's* why I can't explain it to you.'

'I preferred the umming and erring. At least they were honest. I told you when we first met that I love Jenny because she makes me a better person than I can ever be without her. I told you that because it's true.'

'This "better person" is the man who held me captive last night and tried to frame me for assault.'

'You forced me into that.'

283

'Did I really? No doubt I forced you into hounding Denis Maple to his death as well.'

'I wasn't to know he had a heart condition. His death was unfortunate.'

'Unfortunate? Is that the best you can come up with?'

'It was Sobotka's doing, not mine.'

'But Sobotka was working for you.'

'He's been useful to me, certainly.'

'Like when he kidnapped Derek Oswin, you mean?' The traffic had eased and we were speeding along Viaduct Road now, past the very door of number 77.

'You're wrong about that, Toby. I called Sobotka off after Maple died. He didn't go near Oswin. Nor did I.'

'You'll be telling me next he didn't break into the Sea Air and steal my tapes.'

'I would, if I thought it'd do any good. I've no idea what tapes you're talking about.'

'You met Sobotka at Devil's Dyke car park Thursday morning. You were seen there by Ian Maple. So much for calling Sobotka off the day before.'

'*Ian* Maple? Who's he?'

'You can drop the pretence with me, Roger. It's pointless.'

'Sobotka's under arrest, Toby. He's facing a lengthy prison sentence for drugs trafficking. Doubtless he's doing everything he can to chalk up some points in his favour. Pinning something on me would win him a whole load of points. So, if he could lead the police to where you seem to think I'm holding Derek Oswin, he would. But he can't. Because I have no more idea where Oswin is than you have.'

We'd joined the Lewes Road and passed the turning that formerly led to Colbonite. Roger was driving faster as the traffic thinned on the dual carriageway out through the suburbs.

'You're the one who's been cosying up to Oswin this past week, not me,' he continued. 'You're the one who knows how his picky little mind works. So, it shouldn't really be beyond you to figure out why he's done a runner. Or where to.'

Could it be true? Had Derek vanished of his own accord? Had he faked his own abduction? I began to think about the scene at his house: the evidence of a struggle; the carefully scattered clues. It could have been stage-managed. Even the 'commotion' the neighbour had heard on Wednesday night could have been the work of one clever, calculating, painstaking man.

'Want to know what I think, Toby? I think Oswin's been pulling your strings all week. A twitch here, a twitch there. And off you've gone, causing me more trouble than he ever could.'

'No. It's his manuscript you're worried about. It's what he says in it about Colbonite. That's why you removed the original from Viaduct Road and stole the copy I'd sent to my agent.'

'Run past me how I managed that last bit, given that I didn't know you had it to send. I don't even know who your agent is. Or care.'

'Jenny could have told you.'

'Well, we can check that with her, can't we?'

'Derek can't have . . . done it all himself.' The words died in my throat as the implications of such a possibility ramified in my mind. There was more to consider than his apparent abduction. There were the stolen tapes, returned with a threatening message in which only his voice featured. And there was the missing manuscript, the damage it might do Colborn rendered tantalizingly unquantifiable. I hated Colborn because Jenny preferred him to me. It was as simple as that. And Derek knew it. The question was: had he exploited my hatred to serve his own?

'Do you know what the biggest irony is in all this, Toby? It's the fact that none of the digging for dirt you've done would have mattered if Sobotka hadn't gone and got his collar felt. He's been useful. But not useful enough to justify the risk he's exposed me to. I can't afford to have the police sniffing round my business affairs. They might catch a few iffy aromas. Chances are I can fend them off. But not if you feed

285

your suspicions into the works. I have a horrible feeling that would give their investigation more momentum than I can soak up.'

'I'm surprised you think you have anything to worry about,' I said bitterly. And it was true. I *was* surprised.

'That's because you don't know what's likely to emerge. Maybe Oswin does. I'm not sure. Either way, it's time I put *you* in the picture.'

'What do you mean?'

'I mean it's time I told you the truth.'

'You must be joking. *You* tell *me* the truth?'

'It's up to you whether you believe it, of course. But I think you will.'

'I doubt it.'

'Wait and see.'

He paused for a moment, concentrating on the flow of traffic as he joined the A27, eased the Porsche into the outside lane and took her swiftly up beyond the speed limit as we headed east towards Lewes. Then he resumed, his tone of voice bizarrely relaxed.

'You and Jenny would still be together if you hadn't lost your son. Let's be honest, now. You would be. Peter's death was too big a blow for you to bear. You blamed yourselves and each other. And the blame drove you apart. Most of all, though, the loss did that. The grief. The pain. The having him and then the not having him.'

'If you're expecting me to thank you for your six penn'orth of psychological platitudes, then—'

'I'm making a point, Toby. Bear with me. If I'd died aged four and a half, do you think my parents would have parted? I don't. In fact, I suspect they'd have drawn closer together. *Back* together. Because I wasn't theirs. Not wholly. I *wasn't* their son. I was twenty-eight when Mother told me who my real father was. *Twenty-eight.* I thought I knew exactly who and what I was. Then she took it away from me. She had some idea that I needed to understand her. She was egotistical to the last. Suicide's a pretty selfish act, don't you think?'

286

'Depends what leads to it.'

'In my mother's case, the realization that I wasn't going to forgive her. Driving off Beachy Head, where she'd staged so many calculatedly indiscreet assignations with Kenneth Oswin, was her way of making me feel guilty for not stopping her. It was her last mistake. I didn't blame myself for what she'd done. I blamed her.'

'But you never told your father that you knew the truth.'

'My legal father, you mean? No.'

'So there was never any chance *he* might blame you.'

'Ha. You reckon that's why I said nothing to him, do you? Nice try, Toby. But wide of the mark. I said nothing because he said nothing. I wanted to be as real a son to him as I could be. And I believed he wanted the same.'

'Didn't he?'

'Not strongly enough, as it transpired. He hankered after Mother. More and more as he aged. I didn't know about the medium until I was sent the tape. If I had, I'd have put a stop to it. As it was, I had to deal with the consequences as best I could.'

'What consequences?'

'His abrupt change of heart. His U-turn on the question of compensation for Colbonite workers suffering from cancers supposedly caused by exposure to a chloro-aniline curing agent we used in the dyeing shop. Suddenly, he was all for giving them every penny he had. And every penny I stood to inherit from him. The séance was a set-up. I'm sure of it. The medium was probably one of our former employees, or the relative of one. "Whatever wrongs you've done, it's not too late to put them right." Remember that line? Money's what she was talking about. A commodity that doesn't count for much in the spirit world.'

'You don't believe the medium was in touch with your mother, then?'

'Of course I don't. It was a scam. But a clever one, I admit. Father swallowed it whole. He suddenly saw a way to assuage the guilt he felt for not saving Mother from herself by

287

throwing money around in a fit of late-life generosity. I tried to talk him out of it, but his mind was made up.'

'Some would say he simply saw the error of his ways.'

'Only people with soft hearts and simple minds. We've got a National Health Service to look after the sick and dying. None of the so-called victims had any claim on my birthright.'

'Even though one of them was your real father?'

'What had Kenneth Oswin ever done for me? I owed him nothing. The debt was all the other way.' Roger sniggered. 'Though I suppose you could say he paid it off in the end.'

'What do you mean?' I asked, even as his meaning began to dawn on me.

'I couldn't let Father squander the capital the sale of Colbonite had left him with. I'd been loyal to him. I'd done his dirty work. And I wasn't about to be cheated out of my reward. I couldn't make him see reason. He was determined to go ahead. So, I had to stop him.'

'You're saying—'

'Oswin killed him at my bidding, Toby. Yes. You've got it.'

'But . . . why would he . . .'

'I promised to look after Derek. Financially, I mean. Oswin was dying. And he was worried his son wouldn't be able to cope without him. As we've seen, I think he underestimated the resourcefulness of my half-brother, as you kindly defined him. So, the deal was that I'd featherbed Derek for the rest of his life . . . provided Oswin made sure I had the means to do so.'

'You . . . played one father off . . . against the other.'

'That's one way to put it. And I'll tell you what, Toby. They both deserved it.'

'You welched on the deal, didn't you?'

'No. Valerie Oswin did that. I'd made an initial payment to her husband, without which he'd never have gone ahead, and another afterwards. But the cheques were never cashed. After he died, she sent them back to me. Exactly how much she knew, I have no idea.'

'And Derek, what does he know?'

288

'Nothing, I suspect. His father had every incentive to keep our agreement to himself. And that's where it could – and should – have stayed. Our secret. Mine and a dead man's. But now, of course, I've been forced to share it with you.'

'I haven't forced you.' That was surely true. Indeed, I couldn't understand why he'd revealed so much to me, glad though I was that he had – for more reasons than he needed to know. My puzzlement on the point made little impact on me at that moment, however, amidst my astonishment at discovering how coolly and almost casually, by his own admission, he'd arranged his father's murder.

'Blame circumstances, then. Perhaps it's fairer to,' he went on. 'They've conspired against both of us, I'm afraid. Have you noticed, by the way, that we're not on the right road for Tunbridge Wells?'

'What?'

He braked heavily and flicked on the indicator. 'We should have taken a left at the last roundabout but one.' The car slowed sharply to a crawl. Roger steered it up over the grass verge and we came to a juddering halt by an overgrown five-bar gate. 'This is the Eastbourne road.'

I was still trying to absorb all the implications of what he'd confessed to and, come to that, why he'd confessed. The sudden switch of subjects to the banalities of route-finding barely registered. As far as that went, I took him at his word, realizing I'd been unaware myself of our surroundings for several miles. I assumed he was about to turn round and head back, although there hardly seemed room for the manoeuvre. But he didn't attempt to. Instead, he jumped out of the car, strode round to my side and pulled the door open.

As he did so, I saw the gun in his hand, held low, where no passing driver would glimpse it, displayed for my benefit alone. 'Move over, Toby.'

'What the hell's going on?'

'*Move over to the driver's seat.*'

'Why?'

'Just do it. Or, believe me, I *will* shoot.'

I looked into his eyes and read there only deadly seriousness. The fear of imminent death jagged into me. 'All right,'
I said. '*All right*.' I released the seat belt, then cautiously
levered myself over the gearshift and handbrake and settled
behind the steering wheel.

'Belt up,' said Roger. I obeyed. Then he slipped into the
seat I'd just vacated and slammed the door, shutting out the
rush of traffic. He pushed himself well back and away from
me, the gun still held in his hand, still pointing straight at me.

'I thought we had an agreement,' I said, my voice unsteady.

'We do. I just didn't mention all the caveats. But then,
neither did you. Like taping our conversation.'

'I don't know what you mean.' I did, of course, and can't
have sounded genuinely uncomprehending. But I had to
mount some kind of pretence.

'You ran the tape to the end of the séance when I went in to
see Delia, then started recording when I came back out. I saw
you reach into your pocket to press the button as I came down
the drive. I probably wouldn't have noticed, but I was looking
out for it, you see. I was expecting it.'

'Why didn't you stop me?'

'No need. What can be recorded can just as easily be
erased.'

'You want the tape?'

'Not yet. And there's no need to switch the machine off.
Let's just carry on as we are. Start driving.'

'Where to?'

'Straight ahead.'

'To Eastbourne?'

'Just drive. I'll handle the navigation.'

I put the car into gear, edged out into the traffic and took
her up to fifty.

'Give her a bit more. She likes to cruise.'

I accelerated. We flashed past a sign: EASTBOURNE 10,
HASTINGS 22. The road ahead was a ribbon of drizzle-glossed
black between dun-green fields. Low grey cloud had camped
on the downs to our right. The chilling thought struck me that

I might never see the sun again. This could be it: a dull winter's day my last on Earth.

'Nothing to say, Toby? Perhaps you should stop recording after all.'

'Why don't you do the talking?' I cast him a quick glance. 'You've done most of it so far.'

'Why do you think I've told you the truth?'

'I don't know.'

'Think about it.'

'*I don't know.*'

'I'm serious. Think, Toby. What possible purpose could it have served? Take your time. Mull it over. We've a few miles to go yet.'

'I could never prove you conspired with Kenneth Oswin to murder your father.'

'Without the tape, you mean? No. I don't suppose you could. But you could tell Jenny what I've told you. If you could convince her it was true, she and I would be finished.'

'She wouldn't believe me.'

'Maybe she would. Maybe she wouldn't. Who can say? If someone else corroborated the story, of course, she'd have to believe it. She'd have no choice.'

'No-one else knows. You said so yourself.'

'Did I? I must have forgotten Delia.'

'*Delia?*'

'She prevaricated when you challenged her about her hospital visit to Oswin. I noticed the way she avoided my eye when she said she had a few "doubts" about Oswin's truthfulness. I could see it was more than that. She knew he'd lied when he denied I'd spoken to him about my parentage. And she knew why he'd lied.'

It was suddenly as clear to me as it was to Roger. '*Why should he lie?*' I'd asked her. '*Ah,*' she'd replied. '*Clearly there are limits to your perceptiveness.*' Yes. There were limits to my perceptiveness. But not, apparently, to hers.

'When did she rumble me, I wonder?' said Roger, musingly. 'There and then in the hospital with Oswin? Or later? Well, it doesn't matter now. It doesn't matter at all. Because I've devised a solution to all my problems. And you're it, Toby.'

'What?'

'I'll explain when we reach our destination. Speaking of which, I need to set up our rendezvous there with Jenny.' He plucked a mobile phone out of his pocket with his free hand.

'Don't drag her into whatever you're planning, Roger.' I glanced pleadingly at him. 'For God's sake.'

'Don't worry. At least' – he gave me a lopsided grin – 'don't worry about Jenny. She's going to be fine. I'll make sure of that. Now, keep your mouth shut.' He extended his arm until the barrel of the gun was jabbing into my ribs, then punched in some numbers on the phone and held it to his ear. A few seconds later, he got an answer. 'Good morning. I need to speak to one of your guests urgently. Her name's Jennifer Flood. My name's Roger Colborn. Yes, I'll hold.' A few more seconds passed. 'Thanks.' Then a few more. When he next spoke, it was in a tone I hardly recognized as his. 'Hello, my sweet . . . Look, I'm sorry, but I persuaded Delia to tell me where you were staying . . . I know, but . . . Well, this *is* an emergency, I'm afraid. It's Toby. He's become completely unreasonable . . . None of my doing, I promise . . . I'm on my way to meet him now . . . I had to agree for Delia's sake . . . Well, naturally that's a worry, especially after what happened yesterday . . . He came to the house . . . Not pleasant, no . . . Look, I can't see this ending well unless you're there to talk him round . . . You will come, won't you? . . . It's for the best. We need to put a stop to this . . . Beachy Head.' So. Our destination was the place where Ann Colborn had gone to kill herself twenty years ago. My heart was racing now, sweat beading on my upper lip. Most of what Roger was telling Jenny he seemed to be making up as he went. But his prediction was spot-on. I couldn't see this ending well either. 'I don't know,' he continued. 'It makes no sense. But then he *isn't* making sense . . . Yes . . . The lay-by closest to the lighthouse . . . Right . . . You'll see the car . . . OK . . . Yes, I will be . . .

292

See you soon . . . Love you . . . 'Bye.' He rang off and dropped the phone back into his pocket.

A minute or so of silence followed. Then I asked a question I wasn't sure I wanted answering. 'Why are we going to Beachy Head?'

'I'll explain when we get there.'

'But we're not just going to talk to Jenny, are we? We could have done that in Tunbridge Wells.'

'No, Toby. We're not just going to talk.'

'You said that if I could convince her you'd paid Kenneth Oswin to murder your father, she and you would be finished. You must realize the same certainly applies if you kill me.'

'That's true. So, maybe I won't kill you. *Maybe.* You'll find out soon enough. Until then, I'm not sure we have anything more to say to each other. Just drive. I'll give you directions when you need them.'

'But—'

'*Shut up,*' he shouted so loudly that I flinched. 'Question time's over.'

Aside from telling me which turnings to take and when, Roger Colborn didn't say another word as we skirted Eastbourne and headed south across the empty, rolling downs towards the end of the land and the end of our journey.

My fear didn't diminish as we went on. If anything, it increased. But I began, slowly and slightly, to control it, to calm my mind just enough to think about what he might be planning.

Little good it did me. If he meant to kill me, he surely wouldn't have told Jenny where we were going. But, if he meant to let me live, how could he guarantee I wouldn't, sooner or later, tell her what he'd confessed to me and play her the tape to prove it? How, come to that, could he be sure Jenny wouldn't phone Delia and be given a version of events wildly inconsistent with the one he'd just presented?

It made no sense. And yet it had to. Colborn was calm and confident. He knew exactly what he was doing. He'd thought of everything. He had a plan. And I was central to it.

293

The next words I spoke were, 'Is this where your mother came?' We were in a lay-by on a sharp curve in the road along Beachy Head. Beyond a low bank, the ground sloped up ahead of us for less than a hundred yards to the cliff top. It was cold and grey and drizzly, cloud drifting like gunsmoke across the hummocked turf and wind-sculpted patches of gorse, the disused lighthouse on the bluff to the east blurred by the misting fret. There wasn't another car – another human – in sight.

'Yes,' said Colborn, in laggardly answer to my question. 'Witnesses reported that she sat here in the Jag, engine running, for several minutes, then drove straight up the slope – and over.'

'If you're planning some kind of double suicide . . .'

'No. Turn the engine off if it'll reassure you.'

It did, though not a lot. Silence wrapped itself around us, broken by the mournful wail of the foghorn on the new lighthouse out of our sight at the foot of the cliff.

'There was no bank round the lay-by when Mother killed herself,' Colborn resumed. 'But then it's only really intended to prevent accidents. You could get over easily enough with a few runs at it. Then it's a straight drive to a sheer drop of more than five hundred feet. Death guaranteed. It's a popular spot for suicide. Twenty or so every year. And the number's climbing. It draws them. The closeness to the road. The certainty. The symbolism. End of land. End of life.'

'Why are we here?'

'For you to make a choice, Toby. For you to decide what happens to us – you, me and Jenny.'

'What choice do I really have? You're holding the gun.'

'It'll be another half an hour at least before Jenny arrives. We have some time. Just enough, in fact.' He stretched forward, opened the glove compartment, took out a pair of thin leather driving gloves and tossed them into my lap. 'Put those on.'

'Why?'

'Do it. Then I'll explain.'

'All right.' I pulled them on. 'Now, why?'

'Because there has to be some way to account for your fingerprints not being on the gun. *If* it's ever recovered.'

'What are you talking about?'

'It may have struck you that if Jenny phones Delia – as she well might – she'll realize I've lied to her.'

'It's struck me.'

'Not actually a problem, however, because if Jenny does phone Delia, she won't be able to speak to her.'

'Why not?'

'Delia's dead, Toby. That's why not.'

I looked round at him. 'You . . .' The horror of what he was saying burst into my mind. 'You . . . killed her . . . when you went back . . . into the house?'

'I had to. She knew what I'd done. I mean, she probably knew a long time ago. But this morning she knew without a shadow of a doubt. And with you as an ally, she wouldn't have let it lie. Believe me. I had no choice. It was her or me. I asked her for the phone number of the Spa Hotel. She'd written it on a post-it note stuck to a cupboard door in the kitchen. I shot her through the back of the head as she reached up for it. There was a lot of blood. More than I'd expected.' He took something out of his pocket – a small, crumpled piece of bright-red paper – and stuck it to the dashboard: it was the post-it note; as it curled up, I saw that the back was still the original yellow. 'Lucky I was standing out in the hall. I didn't get a speck on me.'

'My God.'

'I left the car engine running so you wouldn't hear the shot.'

'You're mad. You must be. To . . . murder your aunt.'

'I don't feel mad. And it was you who reminded me that she wasn't really my aunt at all. Besides, I didn't do it. You did, Toby. You went back in and shot her, then forced me to drive here at gunpoint, phoning Jenny on the way.'

'No-one will believe that.'

'I think they will. You intended to kill us both and have

Jenny arrive to be confronted by the tragic consequences of rejecting you. But the enormity of what you'd done to Delia got the better of you. You decided at the last moment to spare my life. You let me get out of the car. Then you drove it off the cliff.'

'I won't do it.'

'I can't force you to. But if you don't, when Jenny arrives . . . I'll kill you both.'

'*What?*'

'I won't let you have her, Toby. There's no way in this world I'll allow that. If you try to drag me down, I'll take us all down.'

'You said . . . you love her.'

'I do. More than life itself.'

'You *are* mad.'

'That's your opinion. And this is your choice. Prove *you* love her. By sacrificing yourself to save her. I'll look after her. I'll help her get over it. I'll make her happy. Happier than you ever could. I'll even keep the tape in a safe and secure place so that one day, after my death, the truth will be uncovered. You'll be a hero. A posthumous one, it's true. But a hero none the less.'

I stared at him, sick with the certainty that he wasn't bluffing. He'd already killed once. Twice, if you counted his father. He had nothing to lose. If I didn't take the blame for what he'd done, he'd destroy us all. The offer to salvage my reputation one day was so unlikely it might even be genuine. But we'd both be dead by then, in my case long dead, though probably not forgotten. Abandoning Jenny to a man I knew to be a murderer was a strange way to prove my love for her. Yet the alternative was worse. Only one question mattered. Would he do it? Would he kill her if I refused to co-operate? *Would he?*

'What's it to be, Toby? Death and glory? Or just death?'

'You said I had a choice.'

'So you do.'

'It doesn't feel like it.'

'Should I take that as a yes to death and glory?'

'Maybe.' It was a yes to something. But to neither of the options he'd presented. I could see only one way out. And it was by no means certain.

'I'll leave you to it, then,' he said. 'Hand over the tape.'

'I'll swap it for the gun.'

'Nice try, Toby. But the gun stays with me. You might reckon killing me is a smarter choice than suicide. Or you might bottle out at the last moment and try to drive away. I can't risk that.'

'The police won't buy your story unless the gun's found on me.'

'I'll drop it over the cliff after you. They'll conclude it was thrown out on impact.'

My escape was barred. It had been a frail hope that in truth was no hope at all. 'Don't do this, Roger. Please.'

'Too late for appeals to my better nature, Toby. Far too late. My mind's made up. Is yours?'

'Hold on. Let's—'

'No. Let's nothing. You give me your answer. Now.'

'All right. I . . .' His gaze was fixed and unblinking. I took a deep breath. 'I'll do it.'

'Good. I knew you'd see it my way.'

'You mean you knew I'd have to.'

'Exactly. Stop recording now and give me the tape.' He held out his left hand. 'The rest . . . will be silence.'

Flood, Toby (1953–2002)
Bland English character actor. Started on the stage,
then broke into TV as *Hereward the Wake*. A few
film appearances, but Hollywood did not take to
him. He returned to the stage, without his former
success. Committed suicide at Beachy Head after
murdering a woman in Brighton, where he was performing in a play.

Some such form of words, from a future edition of *Halliwell's
Who's Who in the Movies*, recited itself in my head as I sat at
the wheel of Roger Colborn's Porsche and he climbed slowly
out of the passenger seat, closing the door behind him with
perfectly judged force. I saw him move away, then stop and
look back at me.

I felt sick. My hand trembled as I reached for the ignition
key. My breathing was shallow, my pulse racing. My palms
were moist with sweat. I cursed Colborn and fate and my own
stupidity for finding myself seemingly only a few minutes
away from the death he'd arranged for me. I was going to end
my life on Colborn's terms. I had to. Because every alternative was worse. That, apparently, was to be Toby Flood's
quietus.

I started the engine, clunked the gearstick into reverse and
edged back from the bank bounding the lay-by. Tears were
fogging my vision now, tears of anger and fear and utter
despair. I blinked them away and looked up the slope to the
broken, dipping edge of the cliff. Beyond it, I knew, was thin
air and the sea far below – a plummet to certain death. 'Dear
Christ,' I murmured. 'What a bloody awful way to go.' I
slipped the gearstick into neutral.

Then I saw movement ahead of me. A figure had emerged
from behind one of the clumps of gorse and thorn dotting the
slope and was hurrying towards me across the grass. It was
a mop-haired man, dressed in duffel-coat, jeans and desert
boots. It was Derek Oswin.

I glanced at Colborn and realized he hadn't yet seen the

approaching figure. I couldn't even guess what would happen when he did. And I had only a few seconds in which to forestall him. I yanked on the brake and jumped out.

'What the hell are you doing?' shouted Colborn. 'Get back in the car.'

'We have company, Roger,' I responded as I rounded the bonnet. 'You'd better put the gun out of sight.'

Colborn glanced round and saw at once what I meant. He drew his right arm in close to his side, shielding the gun from Derek's view. A spasm of cold fury crossed his face and he shot me a glare that implied I was somehow responsible for this apparition.

'Mr Flood,' Derek called. 'And . . . Mr Colborn.' He reached the top of the bank and stood there, looking down at us. He was breathing hard, his cheeks flushed from exertion. 'I th-th-thought . . . I'd f-find you here.'

'Where have you been these past few days, Derek?' I asked. 'I've missed you.'

'A . . . guesthouse in Bognor Regis. Very . . . r-reasonably p-priced . . . at this time of the year. I'm . . . sorry if I . . . caused you any . . . anxiety.'

'You trashed your house yourself, didn't you?'

'I . . . m-messed it up a little, it's . . . true.'

'Stole my tapes.'

'B-borrowed them . . . Mr Flood.'

'And stole the manuscript from my agent.'

'R-reclaimed.'

'I told you,' said Colborn, in a steely undertone.

'Why?' I asked softly, the anger I should have felt at being manipulated by Derek Oswin supplanted by a steadily growing hope that his intervention might somehow save the day.

'To . . . see what would happen.'

'"*See what would happen*"?'

'But I . . . think I went too far.'

'That, Derek, is the understatement of the century.'

'It's a b-bit early to say, d-don't you think . . . Mr Flood? W-with . . . ninety-eight years st-still to go . . . I mean.'

'How did you know we'd be here?'

'I d-didn't. Not for certain. It was just . . . a hunch. I've been ch-checking the house each day . . . to see if you'd discovered the t-tape in the globe. I must . . . have just missed you this morning. When I found the tape was gone, I knew you were on the last lap. Thanks for pinning Captain Haddock back on my coat, Mr Flood.' He was talking more confidently now, the stutters and hesitations fading. 'I went to see Uncle Ray, to find out if you'd spoken to him . . . about Dad . . . and Mrs Colborn.' Slowly, as Derek continued, Roger Colborn turned to look at him, crooking his arm behind his back to obscure the gun. 'He told me you'd gone to see Mrs Sheringham, so I got him to drive me round there. P-Powis Villas was cordoned off by the police. There'd been a m-murder. Of Mrs Sheringham . . . one of the neighbours said. She'd seen Mr Sheringham, looking . . . very upset. And a P-Porsche had been spotted . . . driving away. Well, I knew what that meant. I g-guessed . . . Mr Colborn . . . would bring you here . . . b-because of his mother. I left Uncle Ray . . . in the car park . . . at the Visitor Centre.' He nodded in the direction of the building whose roof I could just make out through the murk on the eastern skyline. 'I . . . suppose, logically, I shouldn't have come. I mean, you could argue my plan's . . . worked out b-better than I could ever have hoped.'

'Go on, then,' said Roger. 'Argue that.'

'Well, you're . . . finished, aren't you . . . Mr Colborn?' For the first time, Derek was addressing his half-brother directly. 'I've b-brought you down.'

'It wouldn't have worked if you'd stayed away, Derek,' I said, edging closer to Colborn. 'He'd devised a way to pin the murder on me. After I'd conveniently driven off the cliff.'

Derek blinked at me in surprise. And then at Colborn. 'R-really?'

'Yes,' said Roger. 'Really.'

'That's t-terrible. I'd . . .' Derek looked back at me. 'I'd n-never . . . have let him . . . get away with that . . . Mr Flood.'

300

'No,' said Roger. 'I don't suppose you would. Which makes your arrival here . . . quite fortuitous.'

I saw the decision taking shape in the sudden tensing of Colborn's face. He could still pull it off, by blaming a second murder on me, one that only increased his chances of laying the first at my door as well. He swivelled to face Derek, swinging the gun out from behind him and taking his eyes off me as he did so.

I slammed into his midriff in a stooping charge, capitalizing on the only advantage I had: weight. I caught him off balance and he fell. The gun went off with a deafening crack close to my left ear. We hit the tarmac hard. For the moment, I could hear even less than I could see. I looked up in desperate search of Derek. And there he was in front of me, hopping down the bank and bending to grab the gun which had slipped from Colborn's grasp as we fell.

'Run,' I shouted. And Derek did run, back up the bank and away across the grass towards the cliff, the gun clutched by the barrel in his right hand.

Then Colborn's elbow struck me hard under the chin, hurling me sideways with my tongue viced agonizingly between my teeth. I rolled onto my back, then struggled up to see Colborn already over the bank, racing in pursuit of Derek. I scrambled to my feet and headed after them.

They were about ten yards apart and stayed that way, fear offsetting for Derek any edge Colborn's greater athleticism should have given him. They were running hard across the wet turf, following a beeline to the edge of the cliff. My lungs strained as I followed them, my chest tightening, my left ear ringing. I could hear nothing except my own panting breaths, could see nothing but the two figures ahead of me, one in black, one in brown, moving like fleet ghosts in the thickening fret.

Derek came to a stumbling halt a few feet short of the edge and tossed the gun over. Then he turned to face Colborn, who'd stopped in the same instant, those vital ten yards behind. But I kept running.

Derek was smiling. He opened his mouth and spoke, but I couldn't catch the words. Whether Roger said anything in reply I had no way of telling. He glanced back over his shoulder at me, judging my distance, measuring his moment. Then he turned and ran straight at Derek.

Derek's only chance was to run away from the edge, towards Roger. But he shrank back, if anything closer to the edge. Maybe he hadn't realized what Roger's final way out of all his problems was to be. Or maybe he *had* realized. Maybe that was why he didn't try to evade his brother's embrace.

They went over together, Roger's arms wrapped round Derek's waist, the momentum of his charge carrying them out a yard or so into the grey void before they began to fall.

They were still together when I reached the edge. I dropped, gasping, to my knees and watched the few remaining seconds of their descent.

They struck the foot of the cliff and rolled apart down the beach. The sea lapped in around them. And retreated, foaming red.

That was then. This is now. Late. Very late. Too late, for Derek Oswin and Delia Sheringham. And for Roger Colborn too. Three deaths. And every one of them could have been mine.

Late, like I said. But still too early to impose a strict order on the events that followed that double fall from the cliff. I remember the lighthouse offshore, banded the colours of blood and chalk; the cliff face, pale as bleached bone; the seagulls, muted by my deafness, gliding wraithlike in and out of the mist; and Derek's strange, triumphant smile. I remember all those things. Their clarity seems to grow, indeed, as much else fades.

I flagged down a car and the driver called the police on his mobile. He ferried me the short distance to the Visitor Centre, where I found Ray Braddock waiting patiently for his godson to return. I can't recall how I broke the news to him, nor how he reacted. He was sitting in his car, hunched at the wheel, staring straight ahead, when I walked away.

I returned to the lay-by and waited by the Porsche for Jenny. Maybe it was just as well, in the circumstances, that the police arrived before she did.

Initially, it was just one patrol car. The two policemen in it got the message in the end that this was no routine suicide and contacted Brighton CID. A coastguard crew followed and surveyed the scene down on the beach from the cliff top. They started to set up some sort of derrick preparatory to winching down with stretchers to recover the bodies.

Then Jenny did arrive. Exactly what the police told her I couldn't catch. Whatever it was, she clearly couldn't take it all in at first. The officers tried to keep us apart. I remember the look on her face as she stared at me between their broad shoulders across the lay-by. She probably still thought Roger had been telling the truth when he phoned her from the car. She probably thought I was mad. She started shouting. '*What have you done?*' And crying. '*What have you done?*'

Two more police cars arrived. I was bundled into one of them and driven to Eastbourne General Hospital. On the way, I noticed that my ear had been bleeding. I was fast-tracked through Casualty and into a cubicle, burly policeman in attendance. A young doctor looked me over. He pronounced the eardrum intact and said my hearing would slowly recover over the next twenty-four hours. It already was recovering, in fact, though shock prevented the improvement doing much for my coherence.

Then a familiar face showed up: Sergeant Spooner. I was loaded into another police car and driven to CID head-quarters on the northern outskirts of Brighton. There I was put in a blank-walled interview room, given a mug of tea and a ham sandwich and left alone for more than an hour. What they were waiting for I didn't know. Most probably they were listening to the tape I'd told them they'd find in Roger Colborn's pocket and trying to decide for themselves what

303

had happened that morning at Powis Villas and Beachy Head – and why.

Eventually, Spooner came in with Inspector Addis and the questioning began. They knew now that I'd lied to them yesterday when they'd asked me about Ian Maple. But, thanks to the tape, they also knew I'd stopped lying. We went through everything, step by step. At least, I suppose we did. I can't recall more than a fraction of what was said. I should probably have asked for a lawyer to be present. They may even have encouraged me to. But I couldn't see the point. There was only one story to tell now: the truth.

In the end, Addis couldn't seem to decide whether to reprimand me or sympathize. The gist of what he said was that Ian Maple and I should have come to him with our suspicions on Thursday. Then none of this need have happened. Three people who were now dead would still be alive, Ian wouldn't be in hospital with a smashed leg and I wouldn't be . . . I think he left me to sum up my condition for myself. I didn't argue. I didn't have the strength, let alone the will.

'You can go now, sir,' he said at some point, after I'd signed a statement and drunk some more tea. 'When will you be returning to London?'

'Tomorrow, I expect.'

'I dare say we'll be in touch with you there. The press will be on to you for certain, you being a bit of a celebrity and all. Tell them nothing. If I hear you've sold your story to one of the tabloids, I may have to take a serious look at whether you should be charged with breaking and entering, or wasting police time, or . . . whatever. Catch my drift?'

'You seriously think I want this splashed over the papers?'

'I don't know, sir. You might decide it'd be helpful to your career.'

'Talking of which, sir,' put in Spooner, 'we spoke to a Mr Sallis at the theatre and explained the situation. As best we could.'

'Thanks.'

'Will you be wanting to be dropped somewhere? We can arrange a car.'

'I'd like to . . . see my wife.'

'Not sure I'd recommend that, sir. I gather she insisted on remaining at the scene until they'd brought up the bodies. Wanted to be certain Mr Colborn really was one of them, I suppose. That was pretty upsetting, as you can imagine, given the state they were in and the fact that Mr Braddock was there as well. A WPC's with her out at Wickhurst Manor as we speak, waiting for Mrs Flood's sister to arrive. A Mrs Butler. I presume you're acquainted with the lady.'

'Yes. We're acquainted.' It was natural enough for Jenny to turn to Fiona in a crisis.

'We'll be seeing Mrs Flood later to report our preliminary conclusions. It might be best if you postponed a visit until after that.'

'Perhaps I could . . . phone her.'

'Be our guest.'

'And those . . . preliminary conclusions. What are they?'

'You already know, sir,' said Addis. 'You knew before we did.'

Spooner brought in a phone for me to use, then I was left alone. I stared at the thing for several minutes, struggling to form some words into a sentence that might somehow measure up to the bloody havoc I'd played no small part in inflicting on Jenny's life that morning. I still hadn't succeeded when I picked the phone up and rang her mobile. It was switched off and I didn't leave a message. I tried the house number instead.

The WPC answered and seemed reluctant even to ask Jenny if she wanted to speak to me. She came back to say that Jenny was too upset to come to the phone. I sensed a wall was being thrown up between us. But for the moment there was nothing I could do to break it down.

*   *   *

305

In the end, I declined the offer of a lift and left the police station on foot. Business was frenzied at the nearby super-store. I walked past the jam-packed car park and looked up at the shoppers wheeling out their laden trolleys. It was a normal pre-Christmas Saturday evening for them. The murder at Powis Villas and the deaths at Beachy Head were minor news items. Their futures were unaltered, their lives unaffected. The world went on its way. As it always does.

I can't remember how far I was intending to walk. I doubt in fact if I had much in the way of intentions at all. Somewhere in the seemingly endless sprawl of housing I found myself wandering through, I boarded a bus to the Old Steine. I sat at the back and kept my head down. No-one noticed me.

I felt numb, disconnected, overwhelmed by events. My hearing had recovered, but my thinking hadn't. I slunk into a crowded pub in St James's Street and downed several whiskies. Probably more than several. Then I headed for the Sea Air.

Eunice's greeting was double-edged. She was relieved to see me in one piece, alive and relatively well. But she was also angry over my failure to keep in touch.

'It's only thanks to Brian Sallis and the police that I haven't been worried sick about you. Though what they told me didn't exactly stop me worrying. Seems you've been through the mill, Toby, and no mistake, so I suppose I'd better not be as hard on you as I'm tempted to be. Come downstairs and I'll rustle you up something to eat.'

Protesting that I wasn't hungry did me no good and I was soon perched blearily at the breakfast bar in her kitchen, picking at cauliflower cheese and admitting to myself that, of all the various ends to the day that had seemed possible to me in the course of it, this had certainly not featured.

'What did Brian say?' I wincingly enquired.

'That you'd got mixed up in some dreadful goings-on and been taken hostage by a murderer. Is that really true, Toby?'

'Oh yes. It's true.'

'But the murderer threw himself off Beachy Head?'

'Yes.'

'And you were there at the time?'

'Yes. I was.'

'It's mortifying just to think about it.'

'So it is.'

'The things that happen while we law-abiding folk are going about our daily lives.'

'I'll tell you all about it . . . when it's not so raw in my mind.'

'But the murderer . . . was your wife's . . .'

'Can we leave it, Eunice? I honestly can't—'

'Sorry.' She gave me a sudden and genuinely affectionate hug. 'You don't want me rabbiting on.'

'It's all right. I . . . What did Brian say . . . about the play?'

'Nothing. Except that . . . well . . .'

'What?'

'They're coping without you.'

I managed a rueful half-smile. 'No doubt he meant that to be reassuring.'

'You could always . . . phone him.'

'I don't think so.'

'Are you still planning to go back to London tomorrow?'

'I suppose so. It's probably best, after all. Look at what's happened in the six days I've been here.' I thought about that for a protracted moment, as a forkful of cauliflower cheese congealed on the plate in front of me. 'Yes. It's probably best.'

That was not so long ago. This is now. Late. Very late. Too late, for Derek Oswin and Delia Sheringham. And for Roger Colborn too. But for Jenny and me? I don't know. She should be grateful to me for discovering Colborn's true nature before she married him. But I doubt she feels grateful. I doubt that very much.

I should give her a chance for the shock to fade, of course, for the grief to give way to an understanding of what he was and what he did. I should go back to London and bide my time. I should let my own wounds heal as well as hers.

Yes. That's what I should do. That's definitely what I should do. It's for the best.

Probably.

SUNDAY

I have no memory of lying awake until the small hours last night, struggling to accommodate in my mind everything that had happened. I would have expected sleep to be as hard to come by as hope and consolation, but, strangely, it wasn't. Exhaustion asserted its imperative. I plunged into a deep, absolving unconsciousness.

I hadn't closed the curtains of my room and was woken by the stealthy grey onset of dawn. A few seconds later, I realized that, no, I hadn't dreamt the events of yesterday. Only in a fast-fading dream, in fact, could I walk along a railway viaduct with Derek Oswin high above Brighton and pull him back from the parapet when he seemed about to fall. In the real world, where I dwelt and had to go on dwelling, he was beyond saving. Nor was he alone in that.

I showered and shaved hurriedly, then dressed and packed for my departure, sensing it might be best if, when I returned later, I could just grab my bag and go. Whatever logic and calculation had suggested was my wisest course of action, it wasn't what I meant to do. I had to speak to Jenny. I had to *see* her. Without delay.

But someone else had decided to see *me*, also without delay. As I closed the door of the Sea Air quietly behind me and stepped out into the dank, chill, silent morning, there was a

311

beep on the horn of one of the cars parked on the other side of the street.

It was a battered old Metro. The driver's window had been wound down. And Ray Braddock was staring out at me.

I walked slowly across to speak to him, wondering what I'd find to say and remembering Colborn's taunt about actors needing lines to be written for them before they could sound convincing.

'Sneaking off back to London?' Braddock asked. He was unshaven, his eyes red-rimmed, his manner bleak.

'I'm sorry about Derek, Ray,' I said, holding his gaze determinedly. 'Truly I am.'

'You said you'd look after the boy.'

'I don't think I—'

'You said it would all blow over.'

I let his accusing glare seep into me. 'I was wrong.'

'I tried to stop him going round the cliff to find you and Colborn. I told him to think of himself. But he wouldn't have it. "I got Mr Flood into this," he said. "I've got to get him out."'

'He said that?'

'He did.'

'Well, he was as good as his word, Ray. He got me out.'

'He saved your life.'

'Yes.'

'At the cost of his own.'

'No doubt you wish it was the other way about.'

'I do.'

'But you can be proud of him. You really can. Isn't that something?'

'When you're old and poor and lonely . . . it's sod all.'

'I'm sorry.' It was true. I *was* sorry. But it was also true that my sorrow wasn't enough. For either of us.

'I don't think Derek got you into anything,' said Braddock. 'I think you got yourself in. And I wish to God you hadn't.'

'You may be right. In which case . . .' I shrugged. 'I wish the same.'

'Do you now?' Braddock's anger suddenly ebbed. His

312

expression softened marginally. He shook his head dolefully. 'Fool to himself, that boy. Just like his father.'

'There are worse things to be.'

'So there are.' He sighed. 'If you want to . . . show your respect . . . for what he did . . .'

I suddenly noticed that he was proffering something to me through the window: a small white card. I took it and found myself looking at the name, address and telephone number of a local undertaker.

'They'll be able to tell you when the funeral is.'

'Thanks. I . . .'

'It's up to you.' Braddock started the car. 'I'd best be off. Looks like someone else wants to speak to you.'

'What?' I turned and saw Brian Sallis standing on the pavement outside the Sea Air in his jogging kit.

'Good morning, Toby,' he said solemnly.

'Brian. I . . .' I walked across to him, glancing round as I heard the Metro draw away.

'Who was that?'

'Derek Oswin's godfather.'

'I see.' Brian gave me what was meant to be a sympathetic pat on the shoulder. 'This has been a bad business.'

I nodded. 'You can say that again.'

'I've been trying to raise you on your mobile.'

'I . . . mislaid it.'

'Where are you off to now?'

'The taxi rank in East Street.'

'Can I walk with you?'

'Sure.'

We set off and reached the end of Madeira Place before another word was spoken, the right thing to say proving equally elusive for both of us.

'I'm sorry . . . not to have been in touch,' I said as we rounded the corner into St James's Street.

'Don't worry about that. At the time, we were all pretty narked, but . . . well, from what the police tell me, the circumstances were about as extenuating as they come.'

'I gather you coped without me.'

'I went on for you.'

'Yes.' I winced at the thought of Brian stumbling through my part, script in hand. 'I suppose you had to.'

'It's been a while since I did any acting, I know, but . . . I quite enjoyed it, as a matter of fact.'

'I've never experienced someone going on with the book. I can't believe it's enjoyable, though.'

'Well, actually . . .'

'What?'

'By last night, I was word perfect. I'd already boned up on the part, you see. With Denis gone and you . . . behaving erratically . . . I . . .'

We were crossing the Old Steine as Brian mentioned Denis, no more than fifteen yards from the fountain where I'd found him dead on Tuesday night. I kept my eyes fixed on the middle distance, straight ahead. 'You saw it coming, did you, Brian?'

'Not . . . what happened. Of course not. I mean . . .'

'It's all right. I understand. How did Leo react to news of my absence?'

'Ballistically. But he doesn't know the reason yet. When he does . . .'

'He'll soften. But not enough to hire me again in a hurry.'

'I wouldn't say that.'

'You don't need to.'

'Look, Toby, you've been through a terrible experience. I don't want to add to your woes. I'll make sure Leo appreciates that you missed the last three performances through no fault of your own.'

'Thanks.'

'When are you going back to London?'

'Later today.'

'Probably wise. I haven't heard from the press, local *or* national, so I'm guessing they haven't tied you in with yesterday's events yet. But they will. It'll be easier to lie low in London than here. Unless you're going on somewhere else, of course.'

'I haven't thought that far ahead.'

'Most of us are catching the eleven fifty up to Victoria, if you want to—'

'There are things I have to do first, Brian.' I stopped at the corner of East Street and signalled to the driver of the only taxi on the rank. 'I doubt you'll see me on the eleven fifty.'

'How's Jenny taken all this?'

'I don't know. That's one of the things I have to do.'

There was no sign of the press out at Wickhurst Manor either, which was a blessing. I had the taxi driver, a mercifully tight-lipped bloke, drop me at the end of the lane leading to Stonestaples Wood as an additional precaution and approached the firmly closed gates on foot.

At first, there was no response to the intercom button. But I persisted, reckoning there was close to no chance that Jenny would be anywhere but at home. If Wickhurst Manor could properly be regarded as her home any more, that is.

Eventually, there *was* a response. I recognized the voice as Fiona's. 'Yes?' She was probably expecting the press. She sounded as if she meant to see off whoever it might be in short order.

'It's me, Fiona. Toby.'

There was a brief silence. I thought I heard a sigh. 'You shouldn't have come here, Toby.'

'I have to see Jenny.'

'That's really not a good idea.'

'Let me in, Fiona. Please.'

'I . . . don't think I can.'

'For God's sake . . .'

'You should have phoned first.'

'I'll go into Fulking if you like and phone from the call box for an appointment.'

'Don't be ridiculous.'

'Then, let me in.'

'No.'

'Fiona—'

315

'Sorry, Toby. I have to put Jenny first. Phone later. Maybe tonight. Or tomorrow. But not now.'

She switched off the intercom and I was left staring at the grille, rooks cawing around me in the trees, a fine drizzle filming the steel plate set in the pillar in front of me. I pushed the button again. There was no answer.

I stepped back and surveyed the gates. It looked as if someone younger and fitter than me could climb them.

But they weren't about to try. I was.

Fiona opened the front door of Wickhurst Manor five minutes or so later with the weary look of someone who knows what they're going to see. A sororial resemblance to Jenny has never extended in her case to a fondness for me. She's always regarded actors as suspect by definition – unstable, unreliable and essentially undesirable.

'Couldn't you just for once have taken my advice?' she snapped, pursing her lips irritably.

'It didn't sound like advice.'

'That's because you weren't listening properly.'

'Can I come in?'

'What have you done to your leg?' She glanced down at my left ankle. There was a V-shaped tear just above the hem of my trousers where I'd snagged them on the spike at the top of one of the gate pales. When I looked down myself, I saw there was blood seeping through the hole. Fiona gave a heavy sigh. 'Come into the kitchen. And keep your voice down. Jenny's asleep. I'd like her to stay that way.'

I followed her into the hall and round to the large north-facing kitchen at the back of the house. Its windows looked out onto the lawn I'd crossed under cover of dusk on Friday afternoon. My last visit to Wickhurst Manor felt far more distant to me than it really was, almost from a different age.

'Sit down there,' said Fiona, pointing to a chair by the kitchen table as she closed the door behind us. 'And roll up your trouser leg.'

For the next few minutes, she busied herself with soap,

water, Dettol and sticking plaster in a fashion I guessed her two sons would easily recognize, repeating phrases like 'Such a very stupid thing to do' under her breath as she cleaned me up. The dog wandered in from the scullery, regarded us mournfully, and wandered back out. Then Fiona pronounced the job done and turned briskly to more serious matters.

'You shouldn't have come, Toby, you really shouldn't. Have you any idea how big a shock this has been to Jenny?'

'Yesterday didn't exactly pan out as I'd expected either.'

'But you haven't lost a fiancé, have you? Or a close friend. Delia's death seems to have affected her almost as deeply as Roger's. And it's hard for her at the moment not to blame you for both.'

'*Me?*'

'She loved Roger, Toby. Learning he was capable of murder doesn't alter that overnight.'

'More than capable. Guilty.'

'Yes. I know. He was a monster. A bigger one than I ever suspected. But, let's face it, if you hadn't—'

The door sprang open and Jenny walked into the room. She was in a dressing-gown and slippers, her hair scraped back, her face pale, almost grey, but for the moist redness round her bloodshot eyes. She'd been crying and was clearly still on the verge of tears. And she was trembling, her fingers shaking as she smoothed the collar of her robe, her lips quivering as she looked at me and tried to speak.

Fiona and I both stood up. Fiona moved towards her. But Jenny held up a hand, signalling that she needed a little distance, a little space in which to compose herself.

'I thought you were sleeping,' said Fiona.

'I heard the door,' Jenny responded after a few seconds' delay, like someone communicating via an interpreter. 'And Toby's voice.'

'I had to come,' I said, willing Jenny to hold my gaze over her sister's shoulder.

'I suppose you did.'

'Can we talk?'

'Would you be able . . . to drive Toby back into Brighton, Fiona?'

'Of course,' Fiona replied.

'Good. Just . . . give us a few minutes . . . would you?'

'OK. I . . .' Fiona glanced round at me, then back at Jenny. 'OK.'

She slipped out of the room then, closing the door gently behind her. I heard myself swallow nervously in the silence that followed. Then the dog pattered back into the room and ambled to Jenny's side, where he nosed at her hand.

'He misses his master,' she said neutrally, almost observationally.

'How are you—'

'*Don't*. Please don't.' Her voice cracked. She took a deep breath. Then another. 'Just listen to me, Toby. Please. The police told me everything. I know it all. What Roger did to his father. Both his fathers. And to Delia. And to Derek Oswin. What he *tried* to do to you as well. I never . . . saw that side of him. It seems I never . . . grasped his true nature. I've been a fool. An utter fool. Maybe I should thank you for forcing me to understand that.'

'I never meant it to turn out like this.'

'Of course not. Who would? But if you'd waited till I got back . . . If you'd only . . . bided your time . . . nobody need have died yesterday, need they? That's what I can't help thinking, you see. Delia, Derek Oswin, Roger. They'd all be alive. With plenty to face up to, it's true. With a great deal to answer for, in Roger's case. But they'd be *alive*. Living and breathing. However dreadful it would be, at least we could talk about it, Roger and I. At least—' She stifled a sob. 'I blame myself. For involving you. For letting you . . . back into my life. I should have known better. I really should. You kill everything you touch.'

Grief and anger and a measure of shame were mixed in what she'd said. I knew that. The one victim she hadn't mentioned – our son – had been added implicitly to the list. Fiona was right. I'd come too soon. And Jenny was right too. I hadn't known when to bide my time. I never had. There was nothing I could say in answer to the charge. I stared at her with a tenderness I couldn't express. I forgave her. For not forgiving me.

'I can't think about the future now,' she went on. 'There's just . . . too much to contemplate. John – Delia's husband – is distraught. The police will be back. And the press will be onto the case. It's all . . . horrible. Too horrible for words. That's why I can't bear there to be any between us, Toby. Words, I mean. I just . . . can't do it.' She pressed the heel of her hand to her eyes and looked at me. 'Please go. We'll talk. Of course we will. We'll have to. But not here. Not now. Not . . . any time soon. You understand?'

I didn't speak. I didn't even nod. But she took some fractional narrowing of my gaze as a kind of confirmation. I didn't agree. I didn't accept. Yet, nevertheless . . . I understood.

'Please go.'

Nothing was said during the drive into Brighton. Fiona, never one to waste her words, didn't bother to point out how big a mistake my visit to Wickhurst Manor had been. It was as she'd tried to warn me it would be. It was too soon. And it was probably too late as well.

'Shall I wait outside while you pick up your luggage, then run you up to the station?' Fiona asked as we headed down Grand Parade towards the Sea Air. She'd broken her lengthy silence, I noticed, only for the most practical of reasons.

'Thanks,' I replied. Then I remembered what the numbing anguish of my parting from Jenny had blotted out. I wasn't yet free to go – even if I wanted to. 'Actually, no. Drop me at the hospital. There's someone I have to see.'

Ian Maple was in a room of his own, off a ward deep in the rabbit warren of the Royal Sussex. His right leg wasn't in a plaster cast, as I'd expected. Instead, the section between the knee and the ankle was held fast in an armature of wires and

319

pins. That apart – which was a lot to disregard – he looked well. And his greeting was somewhat warmer than I'd expected.

'I wondered if I'd see you before you left,' he said by way of lightly ironic opener.

'I must have caused you a lot of anxiety by holding out on the police,' I responded, lowering myself onto a bedside chair. 'I *am* sorry.'

'I guessed you had good reason.'

'I thought I did, certainly.'

'I'm not sure they ever seriously thought I was in business with Sobotka, anyway. They just couldn't see the big picture, that's all.'

'They see it now.'

'Yeah. Three dead, including Roger Colborn.' Ian shook his head. 'I wanted to make someone pay for what happened to Denis. But this . . . is too much.'

'Jenny blames me for the way it's turned out.'

'You didn't force Colborn to murder his aunt. Or Derek Oswin. You couldn't have predicted how the guy would react under pressure.'

'No. But I'll tell you something, Ian. I was determined to find out.'

'And now you have.'

'Yes.' I looked past him. 'Now I have.' My gaze wandered to his braced and cradled leg. 'What do the doctors say about that?'

'That it'll mend. Slowly. I might need another operation. I'll definitely need a lot of physiotherapy. I'll be off work . . . for months.' What was his work? I realized I'd never bothered to ask. 'I'll have to go to Denis's funeral in a wheelchair.'

'When will it be?'

'Thursday. Golders Green Crematorium.'

'I'll see you there.'

'Yeah. Time enough to worry about the future after that, hey?'

'Oh yes.' I nodded. 'Plenty of time.'

*   *   *

I headed down to Marine Parade after leaving the hospital and walked slowly west towards Madeira Place through the cold, dank morning. The sea and the sky were two merged planes of grey, the horizon as murkily indefinable as the future. The pier, where I met Jenny a week ago, loomed ahead of me, just as our meeting, and the foolish hopes I'd vested in it, faded behind me into the past. It was time to leave. But I had nowhere to go.

It was nearly noon when I reached the Sea Air. Brian and most of the cast and crew of *Lodger in the Throat* would be on the train to London by now. It was safe to make my own exit from Brighton, to beat my solitary retreat. I went straight down to the basement to say goodbye to Eunice and settle up. That would be it, I reckoned. I'd be on my own then.

How wrong can you be? Eunice had a visitor. More accurately, *I* had a visitor.

He was perched at the breakfast bar in her kitchen, a mug of tea cradled in one hand, a grin plastered across his face. Blazered, cavalry-twilled and cravatted, Sydney Porteous was lurking in wait for me.

'There you are, Tobe,' he said, winking. 'Eunice had me half-believing you were going to stand me up.'

'What are you doing here, Syd?'

'Our lunch date. Don't you remember?'

Sunday lunch at Audrey's, with Syd. Yes, I did remember, albeit hazily, though why I'd agreed I certainly couldn't recall. 'I'm sorry. I'm going to have to cry off.'

'On account of these desperate goings-on Eunice has been telling me about? Understandable reaction, Tobe, entirely understandable. But let me urge you to reconsider. Not only because of Aud's legendary roast spuds, but because I reckon a spot of company could be just the ticket, given the doleful circs. You need taking out of yourself. And you can trust me to do the taking out.'

'I don't think so.'

321

'Syd's right, Toby,' Eunice put in. 'Go and have lunch.'

'Do you two know each other?' I asked, the conviviality of the atmosphere finally registering with me.

'Syd and I were in the same year at Elm Grove Primary,' Eunice trilled.

'Until the old man hit the jackpot and enrolled me at Brighton College,' said Syd. 'Who knows what might have happened if we hadn't been split up?' He rolled his eyes.

'Sorry, Syd. It's still no go. I've got to get back to London.'

'Why the big hurry?'

'It's . . . complicated. I just . . . have to go.'

'You won't regret staying on for a few hours, believe me.'

'Even so . . .'

'Truth is, Tobe, you *have* to stay.'

'Sorry?'

'You can't leave. Not yet.'

'What?'

'You see . . .' Syd cleared his throat and grew suddenly serious. 'There's something I need to tell you. And you *do* need to hear it.'

I couldn't decide whether Syd was bluffing or not. In the end, it seemed easier to let him reveal the answer in his own good time. We loaded ourselves into his undersized and under-powered Fiat and set off towards Woodingdean, where I was given to understand Audrey Spencer lived and was even then labouring for our benefit over a hot stove.

'Bloody awful what happened yesterday, Tobe,' Syd said, much of his *bonhomie* gone now we'd left the Sea Air. 'Worse for you than anyone, of course, but a real choker for anyone who knew the people involved, even so.'

'How did you hear about it?'

'Gav was on to me last night with the gory details. Cold-blooded bastard, that bloke. No love lost between him and Roger, it's true, but you'd think Delia's death would knock him back. It certainly knocked me back. Not Gav, though. All he seemed bothered about was his inheritance.'

'Inheritance?'

'Roger's estate. Gav is sole surviving heir. Unless Roger bequeathed the lot to Battersea Dogs' Home. Which I doubt, worse luck. You'd have thought Gav had won the Lottery the way he was going on.'

'As you say. Cold-blooded. Like his nephew.'

'You ought to know I had a chinwag with Ray Braddock this morning. He told me what happened out at Beachy Head. I had a word with a copper I know as well. Seems you're a lucky man, Tobe.'

'I don't feel lucky.'

'Derek saved your life.' Syd glanced round at me. 'That's how I read it.'

'You read it right.' Something in the tone of Syd's voice and the look on his face when he mentioned Derek was strange, familiar, almost . . . affectionate. 'You talk as if you knew him.'

'I did.'

Syd slowed abruptly. We were driving along the open northern side of the Racecourse now. He flicked the indicator, pulled into a gateway and stopped. The passing traffic rocked the car as it sped by. Drizzle began to mist the windscreen. I said nothing.

'I've got you out here under false pretences, Tobe. There's no lunch waiting for us at Aud's. She's too upset to eat, let alone cook.'

'Why is she upset?'

'Because she knew Derek too.'

'How come?'

'She's a psychic, Tobe. A medium.'

'Audrey Spencer is a medium?'

'Yup.'

'A *practising* medium?'

'Now. *And* seven years ago. When Sir Walter Colborn consulted her.'

'My God.'

'Not sure if God comes into it, Tobe. Heaven. Hell. Purgatory. That's all down to your choice of religion, if you want to choose one. I'm strictly Church of Agnostics myself. But the spirit world? It's out there somewhere. Aud's convinced me of that. Her . . . powers . . . don't brook many quibbles, take my word for it.'

'You're saying she really put Sir Walter in touch with his dead wife?'

'I didn't know Aud then. But she's no con artist, that's for quite sure and absolutely certain. She believed it. Wally believed it. Well, you know that, don't you? You've heard the tape.'

'Yes. I've heard it. But I didn't recognize the woman's voice on it as Audrey's.'

'You wouldn't. She sounds different . . . in her trances. Halfway between herself and . . . whoever she's contacted.'

'Hold on.' A thought had struck me. 'You must have known about the tape hidden at Viaduct Road all along.'

'I gave Derek my word I'd keep out of his . . . campaign. Bumping into you at the Cricketers was a pure-as-the-driven-snow coincidence. Seeing where it might lead didn't mean I'd broken my promise – as long as I didn't blow the whistle on Derek.'

'Audrey gave him the tape?'

'Wally left her in no doubt that he meant to do right by the Colbonite workers who were ill and the families of those who'd already died, as per Ann's urgings from beyond the grave. When he went to his own grave so soon after, Aud smelt a rat. She didn't do anything about it at first. But as the cancer cases kept mounting and Roger aren't-I-a-smart-arse Colborn kept popping up in *Sussex Life* society spreads, she . . . decided to act. She contacted Derek Oswin and told him what she knew. She records all her séances. Once Derek had listened to the tape of the one she'd held for Wally, there was no holding him. He went after Roger . . . in his surprisingly effective way.'

'You should have told me.'

'I'm a man of my word, Tobe. Hard though you may find that to believe. My hands were tied.'

'You should have stepped in. Before everything . . . got out of control.'

'I would have done, if I'd known what was going to happen. Just as you would have done, I guess.'

'Don't Audrey's powers extend to foreseeing the consequences of interfering in people's lives, then?'

'No.' Syd smiled at me ruefully. 'Since you ask, they don't.'

We sat in silence for a moment. Such anger as I felt faded as quickly as it had flared. It seemed we both had regrets aplenty.

'How's Jenny?' Syd asked eventually.

'Much as you'd expect.'

'Taken it hard, has she?'

'What do you think?'

'I think she's taken it hard. Aud's pretty cut up too. You ought to be prepared for that.'

'I thought lunch was off.'

'It is. But meeting isn't. She wants to see you.'

'Any particular reason?'

'Oh yes.' Syd started the car and squinted into the wing mirror. 'A very particular reason.'

A modern semi-detached house in a Woodingdean cul-de-sac isn't exactly the *locus operandi* I'd have imagined for a medium, genuine or otherwise. There were certainly no occupational trappings on view when Syd and I arrived. Audrey Spencer was waiting for us in her neatly decorated home, the sparkle in her eyes I remembered from our previous meeting replaced by welling tears, some of which she transferred to my cheek in the course of a welcoming hug.

'There are no words to describe how I feel, Toby,' she said, leading me into the lounge. 'Nor you either, I dare say. What a terrible, terrible thing to have happened.'

'Tobe reckons we should have levelled with him sooner, darling,' said Syd.

'It's useless to think such things,' Audrey responded, sinking into a sofa. 'Yet it's impossible not to.' She waved me into an armchair on the other side of the fireplace and gazed across at me. 'You can be no harder on me than I've been on myself, Toby. Blame me if you like. I don't mind.'

'I blame all of us,' I said, truly enough.

'Well, there's sense in that,' said Syd, settling on the sofa beside Audrey and closing his sausage-fingered paw round her clutched hands and the damp tissue squeezed between them. 'But blaming isn't undoing, if you know what I mean.'

'I wanted to punish Roger Colborn for thwarting the good intentions Ann had inspired in Walter,' said Audrey. 'It's not often my calling has such an obviously beneficial effect. To see it frustrated as it was rankled with me. Through Derek I saw a way to do something about it.'

'You succeeded,' I said. 'Roger was certainly punished.'

'Yes. But for Derek to die as well . . . and poor Mrs Sheringham . . .' Sobs overcame her. Syd released her hands so that she could staunch her tears with the tissue while he wrapped an arm round her shoulders and whispered some soothing endearment in her ear. 'I'm sorry, Toby. Please forgive me. I feel things . . . perhaps a little more deeply than I should.'

'Don't worry. It's all right.'

'You should tell him now, darling,' Syd prompted. 'About the tape.'

We'd come, then, to Audrey's *very particular reason*. Syd swivelled round to pluck some replacement tissues for her from a box on a shelf behind the sofa. She dried her eyes and blew her nose.

'Well, Toby, the thing is this. None of us may have foreseen these dreadful events. But it seems . . . Derek had some inkling . . . that it might all go terribly wrong.'

'How do you know that?'

'I . . . sense certain things, Toby. It's part of my calling. Or my curse, depending how you look at it. Anyway, this morning I . . . played the tape of the séance I conducted for Walter. Derek copied the original and returned it to me several months ago. Something made me . . . play it to the end. And there I found . . . waiting for me . . . for us . . . a message . . . from Derek.'

'What did it say?'

'Hear for yourself.' She picked up a remote that had been lying, unnoticed by me, on the arm of the sofa, aimed it at a hi-fi stack in the corner of the room and pressed a button.

There was a click from the tape player, followed, after a pause of a few seconds, by Derek's voice.

'I don't know whether you'll ever hear this. Perhaps I'm being too clever by half. Dad often said I was. And Dad was right about most things. Not everything, though. He shouldn't have accepted Roger Colborn's offer. He shouldn't have agreed to kill Sir Walter. The fact that he did it for my sake only makes it worse. But he was ill. He wasn't thinking straight. I forgive him. Roger Colborn wasn't ill, though. He knew exactly what he was doing. I don't forgive him. And I won't, until he's paid for what he did. I've thought of a way to make him pay now. It involves Toby Flood, the actor. He's coming to Brighton in December to perform in a play. His estranged wife, Jennifer, lives with Roger Colborn. That's the connection I propose to exploit. I'll tell you about it soon. But not all about it. There are risks, you see. More than I'll let you know of. They'll be worth running, though. I hope to do more than punish Roger Colborn. I hope to make him see the error of his ways. And to atone for them. I also hope to persuade him to acknowledge me as his brother. Because that's what we are. Brothers. And brothers shouldn't be apart. They should be together. Which is what I think Roger and I can be, at the end of this, if all goes well. But if it doesn't go well, I want you to know that it's my fault. Not yours, Mrs Spencer, or Mr Porteous's, or even Mr Flood's. But mine. I accept full responsibility for the

consequences of my actions. Dad would have said
that's what growing up is all about. Thanks for
helping me understand what I have to do, Mrs
Spencer. And just in case I need to say it: goodbye.'

'Derek exonerates us, Toby,' said Audrey, after the tape
had run to the end and clicked off. 'One and all.'

I looked across at her. 'But can we exonerate ourselves?'

'I don't know. I only know he'd want us to. And therefore
. . . perhaps we should.'

'Will you try to contact him?' I asked Audrey a little while
later, as I stood in the open doorway of her house. Syd was
already sitting in his car, waiting for me, with the engine
running. I'd left the obvious question late. But not too late.

'Of course,' she replied. 'But the dead speak – or not – as
they please. I don't contact them. *They* contact *me.* I'll try.
But the question is: will he? He may have said . . . all he has to
say.'

'Do you think he really knew what was going to happen?'

'Yes. But without necessarily knowing that he knew. They
died together, didn't they, he and Roger? Together. Not
apart.'

It was true. I'd seen them fall. I knew. Derek had been
acknowledged by his brother. In the end.

Neither Syd nor I felt the need to say much as we drove back
to the Sea Air. Syd's loquacity had reached its limit long since.
And my thoughts could no longer be expressed in words.

It was a relief in a way to find that Eunice wasn't at home. I
fetched my bag from my room, left the key, a farewell note
and a cheque on the hall table, then let myself out.

'That was quick,' said Syd as I climbed back into his car.

'Eunice wasn't there,' I explained.

'We can wait, if you like.'

'No need.'

'Had a bellyful of goodbyes, have you, Tobe?'

328

'Yes. I think I have.'

'Understood.' He started away. 'I'll keep ours short and sweet.'

'Thanks. In return, I won't take you to task for playing fast and loose with the facts during our sessions at the Cricketers.'

'I never told you any out-and-out porkies, Tobe.'

'Didn't you?'

'Well, maybe just the one. And it didn't amount to anything.'

'Which one was that?'

'When we first bumped into each other in the Cricketers last Sunday, I told you I'd met Joe Orton there on a Sunday night in the summer of 'sixty-seven. Not strictly true, I have to admit. In fact, not true at all.'

'You made it up?'

''Fraid so.'

'Why?'

'Sensed our chance encounter was slipping through my fingers. Needed something to get your attention. Keep us talking. Simple as that.'

'But how did you know you could get away with it? I've read Orton's diaries. He was in Brighton the last weekend of July, nineteen sixty-seven. And he was out on the town, alone, on the Sunday night. So, theoretically, you could have met him. I can't believe you just got lucky with your choice of day.'

'Ah, well . . .' Syd treated me to a sly, sidelong grimace. 'Truth is, there was this dwarf lodging in the same house as me back then. Used to perform on the pier. Made up in personality what he lacked in height. After Orton's murder was splashed all over the papers, he told me he'd—'

'It's OK,' I interrupted, recalling Orton's matter-of-fact account of oral sex in a Brighton public convenience on Sunday, 30 July 1967. 'I get the picture.'

'You do?'

'In Cinemascope. Besides . . .' We'd passed the Royal Pavilion by now. It wasn't much further to the station. 'You don't have time to do justice to the story, Syd. Leave me to imagine the details.'

Fifteen minutes later, I was sitting alone at a table outside Bonaparte's Bar at the edge of the station concourse, sipping a whisky to while away the half-hour I had to wait for the next train to London. I'd pulled my copy of *The Orton Diaries* out of my bag to double-check Syd's story. Orton's encounter with Syd's neighbour, the cottaging dwarf, was much as I remembered it.

What I'd forgotten, though, was that afterwards Orton had gone into the station for a cup of tea. The café he'd used had presumably transmogrified itself since into Bonaparte's Bar. Selling whisky on a Sunday afternoon back then would have been inconceivable as well as illegal, of course. But that and most of the other changes were largely superficial. Thirty-five years, four months and one week ago, Orton could have been sitting exactly where I was sitting today.

'*I had a cup of tea at the station,*' he wrote. '*I thought a lot about* Prick Up Your Ears.' (The next play he was planning to write, but, in the event, never did.) '*And things in general.*'

Ah yes. Things in general. 'They can be a bugger, can't they, Joe?' I murmured.

The train was announced. I went through the barrier and boarded one of the front carriages, hoping that would mean no-one would sit next to me. I'd bought an *Observer* to hide behind if I needed to.

I looked out of the window. There was a view across the platforms of the station car park, washed with rain, and, beyond that, the soaring flank of St Bartholomew's Church. I checked my watch. We'd be under way in a few minutes. I was taking my leave of Brighton. My week was over. My time was up. In so many more ways than one.

Then I saw something I couldn't quite believe. A woman was hurrying across the car park towards the station: a woman in jeans and a short waterproof; a woman I recognized very well.

I watched, transfixed, as she moved out of the rain into the shelter of the station canopy and headed along the far platform towards the concourse, her pace quickening as she went.

Then I too started moving.

I forced a passage to the barrier through a ruck of London-bound passengers. Jenny was standing beyond them on the concourse, staring at me between their shoulders and hoisted bags. They were there, jostling past me. But, in another sense, they weren't there at all.

My ticket wouldn't operate the exit gate. I kept looking at Jenny as I moved to the manned barrier, mumbled a request to be let out and was ushered through.

'I didn't expect to see you,' was all I could manage to say when I finally reached her.

'I didn't expect you would either,' she said softly.

'How did you know which train I was catching?'

'I didn't. I went to the Sea Air first. Eunice had just got back and found your note. She hadn't been out long, though, so we reckoned it was worth me coming on here. I very much wanted . . . not to leave things as they were.'

'How do you want to leave them, then?'

She shrugged. 'I'm not really sure.'

I went back to Bonaparte's Bar. This time, I wasn't alone. I bought Jenny a cup of coffee. And myself another whisky. We sat at the table I'd only recently vacated. The London train pulled out. The hubbub it had generated died. The concourse grew quiet enough for me to hear the cooing of a pigeon from some perch above us in the station roof.

'I don't know what to say,' I admitted.

'Neither do I,' said Jenny.

'Shall we just sit here, then?' I suggested. 'Until we think of something.'

We looked at each other. Several seconds passed. Then Jenny smiled hesitantly. 'Yes,' she said. 'Let's do that.'
And we did.

End of transcription

LATER DAYS

Lodger in the Throat by Joe Orton ran for five months on the London stage. The part of James Elliott was played throughout the run by Toby Flood. He never missed a performance.

The High Court upheld a claim by a group of twelve former employees of Colbonite Ltd to the estate of Roger Colborn, who was found to have died intestate. Under the rules of intestacy, his estate devolved upon his half-brother, Derek Oswin, who had died with him, but, being the younger of the two, was deemed to have died second. Derek Oswin had on the other hand made a will, the terms of which were therefore held to apply to Roger Colborn's estate. Derek Oswin's property was left to be shared among any former employees of Colbonite Ltd in need of financial assistance. Gavin Colborn, Roger Colborn's uncle and only surviving blood relative, appealed against this decision, but died before the appeal could be heard. An inquest subsequently found that he had suffered a fatal head injury in a fall down a steep flight of stairs at his home in Brighton while under the influence of alcohol.

Jennifer Flood never made the necessary application to the High Court for her divorce from Toby Flood to be declared final and absolute. The couple remain married.

ACKNOWLEDGEMENTS

I am indebted to the following for the help they generously gave me in the writing of this book. My dear friend Georgina James plied me with invaluable information about Brighton as well as various nuggets of legal advice. Peter Wilkins, David Bownes and the great man himself, Duncan Weldon, ensured my portrait of an actor did not stray too far from the reality with which they are so familiar. Veronica Hamilton-Deeley provided a diligent coroner's perspective on events. And Renée-Jean and Tim Wilkin ensured that those fictional events took place in genuine Brighton weather. Thank you, all.